ALSO BY JEANNETTE WALLS

The Silver Star
Half Broke Horses
The Glass Castle

Jeannette Walls

HANG THE MOON

A NOVEL

SCRIBNER

New York London Toronto Sydney New Delhi

Scribner
An Imprint of Simon & Schuster, Inc.
1230 Avenue of the Americas
New York, NY 10020

First Scribner hardcover edition March 2023

SCRIBNER and design are registered trademarks of The Gale Group, Inc.,
used under license by Simon & Schuster, Inc., the publisher of this work.

For information about special discounts for bulk purchases,
please contact Simon & Schuster Special Sales at 1-866-506-1949 or
business@simonandschuster.com.

The Simon & Schuster Speakers Bureau can bring authors to your live event.
For more information or to book an event, contact the Simon & Schuster Speakers
Bureau at 1-866-248-3049 or visit our website at www.simonspeakers.com.

Interior design by Lexy East

Manufactured in the United States of America

1 3 5 7 9 10 8 6 4 2

Library of Congress Control Number: 2022949645

ISBN 978-1-5011-1729-9
ISBN 978-1-5011-1731-2 (ebook)

To John. When I was lost, he helped me find the way.

I know I have the body of a weak and feeble woman,
but I have the heart and stomach of a king.

> *Queen Elizabeth I, 1588, rallying her troops*
> *for the arrival of the Spanish Armada*

Quality? Hell, the only time our whiskey aged was
when we got a flat tire.

> *Rex Walls, the author's father, who ran bootleg*
> *liquor in the late 1940s and early 1950s*

HANG THE MOON

PROLOGUE

THE FASTEST GIRL IN the world. That's what I'm going to be.

I decided this morning. It was the best kind of morning, sunny but not too hot, white clouds that looked like dumplings way up in the bright blue sky, birds chirping away at each other, and little yellow butterflies dancing around. I'd buttoned up my sailor suit and was buckling my shoes when the door opened. It was my daddy. The Duke. That's what everyone calls him.

"I got a surprise for you, Whippersnapper," he said. "A present."

"A present? But it's not my birthday."

"I don't need some special occasion to give my own daughter a present. If I say today is a present-giving day, it is. And mark my words, girl, this present is going to change your life."

"What is it?"

"Why you little sneak. Are you trying to trick me into telling you?" The Duke was using his pretend-to-be-angry voice and that made me laugh. "Then it wouldn't be a surprise." He smiled. "Up in the carriage house. Come with me."

If I live to be a hundred years old, I'll never forget today. The Duke took my hand in his and the two of us walked down the hall, past the parlor where my stepmama, Jane, was playing scales on the piano with my half brother, Eddie. He loves that piano and didn't even look my way. In the kitchen I told our cook, Old Ida, where we were going and she said she loves surprises and tugged one of my braids and then we went into the backyard.

When something good's about to happen, that makes me feel like skipping—I don't understand why so many people walk when they could skip instead—but this morning, I couldn't bear to let go of the Duke's hand, so I behaved myself for once in my life—like Jane is all the time telling me to.

The Duke and I walked past the stone wall we built together for Jane before Eddie was born—it's low, like a bench, so I can sit on it, and wide enough for me to run along the top and then jump as high as I can into the air. Behind the wall are Jane's pink and red and white peonies that look like big scoops of ice cream. She's the only one allowed to pick them.

We headed up the long driveway, under the big poplars, past our chicken house and icehouse and smokehouse and springhouse, all of them painted white with green tin roofs just like the Big House, and all of them empty now because we buy our meat and eggs in town and the iceman brings blocks of ice for the icebox in the kitchen. Still, it's fun to go poking around in them. Eddie's only three, five years younger than me, but as soon as he gets old enough to really play, they'll make great cowboy-and-Indian forts.

When we walked by the paddock, I gave a great big wave to the carriage horses, who were chewing away on grass and swatting at the flies with their tails. They're getting fat because we don't harness them up much now that the Duke bought himself the Ford, first automobile in all of Claiborne County. I feel a little sorry for the horses, but the Duke says in a matter of time only cowboys and fox hunters and circus riders will have horses.

The carriage house at the top of the hill is also white and green and by the time we got there I was just about to bust from wanting to know what my surprise was. The Duke grabbed ahold of the door handles and said, "Close your eyes, Whippersnapper."

So I did. I heard that low, rumbly sound the big double doors make when they're sliding apart.

"Now open your eyes," he said.

So I did.

That's when I first saw it. A wagon. Sitting there pretty as you please on the brick floor right between the Ford and the carriage, an honest-to-goodness coaster wagon, with great big red wheels—bigger than dinner plates—and a shiny black metal pull handle and smooth wood sides with big black and red letters that read DEFIANCE COASTER.

"Is that for me?"

"You bet it is. Saw it in a catalogue and right away I said, that's for my gal Sallie." I looked up at the Duke. He was staring at the Defiance Coaster with a smile in his eyes. "You like it?"

Most times, I've got so much to say that no one can get me to shut up, but right then, I was too happy to say a word, so I just nodded and then kept nodding about twenty times.

"Had one of these wagons myself when I was your age. Couldn't get me out of it. How about we take her for a spin?"

"Me and you?"

Old Ida all the time says I think the Duke hung the moon and scattered the stars. Maybe I do. Right then, I sure did.

The Duke pulled the wagon out to the driveway and squatted beside it. I squatted next to him while he showed me how you steer with the handle, how the brake lever on the left side stops the back wheels, not the front.

"Now why do you think that is?" he asked.

I jiggled the handle back and forth and watched the front wheels waggle. "Because the front wheels turn from side to side?"

"Right. The back wheels are fixed. You're a natural at this, Whippersnapper. Let's go."

He pulled the wagon to the top of the driveway and set the brake. The Duke is big even for a grown-up man, but he sat down in the wagon. I crawled between his legs and tucked my back up against his chest. He smelled good, like cigars and the stuff they splash on his face at Clyde's Barbershop after they trim his beard. It was mighty crowded, with the Duke's legs on both sides of me, his knees at my shoulders like a big pair of dark wings, but it felt good, felt like I could do anything, like nothing could go wrong, nothing could hurt me.

He put my right hand on the steering handle and my left hand on the brake.

Together we released the brake.

We started to move, rolling down the driveway, slow at first, bumpy over the gravel, then we picked up speed, faster and faster, and we zoomed right past the horses and I was leaning forward, staring down the hill, the big poplars coming right at us, the Duke's arms around my shoulders while we both steered, his cheek pressed up against mine, his beard tickling my neck, his voice in my ear. "Steady, girl. You've got it. Steady."

We barreled through the curve at the biggest poplar, leaning into the turn, then we straightened out the steering handle and got to that flat part of the driveway at the Big House. Jane was standing in the yard, holding Eddie on her hip and watching us and we waved at her, but real quick, we needed our hands for steering because below the Big House the driveway heads downhill again, under more trees, so we picked up speed, the gravel crunching below us, the wind in my face, in my hair, my braids bouncing. At the bottom of the hill we got to the little stone bridge that crosses Crooked Run. There's an old weeping willow right beside it and we hit the big bump where a root snakes beneath the driveway. That jerked our wheels and popped us up, but we kept her steady and next thing I knew we were hurtling across the bridge toward the stone pillars at the bottom of the drive-way when the Duke hollered, "Now!" We pulled back on the brake—hard—and skidded to a stop right at Crooked Run Road.

My face was all tingly and so were my hands and I could feel my heart thumping hard inside my chest. I have never, in all my life, ever felt anything like that. We were fast, so very fast, the Duke and me. We were flying.

I started laughing, out of nowhere. It just came out of me like soup boiling over, and the Duke started to laughing too. Then I jumped out of the wagon and danced a happy jig right there, kicking out my feet and throwing up my arms and swinging my head around, and that made him laugh even harder.

"You've found your calling, Whippersnapper," he said. "Keep at it and you'll be the fastest girl in the world."

I keep thinking about what the Duke said.

When I grow up, I can't become a senator or a governor or explore the North Pole or take over the family business like the Duke wants for Eddie. Jane's always saying that ladies don't engage in such pursuits. But becoming the fastest girl in the world, well, that's something I can do. The Duke himself says so. He likes to read out newspaper stories about automobile racing—cars that go faster than two miles a minute. He is mightily impressed by such stuff—people who are fastest, strongest, first—and that's what I'm going to be.

School's out now and the whole summer is ahead of me so every day that I don't get to go to the Emporium with the Duke, I practice. The Duke gave me one of his old pocket watches and it has a second hand so I can time myself racing through The Course. That's what the Duke and me call it. The Course. We gave names to the different parts of The Course. There's the Starting Line, the Drop, the Curve, the Straightaway, the Twist, the Dip, the Hairpin, the Snake—that's what we call the little ridge where that big willow root crosses under the driveway—the Bridge, and the Finish Line.

I figure out ways to make each run quicker than the last, even if just by a second. Or a split second. I use a running start like the Duke showed me, pushing the wagon and then jumping in. Once I get going I scrunch down my shoulders and tuck my chin into my chest so there's less of me to catch the wind—less resistance, the Duke said when he told me how to do it. I hug the insides of the curves like the Duke told me to, picking up speed for the flatter stretches, and after a few days I get so I only need to use the brake at the end, when I reach the stone pillars—the Finish Line.

Then I pull the Defiance Coaster back up to the top, and do it again. And again. I do it for hours. It keeps me out of the Big House all day long, except for lunch, and I eat that in the kitchen with Old

Ida. I think maybe that's one of the reasons the Duke bought me the wagon—to get me out of the house, out of Jane's hair. She says I'm too rambunctious—that's the word she uses—because when I'm cooped up inside I slide down the banister, do handstands in the front hall, accidentally break the glass figurines you're not supposed to play with because they're not toys, start pillow fights with Eddie, and give him rides in the dumbwaiter.

Jane says I'm a bad influence on Eddie but I think we get along just fine. He's very sweet and also very smart. He already knows all his letters and numbers and he practices that piano all the time without Jane having to tell him to. But Eddie gets lots of colds and earaches and Jane gives him an orange every day so he doesn't get the rickets. Also, Jane won't let him spend all that much time outdoors because the sun burns his skin and the flowers make him sneeze. So most days, it's just me and the Defiance Coaster. That suits me fine.

I got my best time ever today. It was windy as heck this morning, the branches of the poplars were waving around like crazy and I had trouble getting into the Defiance Coaster because that old wind kept wanting to push the wagon down the driveway on its own. That gave me an idea so once I finally got in the wagon, instead of scrunching over like I usually do, I kept my back straight and my shoulders up. With that big wind behind me, I really tore down the driveway. I could hardly wait to tell the Duke.

As soon as he comes home, that's what I do, and he throws back his head and laughs. "That's what you call ingenuity, Whippersnapper. Making the wind work for you like that." He points his finger at me. "I said it first, you're going to be the fastest girl in the world. Something like that's in your blood. It's what makes you a Kincaid." That warms me up like sunshine. He turns to Eddie. "What do you think, Son? It's in your blood too, right?"

Eddie nods. Jane gives the Duke a look, a cold one, and he shoots back a cold look of his own and my warm feeling is gone. I hope they don't argue. Sometimes the Duke and Jane have cross words because he thinks she babies Eddie. "For crying out loud, woman, Sallie was doing that when she was the boy's age," he'll tell her. Then she'll give me that cold look, like I'm to blame.

So that's when I come up with the plan. I'll teach Eddie how to drive the Defiance Coaster. I'll teach him the same way the Duke taught me and as soon as he's really good at it, we'll show the Duke. It'll be a surprise, our present for him, and he'll be so proud of his son and if the Duke is happy with Eddie, Jane will have to like me. But I'm not going to tell her about my plan. She might say no. If I don't tell Jane then I'm not doing anything she's told me not to do, not breaking one of her rules—not exactly.

The next morning after the Duke goes to work, I wait until Jane's in the room she calls her boudoir, fixing her hair—which takes a really long time—and I lead Eddie up to the carriage house. He likes my plan, he studies the coaster, and listens close to everything I say, nodding. I can tell he understands and I can also tell he's excited. But he's also very serious. He wants to make the Duke proud of him.

It's sunny and warm, just like the day the Duke taught me, a blue sky with puffy white clouds but no wind. A great day for a beginner. I set the Defiance Coaster at the top of the driveway, pointing downhill, then I climb in and fold my legs up like the Duke did and Eddie sits between them like I did. I put my right hand over his on the steering handle then with my left hand I let go of the brake.

We start to roll, slow at first, then we pick up speed, and I'm guiding Eddie just like the Duke did me, whispering, "Steady, boy, you've got it. Steady."

The wagon wheels rattle over the gravel and Eddie's corn-silk hair blows back while we race downhill past the horses and through the Curve under the big poplar, then along the Straightaway and down into the Twist, picking up speed again, and now we're heading right for the Snake at Crooked Run that always gives the Defiance Coaster that fun little pop.

"Steady," I say. "Steady."

*   *   *

I'm in trouble.

I'm sitting by myself in the parlor. The big old grandfather clock is ticking in the front hall and I can hear the muffled voices of worried adults coming from upstairs.

I hope Eddie's going to be okay.

We were doing great until we hit the Snake. I had warned Eddie that we'd get popped up a little but I guess we got popped more than Eddie thought we would because he yelled and then he jerked the steering handle and so we hit the stone bridge and the wagon flipped on its side and we both got pitched out. I got my knees and elbows skinned up but Eddie was lying facedown in the gravel on the bridge, his arms stretched out on both sides. He wasn't moving. Was he hurt? Was he . . . ? I couldn't finish the thought. I touched his shoulder but he still didn't move.

Then Jane came running out of the house, screaming something awful. She kept yelling at me to stay away from her son, and then she picked him up—his face scratched, his arms and legs limp like a rag doll—and took him into the Big House.

I followed Jane inside and started up the stairs behind her, but she again screamed at me to stay away, so I went to the parlor and that's where I was when the Duke and Doctor Black got here and ran upstairs.

I think I can hear Eddie's voice. I think he's alive. I sure do hope he is. I didn't mean to hurt him. I was just trying to make everyone happy. But I know I'm in trouble. Big trouble. I just don't know how big.

I'm still sitting in the parlor by myself when I hear a door shut on the second floor, then the sound of footsteps coming down the stairs. The Duke. I know the way he walks, heavy but quick. He comes into the parlor. Most times when the Duke sees me he smiles and pats my head or squeezes my shoulder or wraps me in a hug, but not now.

Instead, he kneels down in front of me so he can look me straight in the eyes.

"Is Eddie okay?" I ask.

"He was out cold but he's come to."

I feel myself breathing out, like I've been holding it in all this time.

"So we'll see," the Duke goes on. "Doctor Black wants him to stay in bed for a few days, in case he's had a concussion of the brain."

"I'm sorry."

"Aw, heck, I got knocked out plenty when I was growing up. Part of being a boy."

"It was an accident."

"I'm sure it was. But, Whippersnapper, we got us a predicament. The way Jane sees it, you almost killed your little brother."

"I was teaching him how to drive the Defiance Coaster. As a surprise for you."

"I understand. Thing is, Jane believes you're a danger to the boy. She's angry. Mighty angry. We got to calm her down, Whippersnapper, you and me. And you can do your bit by going to stay with your Aunt Faye in Hatfield for a little while."

Aunt Faye? My mama's sister? My throat swells up until I almost can't breathe. I barely remember Aunt Faye. She used to live with us and help look after me and she sends a birthday card every year, but I haven't seen Aunt Faye since Mama died and the Duke married Jane back when I was three. And Hatfield is way up in the mountains on the other side of the county, far away from the Big House.

From the way the Duke's looking at me, I get the feeling that he doesn't want to do this. Maybe I can beg him not to send me away, promise I'll be good, I'll never be rambunctious again, I'll do whatever it takes to calm Jane down and I'll never do anything that might hurt Eddie, I'll swear it on a stack of Bibles. But the Duke's also talking in that voice he uses when his mind is made up and if you try to change it, his eyes get squinty and angry and you only make things worse.

So I ask, "For how long?"

"Just till this blows over."

PART I

Chapter 1

THE SUN WILL SHOW itself soon. Our house is near the bottom of the mountain—not too far from the train tracks—with another mountain rising directly across from us, so we've got ourselves only a narrow stretch of sky overhead. Most mornings that sky is shrouded with a mist thick and heavy as a wet wool blanket and some days the sun doesn't burn it off until near noon. We'll have boiled and beaten the stains out of these darned sheets by then and we can hang them to dry, take them to the clinic tomorrow and collect our money. That will get us through another week.

But we need the sun.

I keep glancing east, willing that old sun to shine, and that's when I see the car. It's coming down through the switchbacks on the mountainside across from us, moving in and out of the mist. Aunt Faye sees it too. We stop stirring the sheets and both watch wordless while it crosses the Shooting Creek bridge at the very bottom of the mountains, goes into the little town and out of sight, then comes through the mist on our road, the one running alongside the creek and the train tracks. It's a big car, long as a locomotive and green—the dark, hard green of a new dollar bill. No one in these mountains drives a car like that. Far as I know, only one man in the whole county could afford such a car. It rolls to a stop at the faded sign that says FAYE'S DRESS-MAKING AND HAIR-STYLING.

"I look a fright," Aunt Faye says while she dries her hands on her apron and touches her hair. "Be right back." She ducks into the house.

I know I must look a fright, too, and I'm mopping my face with my sleeve when a tall, lanky man in a dark suit steps out of the car.

"Tom!" I shout, dropping the ladle and running toward him like a kid let out of school. I've known Tom Dunbar my whole life but haven't laid eyes on him since he headed off to college. If Tom's back, if he's driven all the way to Hatfield in a fancy green automobile in the middle of the week, he's not here just to ask how I'm doing. Something has happened. Something very good. Or very bad.

I hug Tom hard and he hugs back every bit as hard, then he takes my hands and we just stand there, grinning at each other.

"You're looking good, Sallie Kincaid."

"That's a lie." My work dress is soaked, my hair slipping out of the loose bun I put it in this morning, and my red, chapped hands smell of lye. "But it's a white lie, so I won't hold it against you. I'll tell you something that's true. It's darn good to see you. And you look good, too."

He does. His dark hair is already thinning at the temples but some color has come back to his face since the last time I saw him, when he returned from the war looking drained of all hope and joy, his skin the color of ash and his eyes fixed in that faraway, shell-shocked stare you see in so many of the boys back from France. Now, he looks like my friend Tom again.

I glance past Tom to the green car with its long hood and longer body, its sharp angles and smooth curves, its shiny paint job and shinier nickel plating, so sleek and modern and out of place here in Hatfield, where the mist and rain and dew soften the edges of the sagging houses and coat anything made by man with mildew and rust. "That peacock of a car has got to be the Duke's. What is it? And what the heck are you doing driving it all the way up here?"

"It's a Packard Twin Six, just off the factory floor. And, Sallie"— Tom squeezes my hands and his eyes search mine—"the Duke sent me here. To bring you back."

Bring me back. Nine long years I've been waiting to hear those words. Bring me back. Bring me home. I believed the Duke when he said I'd be staying in Hatfield for just a short while and I kept telling myself he'd send for me any day now, but the weeks passed, then the months, and I stopped thinking any day now. The Duke used to drop by once or twice a year when he was in this corner of the county, but the visits were short, he was always in a hurry, and when I asked about coming home, he'd say the time's not right and I learned to stop asking. In the last few years, he hasn't visited at all. Still, I always knew that one day, one day, I would leave this little town in the mountains. Now that day is here. "Why? Why now?"

"Jane's dead," Tom says. "The influenza took her in three days."

Jane's dead. Tom said the words softly, but I hear them roaring in my head. All those times I thought about Jane, how she had ruined my life, how she'd taken away everything I loved. I couldn't help but wish something would happen to her, but I always did my best to push such thoughts away, praying instead for Jane to have a change of heart, to see that I never meant to hurt Eddie, that I ought to have a place in my daddy's house along with my brother. I swear I'd never prayed for God to take her like this, to leave Eddie without a mama. No child ought to go through that.

"All the Kincaids are gathering at the Big House," Tom says.

Aunt Faye comes back outside just as the sun burns through the last of the mist. She's changed into her good dress and she's tidying her thick black hair with those slender fingers she hates to ruin by doing the laundry. Folks say that in her day, Aunt Faye was a true beauty and you can see it even now, with her doe-like eyes and ample curves. But life in Hatfield ages a body real fast, that thick black hair is streaked with gray, and the skin at the corners of those doe-like eyes has tiny creases.

"Tom, you handsome college boy, what a surprise. What brings you here?"

"Jane died," I say. "Of the influenza."

"Oh my." Aunt Faye's hand goes to her mouth. "May God have mercy on her soul."

"Funeral's tomorrow," Tom says. "The Duke's sending for Sallie."

Aunt Faye smiles. "I told you, Sallie. I told you this would happen one of these days." Then she gives a nervous little laugh. "What about me, Tom? I'm coming too, right?"

"I'm sorry, Miss Powell," Tom's voice is kind. "The Duke didn't say anything about you."

Aunt Faye turns back to me, pulling on those slender fingers, a panicked look in her eyes. I can't leave her here—the woman who raised me for the last nine years—I can't leave her here on her own with a kettle full of stained bedsheets.

"Aunt Faye ought to be there," I say. "She's family too."

Tom nods. "Of course she is. But you know the Duke. He hates surprises—unless he's doing the surprising—and he said, 'Fetch Sallie,' not 'Fetch Sallie and Faye.'"

"I won't go without her."

Aunt Faye takes ahold of my arm. "Sallie, don't be crossing the Duke. You go. You won't be gone long. Because you are coming back, aren't you?"

Am I? Or could the Duke possibly want me home for good? If it's just for the funeral, Aunt Faye will be all right for a few days on her own. The sheets are almost clean now, the sun's out, she can hang them by herself and get them to the clinic in the little red pull wagon, the Defiance Coaster. But what's she going to do if the Duke wants me to stay?

"Am I?" I ask Tom. "Coming back here?"

"Duke didn't say. But the wake's already started. We best be getting off."

Aunt Faye follows me through the house, past the dressmaking dummy and the fashion advertisements from ladies' magazines pasted to the walls. In our bedroom, I pull the pillowcase off my pillow. I don't have much and it'll all fit inside with room to spare.

"You are coming back, aren't you?" she asks again. Her voice is so small and fragile.

"Aunt Faye, you know as much as I do."

"The Duke said he'd take care of me as long as I took care of you. What's going to happen to me if you don't come back?"

"I'll take care of you," I say. "One way or another."

"How?"

"I'll find a way."

I hope. I just don't know how. And Tom's waiting and the Duke's waiting and I've got to go.

It might be tempting fate to pack as if I'm not coming back, but I do it anyway. My second set of underclothes, my summer socks, my boar-bristle hairbrush, my dog-eared Bible that I don't read as much as I ought to—they all go into the pillowcase. I turn my back to Aunt Faye and pull off my brown muslin work dress and, even though it's still wet, roll it up and pack it too. I put on my other dress, a blue gingham with rickrack trim I keep for special occasions. There's only one more thing. My rifle, my most valuable possession, is leaning in the corner.

"Aunt Faye, I'm going to leave my Remington here with you. Don't be afraid to use it."

CHAPTER 2

"ARE YOU READY FOR this?" Tom asks as we pass through Hatfield.

"I'm fine." It comes out sharper than I mean for it to. I'm more on edge than I thought. Tom nods like he knows how I feel. We cross over Shooting Creek and Tom starts talking about how he loves that creek, the way its water shoots into the air from the side of the mountain and then falls almost straight down, tumbling, spilling right over the rocks, cold and fast and narrow but then, at the bottom of the mountain, when the land gets flatter, the water slows and starts winding and wandering, meeting up with other creeks and runs, losing its name to theirs, sliding around rocks and rises, slipping into the low spots where it can flow most freely. "And that's why your Crooked Run is crooked."

Tom tells me the Duke's other car, the Ford, is being used to tote food for the wake so the Duke sent him in the Packard, saying, "I'll have your hide if you get so much as a scratch on it." Tom has always been a careful driver and now that he's behind the wheel of the Duke's fancy new car he is downright inching along, easing through switchback turns, steering clear of the ruts from the lumber wagons, and slowing to a crawl at every mud puddle.

So the trip back to Caywood is slow. Or maybe it just seems slow because my mind's racing. So many thoughts in my head. Thoughts that are at odds with each other. I can't wait to get to the Big House, but I have no idea how I'll be greeted. I had hoped for this day for years, aching to get back home, but all that while I never gave proper thought to what I'd be leaving behind and I can't shake the sight of Aunt Faye standing there on her own beside her dressmaking sign, waving goodbye, doing her best to smile for me.

We make our way down out of the Blue Ridge mountains in the western part of Claiborne County and into the valley where the fine Virginia land is flat enough for good farming and the fields and pastures are divided by fences and hedgerows. Winter hasn't yet let go of its grip up in the mountains, but down here, spring has softened the ground, coaxed out the first tender shoots of green along the roadside, and the buds on trees are fat as ticks.

When we reach the rolling hills in the east I start seeing sites I recall from when I was a little girl—an abandoned stone farmhouse with an old stone wall slowly collapsing, a bullet-shaped grain silo beside a blood-red barn, weathered tobacco sheds.

On the outskirts of Caywood we turn onto Crooked Run Road and pass small houses with smaller porches. Farmers tight for cash would sell off plots of roadside land and the Duke was often the buyer, putting up the little houses and renting them out.

Finally, we reach the stone pillars in front of the Big House. Across the road are two new houses, but the driveway looks just like I remember, flanked with thick-trunked trees that arch overhead.

We cross the little bridge over Crooked Run and I can't help but see three-year-old Eddie lying there, facedown. Beyond the bridge, cars and carriages are parked alongside the driveway and further ahead, a long line of people snakes up to the Big House.

"Don't wait your turn, Sallie," Tom says. "Walk right in."

"That would be rude."

"You were born here, Sallie. You don't have to wait. And leave your bag in the car. I'll bring it in the back door for you."

I give his hand a squeeze and open the door before he can do something foolish like run around to open it for me. Folk glance my way when I get out but no one gives me much mind, they go back to their conversations and I stand there alone, staring at the Big House.

It's a peculiar feeling to finally see something that has been lodged in your head for so long and truth is, I was afraid that when I did get back, the Big House would not be as big as my memories made it out to be. But that is not the case.

The Big House is a sprawler. On one side is the original stone farmhouse, small and sturdy, two rooms over two rooms, made with the field stones my great-grandpa Bull Kincaid gathered when he first cleared this land. Affixed to the stone house is the clapboard wing that the Colonel—the Duke's daddy—added on some fifty years ago, when the family came into its own. Finally, there's the fancy high-windowed wing the Duke built when the Big House became his.

I make my way up the driveway, past the poplar trees that have grown taller and the boxwoods that have grown wider, wondering once more if I am home for good or if I am just paying a visit like all these folk in line. I climb the porch steps and try to ease my way through the crowd at the door but someone hollers, "The line starts back there."

"I'm family."

"We're all family."

"I'm the Duke's daughter."

"Good Lord," a woman says in a near whisper. "It's Sallie Kincaid."

Heads turn, the crowd parts, and I walk through the door.

I am inside the Big House. Mourners fill the front hall but for a moment I don't see them. The flowered wallpaper, the rug that came all the way from Persia, the brass hat rack and umbrella stand with lion-head knobs, the grandfather clock with the sun and moon on its face—it's all so familiar and at the same time, it's a world apart from the life I've been living with Aunt Faye. There is no want here, no pinching of pennies—and it's hard for me to believe I once lived here, that I took this comfort, this abundance for granted, but the memories come flooding back, sliding down that ornate banister, squeezing into that closet while playing hide-and-seek with Eddie, running down this hall when the Duke shouted, "I'm home," and jumping into his arms. I grab ahold of the newel post to steady myself. I'm home.

I walk down the hall, wary, minding my posture—comport yourself with grace, Aunt Faye always says. Mourners are dressed up in their good church clothes, some talking solemnly in small clusters, others nipping at bottles and throwing back their heads in laughter, because a wake is also a chance to meet up with friends and kin.

I think I hear his voice, the Duke's voice, booming out over the chatter of conversation and clatter of dishes, so I follow the sound of it, turning left into the parlor, where the red velvet curtains are drawn, and there in the midst of all the people I see Jane's body, stretched out on the long walnut dining table, her fair face and white silk dress glowing in the soft light of the candles that surround her.

Then I see him. The Duke. Sitting next to Jane's body in his big leather wing chair, greeting guests. Everyone else, everything else, disappears. He is so big, so beefy, towering even when he sits, his rust-colored beard clipped close, his white collar crisp, a white carnation pinned to the lapel of his black jacket, gesturing with his fat cigar.

He glances my way. My face tingles. I wave, I smile, and the Duke nods slightly, dutifully, and then his eyes shift back to the fellow he is talking to, and the tingle is gone, replaced by a sting of shame. Could the Duke possibly not have recognized me? He flicks his eyes my way again, like he's reconsidering, then they light up and he gives me that famous Duke smile of his and slowly rises up out of his wing chair.

"Sallie," he says, "my little Whippersnapper."

I cross the room—I'm doing my best not to run, not to skip. I give him a big hug and he hugs me back, but he lets go before I do, then he holds me out, arm's length, and looks me up and down.

"Not so little anymore, are you?" he asks.

"Not anymore." He doesn't look the same either. He is thicker now, has a gut, his rust-colored hair and beard are streaked with white.

"Good to have you back, girl. How long you been gone? Eight years?"

"Nine," I say. Nine years, eight months, and five days. I was eight when I was sent away. Eight years old. I'll turn eighteen next month.

"Nine." He shakes his head. "Time. Money comes and goes, but time only goes."

"I'm so sorry about Jane."

He looks me in the eyes, grips my shoulders, pulls me close, and kisses me on the cheek. His whiskers tickle. "Don't bullshit a bullshitter," he whispers. "We'll talk later."

Then he looks past me, to the next person in line, his hand slides down my back, and he gently pushes me along.

That's when I notice the thin young fellow sitting slumped beside the Duke. His head is bowed so low I can't see his face, but I know him, know that corn-silk hair. I kneel down in front of him.

"Eddie."

He looks at me blankly. He is small for a boy who just turned thirteen, frail too, with his mama's gray eyes and thin hair. I'm taken aback by the rush of feelings I have for my brother. There's love, yes, but I'd be lying if I didn't admit there's also some envy. He had the Duke for the last nine years—and everything else I didn't have—but now he looks so grief-stricken that my heart truly aches for him.

"It's me, Eddie. Sallie. Your sister."

"Sallie." His gray eyes study mine for a moment. "Mother said you almost killed me."

"It was an accident." My words come out louder than I mean for them to. The Duke glances my way and I lower my voice. "I was trying to teach you to drive the wagon, like I explained in my letters."

"What letters?"

So Jane kept them from him, the letters I wrote when I thought Eddie was old enough to understand what happened, old enough to possibly forgive me. I can only imagine the kinds of things she's told him about me. I can't expect him to be glad to see me. If my feelings about him are mixed up, his feelings about me must be even more mixed up.

"I am sorry. For hurting you. It was an accident, but still it was my fault. I was pretty darned rambunctious, as Jane used to say. And I'm also sorry for your loss. I know what it's like to lose your mama."

Eddie's gray eyes turn chilly, just like Jane's always did. "My mother was nothing like your mother."

I stand up, stung again. "You're right. My mama was nothing like your mama."

Eddie turns away from me, toward his mama. I look at Jane, too. She is so light, so still in this dark, noisy room, her face is powdered white, the wispy, corn-silk hair is perfectly arranged. Even in death, she manages to look superior.

She wasn't a beauty—her eyes are close set and her lips are thin—but by the time Jane came along, the Duke had had his fill of beautiful women. Besides, Jane had what folks called good breeding—she came from the most prosperous family in a not-so-prosperous town—and you can still see it in her delicate folded hands and her small, oval face, unlined except for the little furrow between her brows, the furrow that deepened whenever she disapproved of something. Which was often. There was that time, not long after the Duke married Jane, when the photograph of Mama that I kept on my bedside table disappeared. I was four then, and it took me a long while to work up the courage to ask Jane if she knew what had become of it, and when I finally did her eyes grew chilly, the little furrow in her brow deepened, and she said, "My husband wants no reminders of that woman."

I reach down and touch Jane's cold cheek. Goodbye, Jane. Did you die with any regrets? Did you ever have the urge to make peace with me? I doubt it.

Wandering through the crowd, looking for a familiar face, I nod at people I don't recognize and everyone nods back but as they walk by I feel them looking me over, figuring what to make of me. Comport yourself with grace, I hear Aunt Faye saying, but I had only a small piece of corn bread this morning and right now I could eat a horse and I can smell fried meat and fresh-baked bread. In the dining room, the tables are crowded with all manner of bereavement dishes—rich mincemeat pie, glistening spiced peaches, golden creamed corn, baked apples coated with cinnamon, squash casserole covered with oven-browned cracker crumbs, sweet potato casserole topped with puffy whipped cream, pigeon pie with a mashed potato crust, fried chicken with crackling skin, thick slices of fat-veined ham, loins of dry-aged venison, and pulled pork soaking in sauce the color of molasses.

The smell of it all is making my mouth water, but I'll be darned if I'm going to start wolfing down food in front of people trying to decide what to make of me, and I'm wondering if there is a way to sneak a plateful into the basement without being noticed when I see Tom and his dad, Cecil, out in the crowded hall. I start toward them, but then a woman behind me says, "So the Duke brought her back after all."

The words are said in a loud whisper, like the woman saying them wants to be overheard. She's strong-jawed and broad-shouldered with steel-colored hair and those hard hazel eyes you sometimes see in Kincaids. My Aunt Mattie. Beside her is a young woman, both pretty and mousy. It's been nine years, but I recognize Mattie's daughter, my cousin Ellen.

"Aunt Mattie. Ellen."

"Sallie," she says. "You've grown."

"Surely do hope I have. What is that you were saying?"

"That you've grown up."

"Before that."

"Before that I wasn't talking to you."

"No. You were talking about me."

"Sallie, you've just got back. Don't create a scene. Everyone will say you take after your mother."

Kicked. That's how I feel, like I've been kicked and I feel like kicking back, but people are listening—comport yourself with grace—so I wheel around to leave only someone's right there behind me and I try to stop, but it's too late and I crash headlong into her. She's carrying a tray loaded with dishes and they all clatter to the floor and collard greens, beet salad, and whatnot go flying through the air and splatter on the Persian rug and across the front of my nice blue gingham dress.

I holler out a cussword—or maybe a few—and that stops all conversation. I push through the kitchen door, grab a rag from the sink, and start scrubbing at the stains on my dress. In comes the woman, she's wearing a white apron and she falls all over herself apologizing, saying she is awful sorry, it was all her fault, what a clumsy thing to do and I'm nodding and scrubbing away and just then the Duke walks in.

"What's the trouble here?" he asks.

"My dress just got ruined," I say.

"It was an accident," the woman says. "It was my fault."

"Nell here's pretty careful, but accidents happen, Sallie."

"It all started with Aunt Mattie saying you shouldn't have brought me back—"

"Who cares what she thinks? I make the decisions around here. Lock horns with my sister, you'll give her the fight she wants."

"But it's my one good dress and I look like I've been butchering hogs in it."

"I can get it out with a little elbow grease," says the woman the Duke called Nell. "But I got to soak it and right now that mess in the dining room needs tending to."

"Don't worry about the dress," the Duke says. "Sallie, you come with me."

Don't worry about the dress. Said by someone who's got a different suit for every day of the week. There are plenty like Mattie who believe I don't belong here, and the big red stain on my dress is like a mark that proves it. I cross my arms, hoping to hide the stain, and follow the Duke outside to the back porch, then down the steps and into a crowd of men standing in the garden. The sun is setting and smoky flames from kerosene torches light their faces and flicker on the whiskey bottles that line the table while the men share news of crops and weather—this late frost might kill the strawberries, time to break ground for corn, Fred Mullens wants a ten-dollar stud fee for his new Percheron stallion. The Duke pats a few of them on the back as we walk past and they nod, grateful to be singled out, then we sit on the low stone wall that edges the garden.

The twilight air is chilly. The Duke takes off his black jacket and puts it over my shoulders—the silk lining is still warm from his body—then he pats the top of the wall.

"Remember that summer we built this?"

"Sure do." How could I forget? It's one of my most treasured memories, that summer when I was four and Jane was expecting and the Duke and I spent every Sunday afternoon fitting together these rocks like the pieces of a jigsaw puzzle.

"You worked hard, Whippersnapper. Even on the hottest days. You're good with your hands. Got a decent head on your shoulders, too." He ruffles my hair like he used to when I was a kid. "I know it's been tough on you these last years, but that was the way it had to be. Understand?"

"I understand." And part of me does, the part that is thrilled to be having this talk, the Duke fussing over me, making sure I'm warm, recalling our times together. Another part of me never will.

"Nine years," the Duke says. "That's a long time. It was supposed to be a month, maybe two. But I got to tell you, once you left, Jane became a lot easier to live with." The Duke sighs and studies his fingernails. "Maybe I should have sent Eddie away instead. To military school. Harden his bark. But Jane said it would kill him. Probably would have. So you're the one who got toughened up. But now you're back."

"For good?" I blurt it out. Couldn't help myself.

"For good. To look after Eddie." He nods, pleased with his own decision. "Now that Jane's gone, he needs someone taking care of him. You up to that?"

"I'm up to it. In Hatfield, I helped the teacher, Miss Cain, with the younger students."

"I know. Miss Cain sent me reports on you." He rubs his hands together. "That boy means everything to me. I don't want any more accidents. Got that?"

I nod, doing my best to ignore the jab.

"He's going to be governor one day," the Duke says. "Maybe senator."

I nod again.

Just then, the big windows in the parlor light up, bright and dazzling. I gasp. Electrical wiring. When I left the Big House, it was lit with candles and gas. I watch Nell moving from room to room, lights blinking on in each one, the windows all glowing magically in the dusk.

"Welcome to the modern age," the Duke says. He stretches his arms over his head and cracks his knuckles—a sound I've always loved. "I'm feeling a little stiff, but I best get back inside. Still got plenty of glad-handing to do before the night's through. Better give me that." He pulls his jacket off my shoulders—the chill is sudden and startling—and looks at my dress as if he's seeing it for the first time. "Hell's bells, girl, you do look like you've been butchering hogs."

"I don't have anything to change into."

"Tell you what"—he works his arms into his jacket—"Jane's room is full of dresses. Put one on. There's a black dress she bought a few months ago for funerals. Never wore it. Didn't know that the next funeral she'd be attending would be her own." He lets out a joyless laugh, then wipes his eyes. "I know you two had your differences, but I do believe I'll miss that woman. I know the boy will."

The Duke takes one last deep breath of night air to brace himself then heads into the house.

So I'm back. For good. If I can make it work. And I'll figure out some way to help Aunt Faye from here.

Jane's smell—that is, her lilac perfume—hits me when I open the door to her boudoir. I can't smell lilacs without Jane coming to mind. Inside, the racks of dresses, the row of shoes, the boxes of hats, the drawers filled with corsets and such, all Jane's. The stenciled wallpaper is Jane's and so are the hatpin cushion and ring stand and the pale yellow hairs entwined in the bristles of her sterling silver brush. Seeing Jane's hair makes me feel like an intruder. I shouldn't be here—so I'll hurry.

So many dresses—delicate silks, soft cashmeres, fragile laces—and then, here it is, the black dress. I peel off my stained gingham. Standing in Jane's room wearing nothing but my underthings feels downright indecent, and I quickly slip her dress over my head.

It fits, meaning I'm now the size of the woman who sent me away when I was a little girl. It's like she's doing me a favor from beyond the grave, and the last thing I want is to feel beholden to her, but I don't have much choice and the dress is well-tailored, unlike anything I've ever worn, with a lining and tucks and pleats, darts and padding.

Hooking it closed, I study myself in the full-length mirror. I am not what you would call a raving beauty. Not by a long shot. I have the Duke's hazel eyes and rust-colored hair, but my mama's wide jaw and sharp chin. Mama. This used to be her room. Come to think of it, there might be some trace of her still here, and so despite my promise to leave quickly—can't seem to help myself—I start rifling through drawers and boxes and then open the rosewood jewelry box on the vanity and dig through the thickly jeweled chokers and bracelets and brooches collected by three generations of Kincaid women. Finally, on the very the bottom, I find it. The necklace the Duke gave Mama. It is simple and graceful, with three glowing moonstones that hang from a silver chain like raindrops. Jane must not have known it was Mama's. I put it on. Does it make me look at all like Mama? Wearing it downstairs is out of the question, so I take it off and put it back in the jewelry box. That feels wrong too, and I slip it into a pocket in Jane's dress. I am not a thief, but I have no problem taking what is mine. And the way I see it, Mama's necklace belongs to me.

Downstairs, the wake is even more crowded now, bustling, hot, sweaty, and I raise my arm to wipe my forehead. That danged lilac perfume. The black dress reeks of it. I'll go to the back porch, air the dress out.

Eddie's sitting on the steps. He looks at me, startled and confused at first, but then his gray eyes fill with hurt and anger. "That's my mother's dress!" he shouts.

Down in the garden, all talk of crops and weather comes to a stop. The men stare up at us. "Poor woman ain't even in the ground yet," a big bearded fellow calls out. "And Annie Powell's daughter is already making off with her clothes."

Nervous laughter follows.

"It was the Duke's idea," I tell Eddie, loud enough for all to hear. "My other dress got stained."

"And you can't be talking to the Duke's daughter like that," a short man hollers at the big man.

"No one tells me how I can and can't talk, little man."

More nervous laughter. Then the bearded fellow shoves the short guy against the table. Whiskey bottles tumble to the ground. The small guy stands up and in the torch light, I see the glint of a knife blade in his hand. The bearded man grabs a whiskey bottle off the ground and charges, the two shove up against each other and struggle arm in arm, moving almost like they're dancing, then the big man slowly sinks to his knees. He drops the bottle, clutches at his chest, there's a confused look on his face, and he pitches forward.

I turn to Eddie, who's gasping for breath. I grab his shoulders and press his face to my chest so he can't see what's going on down in the garden, where men are shouting and pushing each other. Just then the Duke comes busting out the back door.

"Enough!" he shouts. "What the Sam Hill's going on here?"

Eddie twists out of my arms and moves away from me, ashamed, I figure, for the Duke to have seen me shielding him. "A knife fight," I say. "Happened in a flash."

The Duke looks at the men standing around the slumped body. "Is that Dutch Weber?"

"Yes sir," someone calls up.

"How is he?"

Two men bend over Dutch for a close look.

"Dead, sir," one of them says.

The Duke shakes his head, more disgusted than upset. "Can't even lay a woman to rest around here without these boys causing a ruckus." Then he starts barking commands like he's the foreman at a work site. He orders the two men holding the short fellow to take him to jail, tells the men kneeling beside Dutch to get the body to the undertakers, sends another man to break the news to Dutch's wife, and has the rest of them clean up the mess. "And do it now. I'm not going to let some drunken brawl ruin my wife's wake."

CHAPTER 3

JANE ALWAYS LOVED HER flowers and the next day there are hundreds of them beside her open grave, hothouse roses and lilies woven into wreaths and crosses and crowns and hearts. I'm sitting beside the grave next to Eddie, wearing my muslin work dress. It still gives off a whiff of lye from washing those sheets, but the wind is coming and going in bold gusts, the last gasp of winter, and we're all wearing overcoats so I'm hoping no one else can smell the lye.

There was no way I was going to put on Jane's black dress again, the one that set Eddie off and led to a man's killing. I keep telling myself it wasn't my fault, but truth is, it wouldn't have happened if I hadn't been there. I also keep coming back to the idea that maybe Aunt Mattie was right, that maybe the Duke ought to have left me in Hatfield.

Everyone is sitting in silence, then the Duke gets up and faces the crowd, and I know he's grieving but somehow, right now, here at the cemetery, standing over the coffin of the woman who finally gave him the son he always wanted, he is at his best. He is the Duke, holding his audience, pausing at the right moment, openly shedding tears while talking about the great loss that is felt, not just by him but by all Kincaids, indeed by all of Claiborne County. "My wife was the very heart of hospitality, her door was always open to the visitor, her purse to the needy," he says, but he also cracks a few jokes—"if Jane cooked a meal, it wasn't the dinner bell that rang but the fire alarm"—which gets everyone to chuckling and you can see how glad they are to laugh, grateful that the Duke is saying it's okay.

As for Eddie, he's not laughing. He's staring at his mama's coffin as if he doesn't really see it. The Duke finishes eulogizing, tosses a handful of dirt on the coffin, then takes Eddie's hand and they file out of the gate. The other mourners follow, but I hang back until I'm alone save for the gravediggers pulling shovels off a truck. When they're not looking, I pluck a rose from one of the floral tributes. There are so many it won't be missed.

It's here somewhere, Aunt Faye brought me to see it once, and in the far corner of the cemetery, I get down on my knees and brush away the dead grass and dried leaves until I find it, not a headstone but a small granite marker set flat in the ground.

ANN POWELL KINCAID
1878–1904

The rose is real pretty, white with a bit of pale pink, and I set it on Mama's gray stone marker. My few memories of Mama are like brightly colored birds you see out of the corner of your eye that are gone when you turn to look. Mama is jumping up on a table and dancing, shaking her skirt and kicking out her feet. She is laughing—a bold, flowing, sparkling laugh—and the Duke is laughing with her, deep and lumbering. They are also fighting, Mama and the Duke, shouting and cussing at each other, she is throwing things, breaking glass, and he is slamming doors. And then there is the night Mama died, more shouting, more cussing, and then a loud crack, nothing else.

The wind is picking up. I stand, dust off my knees, and find a rock to put on the stem of the rose so it won't blow away, then make my way through the rows of tombstones toward the gate. The Big House is three miles away, a long, cold walk from here, but Tom Dunbar is there at the road, leaning on the hood of the Lizzie, as everyone calls the Ford the Duke uses for errand running.

"You up for a drive?" he asks.

"Wouldn't mind that one little bit. I was putting a flower on my mama's grave."

"Figured that's what you might be doing."

"Tom, I barely remember her."

"I remember her." He grins. "Two things. First, she took me seriously, even though I was a kid, she never talked down. Second, she had a laugh that could turn sour milk fresh, a laugh that made you start laughing, too."

"I do remember her laugh."

"Almost as loud as yours."

That makes me smile for a moment. Mama. I didn't choke up looking at her little stone marker, but now, hearing Tom talk about her like this, I do just that and I look away so he won't see.

"You almost never talk about her," he says, "but I know how that goes. Sometimes it's hard to talk about the things most on your mind."

Tom does know how that goes. He came back from the war a hero—for saving lives, not taking them, dragging wounded men back from German lines—and all of Caywood greeted him at the train depot along with a brass band. But Tom spent the next month holed up at home and when he visited me in Hatfield, he wouldn't talk about what happened over there. I've stopped asking.

"You drive," Tom says. "It's hard to feel blue behind the wheel of a car."

I smile again, and Tom sees it, so I climb into the Lizzie and Tom cranks her. She coughs then chugs to life, trembling and throbbing under my rump, and he jumps in.

"I hear the Duke wants you back for good."

"To look after Eddie."

"Good. Caywood hasn't been the same since you left."

Nice to think that could be true, only everything's gone wrong since I got back. But I'm not going to talk to Tom about that, not going to ask him to take pity on me or buck me up. Instead, I step on the gear pedal, push up the throttle, and the Lizzie lurches forward, begrudgingly at first, but then obligingly, and we kick up a cone of dust.

Tom's right. The cure for feeling down is going fast. I gear up and glance over to see Tom smiling as we race past the wild plum trees blooming white in the woods beside the cemetery. The Duke taught me to love going fast, but it was Tom Dunbar who taught me how to drive, back before the war, when he used to run errands for the Duke and came to Hatfield on the second Saturday of every month, bringing the fifteen dollars the Duke sent Aunt Faye for my upkeep, along with books, magazines, newspapers, and the latest scuttlebutt from Caywood. He was a good teacher, a patient one, showed me the basics of brakes and steering, and then the finer points, high-speed tactics, the line to take into a tight turn, how to shift into low as you approach and back to high as you throttle up out of it.

I don't want to talk about Mama, but all of a sudden I do want to talk—about him. Tom's like a brother to me. He has that slow way of moving and talking, but he's whip-smart. That's why, when he got back from the war, the Duke sent him off to college. Said it would be a fine thing to have a college boy working at Kincaid Holdings and maybe one of these days Tom could take over from his daddy, Cecil, as the Duke's counselor.

"Make many friends up there in Georgetown?"

"A few."

"Meet any pretty girls?"

"A few."

"What's college like?"

Tom tells me about Georgetown, the late nights arguing the Constitution with professors, how the classes are easier than he thought they'd be, how those fraternity boys from the Tidewater lowlands make fun of his mountain accent as if they don't have any accents at all, when in fact there's nothing thicker and lazier than some taffy puller's Tidewater drawl, only he says it in a Tidewater accent—nothin thickuh and laziuh than some taffy-pulluh's Tahdwatuh drawl.

That gets me to laughing and I must say, it feels good, just letting go, laughing and racing along in the Lizzie through the bright March sunshine, and that gets Tom to laughing—good, he doesn't laugh as much as he did before the war—and in no time at all we sound like a couple of braying donkeys.

Out of nowhere, Tom stops laughing. "I hear that the Duke thinks it's time you got married."

I take a sharp turn a little fast and the wheels skid across the gravel. Marriage. I'm not yet eighteen, never been courted, never been kissed, but there are girls my age around Hatfield who already have husbands and kids.

"The Duke may think it's time, but I don't know if I do. If I ever will."

"So you're telling me not to wait around."

I glance at Tom. He's smiling, like he's trying to make light of what he's saying, but when we were growing up, people used to say Tom and I would get married one day and over the years Aunt Faye— who never got married but thinks all women should—told me countless times that he would make a wonderful husband. He deserves an honest answer.

"Tom, if I ever do marry, I'd want it to be you, but truth be told, marriage scares me. It didn't work out so well for my mama. I'm not sure I'll ever want to get married. Maybe I'll have a change of heart one day, but I surely can't promise you. So no, don't wait around."

Tom's still holding on to that game smile. "I had to ask."

Chapter 4

THE DUKE CALLS ME into his library the next morning. He's leaning against his desk and on the wall behind him is the big oil painting of him in his prime, strong and prosperous, staring boldly into the distance. On the opposite wall is the painting of the Duke's daddy, the Colonel, in his Confederate uniform. It's almost like the two of them are sizing each other up, and when I was a kid, I used to think of it as the staring contest.

"I need a witness in the death of Dutch Weber," he says. "Sallie, you saw it all."

"I can't help but thinking that man died on account of me."

"Dutch Weber died because he was a bully and a drunk. That's the final word on the matter."

"But if I hadn't—"

"People choose their own fates. You got to remember that, Sallie." I'm not sure I agree, but still, the words are comforting and now's not the time to argue it. The Duke goes on, "Otherwise, you fall to pieces. And I got to say, you seemed pretty calm, given that a man was stabbed right before your eyes."

People have told me that before, both in praise and in reproach. Back in Hatfield, a man was trampled to death by runaway horses right in front of me, and while some folks started shaking and shrieking, I got oddly calm. That's also what happened when Dutch was killed. Don't know why. Could be I was born this way, could be because when I was a little girl the Duke was always telling me not to air my fears, or could be on account of what happened when I was three that no one ever talks about.

"Nothing to be gained by falling to pieces."

"Good, I like that way of thinking," the Duke says. "Now, Chalky Hurd killed Dutch Weber, but from what I'm hearing, it was just a stupid knife fight, so there's no point in sending Chalky off to the penitentiary, much less the electric chair."

"Isn't that up to the jury?"

"We don't need a trial in a case like this. Waste of taxpayers' money, and we're the taxpayers. Dutch started it, right?"

"I suppose. It all happened so fast."

"Don't suppose. You either know or you don't. What started it?"

"Dutch Weber said spiteful words to me about wearing Jane's dress and Chalky Hurd called him on it."

"All the more reason not to send the boy to jail. So we've established that Dutch attacked Chalky and Chalky pulled his knife in self-defense, correct?"

"Correct."

"Good. You sound certain." He reaches for his hat. "You're coming with me to the Emporium. We're going to dispense a little Kincaid justice."

Caywood is the biggest town in Claiborne County, with a lively main street that runs four blocks. Big sycamores shade the wooden sidewalks and the pharmacy and the ice cream parlor look as they did. So do the Central Café and Clyde's Barbershop, and the optometrist office, but wires now cross the air above the street and the sides of buildings are bright with freshly painted advertisements for Coca-Cola and Penn-Way motor oil.

What folk call the beating heart of the town is not the grand limestone courthouse, nor is it the depot, where travelers come and go and folk pick up the packages they've ordered from Sears, Roebuck and Company. It's not even the Presbyterian church, where some folks go to get right with the Lord and others go to be seen going. The beating heart of Caywood—smack-dab in the center of town—is the Emporium. It's where people from all over the county come to shop, some from in-town once a week, some from up-hollow once a month.

The bells on the front door jangle to announce us as we walk in. The Kincaids have owned the Emporium for fifty years and I spent Saturday mornings here when I was a girl. It was my favorite place on earth back then and now, seeing it after nine years, it still is. It's crowded and noisy, farmers trading canned goods and whiskey for dry goods and gossip, old coots playing cards at the woodstove, women roaming the worn wooden floors with baskets, children ogling the candy inside the glass counter.

Mr. Lewis, a slight, bent man who's always seemed to me as much a part of the store as the cash register he's often behind, is on the rolling ladder fetching an item from the shelves that reach all the way to the stamped tin ceiling. Those shelves are stocked with bottles of every shape and color and little boxes, some metal, some cardboard, all painted so pretty you want to buy them just to display them in your kitchen. There's black tea from China, English soap and Irish crackers, instantaneous coffee, and all six flavors of Jell-O. Also, roller skates and stick horses, hair tonic and toilet water, fountain pens and writing paper, spools of thread and bolts of fabric, deerskin riding gloves and cowhide work gloves, broad-brimmed men's hats and be-ribboned ladies' bonnets, stiff new overalls that still smell of dye—pretty much everything you can't make or grow on your own, and more than a few that you can because everyone knows that store-bought is better.

The cardplayers at the woodstove look up at us and nod. The Duke slaps a couple of them on the shoulder and we head to his office at the back of the store. It has a one-way window so he can keep an eye on the doings in his store, but folks on the other side see only a mirror. It's where the Duke runs the businesses called Kincaid Holdings, meaning the store, the warehouse, the lumber mill, the hauling company, the rental properties, and such. The Duke is the richest man and the biggest landowner in the county. Plus, he's chairman of the Claiborne County Democratic Party, meaning he decides who gets elected to what job. People come to the Duke's office with their troubles, and when I was a little girl, I'd sit in a corner on Saturday mornings pretending to read while listening to folk ask the Duke for a loan to tide them over until the harvest, or a bail bond to get their son out of jail, or to make things right between their daughter who was in a family way and the daddy who wouldn't own up.

Today, Chalky Hurd is in the office, sitting in a chair facing the Duke's cluttered desk, scratching his whisker-stubbled chin. Next to him is a stout young woman with puffy eyes I take to be Dutch's widow, Vera Weber—the Duke said he'd sent for her. Sheriff Earl Johnson, who is married to Aunt Mattie, is leaning against the wall, and Cecil Dunbar, Tom's father and the Duke's counselor, is sitting in his regular chair next to the Duke's desk.

The Duke eases into his heavy wooden armchair. "Sallie here is my key witness." He rolls his chair back and puts his arms behind his head. "Sallie, tell them what happened."

"It was a clear-cut case of self-defense," I say.

The Duke nods. "Can you elaborate?"

"I was standing on the porch and had an unobstructed view of the events that transpired. An argument broke out, words got heated, Dutch Weber shoved Chalky Hurd, knocking him down. Chalky pulled out a knife. That was when Dutch picked up a whiskey bottle and commenced to charging. Chalky was just protecting himself."

"As you said, a clear-cut case of self-defense," the Duke says. "That's what we'll tell the grand jury. I figure there'll be no need for a trial."

"You're going to let him just walk away?" Vera's voice rises with indignation. "He killed my Dutch. He ought to go to prison."

"Now what good would that do?" The Duke's voice is certain and calm, almost gentle, like a parent soothing an overwrought child. "Here's what we're going to do instead."

He walks around the desk and puts his foot up on the edge of

Chalky's chair, looking down at the man. "Son, this here fine widow-woman and her two kids don't have anyone to support them now that you've gone and killed her husband, self-defense or no. This is a tragedy, got that, a deed that can't be undone. So, to help make things right, I want you to marry this woman."

Before Chalky says a word, Vera's on her feet. "Marry me?" she shouts and glares at Chalky. "He killed my Dutch."

"Chalky here's a good boy," Sheriff Earl says. "He'll treat you better than Dutch ever did."

"Mrs. Weber," the Duke says, still using that gentle voice, "please take your seat. I'm doing what's best for you and your kids. With all due respect for the departed, you, me, and the good Lord above all know the truth, that Dutch was a drunk, a mean drunk. He was drunk when he started this here fight that got him killed and I guarantee you in three months those kids will be calling Chalky here Daddy."

"Don't I got no say in all this?" Chalky starts to get up out of his chair.

"Not unless you want to stand trial." The Duke squeezes his shoulder and pushes him back down.

"And you don't have the sort of face a jury likes," Sheriff Earl says.

"I can't support her—them," Chalky says. "I don't even got a job."

Cecil has been sitting there silent the whole time, but now he leans over and whispers in the Duke's ear and the Duke nods.

"Tell you what," the Duke says to Chalky, "there's an opening in the Wrightsville Post Office. Federal job. Lifetime employment. Benefits and pension. If you make sure you take care of Vera and those two kids, I'll make sure you get that job." He pauses. "Unless either one of you wants this to go to trial. Vera? Chalky?"

Vera and Chalky eye each other warily.

"Sheriff Earl," the Duke says, "why don't you take them over to Town Hall. Pick up a marriage license."

Sheriff Earl and Cecil escort Chalky and Vera out the door. Now it's just me and the Duke. So that's Kincaid justice. Sure was swift. High-handed too. Still and yet, the Duke had a problem and he solved it, didn't hold a shotgun to their heads, just had an answer ready for their every question. And I played the part he wanted me to play, so maybe now I can ask him for something.

"You did good," the Duke tells me. "'An unobstructed view of the events that transpired.'" He chuckles. "Pretty good vocabulary for someone with an eighth-grade education."

"I read whenever I have free time. Miss Cain lent me her books. I just have to be careful about saying words I've read but never heard spoken."

The Duke clips a cigar then pats his vest pocket. "Where's my matches?" he mutters. "Go get me a light from those boys outside."

When I get back with the matches, the Duke just sits there with his cigar and it dawns on me that he wants me to light it for him. So I do. "Well, I got Chalky and Vera hitched." The tip of his cigar glows orange as he draws on it. "That's what I got to do for you."

"I'm not certain I want to get married."

"There you go again with that 'not certain' nonsense. We'll make you certain. What else are you going to do? You can get married or you can become a schoolteacher or a nurse. Other than that, it's slim pickings—a nun or a whore or a spinster peeling potatoes in the corner of some relation's kitchen."

"Women these days are doing all kinds of things—"

"Lady sharpshooters, lady race car drivers, ladies who walk on airplane wings. I've read all about them. But they're oddities, peculiarities. If a woman wants to get ahead in this world, she marries well and mark my words, Sallie, no man worth the clothes on his back is going to let a woman outshine him." The Duke looks at me as if he's sharing wisdom with me that I must never, ever forget. "And I need grandsons."

"I could come work for you. You said I did good just now. I'm hardworking, I'm not a complainer. Give me a job."

The Duke sighs, leans back, and gazes at the ceiling. "You got a job. Looking after Eddie."

"Aunt Faye could do that. You could bring her back and she could look after Eddie and I could come work for you here."

He stops gazing at the ceiling and stares me square in the eye. "Faye Powell is not going to raise my son."

"Aunt Faye needs to make a living." I straighten my shoulders, trying to look like someone who doesn't cave in when the Duke gets high-handed—the way Chalky and Vera just did. The Duke doesn't respect spineless people who let him push them around—but he truly hates it when you argue with him. I'm hoping I can find the ground in between. "Unless you're going to keep sending her money."

"I was paying Faye Powell to do a job. She's no longer doing it. I'm letting her live in that house rent-free and I'm not going to send her money on top of that. I've got my hands full taking care of orphans and widows, folks who can't survive on their own, like Vera and her young ones. I'm not going to start providing for an able-bodied woman perfectly capable of working. Do that and half the women in the county will have their hands out."

Can't let it go at that. It's been three days now since I left Hatfield. I wrote Aunt Faye telling her I wouldn't be coming back but I'd figure out a way to help her and I haven't stopped worrying about her, sitting alone in that little house fretting about how she'll make ends meet. "Aunt Faye raised me. She's my mama's sister."

The Duke points his cigar at me and I see it in his eyes, the cold rage that's even more terrifying than his hot temper. "If you want to be a part of this family, you will never again mention your mother."

"But I—"

"Got that? Ever."

CHAPTER 5

NELL'S AT THE COOKSTOVE. We say our good mornings and I take a seat at the long pine table. It was made by Great-Grandpa Bull Kincaid from a single tree that once stood on this very spot—first piece of furniture he built for this house—and the wood is stained and scarred from four generations of Kincaids eating and cooking on it. Jane did her darnedest to steer clear of the kitchen—"the servants' quarters," she always said—and we took family meals in the dining room, but I've always felt at home here. This is where Old Ida used to feed me cracklings or peanut butter and pickle sandwiches or biscuits soaked in sugar milk while telling me stories about her people on her mama's side, the Cherokees.

I love the swinging oak door with its scuffed brass kickplate, the chipped soapstone counters, and the checkered linoleum floor worn down in front of the sink to the old flowery linoleum underneath. The kitchen has new gadgets now, state-of-the-art appliances like an electric toaster and an ice cream maker. There is also a fancy new Hoosier cabinet with a flour bin and sifter, spice jars on a revolving rack, and a pullout zinc tray for kneading. Everything in its place so you can find it when you need it.

"Nell, you run yourself a tight ship here," I say as she sets a cup of coffee in front of me.

"Thank you, ma'am. I do my best." She smooths her dark hair back like she's tidying it, even though it's tightly cinched in a knot bun atop her head, the size and shape of a goose egg. "I've been soaking your dress. Had my hands full with the guests and all, but I'll get that stain out today. Kerosene, lard, and a little elbow grease will do it."

"Thanks, Nell," I say as if having a maid fetch my coffee and clean my clothes is the most natural thing in the world—and then I catch myself. When I heard Jane talk down to Old Ida I swore to myself I'd never speak that way to anyone. "How long you been working here, Nell?"

"Six years, ma'am."

That must have been around the time Old Ida died. I remember Tom telling me the news on one of his trips to Hatfield. I never got a chance to say goodbye to her, even though after my own mama died, Old Ida was the closest thing I had to a mama in the Big House. I used to dream of Old Ida up in heaven with the ghosts of her mama's people. "They treat you well?"

"Yes, ma'am." Nell's hands go up to her hair again. She is a few years older than me, I figure, tall and rawboned, and she draws herself up to her full height, then adds, "I'm family."

"You're a Kincaid?"

"No, ma'am, a Porter. The Duke's ma, your grandma Edith, was my grandma's cousin. So we're cousins. Third cousins, ma'am."

It's my third cousin waiting on me and calling me ma'am? That doesn't feel right. Still, I reckon one way of helping out poor relations is giving them a job. I've always been treated like a poor relation myself—after all, the reason the Duke brought me back was to give me a job—so I know what it's like to be beholden to kin, to be dependent on their kindness, all the while knowing they can cut you off with a snap of the fingers.

"Call me Sallie."

"I'll do that, ma'am. Pardon me. Sallie."

There's a moment of quiet, the both of us trying on this way of looking at each other, as family, seeing if it fits, and I start to ask Nell about the Porters, but just then we hear the sound of piano music coming from the parlor—slow and sad, dark and yet somehow soothing. The Duke pushes through the kitchen door. "Nell, give me a moment alone with Sallie."

"I'll get on that dress, then." Nell lowers her eyes and heads back toward the wash room.

"Today, you start working with Eddie." The Duke gestures toward the parlor and on the arm of his mole-gray suit I see he's wearing a black mourning band. "My son, the pianist."

"He's pretty darned good."

"At tickling the ivories." The Duke shakes his head. "Sallie, you got to bring out the Kincaid in that boy. He's smart. That's not the problem. He was the smartest kid in school by a far sight, a prodigy, Jane always called him, smarter than his teacher by God, but he just had to go and let everyone know it. He was all the time correcting everyone else, including the teacher for Pete's sake, so even though he's a Kincaid—or who knows, maybe it's on account of him being a Kincaid—the other kids were always giving him a hard time, trying to get his goat, testing him with stupid little pranks, stuff they could pass off as an accident, jostling him, tripping him, knocking books off his desk, then making the deepest, truest, sincerest bullshit apologies you ever heard."

The piano goes silent.

"It's what boys do." There's a sheepish tone in the Duke's voice, like he's embarrassed by his own son. "Probably should have made the kid tough it out, learn how to fight back, how to stand up for himself, how to take a punch and how to throw one." He feints, drops his head, and makes a few shadow jabs. "But Jane"—he shrugs—"you know Jane. She always said Eddie became a fearful boy—that was the way she put it—only after he got knocked out, and of course she blamed you. But Jane was a handwringer herself, all the time fretting that Eddie would get hurt at school, pushed off the seesaw by some bully and hit his head again only this time he wouldn't come out of it—so a couple of years back, she started teaching him at home."

The kitchen door pushes open a few inches, and I see Eddie peering in, but the Duke's back is to him and he doesn't realize his son is listening so I give a little cough and nod sideways to signal the Duke, but he just keeps on talking. "Frankly, Jane coddled the boy. What he needs is people smarts, the common touch. He's my son. He's got some Kincaid in him somewhere. Find it."

The Duke heads out the back door, toward the carriage house, where he keeps the Packard. I turn to look for Eddie, but he's gone. And then I hear that sad, beautiful piano music start up again.

CHAPTER 6

EDDIE'S CLASSROOM IS A heck of a lot fancier than the one-room schoolhouse in Hatfield. It used to be a back parlor in the Colonel's wing and it has a carved marble fireplace, a slate chalkboard big as a mattress, and maps of Virginia, the United States, and the solar system. There's also a glass-fronted bookcase with a globe on top and inside are shelves of textbooks, the complete works of Jules Verne, and all twenty-eight volumes of the Encyclopaedia Britannica plus the index. Two desks with thin, curvy legs face each other in front of a window looking out on Jane's bright red tulips blooming in the back garden.

The drawers of one desk are as tidy and shipshape as Nell's kitchen, filled with pencils, a protractor, a drafting compass, a slide rule. Eddie's desk. Inside the drawers of the second desk are dog-eared copies of *The Saturday Evening Post* and *The Ladies' Home Journal*. Jane's desk. There's also an appointment calendar, marked up in Jane's perfect penmanship, entries that don't give me much to work with: "divine ratio," "Fibonacci sequence," "sun spots," "telescope," "Galileo," "Rome," "Caesar."

I sit down at Jane's desk. I can do this. I may not have a high school diploma, but I've had a high school education. In a sense. After I finished the eighth grade and started helping Miss Cain with the younger kids, she tutored me in high school subjects like geometry, biology, and literature. She also lent me her books, saying reading was a way of traveling the world, getting to know people you'll never meet, also traveling through time, getting to know people who lived long ago. I read and reread her copies of my two favorite books, *The Call of the Wild*—which made me see people the way a dog does—and Helen Keller's *The World I Live In & Optimism*, which taught me that if a blind, deaf girl didn't sit around feeling sorry for herself and instead learned to read and write, then I could also do anything I set out to do. Like teaching. Miss Cain told me I'd make a good teacher myself. She also told me that teachers don't know everything, but as long as they stay a step ahead of the students, the students think they do. That's my plan with Eddie.

When Eddie shows up, his thin, pale hair is combed back and his plaid shirt is pressed, but he has dark circles under his eyes that look almost like bruises and you can see the faint blue veins in his forehead. He's carrying a copy of a magazine called *Scientific American* and he sets it on his desk, then sits down and crosses his arms.

"It's awful soon after your mama's death," I tell him, "but the Duke thinks it doesn't do to worry on it, that getting back to work, keeping busy, will help us all move on. If you have a reading list or your mama had a lesson plan, we can start there."

Eddie shoots me a scornful look. "Don't try to be my mother."

"I couldn't be your mama if I tried, Eddie. It's simply that the Duke wants me to help you with your studies."

"I don't need your help. I don't need you tell me what to read. No offense, Sallie, but I'm smarter than you."

This must be the kind of talk that set the other kids to picking on Eddie, and I'm about to let him know that, but I stop myself. My brother's frail, doesn't have friends or pets, doesn't play sports, but he is very, very bright and he can't help himself, he has to let people know it, know he is always right, even if they hate him for it. Maybe, too, with his mama gone, it's the one thing that keeps him going, maybe it's all he has. There are people like Eddie, with plenty of book smarts but no people smarts. Then there are ones like the Duke, plenty of people smarts but a little thin on the book smarts. Then there are those rare few with both, like Tom, and they have enough people smarts to know better than to show off their book smarts.

"Eddie, I have a question for you. If you're the smartest person in the room, is it always smart to let everyone know it?"

"Absolutely. Nothing is more important than the truth."

He picks up his magazine and starts reading. Or pretending to. His eyes aren't moving. He's just staring at the page. Where to go from here? Bossing the kid around won't work, I'm sure as heck not going to outsmart him, so I'll stop trying to stay one step ahead of him, stop trying to play the teacher, and instead, I'll play the student.

"What are you reading?"

"You wouldn't understand," he says.

"Give me a try."

Eddie sighs, but then he starts talking, telling me about some expedition to South America in May to study a solar eclipse. A German scientist claims that light has weight, Eddie goes on, and this expedition could prove his hypothesis—the newspapers are calling it a theory, he says, but it's actually a hypothesis—by showing that the sun's gravity bends starlight. As he talks, his smart-aleck tone fades and he sounds almost awestruck. "It could be momentous," he says and repeats the word, savoring it. "Momentous. If gravity can bend light, then light has weight, and that means light is matter. That changes everything."

"You got me, Eddie. You said I wouldn't understand, and I don't."

"Of course you don't. No one does. Not fully, anyway. Because if he's right, that means the only difference between light and matter is speed. And if we travel at the speed of light, we'll become light."

I pick up Jane's marble paperweight. "This is a rock." I point through the window at the morning sky. "That's light. They're not the same."

Instead of arguing, Eddie stares out the window at Jane's bright red tulips. "Maybe that's what happened to Mama," he says. "She became light." Then he stands up and without saying another word walks out of the classroom.

A few seconds pass, then I follow him, holding back so he doesn't see me, listening to his footsteps slowly cross the hall and climb the staircase. A door shuts. On the second floor, the Duke's bedroom door is wide open and Eddie's is too, but the door to Jane's boudoir is closed. I go up to it, ready to knock, to see if he is all right, but I stop, because he's not all right. And I know what he's doing, burying his face in those beautiful dresses or holding the silver brush with Jane's pale hair still entwined in the bristles. There's something else I know to be true. Eddie needs to be alone with what's left of his mama.

The Duke's always hated being alone, I remember figuring that out when I was a kid. And now, in the weeks after Jane's funeral, he is all the time on the move, catching the latest scuttlebutt at Clyde's Barbershop while he gets his morning shave, eating his breakfast of steak and eggs and fried potatoes all covered with gravy at the Central Café while trading more scuttlebutt with folks who know they can always find him in the first booth. After breakfast, he heads to the Emporium, where he checks bills of lading while holding court, then he races around the county in the Packard, Cecil by his side, going from the mountains in the west, where we have timber stands and a sawmill, through the rolling farmland in the valley, with its tobacco fields and orchards, to the Finch River, fifteen miles away on the eastern border, inspecting the roads, barking orders at work crews, and signing invoices. And at dinner we always have guests. Always.

"Stay busy, you got that?" the Duke keeps on telling me. "That's the secret. Stay busy. It doesn't do to dwell on it." Stay busy. On the move. Keep the wheels turning. It's how the Duke gets out in front of his own grief.

Meanwhile, Aunt Mattie's taken over running the Big House. She's the oldest child and would have inherited the house, along with everything else, if she'd been born a boy—and she makes sure you know it. She shows up each morning at seven on the dot, makes detailed shopping lists, gives Nell her chores of the day and chores of the week, calls the Duke to discuss who to invite for dinner, and just before the guests show up, moves the place cards around like they're chess pieces.

Mattie is polite to me and I'm polite in return, neither of us mentioning our tiff at the wake. Like a lot of folks around here, Mattie was fond of the Duke's first wife, Belle—helped her run the Big House—and when the Duke divorced Belle to marry Mama, Mattie and her friends claimed Mama stole the Duke from Belle. Seeing me reminds Mattie of that whole messy business, even if she says nothing about it, but she seems to figure that if she's going to run the Big House, she'll have to put up with me for the Duke's sake. Jane always kept Mattie at arm's length, making it clear that Mattie had no claim on the Big House and was nothing more than a guest. Now, Mattie's clearly relishing her role as First Lady of Claiborne County and I'm happy to let her play the part. I have no interest in drawing up guest lists or arguing with the butcher's delivery boy about cuts of meat. Besides, I have my hands full with Eddie.

I keep trying to get him out of doors, keep trying to find the Kincaid in him. He follows baseball fanatically in the newspapers but he hates to do something if he's not good at it and I can't get him to play catch. We did go on one hike but we didn't get far on account of his allergies. I gave him a shooting lesson with the Duke's twelve-gauge but the noise startled him and the kickback near about knocked him over. I also wanted to show him how to drive, but he flat out said no, rattling off statistics about automobile fatalities.

So we stay in the classroom, and that's not so bad. Fact is, now that I'm the one with the questions and Eddie the one with the answers, I'm getting myself a pretty good education. And I've got to hand it to Eddie, he does have powerful book smarts. He loves anything to do with numbers, has even memorized train schedules, and has read every single one of the textbooks Jane ordered for him. He's also set out to read the entire Encyclopaedia Britannica. "Not front to back," he says, "that would be pedestrian." Instead he's reading one entry and then a related entry, and then an entry related to that one. "Once I've gone through them all, it will prove that everything is connected to everything else."

I've taken to reading those entries myself—darned if some of it isn't pretty interesting, "Monarch butterfly" leads to "Mexico" leads to "Aztec" leads to "Cortes" leads to "Spanish Inquisition" leads to "black plague" leads to "fleas" leads to "wings" leads back to "butterfly"—and as the days pass we get along better. A lot better. There's a problem, though. Everywhere he looks, he sees reminders of his mama—her roses now in full bloom outside the window, Jane's fountain pen and paperweight on her desk, her hometown circled on the map of Virginia—and whenever the memories become too much to bear, he's got to be alone, so he ups and leaves the classroom. And I let him be.

That's what happens one morning in early June, and I'm sitting by myself reading Eddie's *Scientific American,* trying to figure out this business about the speed of light—186,000 miles per second, dang, that's fast—when the Duke comes home without warning.

He sticks his head in the classroom. "Where's the boy?"

"Jane's room."

"What's he doing there?"

"He misses his mama."

"A steer misses its balls, but it still rejoins the herd. I thought you were going to bring out the Kincaid in him."

"We're working on it," I say.

"And?"

"And, Duke, I got to tell you, Eddie's darned good at what he's good at. He's smart as heck. Understands the speed of light. He's awfully talented."

"I know. The piano. And if he keeps at it, he'll end up like most piano players, banging out honky-tonk in a bordello."

"His heart's in music. Music and math and science."

"I don't care about his heart. I care about his spine. He's going to be running the county one of these days, not squeaking chalk on some blackboard or plunking a piano."

"Miss Cain used to say that teachers and parents can't change children and shouldn't try. What they can do is bring out children's strengths."

"His strengths." The Duke spins the globe then walks to the window and stands there, looking out. "He's not going to change," he says, more to himself than to me. "The boy's not like me. Jane was always going on about how Eddie was going to change, we had to wait for him to come of age, for his growth spurt, but he's not going to change and there's no use pretending he is." He turns around, faces me. "I'm taking the boy to the Emporium. Get Nell to burn Jane's clothes."

"You can't do that!" I blurt it out.

"Don't tell me what I can't do, girl."

"I'm sorry, Duke. I didn't mean that. It's just that, it's that—Eddie's not ready."

"I know it sounds hard, but trust me. It's time for Eddie to be moving on. Boy's got his whole life ahead of him. I know what I'm doing. You and Mattie help Nell. Get it done quick. It's for the best."

Maybe I can talk him out of this. "Those are nice dresses. Expensive. We could just fold them up and put them in trunks in the attic."

"And the boy will end up sitting in the attic all day."

"Or give them to charity."

"I don't want that boy pitching a fit again if he sees some woman wearing one of his mother's dresses."

Like he did when I put on Jane's black dress. I can't win this fight. That's clear. If I keep trying, I'm only going to make the Duke even more angry with me and more disgusted with Eddie. So I nod.

After lunch, the Duke and Eddie head to the Emporium, and Nell, Mattie, and I start pulling Jane's beautiful clothes off their hangers. We carry them outside, along with Jane's dainty little shoes and her boxes of hats and gloves and her chemises and corsets and underskirts and camisoles and stockings, and we dump everything into the burn pit behind the carriage house. The dresses lie there, a heap of pink satins and lavender silks and lemon-colored chiffons and ivory lace and I wonder if this is what happened to Mama's clothes. Burned by the help. I'd never thought about it before and I can't remember anything, but the Duke must have taken me off to the Emporium just like he's done with Eddie while someone—might even have been Aunt Faye, come to think of it, she was there—got rid of Mama's clothes, because by the time Jane showed up, they sure enough had disappeared, along with every other trace of her. Except the photograph and the necklace. And me. Then Jane took the photograph. And then she sent me away. And all that remained of Mama was the moonstone necklace buried at the bottom of the rosewood jewelry box.

And now Jane is disappearing, too.

"This is going to break that poor boy's heart," Nell says.

"How do we tell him?" I ask.

"We don't," Mattie says. "The Duke will never say a word about it. Eddie's got to learn that in this family, there are certain things you simply don't talk about. Nell, fetch the kerosene."

Mattie lights the fire and as the flames go up in a whoosh, I reach into my dress pocket and finger Jane's sterling silver hairbrush, the one with strands of her hair still in the bristles.

Boy's got to have something of his mama's.

CHAPTER 7

"I GOT BUSINESS IN Danville. Back in a couple of days." The Duke puts on his hat and tugs at the sleeves of his mole-gray suit. He stopped wearing the black mourning band two weeks ago, that same day we burned Jane's clothes.

The smell of smoke from that fire still hangs in the air. Or maybe it's only in my head. After the fire burned down, I slipped Jane's hairbrush under Eddie's pillow. Early the next morning, he was standing by the fire pit, staring at the smoldering remains of Jane's shoes and corsets—so he knows what happened—but he hasn't said much of anything since then. Isn't even interested in discussing the solar eclipse or reading the Encyclopaedia Britannica. Just plays his sad, beautiful music on the piano or stares out the window at Jane's roses.

Mattie follows me onto the porch and we watch the Duke drive off. "You know why he's going to Danville?" she asks.

"Business, he told me."

"He's in the market for a new wife."

Could Mattie be teasing me, testing me, trying to see if news like this will upset me? I'll be darned if I'm going to let her know that it does. Because what Mattie's saying could be true. And if it is true, this new wife might turn out to be like Jane, only she'll want to get rid of both me and Eddie, so I have to be prepared.

"Someone in particular? Or is he just kicking tires?"

"He's got a prospect. Newly widowed. No money, but no children, either. Sheriff Earl's brother Seymour knows her. He says she's easy on the eyes, broad in the beam, and has a sweet disposition. The Duke started talking about finding a new wife, so I told him about her."

Mattie's never confided in me like this, as if we're bosom buddies. What the heck is she up to now? I know Mattie loves her role as First Lady of Claiborne County and a new Mrs. Kincaid could well mean she'll have to give that up. So could be she's thinking that as long as the Duke's bound and determined to get remarried she should be the one to steer the right woman his way. It will put both the Duke and the new wife in her debt.

Mattie seems to read my thoughts because she says, "A new woman in the house will change things for both of us, Sallie. We'll have our hands full training her." She says it in a playful way and smiles at me for the first time since I've come home, smiles at me as if—after everything that's happened—we're in this together, we've got to make sure a new woman understands she can't freeze us out the way Jane did. One thing about Mattie, if she does something for you, she's going to want something in return. For every give there's a take, for every to there's a fro. She doesn't want my friendship, she wants an ally. But I don't trust her any further than I can throw her.

"You think the Duke is serious?" I ask.

"He says it's not too late to have more sons."

That Friday afternoon, we hear the trumpet blare of the Packard's horn. Eddie and Mattie and Nell and I file onto the front porch as the Duke opens the car door and helps out a big-hipped woman with honey-colored hair.

"He went for looks again," Mattie mutters.

Not looks, in my opinion. The Duke twice married women from Old Virginia families and now, for the second time, he's married a woman who came from nowhere. He wasn't shopping for a blue-blood name, he wanted a woman with what they call good birthing hips.

The woman tucks her right hand into the Duke's cocked elbow, with the left she's clutching a needlepoint valise. The Duke leads her up the steps, introduces us, and she gives everyone a hopeful smile. There is something candied and creamy about this woman, the lazy, swaying way she moves, her sloping shoulders and round face and muffin-soft flesh.

"Meet Katherine," the Duke says. "The new Mrs. Hank Kincaid."

"You all just call me Kat." Her smile broadens. "I've heard so much about each of you. Eddie the smart one. Sallie the brave one. Mattie the strong one. Nell the hardworking one."

"Soon as I laid eyes on her, I knew," the Duke says. "When it comes to horses and women, I go with my gut."

"And I found out real quick you can't say no to Duke Kincaid." Kat giggles, low and syrupy. "Not that I wanted to."

I watch Mattie sizing up this woman, the fourth woman her younger brother has taken as a wife. A sly little smile comes creeping across Mattie's face and I figure she's thinking, this one's going to be a pushover.

The Duke ushers Kat into the parlor and she oohs and aahs in a surprised, delighted way that gets the Duke to beaming. She runs her hands lightly across the horsehair sofa and the matching flame-stitch wing chairs, fingers the silk fringe on the shades of the standing electrical lamps, plays a few quick notes on the upright piano. The Duke shows her the small portrait of his grandpa Bull Kincaid, a stiff-backed, unsmiling man in a dark coat, and the huge portraits of himself and the Colonel in the library. He explains the three wings of the Big House, how each was built by the new generation, each man making the place his own, adding to the Kincaid heritage. Then we all follow them up the stairs to the second floor.

The Duke has kept the door to the boudoir locked since we burned Jane's clothes and now he takes out the key and opens it. He had Nell scrub the room and air it out—there is no more scent of lilac—and she's polished the mirrors, waxed the vanity, fluffed the pillows on the fainting couch, and put fresh-cut roses in a vase. But the bare clothes hangers are dangling in the open closets and the room feels empty and forlorn.

"This is yours," the Duke tells Kat.

"My own room?"

"Consider it your personal domain."

Eddie stares into the boudoir. It's the first time he's seen it since Jane's clothes were burned. He knew his mama's belongings were gone, but still, the sight of those stripped closets and naked clothes hangers has got to cut him to the bone.

He turns away and walks down the hall, his thin shoulders stiff. Maybe I ought to run after him, do my best to comfort him, but with everyone watching that would only make things worse. Eddie closes the door to his room and Kat glances his way, then at me to see what I make of it. I force a smile. The Duke takes no notice of Eddie's leaving, or least ways acts like he doesn't. His eyes are on his new wife.

"You can do whatever you want with this room," he says to her.

"Anything?" Kat sounds surprised. "I love the color pink. How about I paint the walls pink?"

"You can paint polka dots on the walls if you want. The rest of the house stays the way it is."

Kat's smile tightens. "Of course."

"You reckon she's going to be making any changes?" Nell asks me after dinner. The Duke and Kat have retired for the evening, Kat blushing as she said her good nights to the rest of us. "She going to want me to start making them oysters croquettes or à la mode this or flambé that or whatever fancy food stuff they eat in Danville that I never heard of? Or maybe bring in someone who has?"

"I wish I could tell you, Nell."

"I know you had your differences with Jane, but she treated me fair and square and I'm right sorry to see that little boy watching this new woman sitting in his mama's seat at the dinner table and then going off with his daddy to sleep in his mama's bed."

Nell's right. Dinner was trying, the Duke and Kat exchanging overheated glances while poor little Eddie stared wordlessly at his plate and I sat there worrying about being sent back to Hatfield. But Mattie was right, too. There are certain things in this family you don't talk about—the Duke forcing his new wife on his son like this sure as heck is one of them—and if the Duke barges into the kitchen and hears Nell talking like this, she'll be out on her ear. "Nell, I know you're worried—I guess we all are—and I'm usually in favor of speaking your mind, but right now, I think it's best if we keep our thoughts to ourselves and do everything we can to make Kat feel welcome."

On Saturday morning, the ladies in white gloves come calling. Mattie has arranged it all, and of course she's here to oversee the get-together. Just before the ladies show up, she pulls on her own pair of white gloves. So does Kat.

Wearing white gloves is a way of letting everyone know you don't have to get your hands dirty working but instead have leisure time that you spend on clubs and committees and societies. Such airs are of the utmost importance to some town women—the wives of the judge, the bank president, the undertaker, the clergy—who are eager to set themselves apart from women of the hollows. Myself, I never have spent much time around ladies in white gloves, sure don't own a pair, so I keep on finding reasons to mosey by the parlor, and whenever I do, I slow down, my eyes and ears wide open so I can take in all the white-glove talk and white-glove manners.

Nell brings in a tray of cheese rolls and pecan loaves she's made from her book of recipes. She's trying her best. So is Kat, sitting on the sofa, knees together, ankles crossed, white-gloved hands folded in her lap all proper-like.

While the people of Claiborne County are by and large a friendly lot, they're keenly aware of their stations, of who are the haves and who are the have-nots. I can see the ladies in the white gloves trying to decide if Kat's going to fit in and if so, how, all the while filling her in on the relative merits of the bridge club, the garden club, the needlepoint circle, the Caywood Beautification Society, and the Better

Streets and Sidewalks Society. They also give Kat the lowdown on the Claiborne County families that matter, the families that matter more, and the families that should under no circumstances be invited to the Duke's dinner table. Meanwhile, Mattie passes around teacups and they all sip their tea with their white-gloved hands.

After church on Sunday, the Duke holds a welcoming party in the garden. Kat stands in front of the low stone wall—behind her Jane's fading peonies are so heavy with blooms they bend under their own weight—and the Duke introduces her to the menfolk whose wives she has already met, everyone on their best behavior but also sizing her up like a prize heifer just bought at a cattle auction. Then the Duke raises his glass in a toast. "To my new bride," he says. "I only got her to marry me by lying about my age, my fortune, and my temper."

Everyone bursts into laughter, Kat laughs harder than anyone, and later, as the party winds down, she says we ought to take a walk. I swing in beside her, slowing my pace to meet her easy, swaying gait. Her scent is sweet and flowery, like a magnolia.

"By any chance, do you like to swim?" she asks.

"Flail around to keep from drowning is more like it."

"I love to swim. Truly I do. Every summer, my late husband would take me to Virginia Beach. Are there any places for a body to swim around here?"

"Finch Lake has a dock. Water's cold, though."

"Cold water's good for your complexion. We must go swimming together." She links her arm in mine. "I've met so many new people, I swear I can't keep their names straight, and everyone's got something to say about everyone else."

"I'm sure people have said all sorts of things about me. Some of it might even be true."

"Don't you worry, sugar." She squeezes my hand. "I want to be your friend."

That evening before dinner, Eddie is at the piano, his tuning kit out. I sit down next to him on the bench. Ever since Kat arrived, two days ago, he's been spending a lot of time in his room. I keep quiet, waiting for Eddie to say whatever he wants to say about Kat—or anything else—but he says nothing, so I speak up. "What do you make of her?"

"I haven't formed an opinion." He sets a tuning fork on the piano. "She smells nice."

"She says she wants to be my friend."

"She told me she's not going to try to replace Mother." He taps the tuning fork on his knee, it quivers and lets out a hum, and he strikes one of the keys then listens for a moment. The fork and the key make the same sweet sound. "But she has. She has replaced Mother."

The next morning, Kat knocks on the classroom door. "Mind if I sit in?" She's carrying a plate of fresh-baked gingerbread cookies.

Maybe I do. I've been trying as best I can to make things work in this classroom, and it is working, but just barely, and I surely don't need the new Mrs. Kincaid here.

I glance at Eddie, expecting to see a flash of anger or ill will— the woman who took over his mama's boudoir is now moving into his classroom—but he simply shrugs.

This is up to me.

"Kat, it's a little tight in here," I say, "and Eddie already thinks that I'm one teacher too many."

"Oh, don't worry about me, sugar. I'm here to learn something." She sets the plate of cookies on Eddie's desk. "I can squeeze myself into that little corner chair and I promise I won't be stepping on anyone's toes."

Kat gives me her most disarming smile. I don't want her here. That's my first thought. But after all, we're both in the same tricky spot, both trying to win over the same demanding man and moody boy—and I ought to give the woman a break.

"Have a seat," I say.

Eddie takes a cookie, nibbles, and nods. He's been telling me the latest news about that solar eclipse and Kat begs him to start from the beginning. She keeps on interrupting, saying things like "well, now, isn't that something" and "gracious, I had no idea," and before long, Eddie is eating another cookie and explaining the speed of light to her while she gives him that same disarming smile. Kat's good at this, good at bringing people around and getting them to open up.

That afternoon, the sound of Eddie playing the piano fills the house. It's a new piece, slow like most of what he plays, but tender instead of sad. Then a second pair of hands starts in. It's a duet. I peek into the parlor and see Eddie and Kat side by side.

Kat comes to the classroom again the next day, and the day after that, always carrying a tray of cream puffs or sugar cookies. Then every afternoon she and Eddie play the piano. But whatever else Kat does, she makes sure she greets the Duke at the front door when he gets home. She brings him a tumbler of whiskey, rubs his shoulders, and listens to him talk about his day, the decisions, the plans, the problems solved, the problems postponed.

"I like the woman even more than I thought I would," the Duke tells me two weeks after he brought Kat home. "She's a great conversationalist."

Because she lets you do all the talking, I think, but I say, "She is a great listener." Then I add, "She surely is spending a lot of time in the classroom."

"She told me. Says she's helping you."

"That classroom's a mite small for two teachers." As soon as the words leave my mouth, I know I made a mistake. I sound like a complainer and the Duke hates complainers.

"You're smart," he tells me. "Work it out."

CHAPTER 8

THE DUKE ALWAYS PULLS out something to read when he has no one
to talk to, another one of his ways of keeping busy. He gets newspapers from all over the state and I look over them every day to keep
up my end of the dinner table talk. I'm also starting to make my
way through the books in the floor-to-ceiling bookcase on one of
the walls of the library, grown-up books that I was too young to read
before, like *The Great Rebellion* and *Letters of a Self-Made Merchant
to His Son*, but right now I'm going through the *Danville Bee*, and
there's an article that's filling my head with steam, some writer scolding women who are hanging on to jobs that men need, going on
about how it was one thing for women to work while the men were
away at war, but now that they've returned, women have a patriotic
duty to give the men their old jobs back so they can take care of us
women.

Lamebrain newspaper writer ought to get out of his office and see
the way the world works. He could interview me about it. Or Aunt
Faye. Because sometimes men don't take care of the women. And
that's why we women need our jobs.

Fighting over jobs. They're doing it all across the country, and
that's what I'm doing right here in the Big House, only I'm not fighting a man, I'm fighting another woman, because while I'm reading
newspapers, I'm also listening to Eddie and Kat playing one of their
duets—Kat laughing and taking the blame whenever one of them
messes up—and I know that my days as Eddie's tutor are numbered,

that Kat is edging me out, and I wonder if that means I am headed back to Hatfield.

Just then the telephone in the hallway rings—two short rings followed by a long one, the signal on the party line that the call is for the Big House. Mattie's still coming over every day to plan dinner, still holding on to her role as first lady, and she answers. "Kincaid residence, this is Matilda Kincaid Johnson speaking."

I overhear a few mumbled words of a conversation, then Mattie calls out in a loud voice, "Sallie, it's Faye Powell."

It's been three months since I came back, and Aunt Faye and I write each other once a week. I let her know that the Duke wants me to stay on and she keeps assuring me all is fine, but we haven't talked since I left Hatfield, and seeing as how there's no telephone in her house, I wonder where she's calling from.

Mattie holds out the receiver to me. "Something's wrong, but she wouldn't say what."

"Aunt Faye? Where are you?"

"The clinic." The line is crackling with static and her voice is small and faltering, but it sounds like she's crying. Mattie stands there, all ears, and I turn my back. "Aunt Faye, are you okay?"

"No, honey, I'm not."

"What's wrong?"

"I know you got your hands full there with the Duke bringing home a new wife and all, and I hate to bother you so I didn't write you about it but I am having myself a few little problems."

It takes a while to pull the story out of Aunt Faye, but she lost the laundry job, couldn't get the stains out of those sheets all on her own, so she started working as a waitress at the Roadhouse, like she'd done before. She met a man there and invited him to move in with her. The deal was supposed to be that they'd share expenses and he'd pitch in with the chores. For a few weeks, all was hunky-dory, but then the man started drinking, rooting through her purse to get his hands on the grocery money, and when she tried to take it back, he hit her.

I feel sick. Sick and responsible. This is my fault. I promised to take care of Aunt Faye but I haven't. I've fretted over it, but fretting isn't doing, and this is what happens.

"Where is he now?"

"At the house. I don't know what to do. Maybe you can talk some sense into him."

The Roadhouse.

I remember that night in Hatfield when Aunt Faye came back from the Roadhouse.

The night I found out.

I was thirteen.

The winter wind woke me, shrieking through the hollow, battering our house, whistling between the cracks in the walls, rattling the bedroom window, whipping the roof with the naked branches of the ash tree. I looked over to see if the wind woke Aunt Faye, but her bed was empty. She was working late again. Times were hard. A blight was wiping out the chestnuts—the biggest cash crop in these parts—and the few women who used to pay Aunt Faye to style their hair or fix their clothes had taken to doing it themselves. We were low on food, almost out of coal, and the fifteen dollars the Duke sent every month for my upkeep didn't go as far as it once did, so Aunt Faye took on work, waitressing at the Roadhouse, a rough-and-tumble place a mile down the tracks from Hatfield that was visited by loggers and sawmill men.

During a lull in the wind I heard the rusty front door hinges screech open. Aunt Faye was home. A flicker of light came from the parlor as she lit the kerosene lamp. I got up to check on her.

She was slumped over in the padded armchair, her face in her hands, her threadbare wool coat at her feet.

"Aunt Faye?"

She looked up. One eye was swollen and dark.

"Aunt Faye! What happened?"

"I don't—" She turned her face away from the lamplight and into the shadows, like she couldn't meet my stare. "I don't want to talk about it."

"Tell me," I said gently as I could.

"A customer"—she paused—"he wouldn't give me my token of appreciation."

"You mean your tip?"

"No." Aunt Faye raised her eyes. "From time to time, men ask me for something special." She was speaking in a strange, faraway voice. "In their rooms. Then they give me a token of appreciation."

A token of appreciation? What was she talking about? I waited for Aunt Faye to explain but she didn't, she just stared down at her hands in her lap, the slim ladylike hands she was so proud of. Then it dawned on me. What she was talking about. What the token of appreciation was for.

"But this man hit me instead." Aunt Faye looked so wounded, so desperate, and I figured that must be about the loneliest thing in the world, what she did. And then to get smacked around afterward. That'd be enough to make a woman feel worthless.

Back when the Duke first brought me to Hatfield, he gave me a silver dollar and told me it was "in case of an emergency." If I'd known what Aunt Faye was up to at the Roadhouse, I'd have given it to her. So I went into the bedroom, got the silver dollar from the bundle under my bed, and held it out to Aunt Faye. "I've been saving this for a time when we really needed it," I said. "That time's here."

"Honey, that's yours," she said. "Besides, once it's gone we'd still be in the same boat."

"Aunt Faye, you can't go back to that Roadhouse. I won't let you."

"How are we supposed to make it through the winter?"

"We'll find a way."

That was when I got us the job washing the clinic sheets. Aunt Faye complained that the lye ruined her hands, but it kept her out of the Roadhouse.

Now she's back there. And it's my fault.

* * *

I half-walk, half-run the mile to the Emporium, and when I get there, my breath's ragged, but the words come rasping out. "Aunt Faye's in trouble."

"Not for the first time." The Duke is at his desk and next to him, in Cecil's chair, is Tom Dunbar. He returned to Georgetown after Jane's funeral, but now he's back for the summer, helping out, collecting rent and running errands for the Duke while the regular wheelman tends his crops.

"It's serious," I say.

"And don't tell me," the Duke says, "it involves a man."

I nod. He's not going to make this easy and going into the particulars won't help, so I simply say, "You got to send someone."

"I'm not wasting the deputies' time on this, Sallie. Faye Powell's not a bad woman but she's always getting herself into these jams. If I keep bailing her out, she won't learn to take care of her problems herself."

"I'm going then," I say. "Can I take the Lizzie?"

The Duke considers for a moment then nods. "She is your aunt."

Tom stands up. "I'll go, too."

The Duke nods again, like he figures I could use backup. I'm not scared, at least that's what I tell myself, but if I'm going to walk into Aunt Faye's house and tell this thug to clear out and stay out, I got to let him know I mean what I say.

"I need a gun."

"Don't be a hothead, Sallie," the Duke says.

"Just for show."

The Duke tosses me the key to the gun case by the door. "Take the twenty-gauge. But don't let things get out of hand."

Outside, I break open the shotgun to check if it's loaded. There's a shell in each barrel.

"I'm driving," I tell Tom.

"You're too worked up to drive."

"I thought I sounded calm."

"I've known you too long, Sallie. I can tell when you're calm and when you're only acting calm."

"Driving will settle me down."

I climb behind the wheel while Tom cranks the Lizzie's engine and a couple of minutes later we're speeding across the valley to Hatfield.

Tom is right. I'm not calm. How could I be calm when some lug belts my aunt? Aunt Faye's in a bind, but still, she should have known better than take in this lug to begin with. And the Duke shrugging it off like he doesn't care one hoot about Aunt Faye, that didn't calm me down either.

"Slow down, Sallie." Tom puts a hand on my arm, and then in a gentler voice says, "Your aunt will be okay. We'll see to that."

"She wouldn't have got hurt if I'd been there."

"Sallie, I don't know if that's true, and you don't either. But I do know you couldn't stay in Hatfield when the Duke sent for you. You had to come back. You had no choice. And you'll always do your best to take care of your aunt. Just like you're doing now."

The tightness in my chest eases some and I throttle down. "Are all college boys as smart as you?" I glance at Tom as he smiles and shakes his head to let me know he's not going to touch that question. I wonder if he's feeling any fear. He's been through the war. Does that make you less fearful when it comes to a fight? Or more?

Tom got back from Georgetown only a couple of days ago and this is the first chance I've had to talk to him. "Help me take my mind off Aunt Faye, Tom. Fill me in on what you've learned at college."

"I'm taking a course in psychology. The professor spent an entire lecture explaining how most folks have no idea why they do what they do."

"Tom Dunbar, you're paying good money to learn what any one of the cardplayers at the Emporium would have told you for free?"

Tom laughs that slow, easy laugh of his, then runs his fingers through his dark hair, pushing it off his high forehead—one of his habits, something I've watched him do since we were kids.

"Sallie, there's something I have to tell you." He reaches over and tucks a stray lock of hair behind my ear. "I'm engaged."

"Engaged?" His words jolt me so hard I almost veer off the road. "To be married?"

"You told me not to wait around." He gives me an off-center smile. I try to smile back, but a sudden feeling of panic seizes me.

"Congratulations." I hope the word sounds happy. "This is grand news. She got a name?"

"Amy. Amy Gordon. Her father is my law professor."

Tom is right, I told him not to wait around. Never thought he'd move this soon. Also, I figured that if he did marry someone else, he'd find himself a nice Claiborne County girl, come work for the Duke and we'd stay friends. Guess I took that for granted, Tom's friendship, assumed he'd always be around, but if he marries his professor's daughter, they could stay in Georgetown, I'll lose my dearest friend, just about my only true friend, and the thought makes me sick. Can't let Tom know that. "What she's like?"

"Reminds me of you—in some ways."

"What ways?"

"She knows what she thinks and she's not afraid to let you know it. But in other ways, she's completely different from you."

"Will I like her?"

He looks out the window for a moment. "I don't know."

We're heading up into the mountains, the tree branches above us so thick it's like we're driving through a leafy tunnel. In less than half an hour we'll be in Hatfield and I feel my chest tightening again. In my mind I can see this lug, sauntering through Aunt Faye's open door, sitting in Aunt's Faye's little parlor drinking whiskey, a pistol probably in his belt, and he's still on my mind when we pull up in front of the faded sign that says FAYE'S DRESS-MAKING & HAIR-STYLING. I take a deep breath. My hands are shaking, not with fear, but with fight because I'm a long damned way from calm and I grab the twenty-gauge and charge through the door without stopping to knock.

Voices come from the bedroom, and that's where I find them,

Aunt Faye and some big, slope-shouldered grizzly bear of a man with a flat nose and stubbly jowls, lying under the sheets. Aunt Faye sits up and tugs the sheet around her chest—she has a couple of dark stitches across her cheekbone—and then she starts apologizing and saying how she and Wayne here have straightened it all out, he had whacked her pretty good, but it was more or less an accident, and truth be told, she brought it on herself, she was running her mouth, he is for the most part a good man and Wayne is nodding his block of a head, then he leans across the bed and extends his paw of a hand to shake mine.

He looks hurt when I don't take it.

"I usually stand when a lady enters the room, but I'm sure you can understand why I'll stay right here where I am," he says. "Faye's told me all about you."

"Aunt Faye, you've got to kick this lug out of the house," I tell her, but she keeps saying they straightened it out and everything is fine. I look back and forth between Aunt Faye smiling contritely and Wayne nodding agreeably.

"What am I supposed to do, Aunt Faye? First you wanted me to get rid of him, now you want me to shake his hand."

"Situations change."

"This one surely has."

"I'm on my own. I'm doing what I have to do."

"Situations change, but people don't. This man's dangerous."

"I'll be fine, Sallie."

The fight drains out of me and all of a sudden, I feel empty. Tired. I turn around. Tom is standing in the doorway. "I tried, Tom."

He shakes his head sadly. "You did everything you could. Let's get out of here."

I head through the front door and past that faded sign, breaking open the twenty-gauge and popping out the shells, then climb into the car while Tom, still muttering in exasperation about Aunt Faye, about how you can't take care of someone who won't take care of themselves, bends over to crank the engine. It sputters and knocks, but instead of catching it kicks back. Tom swears and clutches his wrist.

What a disaster. I try to help Aunt Faye and Tom tries to help me but Aunt Faye ends up staying with the lug and Tom gets so riled up he breaks his wrist. The nurse at the Hatfield Clinic fashioned a splint and now we're heading back to Caywood. The Duke was right, I should have stayed out of it.

"Must hurt like heck."

"I won't lie to you."

"I'm awful sorry, Tom. It's my fault and I feel rotten about it."

"It was my fault, Sallie. I know better than to crank with my right hand. Just wasn't thinking. But listen. I have an idea. Since I won't be driving anytime soon, get the Duke to give you my job."

"I can't do that, Tom. It's on account of me that you broke your wrist. I can't go and—"

"Like I said, it's not your fault. And someone's going to get the job. Might as well be you."

"The Duke would never give that job to a woman. A girl. Driving. Collecting money. It's a man's job."

"That's exactly what he thinks but I know you can do it and you know you can do it. You're a better driver than me."

"I don't know about better. Faster, maybe."

Tom laughs. "You're good with numbers, too. And people. You can talk a cat out of a tree."

"I can't just walk out on Eddie."

"You'll still be his sister. Eddie doesn't need a teacher, he needs an audience. From what I hear, Kat is more than happy to do the listening and the clapping. Nothing wrong with that. But that's not what you're cut out for."

"Tell that to the Duke."

"You're the one who has to tell him. Give it a shot. Sell him on the idea. If you get the job you can start sending your aunt a little money and she might not need that Wayne fellow around anymore."

Tom's smart. Maybe the smartest man I know. Why did he have to decide to go and get married? "How do I do that, Tom? Sell him on the idea?"

"You're a Kincaid. Play that up. Get the Duke to think you're exactly like him, except in a skirt. Because sometimes you are."

"You really think so?"

"It's not a compliment."

CHAPTER 9

GOT TO GET THE Duke when he's alone, so the next morning, as he's heading through the back door, I follow him onto the porch.

I can do this. Practiced in front of the mirror last night and again when I woke up. "Make me your wheelman."

The Duke shoves his hands into his pockets and his eyes take on that irritated squint they get when someone asks for something he doesn't want to give. He's looking for a way to brush me off and walk away, so I get between him and the porch steps.

"I'm a good driver."

"So I heard. But you've got a job. Looking after Eddie."

"Kat's better at that than I ever will be. Eddie's taken a real shine to her."

"Driving's not a woman's job."

"Why?"

"It's hard work. Man's work."

"When I helped you build that"—I point to the stone wall in the garden—"you told me I was a hard worker. Took after my old man."

The Duke purses his lips and plays with the coins in his pocket. "Just how good are you behind the wheel?"

"Let me show you."

"You're pushy, Whippersnapper."

"It's the Kincaid in me."

The Duke tries not to smile. "What the hell? Let's take the Lizzie."

The car's in the carriage house, parked next to the Packard. The

Duke climbs into the passenger seat, folds his arms, and watches while I reach inside and set the spark and throttle levers, go around to the front, pull the choke wire with my right hand and give the crank a fierce turn with my left. The engine coughs to life and I scurry back to the driver's side, reset the spark and throttle, climb in, release the hand brake, press my left foot on the low-speed pedal, and the Lizzie chugs forward. I take it slow down the driveway—my old Defiance Coaster Course—then turn onto Crooked Run Road and when we reach the macadam pike to Wrightsville I put her into high gear and throttle up, hitting thirty, then thirty-five on the straightaways.

The Duke is watching my hands move from the throttle to the steering wheel, but he keeps his thoughts to himself. After ten minutes he taps his fingers on the dashboard and says, "Okay. I've seen enough. Let's go back."

I could razzle-dazzle him with a skid turn, slamming on the brakes and spinning the wheel, but I figure I might look like a hotfoot, so instead I go for a crisp three-pointer, left into a cattle crossing, and right in reverse, then straight ahead back to Caywood.

"Right nice move there," the Duke says. "You know how to steer and shift."

The Duke isn't a man who throws his compliments around, so I know he means it and I'm thinking I've finally done something to impress him, but then he adds, "There's a lot more to being a wheelman than knowing how to drive a car."

"I'm up to it."

"You think this job is fun? You think it's an adventure?" I'm staring straight ahead, at the road, but I can feel the Duke's eyes on me, boring in. "You drive around all day on rough back roads, eating dust, getting calluses on your hands and your ass, trying to squeeze money from tenants who don't want to give it to you, who just want to belly-ache about life. This is what you want to do instead of staying at home tutoring a thirteen-year-old boy?"

"Yep. Kat's better with Eddie, better at getting him to want to do things, making him think it's his idea. You said I take after you. I want to work like you do."

"That's not my plan for you."

Don't argue, but don't agree. Find the in-between. "I know. You want me to get married and give you a bunch of grandsons." I turn down Main Street and park the Lizzie in the shade of a sycamore. "And I will one of these days. But right now you need a driver."

"You think you want this job?" The Duke's eyes narrow. "Tell you what. I'm going to give it to you. For a week. We'll see how it works out. My gut tells me that you're going to come to me on your hands and knees begging for your old job back. And out of the goodness of my heart, I'll give it to you. But after that week, Kat's becoming Eddie's tutor and your old job is gone. Got that? Don't come to me in the middle of an August heat wave, pining for your job tutoring your little brother in the comfort of a cool house."

"Thank you."

"Thank me at the end of the week." The Duke opens the car door. "One more thing. Don't expect special treatment. I didn't get special treatment from the Colonel, and you won't get any from me. I'll treat you fair, but I won't treat you special."

Mostly, I collect rent. Rent and debts. Or payment in kind. And the Duke was right, it is a horrible job, grueling and dusty, grimy and greasy, thankless and endless. And I love it. The Duke has tenants all over Claiborne County, mostly poor folk because the people who rent are the people who can't afford to buy and they live in shabby little houses like Aunt Faye's, or in dark, cramped apartments over stores, or on hard-luck farms with land so steep folks joke that they have to shoot their seeds up into the fields with their shotguns.

The tenants with jobs at the lumber mill or the warehouses or on a road crew pay cash. Some tenants pay with Kincaids, as we call the scrip we give out at the Emporium. The dirt farmers pay with corn, tobacco, hams, eggs, sacks of walnuts or potatoes, jars of pickles or fruit preserves, but mostly bottles of homemade whiskey—and we sell it all at the Emporium.

The routes are easy to figure out, the tenants, less so. They keep their hardships hidden, but it's clear that many of them, even families with both a mama and a daddy under the same roof, struggle to make ends meet, struggle even harder than Aunt Faye and I did in Hatfield. My third day on the job I stop at a tidy shotgun house a short ways from the Finch River. Family by the name of Mead, according to the leather-bound ledger the Duke gave me. Three dollars fifty cents, the fifteenth of every month. Laundry is flapping on a clothesline and a woman with a fussing baby answers the door. She doesn't look much older than me, but her face is tired and haggard and her back is already bent, like she's been carrying a heavy load her whole life.

"Afternoon. Name's Sallie Kincaid," I say.

"Heard about you," she says. "You're the Duke's daughter, here to collect rent. Thing is, Miss Kincaid, we're short this month."

Behind her, a man is standing in the shadows, staring down at the floor like he can't bring himself to meet my eye. Must be Mr. Mead, who also couldn't bring himself to plead with me and that's why his wife is doing it.

"We ain't lazy." There's a touch of defiance in her voice. "Carl's a saw man at the mill. Works hard. But the baby had to go to the clinic, needed medicine and we had nothing set aside, so we had to dip into the rent money."

Could be she's testing me, looking to see if I'm soft in the heart, head, or spine. But the tidy house and the shamed husband, the woman's red eyes and colicky baby all tell me they're good folk going through a bad spell. "I'll mark you one month arrears," I say. "We'll work it out. But from now on, you got a problem making rent, and folks do, let me know ahead of time. We can always work it out. But do let me know. The Duke hates surprises." The baby lets out an unhappy wail. "I'll stop by in a few days. If that little fellow isn't better, I'll tell Doctor Black to pay you a visit. Best doctor in the county."

Back at the Emporium, I give the Duke the ledger and tell him what happened with the Meads. He nods in approval. "You got to know how to tell the shirkers from the truly hard up. Know when to cut folks some slack and when to tighten the reins. I told you it was going to be hard."

"And you'd have to beat me with a big old stick to get me to quit."

The Duke chuckles. "People seem to be taking a liking to you."

"It's the Kincaid in me."

"Maybe it is at that." The Duke clasps his hands behind his head, like he's reconsidering me.

"No need to wait until the end of the week to tell you I want the job for good," I say. "So is it mine?"

He nods. "It's yours."

"One more thing."

"What's that?"

"You're paying me, right? Whatever you're paying your wheelman."

The Duke thinks for a moment, then nods again. "Sounds fair. And I said I'd treat you fair."

I'm grinning ear to ear just like a kid, remembering how it felt to get the Duke's approval back when I adored him, back when I was the Whippersnapper. He's grinning too, like he's remembering how it felt to be adored by the Whippersnapper.

At the end of the week, Cecil Dunbar pays everyone who works for Kincaid Holdings, and I stand in line along with the rest. No special treatment. Cecil counts out my five dollars—a dollar a day for five days' work. Back at the Big House I put two dollars in a sock and hide it under my mattress. The other three go into an envelope for Aunt Faye. I write her a note saying that with this extra money she won't need Wayne and I'll send more if she kicks him out. But I can't do that, can't set the rules for the forty-three-year-old aunt who raised me. All I can do is hope. So I throw away the note and send the cash along with my love.

CHAPTER 10

THE FIRST WEEK OF September brings on a late-summer heat wave. The mercury climbs to near one hundred, roadside buckeyes are wilting, and poplars are shedding yellow leaves. It's also dry, the creeks thinned to a trickle, the roads swirling with dust so thick it's sometimes hard to see. I don't want to quit my job, but I am feeling hot and tired and gritty on Thursday evening when I get back to the Emporium. The Duke's at his desk, his black jacket off and his tie loose, dark circles of sweat in the armpits of his white shirt. A sandy-haired fellow is sitting next to him in Cecil's chair, looking crisp and cool in one of those pale blue seersucker suits.

"Sallie, this is Seymour Johnson, Sheriff's brother," the Duke says. "Seymour, this is my daughter."

It's Kat's friend, the one who told Mattie and Sheriff Earl that the Duke ought to meet her. He stands up, tall and lean. When he smiles his teeth are white in his sun-darkened face and the smile makes crinkles in the corners of his yellow-green eyes. "Miss Kincaid. Even prettier than I heard."

"You should see her when she's washed off the road dirt," the Duke says with a grin.

Then this stranger takes my hand and he shakes it and I shake back, but he's doing something kind of peculiar, using both hands, shaking with his right while covering my hand and squeezing it gently with the left, staring deep into my eyes the whole time, and I go stupid. I can't think of what to say. Maybe it's because I'm dazed on account of the heat, or maybe it's because no man has ever looked at me like that or held my hand quite that way or told me how pretty I am but I just stand there staring back at him and feeling his strong hands squeezing mine.

The Duke clears his throat and suddenly I can think again. More or less. "I don't know what you been told," I say to this Seymour fellow, "and I don't reckon I want to know, but welcome to Caywood, Mr. Johnson."

I pull my hand out of Seymour's and pass the ledger to the Duke. Most days he looks at the figures right away, but now he sets it on his desk without a glance. "Seymour here is one of those professional baseball players, but says he's tired of playing games for a living and thinks he may want to get a real job. With us."

"Game's changing," Seymour says. "Fans don't care about skill anymore. All they want to see is home runs."

"And a cleaner game," the Duke says with a smirk.

Seymour shrugs. "So it's time to get out."

"Probably is." The Duke stands up the way he does when he wants the conversation to end.

Seymour nods. "I've taken up enough of your time, Duke. But do give some thought to what I've said."

"I will. And Kat's invited you for dinner tomorrow night."

Seymour gives the Duke a snappy little two-fingered salute, reaches for my hand and squeezes it again, then moves smooth as a panther out the door. I watch through the one-way window as he walks off, his footsteps light and quick. He glances back and I drop my eyes, thinking Seymour caught me looking at him. But of course all he saw was the mirror.

"That boy left the game under a bit of a cloud," the Duke says, "but there's nothing wrong with breaking a few rules. We do that all the time around here."

"You going to hire him?"

"That's a possibility. A real possibility." He pulls a cigar out of his pocket and clips off the end. "He might make someone a good husband."

"You're sure in a hurry to marry me off."

"You told Tom not to wait around and now he's moved on. But you're not getting any younger and there's plenty of men out there who would think that Sallie Kincaid is a right fine catch."

Seymour does come for dinner the next night, along with Mattie and Sheriff Earl. Kat is downright giddy with excitement, telling Nell to cook up Seymour's favorite dish, roast loin of veal, and that makes me wonder how well she knows this baseball-playing fellow. I wonder even more during dinner, wonder if anything ever went on between them, because Kat laughs maybe a little too hard at Seymour's jokes and she swats the top of his head with her napkin whenever he says anything fresh, and then he flashes a cat-that-ate-the-canary smile and says that seeing as how he introduced the Duke to his lovely new wife, the least the Duke could do in return is give him a job.

The Duke lets out a short grunt of a laugh, but I can tell he doesn't find it the least bit funny, just wants to pretend Seymour's joking. Then Sheriff Earl starts needling Seymour about why he really left baseball, saying it was because he'd placed bets against his own team, and Seymour says of course he bet against his own team if it had no chance of winning, but he never threw a game—and he laughs as if that was a joke, and then he needles Sheriff Earl back, says his big brother taught him how to pitch, but never had what it takes to become a pro himself.

That gets Seymour going on about life in the majors. We all listen, but Eddie—who follows baseball the way a pig farmer studies pork belly futures—is soaking up every word of Seymour's stories about winning streaks and losing streaks, about dugout-emptying brawls and fights in the stands with fans, about fastballs and dead balls and scuff balls and dirt balls, and about Seymour's specialty, stealing bases.

The two of them start trading opinions about overrated and

underrated players, rattling off statistics the whole time—batting averages, strikeouts, men left on base.

I start sizing up this Seymour fellow and before I know it, I'm leaning in to listen to him. Maybe he played fast and loose with the rules, but there's something about him that's hard to resist—and I get the feeling he knows it, that he's accustomed to boys asking for his autograph, men shaking his hand, women making goo-goo eyes at him. Seymour loves being the center of attention, loves it every bit as much as the Duke does, and then I look at the Duke. He'd started out the evening the center of attention—opening the wine, making the toasts, telling the jokes—but now he's all quiet and sullen, a sour little smile on his face as he listens to this former baseball player putting on the charm for his son and his new wife and his daughter, this upstart who has taken over his own dinner table.

Seymour did a quite decent job of picking up on the Duke's cues in the office yesterday, but tonight he doesn't seem to notice the change in the Duke's mood, and with the Duke quiet, Seymour talks all the more, laughs louder, gestures more grandly.

"When you see the opportunity to steal a base, it's there for only that one split second, and then it's gone," Seymour tells Eddie, snapping his fingers. He reaches for the bottle of fancy, imported wine—even though it's the Duke who always pours the wine—and refills his own glass. "You got to seize that opportunity, you can't spend time thinking about it. You just go."

"Stealing bases is an empty stunt." The Duke's voice is final.

"No disrespect, Duke," Seymour says, refilling Kat's wineglass, "but I'm the ballplayer here and stealing a base can put you in a scoring position, and that can make the difference between victory and defeat in a close game." He chuckles, adding, "And the good games are all close."

"Base stealers are showboats," the Duke says. "Most of the time they get thrown out."

Kat looks nervously back and forth between the Duke and Seymour, but Seymour won't drop it. "Just because you get thrown out doesn't mean you were wrong to try," he says. "If you go only when it's a sure thing, you'll never become much of a base stealer."

The Duke likes to have the last word in every back-and-forth but before he can say anything, Seymour turns to Eddie. "What you'd be great at, kid, and what you should give some serious thought to, given your grasp of statistics, is managing a baseball team, maybe someday even owning one. Hey, maybe that's what you Kincaids should do, start your own ball team."

"I'm not going to pay a bunch of grown men to run around in short pants," the Duke says. "And my son's going into the family business. Then politics."

A silence falls across the table. Seymour looks around and finally seems to realize he's overstepped himself.

"I have an idea," Kat pipes up. "Let's have a picnic on Saturday. At the lake. Get a break from this heat. Boys and girls, men and women together. It will be the last swim of the summer."

Chapter 11

THE PACKARD STOPS BESIDE the dock on the rocky spit of land that juts out into Finch Lake. It's a long, narrow lake and the sloping mountainsides that rise up on both sides—too steep to farm or log—are thick with dark green trees. The water is also dark green, so dark it's just about black, and at the far end of the lake a steel railway trestle soars high above the water, its arched black beams looking delicate and almost lacy at this distance.

I get out and shade my eyes against the ten o'clock sun. Kat has put together quite a party for our picnic. All of us from the Big House, plus Mattie and Sheriff Earl; my cousin, Ellen, and two of her friends; then Seymour and George and Casey Bailey, the two young deputies Earl treats like sons.

Under my street clothes, I'm wearing nothing but a jersey knit bathing suit, and when I slip off the dress, I feel like a plucked chicken. Never been so bare-skinned in front of so many people. We Kincaids are land people not water people and for us, swimming means splashing around in creeks and frog ponds when we were kids. But earlier in the summer Kat ordered me this bathing suit and asked me along on a couple of ladies-only swims. She also ordered bathing suits for Eddie and the Duke, but this is the first time they've worn theirs. I watch everyone stepping out of their clothes—most of the men's hands and faces are brown as walnuts, but their arms and legs are pale—and everyone's doing their best to act natural but in fact, it's the first time anyone can remember men and women swimming together in Claiborne County—and so everyone is in a racy mood.

Seymour is the last to arrive, in a spiffy Saxon roadster with a black hood and yellow doors. Underneath his street clothes, Seymour is wearing a sleeveless black bathing suit that shows off his ropy shoulders and his legs, long and lean muscled and covered with whorls of sandy hair. I can't stop staring.

Seymour trots to the lake and when he gets near the end of the dock, he raises his arms and I get a peek of sandy-colored hair nestled in his armpits. I try to look away. I can't, but everyone else is looking too, and Seymour skips twice, throws himself into a handstand at the edge of the dock, then kicks his legs out and pushes himself off the dock, doing a somersault in the air before splashing into the water. He comes to the surface and throws himself into a backstroke, fluttering his feet and milling his arms, heading for the far side of the lake.

Sheriff Earl's two deputies whoop and charge along the dock and jump into the water. So does skinny little Eddie and the Duke does too, his gut swagging inside his bathing suit.

I race to the end of the dock, my bare feet loudly smacking the wooden boards, jump up in the air, and plunge in like the men did. The water is bracing, cool but not cold, and when my head pops back out I shake it, whipping my wet hair around, and the water smacks George Bailey in the face, then he laughs and splashes me back.

We watch the other women climb properly down the wooden ladder and ease themselves into the lake. Kat glides through the water, her arms moving smooth and slow as a heron's wings, while the other women dog-paddle in circles with their heads up, careful to keep their hair dry as possible, but everyone is feeling frisky and bold and there is plenty of horseplay and giggling and squealing.

After an hour or so of frolicking, the men sprawl on rocks, sunning themselves, and the women put on big hats to keep off the sun and spread blankets on the ground, then set out fried chicken, corn bread, shucky beans, elderberry pie, and, of course, sweet tea.

I sit next to the Duke on a red-and-white checkered blanket, my bathing suit dripping and heavy. Seymour fetches a baseball and a couple of mitts from his roadster, then he calls over Eddie and explains the grips he uses for his pitches—knuckles turned in for one, fingers splayed along the seams for a second, spit worked into the ball's leather for the third. By now everyone's watching as Seymour shows Eddie the pitching stance, how you stand sideways, shoulder to home plate, raise the left knee for the delivery, plant the left foot just so, release the ball like this, and swing the right leg around in the follow through. Seymour lobs a few pitches to Casey Bailey then tosses the ball to Eddie. "Give it a try," Seymour says.

Eddie takes the ball and studies it, then—you could knock me over with a feather—assumes the pitching stance. Seymour adjusts Eddie's shoulders and moves the ball around a bit in his hand, and then Eddie winds up and throws. It's a game effort. The ball bounces into Casey's mitt.

"Here, buddy," he says as he tosses the ball back to Eddie, "try again."

Kat comes over carrying a plate of chicken and beans along with a glass of sweet tea for the Duke and we watch Eddie throw another pitch. This time it goes right into Casey's mitt, a little low, but another game effort.

"Your son's really taken a shine to Seymour," Kat says. "You could hire him to be Eddie's coach, to teach him sports, develop him physically like you're all the time saying he needs. I could work with him on his lessons in the morning and Seymour could take him in the afternoon."

It's true, that is what the Duke's been saying, but he just gives a sour smile like he did last night when Seymour took over the dinner table. "I could do a lot of things," he says.

He sets his plate of chicken on the blanket, stands up, puts his hands on his hips, and looks down the lake to the trestle. "Throwing a ball doesn't prove squat," he says to everyone. "When I was a boy, we jumped off that bridge. Who's coming with me?"

"Hank, you shouldn't," Kat says.

"Been doing it since I was eight."

"I don't know if it's a good idea." Kat glances around. "Don't you all agree? It might not be a good idea?"

"You're putting it to a vote now?" The Duke gives her a look. "Okay, let's have a vote. I vote we're doing it. So we're doing it. Who's coming?"

"Count me in," Seymour says. Sheriff Earl and the deputies nod.

"Anyone else?" The Duke looks at the rest of us.

Leaping from the trestle is a rite of passage for the bravest boys in Claiborne County. Never done it myself, never even climbed up to it. Is jumping brave? Or downright foolhardy? Both, of course. And of course I'm going. Maybe I can still get the Duke to see me in a new light. "I'm in."

The Duke nods. "Eddie?"

"Please, Hank, he's just a boy," Kat says.

"Are you?" the Duke asks Eddie. "Just a boy?"

Eddie hesitates. He looks at Kat, who shakes her head, then at Seymour, who winks at him and gives a tiny nod.

"Sure," Eddie says. "I'll go."

"That's settled then," the Duke says.

Kat's right. Eddie ought not be doing this. He looks determined but also fearful, just like he did when he first climbed into the Defiance Coaster, aching to impress the Duke when he was three years old. That was my fault, and maybe this is, too. How could Eddie refuse after his sister said she'd go? I could announce that I've changed my mind, decided that's too risky for my taste, but Eddie won't back down now. If anything happens to him, I'll never forgive myself.

Still, I follow the Duke along the edge of the lake. We all do, wet-headed and bare-footed, the air hot and heavy, smelling of lake water and echoing with the clattery song of the cicadas. Ahead of us, startled frogs leap to safety as we approach and all around us dragonflies big as sparrows hoover and shimmer in the tall grass. We pick our way over boulders, sometimes jumping from rock to rock, sometimes wading through the warm, shallow, brackish water, keeping our eyes out for snakes, and finally we reach the base of the mountain below the trestle.

"Race you all to the top!" Seymour shouts and clambers up the slope above us. It's steep and thick with scrub oaks, skinny poplars, thorny locusts, and blood-red sumacs along with brambles and wild grapevines, and there's no clear path so we all follow Seymour, scrambling up, grabbing the vines and branches, hoisting ourselves over the granite outcroppings, knocking loose stones.

We reach the tracks and sit down on the rails. I'm panting and sweaty, plastered with dirt and briars, my knees skinned and my hands and feet raw. Eddie's sitting between Seymour and the Duke, sweaty and panting too, but for someone who hates the outdoors he seems to be holding his own. I take a good look at the tracks. They come out of the tunnel in the far mountain, cross over the water on the trestle, then disappear into the tunnel in the mountain behind us. In the midday sun, the steel is gleaming like silver, so bright it almost stings my eyes, but the bolts holding the tracks down are dull black and the ties beneath them smell of tar.

After a couple of minutes, the Duke stands up, yawns, and stretches. "We got to get out in the middle," he says, "where the water's the deepest."

We follow him out across the trestle in silence, everyone's movements measured and careful, Eddie holding his arms out to the sides like a tightrope walker. There is nothing on either side of us except the still air and nothing between the ties, just empty gaps and the sight of the flat black lake far, far below. Looking down makes me dizzy, but I must—to decide whether to take small, cramped steps from tie to tie, or awkwardly long steps, skipping every other tie. I take the small, deliberate steps, planting a foot squarely each time and ignoring the dizzy feeling because up here you have to pay attention to everything, you can't take anything for granted, and every small step feels like a minor triumph.

At last we reach the middle of the trestle and line up along the tracks. Far away on the rocky spit, the little squares of picnic blankets look like postage stamps and Kat and the other women are tiny figures standing on the dock, shading their eyes from the sun with their hands, watching us.

No one is in a great hurry to jump. Seymour keeps fooling around, windmilling his arms, pretending he's about to lose his balance, and the Duke pretends to push him, and then they both throw back their heads laughing, har-har-har, as if it is all hilarious.

That is when we hear the rumble of the train.

It's in the far tunnel. The rumbling grows louder and the tracks start to vibrate. The white glare of the locomotive's headlight appears inside the dark tunnel. The engineer must see us, because the train whistle gives off loud, urgent blasts.

"Time to go!" Seymour shouts. "Don't think about it. Go!"

Sheriff Earl jumps and the deputies quickly follow.

They slide through the air below us, getting smaller, disappearing into little white splashes in the black surface of the lake.

Now, there is just me, Seymour, the Duke, and Eddie on the track and the train is getting closer, louder, its engine thundering, its whistle screaming, its steel wheels grinding and white sparks shooting up from the tracks. There is no way it can stop.

"Jump, Eddie!" the Duke shouts.

Eddie stares down at the lake.

"You go, Sallie!" Seymour shouts. "Cross your arms and legs." He wraps his arms around his shoulders to show me. "Don't think about it. Go!"

I do it. I leap up and out. I hang in the air for what feels like a very long instant and I am weightless, then I drop. Everything slows down, it seems to take forever to fall through all that empty space—the air rippling my hair skyward, tugging up my bathing suit, the black surface of the lake rushing at me—and I have time to think, so I do what Seymour told me to do, I wrap my arms across my chest and I cross my legs at the ankles.

I hit the water. Hard. An exploding sting. I knife through it, plunge down, pulled deep, the water is colder here and I am pulled deeper, now it is downright icy, and I start to slow and finally I stop. I open my eyes. Nothing. Everything is inky blackness. I start to float upward, but don't know if I can hold my breath all the way back, so I start clawing up, the water is getting warmer and the blackness is now a murky grayness but my lungs are burning, they are about to burst—don't know if I can make it—so I keep clawing until finally my face breaks through the surface, into the sunlight, gasping, heaving, gulping air.

I look toward the sky, toward the bright, bright sun and the trestle, and that is when I see it, see the locomotive come hurtling out of the tunnel—whistle blaring, smoke billowing, the engineer leaning out, waving frantically. Seymour grabs Eddie by the hand. They are tiny. They jump. The two of them fall through the air, then Seymour lets go of Eddie's hand and they drift apart and become bigger until they're full size and then in a rush they hit the water.

Back up on the trestle, the Duke leaps. He is falling slowly at first but then he spreads out his arms and legs and I'm trying to figure out what he's doing and why because he starts to roll backward, then he starts flailing his arms and legs like he's trying to fly but that only brings his feet up more and his head down. Something is wrong. He's almost flat on his back and he's closer now and it's all so fast it's almost a blur and I scream but can't hear myself because the locomotive is rushing overhead and the Duke hits the water and it explodes in a huge, violent splash.

The train goes into the tunnel and everything is quiet except for the rumbling cars and I am staring at the spot where the Duke landed and he comes back up, but just floats there, motionless.

PART II

CHAPTER 12

CECIL DUNBAR IS AT the head of the walnut dining table, looking over the Duke's will, tapping his fountain pen on the tabletop. The sound echoes through the dining room, where we're all gathered, and the house now feels so empty and still that the tap-tap-tap seems loud, too loud, almost deafening.

Eddie's next to Cecil, his head down. He's barely said a word in the last four days. I told the Duke that I'd take care of Eddie, swore I'd protect him, and he surely looks in need of protection, but how do you protect someone from grief? Sudden noises startle him and he wanders around the house fragile as a dragonfly's wing, his skin so waxy and thin you can see the blue veins pulsing in his hands and temples. Some people seek the comfort of others when they're grieving, but Eddie's one of those who hides in the dark corners of his own mind, and I haven't seen him cry.

Kat's been crying nonstop. Eddie at least has us Kincaids to turn to but Kat is surrounded by people she barely knows. She's all alone except for her friend Seymour and she is the kind of woman who craves the comfort of others. At the wake she nodded gratefully at anyone who offered it, even strangers mumbling a few awkward words of condolence.

Like Eddie, I haven't cried. That surprises me. When I was in Hatfield, the Duke was always part of my thoughts. I relived each moment of that day he sent me away, imagined how I'd do it all different if I had the chance, and also planned how, if the Duke ever let me back into his life, I'd show him that I wasn't the disappointment he thought I was. In the last few weeks, I had the feeling that I was close to doing just that, getting him to see me in a new light, maybe even winning him over, maybe even one day talking to him about Mama.

Now that will never happen. Now I will have if-onlys and what-might-have-beens. That creates a hurt, but not the kind that makes you cry.

"Let's get started," Mattie says. She and Sheriff Earl are at the far end of the table with my half sister, Mary, who's come in all the way from Mercer County, where her mama's people live. She's the daughter of the Duke's first wife, Belle, and I've met her only once, when she visited the Big House shortly after Eddie was born. I was five and she was fifteen. I thought she was old, but she was younger than I am now. I know from Aunt Faye that Mary never forgave the Duke for divorcing her mama. Her face is stony and guarded, her dark hair up in a braided coil, and pinned over her heart is a mourning brooch with woven dark hair inside, which I take to be her late mama's.

Cecil stops tapping his pen and runs a hand over the thin, silver hair he combs straight back. Cecil, the Duke's counselor, the one man he trusted, is trying to move us all forward, all of us who never imagined a world without the Duke at the center of it.

"As you all know," he says, "the Duke was exceedingly scrupulous about legal documents." He had revised his will twice within the last year, Cecil goes on, once after Jane died and again after he married Kat. Then Cecil pushes his spectacles up his long, thin nose and starts reading. "I, Henry Edward Kincaid, being of sound mind and body . . ."

Cecil continues in lawyer language, telling us what we already know, that it's the Kincaid family tradition going back generations—a tradition that's been the cause for a goodly amount of envy and anger—for the eldest son to inherit everything. Only if there's no son does it go to the eldest daughter. Chop it up and parcel it out, the Duke always said, and it will all be gone in a couple of generations. So the Big House, the Emporium, the land, the businesses, and the investments are all going to Eddie.

Cecil turns a page and reads on. "My daughters, Mary Kincaid and Sallie Kincaid, will each receive twenty-five hundred dollars as a dowry if and when they marry."

Isn't that just like the Duke? Even from beyond the grave, he's trying to bait me into taking a husband.

"My wife," Cecil reads, "Katherine Howard Kincaid, is to receive five hundred dollars."

"But where will I live?" Kat's voice sounds ragged and confused.

Cecil raises a finger. "We'll get to that." He reads on. "In the event of my death my wife may continue to live in the Big House, located at 9136 Crooked Run Road, at the discretion of my heir. Nevertheless, the Big House will remain in the possession of my heirs in the order of succession."

"So," Mattie says, drawing out the word to let us know what she thinks of it all, "this woman who was married to my little brother for less than ten weeks is going to be living on in the house where I was born and raised?"

"At the discretion of the heir," Cecil replies.

"And what about the heir?" Mattie asks.

"He's a minor," Sheriff Earl says. "Who's going to look after him?"

Cecil straightens his spectacles. "The will doesn't address that."

That seems odd, seeing as Eddie's future was so important to the Duke. He must have had his reasons and I'm wondering if I ought to ask what they are when Kat, jolted out of her daze, speaks up.

"Eddie's going to stay here with me, of course," she says. "I'm his stepmother. I've been tutoring him and taking care of him. He's got his sister Sallie here. Eddie belongs here. With me."

"You're not even a blood relation," Mattie tells her.

"That's right," Sheriff Earl says. "Eddie should be living with us."

"Or we should move into this house to take care of him," Mattie says. "I'm the Duke's older sister."

"Eddie ought to come and live with me," Mary cuts in. "I'm the Duke's eldest child and Mercer County is a God-fearing place. Quite frankly, Claiborne County is too wanton for a boy like him."

That really gets my goat—Eddie's feeling a lot of hurt for a bushelful of reasons, but living in a so-called wanton place, the only home he's ever known, is not one of them—and I'm not going to hold my tongue any longer. "Maybe we ought to ask Eddie. He's smart." I turn to him. "Eddie, what do you want?"

He's still looking down at the tabletop, his face hidden, and that empty silence fills the room again. Finally, without looking up, he says, "I want things to stay like they are. I want to live in the Big House with you and Kat."

"Very well." Cecil taps his fountain pen again. "As heir, that's your prerogative. You're a minor but you're old enough to have your wishes taken into consideration." He looks at Mattie. "Eddie will remain at the Big House with his stepmother Katherine Howard Kincaid and his sister Sallie Kincaid."

Cecil slips the will into his briefcase, looks around and nods, and we all stand up, the chairs scraping the floor noisily. The others file out but I haven't been alone with Cecil since the Duke died, and I linger behind to talk.

Cecil never has been a robust or hearty man but now he looks shrunken, lost, with gray skin and a slight tremor in his hands. Ever since the Duke took charge, Cecil has been at his side, and I'm reminded of a lion tamer in a circus that came to Caywood. He was slight, like Cecil, but he could get that fierce beast to roll over and purr. Then one year the lion died. The tamer stayed with the circus, taking tickets, but he looked like a ghost—and it hit me that the man tamed the lion, but the lion gave the man his heart. Maybe that's the way it is with Cecil.

"Cecil. You've been looking after all of us, but this has taken a toll on you, too."

He stares off into the distance. "I keep thinking of things I have to tell him, things that he has to do—we have to do."

"Who's going to run it all now?"

"Sheriff Earl is the Duke's brother-in-law. Until Eddie reaches his majority, there's really no one else. Mattie will be right beside him."

"If the Duke was so scrupulous about such things, why didn't he appoint a guardian for Eddie?"

"Truth is, even when he was rewriting his will, he didn't think he'd die. Not so soon, anyway. And you know the Duke, he believed in playing people off each other—balance of power, he called it. Mattie and Sheriff Earl are already going to be running the business and he didn't want his sister getting any ideas—or acting on ideas she's always had. But he didn't want Kat getting any ideas either."

We join the others on the front porch. I'm surprised to see Seymour Johnson is there. He touches his hat brim as Mary passes him. Eddie and I watch our sister walking toward her hard-topped Studebaker. She's stout and slow-moving. When she turns back, I wave and she gives us a nod, still stony and guarded.

"She sure is in a hurry to leave," Eddie tells me.

"I'd hoped she'd spend the night," I say, "maybe give the three of us a chance to get to know each other after all these years."

Kat puts a hand on Eddie's arm. "I need some air, sugar. You up for a walk?"

"Mind if I join you?" Seymour asks, and the three of them start down the steps. I almost go with them—I could use a little fresh air myself—but I stop. I wasn't invited.

"Your brother has been hovering over that woman like a vulture." Mattie's talking to Sheriff Earl in that loud whisper she uses when she wants other people to hear her. But what she said is true.

At the funeral, Seymour Johnson was downright courtly toward Kat. He helped her out of the Packard and into her chair, and when she broke down sobbing by the grave, it was Seymour who offered her a handkerchief.

"And she is not letting go of Eddie, is she?" Sheriff Earl asks.

"That woman may be staying in the Big House, for the time being," Mattie says to Cecil, "but nothing in it belongs to her. So I'm taking the family jewels—for safekeeping. Don't want anyone to start selling them off."

"Might be for the best," Cecil says.

"Kat Howard is not family," Mattie tells me. "Someone's got to look after our heirlooms."

I watch Mattie head into the house. Our heirlooms? Don't that beat all? I've always been the outsider in Mattie's eyes, an interloper, a Powell not a Kincaid, who ought to have stayed in Hatfield, but now she thinks some kind of rift is coming, so I'm family, we're in this together. Mattie is as much an operator as the Duke ever was.

She comes back with the rosewood jewelry box, and takes out a brooch the size and color of a plum. "The Colonel gave this to my mother when he came back after the war. Every piece in this box was given by a Kincaid man to a Kincaid woman either in gratitude or in penitence. Every piece has a story and I know them all."

Those stones could be rubies, or garnets, or just paste—I'm not one who can spot the difference—but that brooch could mean as much to Mattie as Mama's moonstone necklace means to me. Mattie ought to have it. But I surely am glad I took the necklace when I had the chance. Might have never seen it again.

Mattie tucks the jewelry box in the back of her Buick. "You never knew Mattie's mother, Edith," Cecil tells me. "Edith was the real brains behind the Colonel. Mattie's got a lot of her mother in her. Stay on your toes."

Chapter 13

I can't sleep.

I'm lying in bed and I keep thinking about Eddie saying he wants to stay on in the Big House with Kat and me. We've both lost two parents now, but it's got to be hitting Eddie harder, only thirteen and still grieving for his mama when his daddy dies. I have some notion of what he's going through—but I haven't found a way of letting him know it, a way that matters.

The night breeze rustles my curtains. Fresh air. I need a walk. The walk I didn't take with Eddie and Kat.

Outside, the moon is a thin sliver, a rind, the sky is pitch black and the stars are so very bright. Now that the Big House is wired for electricity—light at the flick of the wrist—I don't give as much notice to the moon and the stars as I did back in Hatfield.

The low stone wall is hard and cool on my rump when I sit down and gaze up at the masses of bright stars. When Eddie and I talked about that solar eclipse, we also talked about how stars are in the sky all day long, you just can't see them on account of the sun being so bright. You need the darkness of night, or an eclipse when the moon briefly blots out the sun, to see the stars by their own light. So most things you can't see in the dark, but other things—like stars—you can see only in the dark. That's what I've been doing since the Duke died, sitting in the darkness waiting for whatever has its own light to show itself.

* * *

Breakfast the next morning is a quiet, sad affair—little eating, no talking—and even before the plates are cleared Eddie and Kat leave for the parlor. It's where they're spending most of their time lately, the red velvet curtains drawn. I hope for the sound of the piano, but there is only more quiet.

When Jane died, Eddie was deep in grief—but he still played those beautiful, haunting songs. Now he's dry-eyed, distant and brittle. Sometimes, he reads or he and Kat play cards. Or he does nothing, just sits slumped-shouldered in a wing chair, then out of nowhere jumps up and paces around the parlor like he's looking for something he can't find. Kat sits on the horsehair couch, fingering her wedding ring, twisting it around, worrying it with her hands, dabbing at tears with her kerchief, and from time to time lets out a small sigh or whimper that she doesn't seem to know she's making.

As for me, I'm making do, I tell myself. But I'm snappish and cross and if someone tries to hug me or offer words of condolence, I push them away. It strikes me as belittling, the idea that a hug or a few words would comfort me.

And I'm getting back to work. That's not defiling the Duke's memory. It's honoring his words. Stay busy, he kept saying after Jane died, stay busy.

Driving into town, I get to thinking about Aunt Faye. She was at the Duke's funeral. We didn't have much chance to talk, but she took his death real hard. A childless old widow is paying Aunt Faye to cook, clean, and just keep company, but I could tell she's barely getting by. I'll get up to Hatfield as soon as I can, but not today. First I've got to see Mattie and Earl. Make sure I still have my job. She seems to have it out for Kat and anything could happen. Like Cecil said, stay on your toes.

On Main Street, the shopkeepers who closed their stores after the Duke's death are rolling down their awnings and setting out stacks of newspapers, chairs for sidewalk sitters, and cases of empty soda bottles to be returned to the bottling plant. Getting back to business as usual. Good for them.

Just as I step into the Emporium, the door to the Duke's office swings open and Seymour comes out, looking flushed and irritated. Then he sees me. "Sallie, how you doing?"

I've been asked that question dozens of times since the Duke died, and I don't know if I can ever find the words for what I'm thinking or how I'm doing. Don't know if I want to, so I simply say, "I can't believe he's gone."

"I know. The great Duke Kincaid. Ran this county like his own darned fiefdom for twenty-five years. You all are going to miss him, that's clear as day." Seymour shakes his head. "Anyway, here to kiss the ring?"

"What do you mean by that?"

"You'll find out soon enough."

Through the office doorway, I see Sheriff Earl sitting in the Duke's swiveling oak armchair. Mattie's on one side of him, Cecil on the other.

"Sallie, come in here," Sheriff Earl calls.

"And close the door," Mattie adds.

Earl looks fidgety and out of place behind the Duke's desk, like he doesn't belong there and knows it. He and Seymour grew up working the sorry soil of their daddy's failing tobacco farm, and marrying into the Kincaids was Earl's way out, just as baseball was Seymour's. There were those in Caywood who believed the Duke's only sister had married beneath her station, but after Mattie became Mrs. Johnson, the Duke made Earl sheriff. He always called the Duke "boss." Now Earl is the boss. But he owes it all to Mattie and neither of them ever forgets it.

"Big changes are coming, Sallie," Mattie says and picks up the Duke's ivory-handled letter opener and twirls it. Sheriff Earl may look out of place but Mattie seems completely at home.

Cecil gestures at the ledgers piled on the desk. "Sheriff Earl and Mattie want a complete review of the books."

"Top to bottom," Mattie says. "Then it's going to be a whole new ball game."

"What does that mean?"

"We'll let you know soon as we finish the review. The question is, Sallie, are you with us on this?"

"My brother was just in here asking for a job," Sheriff Earl says. "Thinks he ought to be my right-hand man. But Seymour's always just been out for himself."

"Like letting us know Kat was looking for a husband," Mattie says. "Thought that would give him an inside track."

"Seymour's not loyal," Sheriff Earl goes on. "Are you loyal?"

Why the heck would anyone ask you if you're loyal? What fool would say no? I look at Cecil and he smiles slightly. We both know the Duke would never ask you if you're loyal. The Duke just knew. But Sheriff's not the Duke. Even so, and even though I don't know what these big changes will be, I nod. "Loyal as the day is long."

"Then you've got a chance to prove it," Sheriff Earl says.

"You saying I still have my job?" I ask.

"Of course. You're family." Mattie points the letter opener at me. "But I've got a bit of advice for you." And then she says very slowly, "Don't disappoint us."

Today was long. And rough. People in these parts don't take well to change—but the Duke's passing means change is in the cards. Some folks loved the Duke. Others found him high-handed, bossy, and overbearing. But they all felt that in a pinch, he'd be there for them. Now, they're sick with worry about what is going to happen—to them, to the whole county. I spent the day reassuring folks that everything would be fine—and doing my best to believe what I was saying.

The peepers have stopped their evening song by the time I scrub my hands and face at my washstand. I pull on my nightgown and my fingers touch the ceiling. It's that low, the ceiling in the stone wing. The Duke moved me here after Eddie was born because Jane complained that my nightmares kept waking the baby. At first I felt cast aside, banished—back before I found out what it was like to really be banished—but Old Ida's room was next to mine, and she told me

stories about what had happened long ago in the forest where the Big
House now stands, stories she said the stones in the walls had told
her, stories about spirits who knew what had passed and what was
coming, stories about children who could fly and beasts who could
talk, and I grew to love my room, with its sloping heart-pine floorboards and the plastered-over fieldstone walls more than a foot thick.
It's solid. It suits me. The one place in the Big House I've always called
my own and when I came back from Hatfield I moved right into it.

I'm about to climb into bed when there's a knock on the door.

"It's Kat."

"Come on in."

"I've never been in here before," she says, sitting down on the bed
next to me. "It's cozy."

"Cool in the summer, freezing in the winter. I'll be building a fire
every night come the frost."

"A sweet little room for one person," Kat says. "Sleeping alone in
the Duke's big bedroom doesn't feel right."

"There are spare bedrooms all over the house."

"That wouldn't feel right, either. Might as well come out and say
it. I don't belong in the Duke's bed. That's what people think. That I
don't belong." She grips my arm hard, pulls me close, and I smell the
sherry on her breath. "It's my fault the Duke died."

"Oh, Kat, don't be doing that to yourself."

"It's true, all the same, and you know that. If I'd never had the
idea to go on that picnic. If Seymour hadn't been there to lead everyone on . . ." Her words trail away. "And now I'm a widow. Again.
It's on account of me that the Duke's gone and people want me gone,
too." She can tell by the way people eyed her the one time she went
into town, the way they pulled back or shunned her, the way the few
neighbors who dropped off bereavement dishes found flimsy reasons
not to come in and visit. "I know everyone thinks I got no business
staying here in the Big House without the Duke."

No one I talked to today asked after Kat—not Mattie, not Sheriff
Earl, not any of the tenants—and I'm pretty sure she's right, folks

think she doesn't belong in the Big House without the Duke here, and they can't help but blame her—at least in part—for his death.

"Kat, you got as much business living here as anyone," I say.

"I'm all alone. Except for Eddie. And you. And Seymour."

"Seymour?"

"He stopped by today. He told me he keeps seeing it over and over in his mind, that he blames himself, that he ought to have stopped the Duke from going up on the trestle. I told him that I blame myself, too. But then we both agreed that no one could stop the Duke from doing what the Duke wanted to. It was comforting to have someone to talk to."

Kat falls asleep with her head nestled in the crook of my arm, and while it's a little tight for the two of us in my bed, I leave her be.

The next morning, Nell's in the kitchen, mixing dough at the Hoosier's pullout zinc drawer.

"Drop biscuits for Eddie," she says, sifting flour with a smooth grace. "It's all he'll eat, if he'll eat."

"How do you think he's holding up?"

Nell shakes her head. "He ain't. Boy's all to pieces. Poor thing. All alone. The widow, too. I had some unkind thoughts about her at first, but I feel for her, I truly do. Not a single caller yesterday but for Seymour Johnson."

CHAPTER 14

IT'S BEEN THREE WEEKS since the picnic at the lake, Eddie and Kat are still spending their time in the parlor with the curtains drawn, but it's the Saturday after payday, the busiest day of the month, and folks from all over the county have made the drive into town, so I'm at the Emporium helping Mr. Lewis behind the counter.

Two boys with toffee-colored skin are studying the candy display behind the glass, arguing in fierce whispers about what they'd buy if they had a penny. Their names are Isaac and Calvin, and their daddy, Abraham Crockett, is one of our tenants. At this moment, he's having words with Mattie and Sheriff Earl in the back, and I slip both Isaac and Calvin a peppermint because I know that when their daddy comes out of that office he is going to be mad as a baited bull.

The tenants haven't taken well to Aunt Mattie's notions for change.

She and Sheriff Earl wrapped up their review of the books and didn't like what they found. They knew that most tenants don't even have leases—just handshake deals with the Duke, or even with the Colonel—and they've been paying the same rent for years. The Duke kept rents low because it meant votes at election time, and, as chairman of the Claiborne County Democratic Party, the Duke decided who ran for office and that's why Cecil is mayor and Earl is sheriff. But when Mattie took a good look at the numbers, she saw low-hanging fruit. She figured no one would dare take on the Kincaid ticket in any election and sent out letters raising everyone's rent.

It hit folks hard. Those tenants squirrel away nickels and dimes in coffee cans labeled RENT that they stash at the back of a kitchen cupboard and dip into only for true emergencies. Seeing as how Mattie always felt cheated out of her inheritance, you'd think she'd feel more kindhearted to other hard-luck folk. That is not the case. Instead, Mattie seems hell-bent on proving that she's as tough as the toughest man out there.

"You don't know how hard these folks have it," I told her.

"Don't presume to tell me what I know and don't know, Sallie Kincaid," she said. "We set the rents. Your job is to collect them. These folks have been taking advantage of the Duke for years. They can all slice their bacon a little thinner."

The tenants took out their anger on me, and I felt about as useless as teats on a billy goat—unwilling to defend what's wrong but unable to make it right. All I could do was tell folk to take their case straight to Mattie and Sheriff Earl.

That's what Abraham Crockett's doing right now in the Duke's office. Suddenly, the office door opens and out steps Abraham, a big fellow, mixed-race with a smattering of freckles, and the anger coming off him is all but making heat waves. He and the Duke hunted and fished together when they were both boys, and when I was growing up, they liked to share a laugh, the Duke clapping Abraham on the back when he brought the Duke a big snapper to make one of the Duke's favorite dishes, turtle soup. I've always liked Abraham, a preacher from Hopewell Road whose name often appears in "Among the Colored People," a column in the *Claiborne Gazette*, but some folk complain that Abraham is a little too quick to speak his mind, not properly deferential, thinks the rules don't apply to him, doesn't know his place—he won't let his wife clean the houses of white folks—and they say that way of thinking is going to get Abraham Crockett in trouble one of these days.

"Ain't right," he announces to all in his big, deep voice.

Mattie and Sheriff Earl follow Abraham out of the office. By now everyone has stopped to watch. "Abraham," Mattie says, "anyone who doesn't like the new terms is free to move."

Abraham looks at me. I meet his eyes, hoping he'll see me as like-minded, but if he does, he's not showing it. "Hear that, Miss Kincaid?" he says. "I'm free to move."

"Watch that mouth, boy," Sheriff Earl warns him.

Abraham ignores Sheriff Earl. He looks down at his sons sucking on their peppermints. "You young'uns give me that candy." His boys bend their heads and the peppermints drop into Abraham's outstretched hand. "The Crocketts don't take handouts." Abraham tosses the sticky peppermints into the spittoon.

"Boy," Sheriff Earl says, "don't you be—"

"It's my fault," I say quickly. "I gave those boys the candies without their daddy's say-so."

Please, Abraham, I'm thinking, please don't go and do something foolish or say something proud that might rile Sheriff Earl and all the white folk watching you. Instead, he takes a swallow, a hard swallow as he packs his anger back down deep inside him where it lives, then he nods at me like now he does see I'm on his side. "Miss Kincaid, I'm sorry for your loss. My loss, too. Knew the Duke my whole life. Was right fond of that man."

"Thank you, Mr. Crockett."

Abraham sets his hat on his head and ushers his boys through the door, the bells jangling, and then there is silence, relief you can almost taste. The moment has passed. Nothing was broken, no blood was shed.

Later that morning, a shiny red Stephens roadster parks right in front of the Emporium. The driver who gets out looks like someone from a Wild West show, with a wide-brimmed hat, a sheepskin overcoat that reaches down to his knees, and britches that are tucked into a pair of lace-up yellow leather boots.

"Get an eyeful of Little Jimmy Bond," Mattie says.

"Six months ago, that boy was riding a worn-out mule," Sheriff Earl adds.

The doorbells jangle as Little Jimmy, who is a good six feet tall in his stocking feet, steps inside and saunters past the cardplayers at the stove. "Morning, fellas," he says.

Little Jimmy, the youngest of the six Bond boys, unbuttons his sheepskin overcoat with tobacco-stained fingers and leans an elbow on the counter. He takes his time studying our wares—and letting the other shoppers study him—then tells me in a loud voice to give him three yards of our very best lace, six tins of chewing tobacco, six boxes of twelve-gauge buckshot, and that whole jar of licorice on the shelf behind me. I collect the goods while Mr. Lewis totes it all up. Little Jimmy reaches inside one of those yellow boots and takes out a fat wad of bills, pulls off a twenty, and, with his stained fingers, flicks it toward me like he's dealing from a deck of cards. Then he holds up the jar of licorice.

"Care for a stick?" he asks me.

"Thank you, no." I don't want a doggone stick of licorice from Little Jimmy Bond—showing off with his tall leather boots and his fat wad of bills—don't want it any more than Abraham wanted his boys to take what I was handing out.

"Well, you all have yourselves a fine day." Little Jimmy grins at me when he takes the package I've wrapped. As he passes the cardplayers, he holds out the licorice jar. None of them wants Little Jimmy's hand-out either. A handout. You think you're being all generous, but what you're also saying is you got what the other person doesn't—so much of it you're giving it away.

Mattie goes to the window and watches Little Jimmy climb back into his sporty red roadster.

"Earl," she says, "that boy's got his hands on too much money."

"And we know where it's coming from," Sheriff Earl says.

Sheriff Earl and Mattie live up in the Heights, above Courthouse Square, in a Sears house. I recall the day it came into the depot. I was five years old and I couldn't believe my eyes. The whole darned house in two box-cars, or all the parts for it anyway—doors, knobs, windows, electrical wires, kitchen sink, shingles—and Aunt Mattie had Earl's deputies put it together like a giant set of Tinkertoys. It's as modern as a house can be, has central heating and an indoor bathroom, and it's tall as it is wide and as deep as it is tall, with green and white striped awnings and a cement walk leading to the door. If Mattie didn't get to live in the Big House, she was hell-bent on having the most modern house in town.

I knock and Mattie answers. She's called me here to a meeting, away from all the eyes and ears at the Emporium, as she put it, but hasn't told me what this mysterious meeting is about or who will be there.

"On time," she says and gives me a smile, the same smile she used to greet the ladies in white gloves, then she drops it. "Everyone else was early."

I let that pass. Mattie can't help but find fault. It's in her nature. She leads me through the parlor. A burgundy settee sits on a burgundy carpet and doilies adorn all the chair backs and tabletops. Framed silhouettes hang on the wall and plates honoring the presidents are displayed in a glass-fronted cabinet, along with a copy of the portrait of Mattie's mama, Edith.

We follow the sound of male voices into the dining room. Sheriff Earl and Cecil are sitting at the table along with Earl's four deputies in their brown uniforms and tan ties, their gleaming leather boots and gun belts squeaking when they move. As I pull out a chair and give Cecil a what's-up? look, he gives me a don't-know shrug. There's no food or drink on the table, so it's strictly business.

"We called you all here—" Sheriff Earl says.

"Because it's time to do something," Mattie cuts in, "about all the money boys like the Bonds are making from the sale of bootleg whiskey."

"Why do we have to do anything?" I ask. People in these parts have always made whiskey, especially folk up in the mountains, where that thin soil and those steep, rocky slopes don't produce much in the way of cash crops. It's always been your business and you never had to pay any taxes or abide by any regulations. For as long as anyone can remember, it's been illegal to make and sell your own whiskey in Virginia, but everyone in the county—from the Duke to the deputies to the Bonds—ignored the law. Now, with Prohibition outlawing liquor throughout the whole country, drinkers looking to stockpile it are buying everything they can get their hands on and next thing you know Little Jimmy Bond is wearing yellow-leather boots and driving a cherry-red roadster. "This is a chance for folks who never had much money to get their hands on a little."

"You're making my point for me," Mattie says. "These boys aren't just selling a pint or two on the side. They've gone into business in a serious way and every business in this county, I don't care if it's a barbershop or a law office or a mill, has to pay taxes."

"So from now on," Sheriff Earl says, "if you're selling whiskey, you're paying a still tax."

This won't go down well. It'll strike folk who are already being squeezed as downright unfair—something the Duke never would have done—but Cecil's not saying a word and I can't help myself, I speak up. "The Duke hated taxes. If he were here, I don't think he'd go for this."

Mattie's eyes get the same riled look the Duke's got when anyone dared question him. "Who are you, missy, to say what the Duke— God rest his soul—would and would not do? I knew the Duke better than anyone in this room. He was my little brother and the truth of the matter is—what with Jane dying and his grieving and then rushing off to marry that new woman—my brother didn't have his mind on business."

"If the Duke were here," Sheriff Earl says, "he wouldn't just support this plan, he'd take credit for it."

"Speaking as mayor"—Cecil's voice is soft but steady—"what the Duke might do is present the plan to the County Council. Get everyone on board."

"We don't want the council involved," Mattie says. "That's why you all are here. We're forming a special committee, a secret committee, to collect the tax."

"Where's the money from this new tax going?" Cecil asks.

"Into a special account," Mattie says. "To help the needy."

"And who's going to control the account?" Cecil asks.

"Me and Earl," Mattie says. "But everyone in this room is getting a cut. You, Cecil. You deputies. You, Sallie."

I'm wondering why I'm included and Mattie must see the puzzled look on my face because she adds, "You're family. It's only right that everyone in the family gets a cut. Your cut also covers Eddie. And you're the only kin your brother's got over in that house so you're also getting a cut to keep an eye on things."

"I don't mean to be disagreeable," Cecil says, "but folks are going to call this a shakedown."

"They can call it whatever the blazes they want," Mattie tells him. "County maintains the roads these boys are driving on loaded down with their liquor. It's causing wear and tear. Someone's got to pay for that."

"Me and my men here provide law and order," Sheriff Earl says, "the protection these boys need to operate the business that's all of a sudden making them all this money."

"They don't get that for free," Mattie adds.

"I don't like it," Cecil says.

"You don't have to like it," Mattie tells him.

Cecil leaves it at that. As the Duke's right-hand man, what Cecil mostly did was give him advice. The Duke made all the decisions. He usually listened to Cecil, but if he didn't, there was nothing Cecil could do about it. And now Mattie's not listening—and there's nothing Cecil can do about it.

"No one's going to like it," I say, even though I know Mattie won't listen to me either. "Folk have never had to pay a whiskey tax before."

"Folk always hate change and they always get used to it and life goes on," Mattie says.

"I've never arrested a single soul for making or selling whiskey in this county," Sheriff Earl adds. "I'm right proud of that. But if these boys don't pay up, I'll send my deputies in after them."

"That's what you're going to explain to them, Sallie," Mattie says.

"Me?"

"That's the other reason you're here," Mattie says. "Why you're getting a cut. You're the Duke's daughter. They'll take it better coming from you."

CHAPTER 15

WHO IS AND ISN'T a whiskey maker in Claiborne County is hardly a secret—everyone knows except those who don't want to know—and Sheriff Earl sends the deputies George and Casey along with me to talk to the stillers. I don't get tied up in knots thinking about the right or wrong of it, the legality or illegality of taxing an illicit enterprise. Mattie's made it clear she's paying me to do what she tells me, and that is to collect this cockeyed whatever you call it—tax, toll, tithe, tribute, revenue, dues, shakedown, bribe—because what you call it depends on whether you're collecting it or paying it.

George and Casey do a heck of a job defending Sheriff Earl and Mattie, telling whiskey makers they ought to blame it on the boneheads in Washington who passed that Volstead Act, turning the making and selling of "intoxicating liquor" into a federal crime. Most of the whiskey makers sigh in disgust or mutter a few words of protest—we never had to abide by no regulations, it ain't fair, it ain't right, they get you coming and going, this country has gone to hell in a handbasket ever since those same thieving federals passed that law forcing us to pay income tax, it's communism, it is, it's downright un-American.

But George and Casey get them to admit that, well, sure, they have been making a bit more money now that you can't buy liquor legally, maybe more than a bit, and one by one, they come around and we keep crossing names off our list. Then we get to the Bond brothers.

Those Bond boys are scrappers, rough as corncobs and more mountain than the Kincaids, known for keeping to themselves, marrying their cousins, and making a particularly eye-watering whiskey. The flu brought down their ma and pa in the winter of 1905—the ma just hours after the pa. None of their kin could take in all six boys and when an uncle came for five-year-old Little Jimmy, fifteen-year-old Billy, being the eldest, pulled a gun and said he'd shoot anyone who tried to split up the family. All six Bond brothers stayed on in the family house, looking after one another. They live there still and some now have kids of their own.

The house is tucked in the pines at the end of a steep drive up Ortney Hollow, a narrow vale way to hell and gone in the mountains. It's a rambling, shambling place, with slapdash tar paper lean-tos the brothers bang together whenever another one of them gets married. The twins and I drive up and see Little Jimmy's cherry-red roadster parked out front next to one of those homemade trucks the Bonds built with parts from other vehicles. The yard is chockablock with rusty tools, old tires, rotting barrels, engine parts, sections of pipe, spare boards, piles of wood chips and gravel, split logs, and chopping blocks. But there's an order to it all. The Bonds have been through hard times, when they had to rely entirely on themselves and what they had on hand, and they operate on the belief that you never throw anything away because it—or some part of it—may be of use someday.

The brothers are all outside. Little Jimmy is on the porch steps in his yellow leather boots, cleaning the barrels of his shotgun with a ramrod. Jonah and Al are next to him cracking walnuts with the butt of a hatchet. Rick is standing beside a pile of wood holding an ax, his shirt off despite the October chill and his suspenders dangling down from his waist. Jesse is in front of him, setting up the logs that Rick is splitting. Behind them, in the shadows of the porch, Billy is sitting on a long bench with a few women and children.

They're all lanky boys with strong shoulders, beady dark eyes, and those sharp Bond cheekbones, and they stare at us as we get out of the car. We Kincaids have history with the Bonds, so I'm bracing myself for a little head-butting.

"Afternoon," I say.

Billy comes halfway down the steps, his thumbs hooked on his pant pockets. "Been a while."

"I'm here on business."

"Course you are."

"Billy, the Bonds and the Kincaids have known each other for a long time—"

"And we always kept our distance."

"True enough."

"And you always thought you was better than us."

"Billy, you know that ain't the case."

"What I know is you all Kincaids treated us Bonds like we was dirt. You always went and took what you wanted. Your grandpa cheated my grandpa out of those eighty-eight acres of good bottom-land."

"My grandpa purchased that land fair and square," I say. "Just got it at a good price."

And that is the by-God truth. At least as the Duke always told the story. The Colonel rose through the ranks during the war between the states, ended up leading a regiment of Virginia cavalry, and when it was over he came home carrying a pair of saddlebags stuffed with federal notes. Never said where he got it—raiding a Union payroll wagon, some said, robbing a Pennsylvania bank others claimed—but the Claiborne County he came back to was hurting bad, sons and husbands buried on distant battlefields, cattle rustled, crops burned, barns busted up for firewood. Slave owners who started the war were crying into tattered hankies, wringing their hands because their slaves were all gone and land that had been fetching $150 an acre before the war was going for $2. With those federal banknotes, the Colonel started buying. And the Bonds sold. Buy when folks need money, the Duke said whenever he told the story, sell when they have it.

"Robbery," Billy says. "Highway robbery without a gun."

"Your grandpa needed money in a hurry. And he got it. But I didn't come all the way over here to rehash old grievances."

"I know what you're here for. Heard all about it. You're going around telling folks they got to pay some ginned-up still tax."

"It's the sheriff's new rule."

"Rule? That what you call it? I call it robbery. More robbery." Billy steps down into the yard, comes at me, stops so close we are all but touching. I can smell his sweat, his tobacco breath, but I hold my ground. "We work our asses off back here, Miss Kincaid, barely scraping by, and now when we finally start making us a little cash money you and these two jokers come here, telling us to hand it over because the sheriff's got a new rule?"

Billy's no fool. I know he's right—and he sees it. But I press on with a speech I cobble together from what Mattie and Sheriff Earl said.

"Making and selling whiskey is a business, Billy, just like cutting hair and shoeing horses. Barber pays taxes, so does the farrier, and the people who make liquor got to pay taxes, too. For protection. And to pave the roads you and your brothers haul your whiskey on."

"Protection? Is that what the sheriff told you to say? The Duke would be ashamed of you, Sallie Kincaid, turning against your own people, shilling for that gelded sheriff. I knowed your daddy my whole life, we had our differences, but for the most part, he let us alone. We asked for no favors. He gave us no grief. Now you show up here with the sheriff's flatfoots, talking big about rules and taxes and protection." He jerks a thumb at the deputies. "The day we need to turn to the likes of those two for protection, we'll give you all a holler."

Casey steps forward, one hand on the pistol at his hip, and in a split second Little Jimmy slides two shells into his shotgun, clicks the barrel shut, and swings it toward us.

"You want to take on the whole sheriff's department?" George asks.

The barrel of Little Jimmy's shotgun is close enough to touch. I've had a loaded gun pointed at me a few times and I know that it's not the gun you have to concern yourself with, but the person holding it. I look up the long barrel to Little Jimmy's unblinking eyes. He's all business.

"Don't threaten a Bond," Little Jimmy says, "unless you're aiming to fight all the Bonds."

"Whoa, boys." I hold up my hands. They're steady, but I can feel the blood tingling in my fingertips. "We didn't come here to start a war."

"Glad to hear that," Billy says. "And now, Miss Kincaid, I do believe it's high time you all get the hell off Bond property."

We start backing up toward the Lizzie, me with my hands still up, George and Casey with their hands on their pistols.

"Sheriff Earl's not going to stand for this," Casey calls out.

"I never lost much sleep worrying about what the sheriff thinks," Billy says.

Word is that over the summer the Bonds built themselves a big new copper still and that it's hidden up in the brambles and thickets of Claiborne County's western mountains, where those cold sweet-water creeks make for fine whiskey. Mattie and Sheriff Earl ordered me and the deputies to find it, and that's why, as I make my rounds, I'm slowing down on back roads, scanning the horizon for a plume of smoke coming from a clump of trees, listening for the telltale thumping sound of stills, all the while telling myself I have no say in all this, that I am just doing what I am told. But those words are starting to feel mighty flimsy.

Back in Hatfield, watching farmers trying to coax a crop out of thin soil only to see it washed away in a heavy rain, I used to think what a fine thing it would be to have a paycheck job—you show up, work your hours, and at the end of the month, doesn't matter what the weather is, you get your money. Now that I have one of those jobs, I see it's not the rain that's your worry, but the whims of the boss man. Some of the times, the things you're asked to do are foolish. Leaves you rolling your eyes, but it can be done. It's when the boss asks you to do something you know to be wrong and you do it anyways. That sort of work whittles away at the soul.

A week after that talk with Billy I stop for a soda at the general store by Pogue's Crossing, where a mule hitched to a tinker's wagon is tied to the porch rail. Inside the tinker is shaking his head, telling the storekeeper how he tried to water his mule by the bridge at Deep Run, but the mule wouldn't drink. "That's always been sweet water," he says, "but not no more."

I head for Deep Run, park beside the bridge, and push through the box elders and dried stalks of joe-pye weed that edge the banks. It's a pretty creek, like they all are in these parts, clear icy water gushing and splashing down the steep rocky creek bed. I fill my hands with water and bring them to my nose. It's there, so faint I can hardly smell it, but it's there, the sour, swampy odor of fermented mash.

I see no flattened weeds, no sign of a path leading up into the hills on the far side of the creek, so I hide the Lizzie in a grove of cedars and lie down behind a fallen log in the trees beside the bridge.

A flight of geese passes overhead, wings beating in time, necks outstretched, honking loudly in the still air. They're so close I can see their black feet tucked under their tails. The lead goose falls back, another takes its place, and the rippling lines close ranks, no fight, no debate, everyone working together, each doing its job to keep the whole flock alive and moving. They make it all seem so easy.

Wagons pass from time to time, also a few cars, and the sun through the trees warms my back. Hunting is waiting, the Duke used to say, and if you never came home empty-handed they wouldn't call it hunting. Finally, late in the afternoon that homemade truck I saw at the Bonds' house comes around the bend and stops in the middle of the road.

Billy, Rick, and Little Jimmy jump out. Billy pulls a couple of long boards from the back while Rick and Little Jimmy unload big burlap sacks. Billy lays the boards across the creek and weeds, then the three of them carry the sacks over the boards and into the woods, leaving no tracks. Billy comes back by himself, tosses the boards into the truck, and drives off. No more than three minutes have passed from beginning to end.

I can't help but admire those Bond brothers, their teamwork, their hustle. They're not just scrappers, those boys have pluck and smarts, and I'm sorely tempted to keep what I've just witnessed to myself. But I can't be drawing a salary from Mattie and Sheriff Earl acting like I don't know what I do know, because holding back is just as bad as an outright lie, and if I was found out, I'd be fired in a flash—and I'd have it coming. So back at the Emporium I tell Mattie and Sheriff Earl about the homemade truck and the burlap bags and the boards. The following morning Sheriff Earl leads his deputies across Deep Run and into the woods. They bring along Morris Nelson, owner and editor and sole reporter of the *Gazette,* and the next week it's the front-page story.

SHERIFF BUSTS BOOTLEG STILL

The article strikes a jaunty tone, calling the raid a "spirited battle" and making it sound like Sheriff Earl and his deputies were brave heroes, and the Bonds were cowardly villains. Seeing as how the Emporium is the *Gazette*'s largest advertiser, that favor-currying Morris always wrote articles he figured the Duke would want to read, so it looks like he's now writing whatever he reckons Mattie and Sheriff Earl want to read.

But all I can think about are the stories I'd grown up hearing about whiskey rebellions and revenuers, about raids and shoot-outs, about a five-hundred-pound woman known to lawmen as "catchable but not fetchable" who raised sixteen children making corn whiskey—and in those stories the whiskey makers were always the heroes and the revenuers were always the villains.

I felt cleaner when I was washing those bloodstained sheets back in Hatfield with Aunt Faye.

CHAPTER 16

THE GRANDFATHER CLOCK IS ticking steadily when I step into the front hallway, but otherwise, the Big House is quiet. I've taken to stopping by for lunch when I can, checking in on Eddie and Kat, and I expect to find them in the parlor, but it's empty, the curtains pulled back and motes of dust floating in a shaft of sunlight that hits the piano—the piano that no one has played in the six weeks since the Duke died.

The rest of the house is empty, too, save for Nell, who is working away at the Hoosier, stirring dough for those drop biscuits that are still pretty much all Eddie will eat these days.

"Where is everybody?" I ask.

"Seymour took Kat and Eddie for a drive." Nell's voice is flat. "Said they'd be back by supper."

"Good."

"In the Packard."

"I suppose that makes sense. Hard for them all to fit into Seymour's roadster."

"I know I'm just the maid, but it ain't proper."

"At least Seymour's getting them out of the house."

"Kat's a widow in mourning. She ought not be driving around with an unmarried man."

I don't want to argue about this with Nell, so instead of sitting down I say something about having a busy day and I wrap wax paper around the egg-salad sandwich she made for me.

A ways down Crooked Run Road I pull over to eat Nell's sandwich. I keep hearing her voice, "Ain't proper." Could be she's right. The sight of the Duke's widow on an outing with an unmarried man—Seymour behind the wheel of the Packard like he owns it, their only escort a thirteen-year-old boy in the back—sure will get the ladies in white gloves talking. But as long as Eddie and Kat are feeling better, who cares?

When the Duke first suggested Seymour might make a proper husband for me, I didn't much like the idea, but I'll admit there is something about the man that turns my head. Seymour loves attention every bit as much as the Duke did, but the Duke always had to be the center of attention, whereas Seymour will, from time to time, make you the center of attention. When he does, you feel like he's seeing something in you, something special, something that everyone else has missed.

That must be what he's been doing for Kat and Eddie. I've been working long hours and haven't been home when Seymour visits, but I know from them that he's been coming by every day, bringing them presents. Wildflowers or a chocolate bar for Kat. For Eddie, a rabbit's foot or a deck of cards or, one day, a book of poetry by some Irish writer. Seymour gets Eddie to laugh and Kat has opened the curtains and let in the light and they all take walks. And now they're out for a drive.

I want to believe that Seymour is no more than a gentleman consoling a bereaved widow. But even back at the reading of the will, Mattie talked about how Seymour's been hovering around Kat like a vulture, and Nell clearly thinks he has his eye on the Duke's widow. Could be I've been so busy staying busy that I've been blind to what's been going on under my nose, that I don't want to know. If it's true, I'll feel like a fool. What I've got to do is find out Seymour's intentions toward Kat. If all this is going on, it is darn well time to consider what's proper and what's not.

By the end of the day, I've made up my mind to have a frank talk with Seymour Johnson. I open the front door and hear voices, then Eddie's high-pitched laugh. They're all in the parlor, looking like they just came back from a day at the races that ended in the money.

"Sallie's here," Seymour says. "The toasts can begin."

A bottle of the Duke's special-occasion French champagne sits on the marble-topped side table. Seymour fills four glasses, raises one, and looks at Kat. "To my new wife."

A hot flush stings my face. "To your what?"

"I'm Mrs. Seymour Johnson now," Kat says, laughing like she can't believe it either.

"Eddie here was best man," Seymour says.

"Why didn't anyone let me in on this?" My head is boiling but I have to keep calm, think straight, figure out what to do.

"They didn't tell me, either," Eddie says. "It was a surprise. I thought we were just going for a drive and we ended up in Roanoke, at City Hall."

There's a willful light in his gray eyes, like he's cast his lot with Seymour and is daring me to question it.

"Surprises are what life is all about," Seymour says. "So, Sal, aren't you going to congratulate us?"

Seymour holds out a glass of champagne, the tiny bubbles dancing and popping. "I need some air," I say.

The headlights cut through the dark, catching the eyes of a doe in the brush beside the road. I thought the deer were all hunted out in these parts, but that doe is staring at me like she's wondering what the heck I'm doing. I'm wondering that too. I'm not one to run from problems, but I left the house and the next thing I knew I was in the Lizzie, on my way to Hatfield to see Aunt Faye, maybe stay for a few days because I had to get away. From the both of them. The newlyweds.

Halfway across the valley, I still feel sick to my stomach. Sick. Am I jealous? Maybe. Hurt? A little. But the truth is, I never wanted to be Mrs. Seymour Johnson.

I feel sick because this marriage is plain wrong. It's too soon. It's reckless. It's an insult to the Duke's memory. An insult to everyone in the county still grieving for him.

What were those two thinking?

The truth about Kat is that she's one of those women who always needs a man by her side, to protect her, care for her, can't get through life on her own, even for a decent period of mourning.

As for Seymour, it's looking like Mattie's right, he's a vulture, a shameless fortune hunter. Kat doesn't have a fortune but she's caring for a boy who will inherit one in five years.

And what about Eddie? Despite giving me that willful look, he's like an unfledged bird that fell from the nest, looking to anyone for protection, and Seymour's taking his hand just like he did when Eddie froze up on the trestle. But if Seymour truly is an operator, I can't leave Eddie on his own. With the newlyweds. I slow the car and look for a wide spot in the road to turn around.

The next morning, Nell's at the kitchen sink, scrubbing a cast-iron skillet. She gives me an unsmiling nod but stays quiet. Fine by me. I pour myself a cup of coffee and sit at the table. The only person I want to talk to is Eddie, find out what he thinks.

"It's wrong," Nell blurts out like she can't keep her thoughts to herself any longer. "Just plain wrong."

"Lot of folks will agree." And I'm one of them. But saying so will only get us both riled up. I worked hard last night to calm myself down, and I'm doing my best to stay that way for my talk with Eddie. "What's done is done. No use complaining about it. And you have to admit, this house is a lot cheerier when Seymour Johnson's around."

"It ain't supposed to be cheery," she says. "It's in mourning."

I'm on my second cup of coffee, pondering Nell's unvarnished words, when I hear the piano for the first time since the Duke died. Eddie's alone on the bench, his narrow back erect but swaying ever so slightly like it does when he plays. He doesn't pause when I sit down beside him and watch his slim hands move, knowing and graceful, across the keyboard. It's haunting and beautiful, a maze of a piece that keeps looping back on itself, one of his favorites and he plays it mostly on the black keys.

"How'd you sleep?" I ask.

"Not so well."

"Me neither. It'll take some getting used to." I wait for Eddie to say more, and when he doesn't I try to prompt him. "It was kind of sudden."

"The Duke didn't wait long after Mother died to marry Kat."

"Does that mean you're in favor of it?"

Eddie stops playing and his eyes take on that willful look. "Sure."

"Mattie's not going to stand for it."

"It's not her concern."

Eddie starts playing again. He lost the daddy who made no secret of wanting him to be someone he wasn't. That has to make for mixed-up feelings. Could be some part of him was even relieved—and if so he probably hated himself for it. Could be why he stopped playing the piano. Now Seymour's in the house—Seymour, who makes you feel he sees something special in you—and Eddie's playing the piano again.

"I wish they'd waited," I say.

"What does that matter?" Eddie asks.

Just then, Kat and Seymour come into the parlor. We say our good mornings, but I can barely meet their eyes, thinking about how the Duke's widow and the man who turned my head spent the night in the Duke's bed.

In the kitchen, Nell's at the stove. Even with her back turned to us, you can tell she's bristling with disapproval. She sets a platter of scrambled eggs on the table. "There's breakfast," she says. "I'll leave you all to it."

She walks out and the kitchen door swings shut.

"Well," Kat says, "we know how she feels. How about you, Sallie?"

"You think this is all too soon," Seymour says to me.

"If you know what I think, why are you asking? Seymour, this isn't some ball game where you steal a base the moment you see that you can."

"Sallie, there's something you ought to know," Kat cuts in. "Getting married was my idea. I was alone, me and Eddie. Alone and grieving in this big empty house. Seymour was the only one I could turn to, the only one to keep me and Eddie from going under."

"When you lose the man you love, you live with the loss for a while. You don't rush out and find another man to take his place. That makes light of the loss."

"I don't have time to mourn the Duke properly, Sallie. Mattie's made it plain as day she doesn't think I ought to be living here. Thinks this house should be hers. Thinks she should be here, taking care of Eddie. I'm not a fighter, Sallie, I need a man to fight for me. I need a husband. Eddie needs a daddy. We need a man in this house."

"You do too, Sallie," Seymour says. "Mattie wants to send you back to Hatfield just like she wants to send Kat back to Danville."

I wonder if that's true. It's certainly possible. Mattie's never thought I belonged here. "Could be so," I say. "But you're moving too fast."

"Sometimes you have to be bold," Seymour says. "What the four of us have to do is stick together. Show everyone we're a family."

"The four of us are a family now?" Kat's six years older than Seymour and they could pass for husband and wife, but he's only eight years older than me.

"That's right," Seymour says. "We're a family. We'll go talk to Mattie. Now. Explain it all. Come with us, Sallie."

Family. Back in Hatfield, what I wanted more than anything in the world was to be part of my family, but ever since I've come home, that family's been falling apart. I have to stay here in the Big House for Eddie's sake, but I want no part of this new family of Seymour and Kat's.

"You got married. That's your business. But I'm not going to go around saying it's wonderful. I'm not going to play that part for you. And when Mattie finds out, Seymour, she's going to want your hide."

* * *

Later that day, I'm pulling up in front of the Emporium when Mattie sees me through the window and comes running outside.

"It's disgusting." The muscles in her neck are throbbing. "Vile. The Duke's barely in his grave and that leech—my husband's own brother—marries his widow. She's supposed to be in mourning." Mattie grabs my arm, her fingers digging in. "Were you in on this?"

"No. They sprang it on me same as they did you."

"Of course they did." She presses her fingers to her head. "They didn't let anyone know beforehand. They didn't want us to know because they knew we'd put a stop to it." She takes a deep breath. "Do you approve?"

"I don't. It was too soon. For one thing."

"Good. But I told you to keep an eye on things, Sallie. The Duke trusted you to protect Eddie and this is what happens."

"Eddie's all for it."

"That's because Seymour's playing that boy like a harmonica. You should have heard him this morning when they all came over, making the case like he was Seymour's attorney. Sallie, if you'd have seen it coming we could have done something before it was too late."

"What could we have done? They came back from Roanoke yesterday married."

"Yesterday?" The color drains from Mattie's face. "Where did they sleep last night? Don't tell me they slept in the Duke's bedroom."

My cheeks turn hot and I look down.

"Fornicating. In my dead brother's bed. Appalling." Mattie takes another deep breath. "Seymour thinks he's so clever, the way he staged this. But Seymour can be too tricky for his own good. This is going to end badly. Mark my words." She grabs my arm. "Sallie, you and Eddie both have to come live with Sheriff Earl and me."

"Eddie won't want to. And if Eddie stays, I'm staying."

"Well, then remember, Sallie Kincaid, it's your job to protect your brother, to open that boy's eyes to what's going on, to how those two are using him. I can count on you, right?" She studies my face. "You're not on their side, are you?"

"I'm doing my best not to take sides."

Mattie cocks her head. "Shame on you, then, Sallie Kincaid. You wanted to come back here to Caywood, assume your place in the Kincaid family, reminding everyone at every possible opportunity that you're the Duke's daughter, but now at the first sign of a family fight, you're saying you want no part of it. If you're truly a Kincaid, you don't have the luxury of sitting this one out."

CHAPTER 17

IT'S EARLY DECEMBER. A hard frost last night. Hog-killing time. I'm adding a log to the fire when Kat knocks on my door. She sits down on the bed, wraps her arms around her belly, and rubs it gently. "Sallie, I think I'm pregnant."

"Congratulations." That was quick. Kat and Seymour got married five weeks ago.

"Thing is, Sallie, it has to be the Duke's child. I haven't"—she blushes—"been with Seymour long enough."

I feel a catch in my throat. So the Duke would have gotten that other child he wanted if he hadn't been so hell-bent on proving he could climb higher and leap further than Seymour. Another Kincaid child. Another brother or sister for Eddie and me. And Mary.

A new life ought to be a cause for joy, but if the family's coming apart, a baby can deepen the divide. I wonder if Kat thought she might be with child when she got married and that was one reason she hurried it along.

"What does Seymour think?"

"He doesn't know. I had to tell someone, so I'm telling you. But no one else can know."

"You must tell Seymour."

Kat shakes her head. "When he married me he didn't know I was carrying another man's child. It's not what he bargained for. He'll feel different about me."

"Seymour's becoming like a daddy to Eddie. He'll take to a new child even more." Seymour and Eddie have been keeping to the house with Kat, studying the sports and business pages, and they even bought a stock that paid off in a big way. He keeps saying things will blow over, just a matter of time, and news of a baby on the way could help. "This might even bring Mattie around. That child is her brother's. She'd see you as kin."

"Mattie won't believe it's the Duke's." Kat shakes her head like she's already thought this through. "She'll say it's Seymour's, that I was lying with him before we got married, as soon as the Duke died. Or even before that. She'll say I'm trying to pass the child off as the Duke's. That's what she'll tell everyone, and they'll believe her. They're all ill-disposed toward me as it is. So no one can know."

Secrets and lies. That's no way to bring a baby into this world. But Kat seems set on it. "People will find out sooner or later."

"I know. I just need a little time. If I wait I can convince Seymour it's his."

"To lie to your husband about this is—"

"Or get him to pretend it's his. Maybe that's best. We can say it's early. We can pass it off as Seymour's."

"Folk know what an early baby looks like. Kat, you're not thinking straight."

"I know I'm not thinking straight, Sallie. I'm thirty-two years of age, I've never been with child before—figured I wasn't meant to be a mama—and marrying Seymour hasn't solved my problems like I thought it would, so of course I'm not thinking straight, but I need someone to talk to, Sallie, and you've got to promise me you won't tell anyone."

Kat sounds like she's hanging by a thread. I take her hand and give it a squeeze. "I promise."

CHAPTER 18

"SALLIE KINCAID?" THE VOICE in the telephone receiver is tinny and crackling. A woman.

"Who is this?"

"You don't know me and my name's not important, but Faye Powell is in danger. She's back at the Hatfield Clinic. That fellow Wayne took after her again."

"Oh Lord. Is she all right?"

"Your aunt was roughed up, but she'll heal just fine."

"That's a relief. And Wayne? Did they arrest him?"

"He's run off. But I'm not calling about him. Reason I'm calling is they're fixing to take your aunt away."

"Away? To where?"

"To that colony in Marion. The one for the feebleminded. Doctor Pruitt decided Miss Powell ought to be locked away and have her female parts fixed. A car's coming over to pick her up tomorrow."

A few minutes later, I'm in the Lizzie, barreling across the valley to Hatfield. Doctor Pruitt, he's new to the clinic and I've never met him, but I have heard of the Marion Colony for the Feeble Minded. Fancy name for an insane asylum. When I was in Hatfield, there were rumors about doctors from places like Marion who were rounding up simple folk, saying they'd treat their ailments then secretly sterilizing them without their say-so. Culling them to improve the stock, like a herd of cattle. And now one of those doctors has Aunt Faye.

She can be flighty and frustrating and she's all on her own, so of course she still needs help, and I've been sending her whatever money I can spare, but she's hardly feebleminded and we don't need some prying do-gooder deciding her fate.

I turn onto Hatfield's muddy main street and I'm startled by the clinic's new coat of chalk-white paint, like it's announcing how much cleaner it is than the dingy, weathered buildings around it. Inside, a woman I've never seen before is at a desk flanked with posters about hygiene and croup and ringworm. Those weren't here before either.

I ask for Faye Powell and can tell from the way she looks at me she's not the woman who telephoned. She tells me to wait and goes into the back.

The room is empty. Outside, grackles screech and a lumber truck rumbles by, its wheels sloshing loudly in the potholes. I'll be darned if I'm going to stand here waiting for that meddling doctor to tell me if I can or can't see my own aunt, so I take a look at the clinic log lying open on the desk. There it is in blocky handwriting:

> *Faye Powell. Admitted Feb. 16, 1920.*
> *Facial bruises & lacerations & minor abdominal trauma.*
> *Rm 3. To be transferred to Marion Col. for the Feeble Minded*
> *pending enfeeblement determination. Feb. 18, 1920.*

Bruises, lacerations. Wayne had it in him to hurt Aunt Faye once and in the back of my mind I knew he'd do it again. They always do. That time I found him sitting in bed with her, I had my Remington in hand. I should have used it.

Room 3 is right down the hall. Inside, Aunt Faye is sitting up in bed, studying her black eye with a small mirror. She cries out in delight when she sees me, but then I feel a hand on my arm. It's that new doctor in a starched white jacket. He's young, his face unlined, his hair cut so short he might as well be bald.

"I'm sorry." His voice is polite and patient and cold. "Visiting hours are over."

"This woman is my aunt."

"Come back tomorrow."

"By then, she'll be gone." I turn to her. "This doctor's planning to send you to an asylum. Tomorrow."

Aunt Faye looks confused. The doctor rests a hand on her shoulder, acting like he cares, but he's keeping her in place.

"It's in your own best interest, Miss Powell." In that same polite, cold voice he tells me, "This patient suffers from acute melancholia and uncontrollable nerves. A medical panel will determine if she fits the criteria for enfeeblement."

"No medical panel is determining anything about her," I say. "Aunt Faye, I'm getting you out of here."

"I can't go home." She looks so worried. "Wayne—"

"I'm not taking you there."

Seymour and Eddie are in the parlor with notebooks and newspapers, rating ballplayers and stock prices. They look up at us startled, but before they say a thing, I tell them as much as they need to know and not a word more—"Aunt Faye here was at the Hatfield Clinic but the doctor wasn't treating her right, so I brought her home."

Whenever she's embarrassed or ashamed, Aunt Faye chatters about everything but the matter at hand. That's what she did on the drive back and that's what she does while I help her wash up, going on about how, goodness gracious, long ago, before I was born, she cleaned this very sink when she was a maid working here for Belle and then after that for my mama, and now here she is a guest, imagine that, isn't life funny, the way the world turns, the way things work out, but then suddenly she stops.

"Thank you, Sallie, thank you for taking care of me today. I took care of you. I wasn't always a saint, but—"

"You did your best."

"I did my best. But you don't know, Sallie. You don't know everything." She sighs. "I should never have let Wayne move in with me, you were right, you don't have to tell me that, but the truth was—"

"You were lonesome."

"So very lonesome. It wasn't only about the money. I've been so lonesome ever since you left."

"I'm sorry. I know it must seem like I forgot you, it's that—"

"None of that matters, hon. You saved me today. I know that. I'm a changed woman now. My days of running around with men from the Roadhouse are over. I swear it."

Once Aunt Faye is in bed, I go back to the parlor. Seymour and Eddie glance at each other like they have something awkward to discuss. "So tell me, Sallie"—Seymour rubs his chin—"how long you planning to let your aunt stay here?"

"Long as she needs. Why?"

"Just wondering."

"Anything wrong with that?"

"Maybe," Eddie says. He's looking at the notebook in his lap like he doesn't want to meet my eyes. "Mother wouldn't have allowed her in the house. She used to say Faye Powell was a fallen woman."

I feel very tired. Is that all people will ever think when they see Aunt Faye? People who've never gone without find it easy to pass judgment on those who've struggled. But there's nothing to be gained by arguing about who has fallen and why. "Your mama was a churchgoing woman, Eddie. She believed in redemption. You should too. And you, Seymour, don't you be getting all high and mighty on me."

"I got nothing against ladies of the night, but people will talk. They're already talking."

"About your marriage," I point out.

"This will give them more to talk about," Eddie says. "Especially Aunt Mattie."

"Things will never settle down," Seymour says.

"Seymour, if there's one thing people in this county understand it's kinfolk in trouble. At one point or another, everyone's had a ne'er-do-well brother or cousin or in-law who needs to be pulled out of a jam."

Seymour and Eddie glance at each other again, like they're weighing what I said. "Let's see what Kat thinks," Seymour says.

"Thinks about what?"

Kat's in the doorway. Her hair's tousled and she's wrapped a heavy shawl over her paisley bathrobe. It's been two months since she told me she's with child and she's been acting tired and sickly lately, but she's always been plump and she keeps that shawl on all day, says she's warding off the cold, and so far no one's guessed.

She sits down and gives me that disarming smile of hers, so I tell her about what happened at the clinic, about Doctor Pruitt and his enfeeblement nonsense. Kat shakes her head in disbelief.

"Of course Faye's staying," she says in a voice that makes it clear there will be no debate about the matter. "We're not sending her back to that doctor. She's family and family is always welcome. Besides, we're going to need some help around here." Kat takes Seymour's hand and puts it on her belly. "Because I do believe I'm with child."

The next morning before breakfast, I catch Kat alone outside the bathroom.

"Thank you for standing by me and my aunt," I say.

"She's family," Kat says with a smile.

Family. I reckon Kat sees Aunt Faye as someone like herself, a woman alone, beholden to people who—for all the talk of family—are more or less strangers. Back when Kat started showing up in Eddie's classroom, I thought she was trying to push me aside, but she sure came through last night. Just like family is supposed to. I was surprised when she chose that moment to let everyone in on her secret, but it sure did put a stop to the quarrel about Aunt Faye.

"Did you talk to Seymour about who's—"

Kat gives her head a quick little shake, cutting me off. "I didn't tell him and he didn't ask. Anyway, I'm not sure it really is the Duke's child after all. And what does it matter? It's my baby. Seymour is my husband. And we are going to raise it. That's all that matters."

"That's all that matters," I repeat. I hope it's true.

At breakfast, everyone is lively and loud, talking over each other,

Seymour going on about how he knows in his bones the baby is a boy, he's going to be a father. Eddie keeps saying he's going to be a big brother. Big. Eddie has always been the smallest person in the family and he's always been treated that way, but now that's going to change. Kat is downright glowing, relieved that at last we all know she's going to be a mama and that we're all truly happy for her.

But it's Aunt Faye who is positively gleeful, heaping grits on Eddie's plate and talking about how Kat ought to get some rest so she is going to throw herself into running the house, then, as Nell brings over a steaming plate of drop biscuits, Aunt Faye pats her on the arm and says, "With this fine young woman's help."

The prospect of a baby has brought even Nell around, and she and Aunt Faye start talking about how, seeing as money is so tight, they'll cut costs, make chitterlings and neck-bone soup, and pudding out of stale bread, brew nettle tea for Kat's morning sickness and melt down candle stubs to reuse the tallow. Maybe it's because Nell is doing the cooking and cleaning just like Aunt Faye did twenty years ago, but the two of them take to each other right away.

We're starting to sound like we really are one big family.

Later that morning Aunt Faye and I make a quick trip back to Hatfield to pick up her things. The Defiance Coaster is on the porch, dented and rusty, reduced to a laundry tote. I'll take it home with me. My Remington is leaning in a corner of the bedroom, where I left it. Unused. It's coming back with me, too. While Aunt Faye puts her few clothes in a box, I check the gun's chamber—it's loaded—then wipe down the barrel and stock and aim the gun through the window, fixing the site on a squirrel scampering across the railroad tracks. I could hit it from here, I know—my aim has always been true.

I favor a long gun over a handgun. Never cared for the way a handgun feels in my grip, way out at the end of my arm, like a carpet beater or a stirring spoon. But now a long gun, when you take aim, it's almost like the gun becomes a part of you, the smooth stock hard up

against your cheek, the butt nestled solid into the crook of your shoulder, left hand cradling the forestock, right at the trigger, and you're
squinting down the long straight line of the barrel through the little
notch of the sight and then beyond, your eye locked onto whatever it
is that's threatening you—or whatever it is that you are threatening—
and you're leaning into it, not leaning back all casual, but into it, into
it—because you got this. You got this. And then, with just the slight-
est, smoothest squeeze of your forefinger—badaang!—you have just
bagged whatever it is—squirrel, rabbit, rabid possum, chicken-killing
fox, two-fisted lug—you are looking to bag.

And you are a force to be reckoned with.

I lower my Remington and watch the squirrel scamper away.

I need a gun.

That's what I told myself right here in this room. It was the day
after Aunt Faye came back from the Roadhouse with that black eye
from the customer who wouldn't give her a token of appreciation.
I needed a gun to keep that from ever happening again. I searched
through Aunt Faye's tattered Sears, Roebuck catalogue. There was a
Winchester for twenty-seven dollars and ninety-five cents, a mighty
fine gun but more than I could ever afford, and there was a thirteen-
dollar Marlin that was also too steep. Then I saw it, a Remington
twenty-two for three dollars. It might just be in my reach. If I used
the silver dollar the Duke gave me in case of an emergency, I needed
only two more dollars. All I had to do was figure out a way to scrape
it together.

Ronnie Webb, a rabbity kid who sat next to me on the bench for
the twelve- and thirteen-year-olds in the Hatfield schoolhouse, had
been carrying on about how he was going to earn the money for his
first gun by helping his pa collect chestnuts once we got a hard frost.
I asked if his pa could use an extra pair of hands, seeing as how I also
wanted money for a gun.

"Why'd you want a gun? You're a girl."

"We don't have menfolk in our house. We got to do our own protecting."

The next day, Ronnie said his pa could make room for one more youngster in the wagon, but I'd best not be a shirker.

The hard frost came that Friday. The sky was still inky black when I got to the Webbs' house and the whole family was loading up the wagon by lantern light, everyone bundled in scarves and caps and gloves against the cold. Mrs. and Mr. Webb climbed up on the seat and the rest of us piled on the burlap bags in back. Mr. Webb snapped the reins and the mule took us up an old logging road high into the mountains. The sun was starting to light up mountain peaks when we reached the chestnut trees, and in that pinkish golden dawn you could see them, like an army of giants, some near a hundred foot high, with gnarled trunks six foot across.

The frost had knocked the nuts out of the trees and the ground was thick with them. Mr. Webb told us we had to make haste, seeing as how bear, deer, boar, and people would all be fighting over these chestnuts and in a couple of days they'd be gone.

I grabbed a basket, jumped out of the wagon, and started picking up nuts as soon as my feet hit the ground. Mr. Webb was paying his kids and me six cents a basket and I had to fill thirty-four baskets to buy that Remington. The chestnuts were big as my fist and covered with bristly burs that made them look for all the world like little porcupines, and soon burs were clinging to my skirt and coat and gloves and hair, but I didn't stop to pull them off.

I filled my first basket without having to move from my spot and ran over to Mrs. Webb, who was already husking the chestnuts, twisting off burs, spilling the fuzzy, dark nuts into a sack. Without saying a word, she took my basket, dumped it in the wagon, then put a check by my name on her list. One basket down, thirty-three to go.

My gloves were making me fumbly, so I took them off but my fingers got numb with cold and bloody with scratches so I put the gloves back on. I filled and emptied my basket so many times—quick quick, faster faster—that my back got to aching so I knelt, but then my knees started aching and I went back to bending.

I skipped lunch and by sunset I'd filled thirty-one baskets. The pickings were slimmer by then, it was getting hard to see, and I was so sore I had to push myself to move but I was still short three baskets. I started back toward the trees.

"Get yourself over here," Mr. Webb hollered at me.

His clothes hung on him like he was a scarecrow and his gray beard fell all the way to his chest but I figured he was not near as old as he looked. He didn't talk much and this was the first time he'd spoken to me direct.

"I got to get three more baskets," I told him.

"We're done here," he said in a tone that was not brooking any disagreement from a thirteen-year-old girl.

Once we got back to the Webb house, I climbed off the wagon and stood there waiting for my money. Even in the moonlight I could see Mr. Webb scowl.

"You're not looking to get paid, are you? Can't pay you till I get paid. Come back tomorrow night."

The next afternoon, I scoured the woods above Hatfield for chestnuts but they were already picked clean. I was not going to earn enough to buy that Remington. And something about Mr. Webb's scowl the night before worried me. I was just a girl, no one to stand up for me, and Mr. Webb might cheat me. If he did what could I do about it? Without a gun, not much.

That night, when I got to the Webbs' house a fire was crackling in the big fieldstone fireplace and the whole Webb family was squeezed around the table. All the kids were shucking chestnuts and watching Mr. Webb stack his quarters, pennies, nickels, and dimes. I waited for Mr. Webb to give me that scowl of his. Instead, he glanced at his wife.

"Ma," he said, "how many baskets the Kincaid girl bring in?"

She could say twenty and I'd have no way of proving her wrong. I clenched my fists and my chin jutted out.

"Thirty-one."

My fists unclenched. I was wrong. I felt like a louse. But I was also relieved. There would be no fight. And I was only fourteen cents away from my Remington. I smiled weakly at them both.

"Thing of it is," Mr. Webb went on, "price of chestnuts wasn't what I figured."

The fight in me rushed back. So he was going to cheat me after all, he was going to say the chestnuts didn't fetch the price he expected, and I couldn't prove otherwise.

"That blight coming down from the north, it's killing the trees," Mr. Webb said. "Turns out chestnuts are in short supply. Got more per bushel than I expected. So I'm paying you seven cent a basket instead of six."

Some folks say they hate to be proved wrong, but I was never happier to be mistaken. And I was getting myself a gun, with a little left over to buy something for Aunt Faye. I felt like hugging Mr. Webb—but he didn't strike me as a hugging man, so instead, I said, "That's right generous of you, sir."

"I make it out to be two dollars, seventeen cents." Mr. Webb counted out eight quarters, one dime, one nickel, and two copper pennies. "My boy says you're saving to get a gun."

"Yes sir."

He looked at me with small, sharp eyes under scraggly gray brows. There was no hint of softness. "Once you get yourself that gun, you bring it on over and we'll make sure you know how to use it proper."

CHAPTER 19

SPRING'S TRYING TO COME too early this year, fooling the confused witch hazel into sending out brave little yellow buds—and when I get back to the Big House at the end of the day everyone has pulled the porch chairs into the yard to enjoy this spot of warmth. I join them, close my eyes, feel the sun on my face.

Three days have come and gone since I brought Aunt Faye back. Mattie keeps asking how things are "over there," and I keep saying everything's fine. Haven't said a word about Kat's condition—Kat wants to be the one who tells her. I also don't say a word about Aunt Faye. It might rile Mattie. None of her business, I tell myself, but like I've always said, withholding is nearly as bad as lying, and it makes everything feel off, like witch hazel budding in February.

My eyes are still closed when I hear the buzzing of a bee, confused as the witch hazel. Kat and Seymour are talking about paying a call on Mattie and Sheriff Earl this coming weekend to tell them about Kat's condition, this could bring them around, they'll have to accept it—who doesn't love a baby?—and I think maybe I'll go with them this time, bring Aunt Faye along too, I've got nothing to hide, and if we show ourselves to be like-minded, maybe, just maybe, this will work out after all.

Then I hear a car.

I open my eyes. Mattie and Sheriff Earl's Buick is coming up the driveway. We stand. Mattie and Sheriff Earl and the Bailey twins get out of the car. Sheriff Earl holds up a piece of paper. "I got a court order here from Judge Barrow."

"Granting us custody of Eddie," Mattie says. "We're taking him."

"Like hell you are." Seymour uses his loud ball-field voice.

"I'm Eddie's aunt," Mattie says.

"And I'm his sister." Mattie glares at me but I hold it and glare back at her every bit as hard.

"You're not old enough to be a guardian," Mattie says. "This boy has got only one blood relative in these parts who is. That's me."

Sheriff Earl waves the paper. "Judge Barrow has declared that as of today, Mattie is to be Eddie's legal guardian because this house has become"—he reads from the document—"a deviant environment."

Mattie points at Kat and Seymour. "You two marrying like you did was shameful enough." She turns to me. "Now, by bringing your aunt, a known prostitute, to live here, you made this place unfit for the Duke's son."

She's heard. I'm caught off guard, and I just stand there, staring at Mattie dumbstruck.

"Eddie's coming with us," Mattie goes on.

"No, I'm not," Eddie says. "I'm staying here."

"It's not up to you," Mattie says. "You're a minor." She puts her hand on Eddie's back. "It's up to us to decide what's in your best interest, young man. We're doing this because we care about you."

"Eddie's my stepson," Kat says.

"And he's not going anywhere," Seymour says, moving in front of Eddie.

The deputies step forward and Mattie says, "Don't make this any harder than it's got to be."

Then the deputies take Eddie by his arms and march him to the Buick. Doors slam, the engine roars, and I can see Eddie's frightened, confused face when he looks back at us through the rear window, standing there in silence while the car drives away.

*   *   *

We stay up past midnight, arguing about what we should do—what is smart, what is right, what will work—worrying how Eddie is taking it, wondering what Mattie and Sheriff Earl are telling him. Listening to the four of us blaming ourselves, blaming each other, blaming Mattie, it dawns on me that this is what happens when you lose your center, the sun that everyone else circles around. I don't trust my head or my heart anymore, so after a sleepless night, I telephone Cecil. His wife, Louise, tells me he's having a dizzy spell and I can try again in the afternoon. Then I call Tom's boardinghouse, but he's in class. I don't know who else to turn to.

Over breakfast, Seymour keeps talking about how one way or another he is going to see Eddie today, no one can stop him, not Mattie, not Sheriff Earl, not the deputies, but the rest of us simply stare down at our plates. We're pretty much talked out.

Nell starts clearing the table and that's when we hear the front door open and shut. Footsteps come up the hall, brisk and confident. Only one person who doesn't live here walks in without knocking like she owns the place, and sure enough Mattie pushes through the kitchen's swinging door.

We all stand but no one says a word. Mattie looks at us one by one. She has the upper hand and knows it.

Finally, I speak up. "How's Eddie?"

"Eddie's fine," Mattie says. "He's coming around. We've been talking to him and he's coming around. I'm here to get his books."

"Some are in the classroom," I say. "Some are in his bedroom."

"Nell, go collect them," Mattie tells her. "I want to speak to the rest of you."

Nell stares at Mattie for a moment, then she wipes her hands on her apron and goes out the swinging door.

"You said Eddie's coming around," Seymour says to Mattie. "Coming around to what?"

"Coming around to seeing that you've been taking advantage of him."

"That's a goddamned lie!" Seymour shouts. "A lie and an insult!"

Mattie ignores him and turns to me. "They're out for themselves, these two." She thrusts her chin toward Seymour and Kat. "They want to get their hands on Eddie's money when he comes into it."

"We love Eddie," Kat says.

"Love." Mattie practically spits the word out. "You call it love?" She looks at me again. "They cater to his every whim, they make his head spin with talk of owning a baseball team and becoming a concert pianist, but they don't have that poor boy's interest at heart." She turns back to Kat and Seymour. "You're not family. You have no roots in this county."

"I'm your husband's brother," Seymour says, "if that's not family—"

"You're not a Kincaid, Seymour," Mattie says, getting inches from his face, then even closer. "You're just a grifter who saw a golden opportunity when the Duke died and his poor widow was suddenly all alone. Unless . . ." She pauses.

"Unless what?" I ask.

"Unless, it's all a plot, Sallie," Mattie says. "Unless it's all been a plot from the beginning. Seymour arranges for the Duke to meet a woman he had a history with. Once the Duke marries her, Seymour just happens to show up and three days later goads the Duke into doing something stupid that gets him killed, then before the Duke's body is cold Seymour marries his widow to get his hands on Eddie's inheritance."

"That's not how it happened." Kat's voice is sharp. She takes Seymour by the arm. "Getting married was my idea."

"Could be it was, Kat," Mattie says. "Could be it was. Could be you were in on it all along, seducing the Duke, urging a snap marriage before anyone could find out anything about you except what Seymour here told us, then begging the Duke not to jump off that trestle knowing all along your words would only make him hell-bent on doing just that."

"That's utterly ridiculous," Kat says.

"Is it?" Mattie asks. "What do you think, Sallie?"

"Kat's right. It's ridiculous." But could Mattie possibly be onto something? No. Impossible. But then again, even if it's not true, it sounds like it could be true, and if Mattie's been talking to Eddie like this, I can see why he might believe her.

Mattie's studying me, like she knows what I'm thinking. "There's been nothing but disaster for this family since Seymour arrived, wouldn't you agree, Sallie?"

"A lot has happened . . ." I pause. Seymour and Kat are watching, waiting, and I feel like one of those witnesses forced to testify against friends. "But some people blamed me for everything that happened when I came back."

"Death. Scandal. People are looking for explanations. They'll believe a story like this. Don't you think, Sallie, that they'll believe it?"

"This is what you're telling Eddie, isn't it?" I ask.

Mattie's eyes gleam. "It's all starting to make sense to him."

"True or not," I say.

"It's true all right," Mattie says.

"Where's your proof?" Seymour asks.

Mattie's still looking at me. "There's just too many coincidences, Sallie. Think about it. Things don't add up otherwise." She turns back to Seymour and Kat. "People will believe it. And it will rile them up something fierce. Then I can't predict what will happen." She pauses. "Because you two have no friends in these parts, no kin, no allies, no property, no nothing."

Kat lowers herself into a chair like this all made her too dizzy to stand.

"Eddie told me you're with child, Kat. Could be the Duke's and could be Seymour's. No one knows but you, and could be even you don't know." Mattie leans forward and spreads both hands on the long pine table. "So I'm going to make you an offer. Him"—she points at

Seymour—"I don't care about. Kat, I'll give you one thousand dollars to leave town. By the end of the day." Mattie takes an envelope out of her purse and holds it up. "Cash. Right here."

"You're trying to bribe me?" Kat sounds like she's having trouble breathing.

"Bribe. Payment. Incentive. Inducement. Call it what you want." Mattie opens the envelope and pulls out a thick stack of bills. "A thousand dollars. That's a lot of money." Mattie's voice softens. "More than the Duke left you. Enough to start over somewhere new."

We're all silent.

Mattie's offer is so brazen, so out of the blue, it catches us all by surprise. She's taken over the room, keeping us all off-balance, her voice booming, her gestures bold, and it hits me that it's the Kincaid in Mattie coming out, she's sounding and acting a lot like the Duke.

Then something else hits me.

Mattie saw this coming from the beginning. Her shock when Kat married Seymour was feigned. She knew Kat was feeling all alone after the Duke's death, and she let everyone know in that loud whisper of hers that Kat had no right to be living in the Big House. Mattie knew Kat would turn to Seymour, her old friend, her only friend. Maybe she even wanted it to happen. She knew it would scandalize the town. Kat thought marriage would strengthen her hand, but Mattie knew it would make her a target of contempt, knew it might even give Mattie some way of taking charge of Eddie.

I've been like a darned, plodding carriage horse, wearing blinders because I was so fixed on staying busy and moving ahead—"doesn't do to dwell on it"—that I've been seeing only what was right in front of me, nothing that was going on around me. But Mattie saw it all. She knew Aunt Faye was always having man troubles. Maybe Mattie was the one who told that doctor to declare Aunt Faye enfeebled, knowing I'd bring her back to the Big House. Cecil said Mattie had her mama's brains. Stay on your toes, he said. I didn't.

"You knew, Aunt Mattie. You saw all this coming."

Mattie's barely hiding a smile, but she says, "I have no idea what you're talking about."

She turns back to Kat. "Offer ends at nightfall." She stuffs the money back in the envelope. "Because once Eddie sees the whole picture, we'll get another court order, this one evicting you from the Big House. Because you have no right to be here. And then you will leave with nothing."

Kat and Seymour look at each other. She's biting her lower lip, his face is grim. They can't talk to Eddie, can't find out if he's really buying into Mattie's claims. It could all be a big bluff, but can Kat and Seymour take that chance?

"You'll want a little time to think this over," Mattie tells Kat. She slaps the envelope on the table. "I'll leave this right here." She taps it with her forefinger. "And I'll come back for it at the end of the day. If it's still here."

Kat and Seymour go up to the Duke's bedroom to talk it over. An hour later, they come back into the kitchen. Kat's carrying the needlepoint valise she arrived with just six months ago.

"We've looked at it every which way, Sallie, and I don't see that we have a choice." Kat sets the valise on the floor. "Mattie made it clear what will happen to us if we stay."

"Once Mattie starts spreading those lies about me, I won't be able to find work digging ditches in this town," Seymour says. "We have no future here."

"And we have the baby to think about," Kat says. "With things the way they are, this is no place for me to raise our child."

They'll head to Roanoke first, they've decided, and then maybe Danville, or heck, Seymour says, maybe get out of Virginia altogether, try their luck in Atlantic City or even California.

"If you leave," I say, "Eddie will think Mattie's right, you were only after his money."

"That's why you have to explain to Eddie that we're not who Mattie claims we are," Seymour says, "that we're doing this for him, too, to make his life easier. Tell him that, Sallie. Tell him we'll miss him."

"Tell him we love him," Kat adds.

"Both of us love him," Seymour says.

Seymour puts the envelope in his jacket pocket. Kat picks up the needlepoint valise. "It's for the best," she says. "I never belonged here."

Kat and Seymour walk toward the front door. I remember that first time I met Seymour, how I watched him walk away through the Emporium with that lightness in his step, how he looked back. The lightness is gone now and he doesn't look back.

At the end of the day, I hear the front door open and shut again, then Mattie's brisk, confident footsteps. She marches into the kitchen, sees that the table is bare, the envelope gone, and gives me a smile.

"I knew they'd take it."

"You think Mattie will start moving in today?" Aunt Faye asks.

"She's never been one to dally," Nell says from the stove.

"You've always gotten along with her just fine," I tell Nell.

"For the most part."

"I haven't," I say.

Yesterday, after Seymour and Kat left I visited Cecil. He told me he'd read the court order and Mattie did have us licked—that Kat and Seymour had no choice but to do what they did.

Sheriff Earl and Mattie will move into the Big House with Eddie, I'm sure of that, and Aunt Faye and I will be on our way back to Hatfield. I'm sure of that, too. Nell sets a plate of drop biscuits on the kitchen table. I hardly ate anything yesterday and I'm still not hungry this morning, but the biscuits are steaming, just out of the oven. Eddie's favorite. Eddie. I have to get him to see that Kat and Seymour did care about him. I'll do it before Aunt Faye and I are packed off to Hatfield. He's not the injured three-year-old he was when I left the Big

House the first time, he's a smart young man with a mind of his own. I know he'll answer my letters this time.

The front door opens and shuts, just like yesterday. It must be Mattie. Footsteps come down the hall, only they sound different. Mattie pushes through the kitchen door. Something's changed. Something's wrong. I've seen Mattie angry, determined, gleeful, triumphant— a woman who has all the answers—but I've never seen Mattie like this. Her face is ashen. Hair astray. Eyes glazed.

"Mattie, what's wrong?" I ask.

"Eddie," she says. Nothing more.

"Is he all right?" I ask.

"I told him. Last night. About Seymour and Kat. How they left with the money. How it proved they were just in it for themselves."

"How did he take it?"

"I did it for his own good. So he'd see things for what they are."

"Mattie! What's wrong?"

"The fool boy. I loved him. I did it for his own good. I loved him."

PART III

CHAPTER 20

THE SKY IS GRAY. Heavy. Like lead. Soggy snow splatters against the window and slides down.

I'm in bed. But I can't sleep. Not for three days. Since it happened. I've stopped crying. Now I'm just lying here, weighed down by the heaviness of my arms and legs. When I close my eyes I start to spin slowly, can't tell up from down. If I do start to drift off to sleep, I see Eddie's coffin disappear into the icy ground then I'm jolted awake.

You were the one, Eddie, who kept saying everything is connected, and that's what I'm trying to do now, put the pieces together, make sense of what happened, but I can't do it on my own. You're so much smarter than me. I need you to explain. But you didn't leave a note.

You gave us none of your last thoughts, shared no part of yourself except for the book Seymour gave you by that Irish writer, the one that you left on the floor beside you, opened to a long poem, some of it underlined.

> *Some love too little, some too long,*
> *Some sell, and others buy;*
> *Some do the deed with many tears,*
> *And some without a sigh:*
> *For each man kills the thing he loves,*
> *Yet each man does not die.*

That's true. We all killed you. All of us.

Everyone you loved left you. You were all alone. There was no one to hold your hand. So you climbed into Mattie's tub. You did it there.

Sweet Eddie. So smart, so talented, so gentle. But you believed everyone wanted to use you for their own ends, to turn you into something you were not, to "bring out the Kincaid in you."

Mattie was right about one thing. I should have seen it all coming. I should have seen how much you were hurting, should have seen what Seymour meant to you, should have stopped him from leaving, should have spoken up, done something. If I had seen it coming, we could've fixed whatever was wrong, you and me, we could have made it work. But I didn't. So we can't. Jane was right. I was a danger to you. I never should have come back.

The wet snow keeps pelting the window, heavier now, hammering on the glass.

The creak of the door hinge wakes me. I must have fallen asleep. I open my eyes and stare at the plastered stone wall, inches from my face.

"Sallie, hon, brought you something special." Aunt Faye's voice is hopeful. She's been trying to feed me spoonsful of soup and bites of toast, but the sight of food turns my stomach.

"Leave me alone." My voice is ragged and raw.

Aunt Faye sits on my bed. I feel her hand on my shoulder. "Sallie, you got to eat something."

"Not hungry."

"And your fire's just about died down."

I watch her stir the flames with the poker then add a log. She's set a tray on the stool next to the bed. Toast and hot tea. A small clear vase holding a single flower. A bloodroot.

"Sallie, I know you're deep in grief, but you got to eat, get your strength up. Your sister Mary's on her way to claim what's hers."

What's hers.

We went over it all at the reading of the will when the Duke died, how the eldest son gets everything, and if that son dies with no children or younger brothers, the eldest daughter gets it all.

That's Mary Montgomery Kincaid. Mary, who hated the Duke as much as her mama did.

Fine by me. "She can have it. I don't care."

"You got to care, Sallie. And you got to think clearly. You can't go on blaming yourself for what happened."

"I can. I do."

"There's plenty blame to go around." Aunt Faye's voice sounds ragged too. Her face is puffy, her eyes red. This has been every bit as hard on her and here she is bucking me up. "If I hadn't come back to the Big House . . ."

Her words trail off. She sits on the bed again and reaches for the bloodroot. Its small, simple white petals surround the bright yellow center.

"Remember," she says, "how, late every winter back in Hatfield, you'd come busting into the house clutching the first bloodroot of the year. Those mountain flowers, they look frail, but they're tough, and that little bloodroot wouldn't let nothing stop it, it'd pushed its way up through the frozen ground to let us know that cold as it felt right then, spring was coming. You've got to be like this little bloodroot, Sallie. You got to push your way up through the cold and the dark. And if you won't do it for yourself, do it for those of us who need you. So eat."

CHAPTER 21

A LOW-LYING FOG HUGS the ground, the late-winter sun is just a blurry glow. I'm standing at the parlor window looking down the driveway, and everything seems soft and colorless. Like Mary. A soft and colorless fog so thick you can't see what's in front of you until it hits you in the face.

I know so little about Mary, only that her mama, Belle, had briefly been married to the Duke's older brother, Arthur, but he died in a horrible boating accident on their honeymoon and the Colonel decided the Duke should marry Belle. They were happy at first but eleven years later, the Duke met Mama and divorced Belle, who took Mary with her back to her family in Mercer County.

I first met Mary when I was five. Eddie had just been born and the Duke sent for her because he wanted his oldest daughter to meet his new son. The Duke almost never talked about Mary or her mama and I could hardly wait to meet my big sister. I figured she'd be just like me, only ten years older, but Mary acted more like a grown-up than a kid, wouldn't play or climb trees, and kept to herself for most of her visit.

The night before she went home she came to see me, saying she had a fairy tale I ought to hear. Once upon a time in an enchanted country, a handsome prince and a beautiful princess fell in love. They got married and had a baby girl and they were all very happy until one day an evil witch decided she wanted to steal the prince for herself. She cast a spell over him, tricking the prince into banishing the princess and her daughter. The witch wed the prince, but once she was married she lost her evil powers—and the spell wore off. Then the prince saw the witch for what she was, saw that she had tricked and deceived him. So the prince killed the witch.

"I didn't like that story one bit," I said.

"You're not supposed to like it. You're supposed to learn from it."

"How could I learn anything from that horrible story?"

"It is horrible, Sallie, but it's also true." Mary's voice was soft and her eyes tender. "The prince was the Duke, the princess was my mother, and your mother was the witch."

"Mama wasn't a witch. She couldn't cast a spell."

"She was a whore, Sallie, and she bewitched the Duke." Mary gave me a smile, but it didn't invite me to smile back. "I'm telling you this for your own good, so that when you grow up, you don't go around casting spells."

At the time, I didn't even know what the word "whore" meant, but from the way Mary said it, I didn't want to know. It was also the first time anyone had said anything to me about the Duke killing Mama and later when I asked about it, no one would say a word. Mary wanted to hurt me that day, and she sure as heck did. But I've come to see how badly Mary was hurt, too. Banished just like me. Maybe there's more we have in common.

Or maybe not. Mary could be looking to avenge the wrong done to her and her mama, to get back at the daughter of the witch who cast a spell on the Duke. She just might send Aunt Faye and me back to Hatfield, and get rid of Nell while she's at it, but we're all determined to do whatever we can to make Mary feel welcome.

From the parlor window I see a black Studebaker—an old-fashioned one with a brass radiator and headlights—turn up the driveway. Mary's here. Except for that one trip when Eddie was born, Mary never returned to Claiborne County until the reading of the Duke's will. She's been living with her mama's family, the Montgomerys, forty miles due east in Mercer County, ever since her mama died seven years ago. Mary's a complete stranger to these parts, knows no one and nothing about the county, but it's all hers now.

A man wearing a crisp clerical collar gets out of the car. The Reverend Phillip Canon, Mary's pastor—and new husband. We Kincaids had figured Mary would never get married, but when news reached Mercer County of Eddie's death, the Reverend Canon proposed, saying Mary ought to have a husband to look after her in the wilds of Claiborne County. An unmarried woman coming into money draws fortune hunters like ants to spilled sugar.

I call to Aunt Faye and Nell and we go to the front porch. The reverend sets a steamer trunk on the ground, Mary takes his arm and walks up the brick path to the steps. She moves slowly, a heavy but graceful woman, peering up at us from under her black bonnet with dark, grave eyes.

"Welcome, Mary." My voice sounds strange to me. I haven't used it much lately, all those days in bed. I present Nell and Aunt Faye to Mary. She nods politely at both and presents her husband. He's more handsome than a minister ought to be, his boyish face at odds with his thick shock of gray hair.

I stick out my hand to shake his. "Reverend."

He squeezes the tips of my fingers. "Call me Phillip."

I open the door and Mary leads the way into the house. "It's good to see you, Sister," she tells me while Phillip helps her out of her black overcoat. "Even though the circumstances are tragic."

"By his own hand," Phillip says.

"May God have mercy on his soul." Mary shakes her head.

"Eddie wasn't a sinner," I say.

"You're wrong there." Phillip's tone is kinder than his words. "The taking of one's own life is self-idolatry. Only God has the right to take and give life."

"You can't say that." I'm still not in control of my feelings, and those words of his set me off. "We don't know what Eddie was feeling. What was going through his mind."

"Judge not and ye shall not be judged," Nell adds. "Forgive and ye shall be forgiven."

Nell's got more mouth on her than I thought, and my pride at that almost overcomes my worry about how my sister is going to handle disrespectful back talk from a maid.

"You know your Bible," Mary says to Nell. "That goes a long way with me."

"Mary," I say, relieved that my sister's willing to give Nell a pass, "I reckon we're all still upset about what happened."

Then, all of a sudden, Aunt Faye blurts out, "It'll take me a couple of hours, Mrs. Canon, but I'll be packed up and gone by the end of the day."

"I'm going with her." I can't let Aunt Faye live alone again. "This is your house, Mary."

"Sallie, you're my little sister. Of course you're staying on." She pats my arm. "We can't be held accountable for the sins of our parents." Then she adds, "Miss Powell, my husband and I believe in repentance. Forgiveness. Salvation. We've been told you've repented for your past. You're welcome to stay."

"Mary," I say, "that's kind of you, real decent."

"What about me?" Nell asks.

"You too, Nell. We have a lot of work ahead of us—"

"Cleaning up this county," Phillip cuts in.

"—and we're going to need all the help we can get," Mary finishes.

"Mary, I didn't expect this," I say. This isn't the Mary I feared, the Mary who wanted revenge and is now in a position to take it. Maybe we'll find that common ground, after all. "How can we thank you?"

"We'll find a way," Mary says.

Two hours later, Mattie is on the horsehair sofa, Sheriff Earl next to her, and she's leaning forward as she talks to Mary and Phillip.

"I did everything I could to save the boy," she says, "but by the time I got to him, it was too late."

When Mattie and Sheriff Earl showed up to greet Mary and Phillip, they'd barely said their hellos before Mattie brought up what had happened to Eddie, going on about how it was all Seymour's doing, his and Kat's. "They fed Eddie lies about his blood relations, turned him against us while he was still sick with grief and it was all too much for the boy. He was too young to understand."

Mattie's talking nonstop, working herself into a state, like she's trying to convince herself of what she's saying, like if she so much as pauses, the doubt will come flooding in. Then she does stop and puts her hands over her red-rimmed eyes. For a moment I think she is going to start sobbing. Instead she shakes her head like she's clearing it, then Sheriff Earl wraps an arm around her shoulders. "My wife," he says gently, "has not been herself ever since it happened."

It's true. Mattie is not herself. Her eyes look fierce and lost at the same time and she's shaking, not from fear, it seems, but from exhaustion, as if sitting here talking has been a terrible strain.

"I should have brought Eddie home with me after the Duke died," Mary says. "He'd still be with us." That's all Mary says. Doesn't try to comfort Mattie, doesn't agree that this was all Seymour's fault or even allow that it wasn't Mattie's. Sheriff Earl and Mattie glance at each other, like they'd hoped for more from Mary, and in the awkward quiet that follows, Nell brings in the tea tray with carefully arranged stacks of quartered sandwiches.

Mary takes the lid off the teapot and sniffs. "I drink oolong," she tells Nell. "Tetley. Please order it. Also, from now on, trim the crusts off sandwiches."

Nell flushes and yes-ma'ams Mary, her eyes downcast.

I didn't expect Mary to be so forgiving, but I also didn't expect her to be so darned particular and grand. We'll all have to get used to that.

"Your mother also used to cut off the crusts," Mattie tells Mary. "And she drank oolong."

"She did indeed."

Mattie picks up her teacup, brings it to her mouth, then stops and looks at it. I recall that time Mattie told me she knew every last silver spoon and china plate in the house, considered it all rightfully hers, and now here she is sitting across from the new lady of the house, her younger brother's daughter, a woman who's inheriting everything Mattie should have inherited. Wasn't fair then, isn't fair now, but there it is.

"As I'm sure you know, Mary," Mattie goes on, "ever since the Duke died Sheriff and I have been running Kincaid Holdings—on Eddie's behalf—and we'll continue doing it for you, of course, for as long as you like."

"Give you all the time you need to settle yourselves in," Sheriff Earl adds, "get to know the people, figure out where the money comes from and where it goes to."

"My husband is a very capable man," Mary says.

"Speaking of where the money comes from," Phillip says, "my wife and I have heard—all the way over in Mercer County—about this still tax of yours."

"You're not only allowing men to engage in an illegal activity"—Mary's voice is stern—"you're profiting from it."

"That money's going to pave the roads," Sheriff Earl says. "Help widows and orphans."

"Essential services," Mattie adds.

"It's illegal," Phillip says.

"I want it stopped," Mary says.

"We could do that." Sheriff Earl is using his peacemaking voice, the one he speaks in to keep a bad situation from getting worse. "That still tax was more in the nature of a let's-give-this-a-try-and-see-if-it-works deal."

"It's not just the tax. Liquor making is wrong and it must stop." Mary turns to me. "When our little brother died, I asked God why. Then it came to me. God wants me here. He has a mission for me."

"To turn this county into a law-abiding, God-fearing place," Phillip adds.

"I'm aware that you are my aunt and uncle," Mary tells Mattie and Sheriff Earl, "but my husband and I do not need the services of whiskey profiteers."

Mattie stands up. I expect her to explode, breathe a little fire, but instead her voice comes out quiet and cold and I can see the Kincaid temper she's reining in. "You just got here, Mary Montgomery Canon. You and your new pastor husband and all your holier-than-thou notions. Your bags aren't even unpacked. You have no idea what help you need. And by the time you find out it will be too late."

CHAPTER 22

CECIL UNLOCKS THE DOOR to the Emporium's cellar. He's still looking tired, but he felt obligated to explain Kincaid Holdings to Mary
and Phillip. So far, they're not liking what they're hearing. On their
first day, I gave them a tour of the county and this morning they in-
spected the Emporium and Cecil showed them the books. When he
told them that the store takes whiskey in trade and that tenants pay
rent with whiskey when they're shy of cash Mary and Phillip were
shocked.

"You store whiskey in this very building?" Mary asked. "I want
to see it."

So here we are. Cecil leads Mary and Phillip downstairs and
switches on the lights. A string of naked bulbs casts a harsh glare on
the aisles of shelves crammed with bottles. There's ale and elderberry
wine and peach and pear and apple brandy. But mostly there's whiskey. White whiskey. Hundreds and hundreds of gallons of it—in fruit
jars, crock jugs, soda bottles, milk bottles, medicine bottles, pretty
much anything you can stick a cork into. Some are fuzzy with years of
dust, some so shiny clean they could have been put on the shelf this
week.

I remember the first time I laid eyes on this place. I was seven,
I'd been in the Duke's little back office, but some men showed up, and
he told me to make myself scarce, he had grown-up business to discuss. So I wandered around the Emporium spying on customers and
wondering what this grown-up business was about. Then I saw that

the door to the basement was open. It was usually locked, no children allowed, so of course I crept down the stairs. I felt like I'd stumbled into some forbidden treasure room, like Ali Baba's cave. Then Tom came around a corner carrying a bottle.

"You're not supposed to be in here." His tone was scolding, and that wasn't at all like Tom.

"Why? What is this place?"

Tom started running errands for the Duke when he was twelve or thirteen, and sometimes he let me go with him and he answered all the questions I pestered him with. Now he looked at me like he was trying to decide if he should answer this question. His face got very serious. "This is where we keep the inventory." His voice was low, just above a whisper, and I knew he was telling me something very important, a secret of the grown-up world. "Whiskey." He held up the bottle. "For customers."

Whiskey. I knew that the Duke, like most men in Claiborne County, drank whiskey, and I also knew some people thought you shouldn't. "Why are you acting like it's a secret?"

"It's untaxed and unbonded." Tom tore a sheet of brown paper off a roll, and started wrapping the bottle. "That means it's illegal."

My daddy, the man who called the shots in Claiborne County, was doing something that was against the law? Did that mean he was a criminal? Did that mean he was bad? He couldn't be. He was my daddy, the Duke. He took care of all of us. But he was breaking the law. Tom just said so. I figured that for the first time I was seeing the true world of grown-ups, the secret world they kept hidden from children, where things were not what they seemed. I wondered if the business the Duke had with those men, the business he didn't want me overhearing, had to do with the world of whiskey, with breaking the law.

"Will the Duke go to jail?" I asked.

"Oh no." Tom finished wrapping the bottle and tied it with twine. "See, Sallie, there's all kinds of laws. Local law, state law, federal law, common law, civil law, God's laws. Then there's the Duke's laws. Some laws are important and some are silly."

"But if there's all these different laws, how do you know what ones you have to follow?"

"Laws made by people far away don't matter all that much. What matters are the laws made by the people right here, the ones taking care of you. Like the Duke."

I believed that then. Still do. So do most folks in Claiborne County—without thinking too hard on it. They accept it the way you accept roosters crowing in the morning and moths burning themselves in candle flames. Thing is, for years no one outside Claiborne County cared or even knew what we did up here. Now, we got outsiders coming in and telling us what's right and wrong.

I watch Mary and Phillip walk up and down the aisles, inspecting the whiskey, saying nothing, and I know that the Duke's laws don't matter one whit to them. Mary turns back to me, and her face is calm, almost glowing. "I told you I was on a mission, Sallie, I told you why God took Eddie. I want this all brought outside," she says, sweeping her hand at the shelves. "I want it destroyed."

"This is our inventory." Cecil says. "It's worth thousands of dollars."

"It's contraband," Phillip says. "And it's poison, pure and simple."

"I know you adored the Duke," Mary tells me, "but he had a taste for whiskey. More than a taste, according to Mother. And it was whiskey that got him eyeing other women." Tears well up in Mary's eyes and she quickly wipes them away. "Mother blamed it for the ruination of her marriage. After we left the Big House, she devoted her life to the crusade against liquor. And at Mother's deathbed, I promised her I'd carry on her work so that no more wives will be betrayed, no more children will be abandoned, no more families will be shattered. Sallie, round up a couple of clerks."

Myself, I don't have much taste for whiskey—after a few sips, my short temper gets shorter and my loud voice gets louder—but for most folk in Claiborne County, whiskey is a part of daily life, like morning coffee and evening prayers, it's medicinal, a pain soother for both the body and the spirit. Still, it's true what Mary's saying. Liquor can destroy families. Dutch Weber was drinking when he started the fight that got him killed. Ever since Eddie's death, I've been second-guessing myself so I look at Cecil. He nods ever so slightly. I find Garland, the second-floor clerk, and Ernest, the stock boy, and we haul up boxes of bottles and stack them in the lot behind the store.

Townsfolk stop to watch. I know most of them by sight and they're a motley lot, I think, seeing them through Mary's eyes, with patched jackets, stained aprons, and work pants worn and baggy at the knees. They stand there, silent and grim, then Sheriff Earl shows up to find out what all the commotion is about.

"You and your deputies ought to be helping out here," Phillip says. "You ought to be enforcing the law."

Sheriff Earl looks at the stack of bottles, then at the crowd. They look back at him, waiting to see if he's going to be carrying out orders from Mary and Phillip the way he always carried out the Duke's orders.

"Way I see it, Prohibition's federal law, not local law," he says. "Sheriff's department enforces local laws. As I recollect, when me and my wife offered you our help, Reverend, you said you didn't want it. So if you're set on destroying your own private property, you go right ahead. But the sheriff's department won't be pitching in."

Sheriff Earl walks off and more than a few people in the crowd nod in approval. Phillip tells Garland to fetch axes and calls out, "Any volunteers?"

Chalky Hurd, who's still working the post office job the Duke gave him, is in the crowd. I'd heard Chalky became a teetotaler after he killed Dutch, and now he steps forward and Phillip hands him an ax.

Mary nods in approval as Phillip holds out one for me. The hickory handle's been worn smooth by all the callused hands that used that ax to fell trees and chop firewood to provide warmth in winter. The eyes of the crowd are on me. And I feel mighty set up by Mary and Phillip. I know these people will feel betrayed if the Duke's daughter axes the Duke's liquor—whiskey some of them made themselves.

And yet, that day back when Tom told me about all those differ-ent laws, he had a thirteen-year-old's spotty understanding of the way the world works but he sure was right about one thing. What matters most are the laws made by the people close to you, the ones you de-pend on. Now that's Mary.

I reach for the ax.

CHAPTER 23

ABRAHAM CROCKETT IS STANDING by the grand old hackberry in his front yard, swept clean to the packed dirt by his wife to keep away snakes that hide in the grass. Mary and Phillip have been riding with me on my rounds, shaking tenants' hands, inspecting their houses, and passing out pamphlets with lurid tales of men, women, and children destroyed by drink. They're also letting folks know that from here on out, the Kincaids will not be accepting whiskey as payment for rent.

The tenants are bewildered and angry—people have bartered with liquor ever since the county was first settled—but so far no one has argued with Mary and Phillip. I know that if anyone does it will be Abraham Crockett.

Sure enough, he turns to me with a puzzled look and asks, "How she expect us to pay her then?" Us. Abraham's the unofficial mayor of Hopewell Road and he's speaking on behalf of all the colored folk who live here.

I wish I could talk to Abraham in private, tell him what was hammered into me yesterday, that Mary's making the laws now, let's abide by them. See how it plays out. I also wish I had the answer to his question, but there's a lot I'm wishing for right now.

Abraham's wife, Gloria, and their five children are watching from the porch of a small house that's never known paint. Rising up behind its rusting tin roof are the dozen or so hilly acres Abraham rents from us, raising the corn he turns into the whiskey that pays his rent.

Abraham's goes down smooth, people like to say, then ambushes you from behind.

"You grow corn," Mary says.

Abraham fixes his attention on her. "Farming since I was about this high." He holds out his hand. "And, ma'am, no one gets a better yield than Abraham Crockett."

"It's simple then," Phillip says. "Sell the corn instead of making liquor with it and pay your rent with that money."

Abraham glances at me again like he can't believe what he's hearing. "Reverend, sir," he says to Phillip, "I hear tell you're a fine preacher but, and I say this with all due respect, sir, a farmer you are not. So allow me to share with you a few facts from my line of work." Abraham has a deep preacher's voice and now he slows down to give each word its due. "I get five dollars for a gallon of whiskey. Five dollars. The corn that goes into making it would fetch me about a nickel. Five cents."

Abraham's never been good at hiding his feelings and I can tell Phillip is mighty offended, but before he says anything Mary speaks up. "Pray on it," she tells Abraham, her voice gentle but firm. "God will help you find honest work."

"The work I do is honest, ma'am." Abraham's voice is every bit as gentle and firm. "No one has ever complained about the quality of Abraham Crockett's liquor. And, sir, you know your Bible so I need not remind you that Genesis tells us, 'May God give you of heaven's due and of earth's richness—an abundance of grain and new wine.'"

Despite the sirs and the ma'ams, the gentle voice and the courtly manner, a colored man is quoting scripture as a way of telling a white man—a white man of the cloth—what's right and wrong. It's simply too much for Phillip.

"Don't be quoting the Bible at me, boy," he snaps. "Isaiah tells us those who run after drink have no regard for the deeds of the Lord."

"We'll give you a month's grace," Mary tells Abraham. "Rent free. To adjust and find honest work."

"After that," Phillip adds, "cash."

There's an angry jut to Abraham's chin. On the porch behind him, Gloria is standing with her hands on her hips. She and the Crockett children are all in the choir at Abraham's church, and he likes to boast that when Gloria starts singing, even the birds stop their chirping to listen. But she doesn't look like she's about to break into song just now.

Phillip looks my way. "You hear that, Sallie?"

I haven't said a word during this whole ugly visit. In fact, I haven't said much since Mary got here, and now, when I do speak up, I don't like the sound of my voice. "I hear."

I knock on Abraham's door in early May. I skipped him in April but now, it's time to collect his rent in cash. I'm dreading it. Abraham opens the door and before he says a word, I just about fall over myself telling him what I wanted to say back in March. "I'm on your side, Abraham, or I want to be, but I have a job to do and I'm just trying to keep my head down."

Abraham surprises me by laughing. "Miss Kincaid, when it comes to keeping your head down, us colored folk not only been there, we were born there."

Now I laugh. "That so? Is that what you were doing when you were quoting scripture to Mary's husband?"

Abraham laughs again. "Well, let's just say I try to keep my head down but sometimes it won't stay there."

He reaches into his shirt pocket and pulls out four well-worn five-dollar bills.

"The Crocketts are not in need of your sister's charity, so this here is for both last month and this one." He winks. "Tell Mrs. Canon I prayed on it and God told me what to do."

I don't ask where the money came from. Don't have to. I have a pretty darned good idea what Abraham Crockett has been up to. He's gone into business for himself, like just about every whiskey maker in Claiborne County has. When Mary stopped trading whiskey at the Emporium all she did was cut out what Cecil calls the middleman.

That was us. Now, our whiskey makers are selling from their back doors or the beds of their wagons or the trunks of their cars to slick-suited men with out-of-county tags, men who keep their hat brims low, asking in clipped, hurried voices about what might be available and at what prices.

"I've been thinking it was high time Gloria lived in a painted house." Abraham grins and raps the siding with his knuckles. "She's always wanted that."

"That's a fine idea, Abraham. Any color in mind?"

"I was thinking white, but Gloria says yellow's more cheerful."

"I would never dare disagree with that woman," I say.

"You got that one right." Abraham lets out that big laugh of his.

Back at the Emporium, Phillip and Cecil are in the Duke's office going over a column of numbers in the Accounts Receivable notebook. Now that Mary has put Phillip in charge of Kincaid Holdings, Mattie's all but gone into hiding, keeping to her house, feeling unwelcome everywhere, mourning Eddie but also blaming herself, I'm sure, regardless of what she told Mary. Sheriff Earl, meanwhile, spends his time at the jail, leaving it to Cecil to deal with Mary and Phillip.

That's no easy task. Mary and Phillip aren't heeding Cecil's advice any more than Mattie did, but they have left the drudgery of daily business to him, and I worry about the strain it's putting on his bad heart.

"Cash flow's way off," Cecil tells Phillip.

"That's the price of obeying the law," Phillip says.

I pass my ledger and satchel to Cecil. "One hundred eighty-two dollars."

"Not bad," he says. "How many still in arrears?"

"Three or four, but they say they're trying and I told them we'd work with them."

"What about our friend Mr. Crockett?"

"Abraham's paid up. Cash. This month and last."

"He found honest work?" Phillip asks.

"Didn't say. What he did say was. 'Tell Mrs. Canon I prayed on it and God told me what to do.'"

A little of Abraham's mischievous tone crept into my voice and Phillip must have heard it. "Is that a joke?"

"Couldn't say."

"Couldn't say? You think it's a joke, too?"

"Sallie doesn't think it's a joke, Phillip," Cecil says. "She's not laughing."

"Maybe not. Not to my face. But there are people in this county treating Prohibition like it's a joke. They're laughing, Cecil, laughing at me and my wife behind our backs. They think we're fools, but we know what's going on and I'll tell you one thing. If we can't clean up this cesspool on our own, we'll find someone who will. And then we'll see who's laughing."

Chapter 24

Nell's knocking on my door. I know by the polite little tap and I figure she's brought my morning cup of coffee the way she sometimes does even though I've told her I don't want to be waited on. But when I open the door, Nell is empty-handed, her face a knot of worry.

"Kat's back," Nell says. "She's going to have her baby any day."

"What the heck is Seymour thinking?"

"Kat's by herself."

"Where's Seymour?"

Nell just shakes her head.

I can hear Kat screaming upstairs. She's been at it for twelve hours now. She didn't think her thirty-two-year-old body could take it, but Aunt Faye, who's midwifed before, told Kat she's helped women older than that give birth, women who cry at a pinprick, and they all find the wherewithal to come through. "Haven't lost a one yet," Aunt Faye said. But we all know that plenty don't make it.

It's late June, three weeks since Kat showed up carrying that same needlepoint valise she'd had when the Duke first brought her to the Big House—but the creamy hopeful woman she'd been back then was long gone. Seymour had been killed in a car crash, she told us, hit by a drunken driver in Knoxville, and she was throwing herself on our mercy. "I have no one else to turn to," she said. "I didn't call ahead, thought if you saw how desperate I am, you might take pity on me, let me stay."

Mary rose to the occasion and welcomed Kat. "Mothers and babies have a special place in my heart—and God's," she said. "But this proves my point. Whiskey ruins the lives of everyone it touches."

Mary deserves a lot of credit for the way she took in Kat. As for me, I was too thrown by the news of Seymour's death to say much. Couldn't shake the memory of him that day at the lake, grabbing Eddie's hand when he was frozen with fear on the trestle. Now they're both gone. I hoped Seymour was happy, looking forward to being a daddy in those last moments before he died.

Kat asked after Eddie, and when we told her what happened, it was all too much for her. She fell into the same sort of hopeless fog I was in after Eddie died, blaming herself for taking Mattie's money, for leaving Eddie, for thinking she and Seymour could simply walk away without fate coming after them. When she finally had her gush of the waters, it was Mary who came through again. Think what you will of her, Mary holds that motherhood—bringing an innocent life into this world and caring for it—is the highest calling for a woman, and Mary helped Kat turn her mind to what lay ahead, to her baby and the joy it would bring her.

I fill a glass at the kitchen sink. It's fresh well water, clear and cold, and I drain the glass then head back upstairs. The birthing room is hot and crowded and we're all drenched in sweat, but there's also a fierce resolve in the air, each of us keenly aware of the two lives at stake here and determined to do our jobs as best we can.

Mary and Aunt Faye are kneeling between Kat's legs. Nell's at the washbasin, keeping towels fresh and hot. My job is to comfort Kat, to wipe her sweaty brow, so I take my seat at her shoulder and she grips my hand hard, like I'm all that's keeping her afloat. I've never been at a birthing, and it's messier, bloodier, louder, more painful than I thought it'd be, and I'm so danged proud of Kat's courage.

Aunt Faye keeps ducking beneath the bloody sheet that covers Kat's thighs, I can't see much but I can tell that her shoulders are working and her arms are busy. Then Kat lets out a scream you can hear across the county.

"Scissors!" Aunt Faye yells.

I still can't see what's happening, but in a moment, Aunt Faye stands up, the baby in her arms—but oh my Lord, the baby's blue. Something's wrong. Kat gasps and digs her fingernails into my hand. "What's going on?" she asks. "What happened to my baby?"

Aunt Faye takes a towel and rubs the baby hard. It starts to squeal and before our eyes, like a miracle, the blue fades and the baby's skin turns pink, a beautiful living pink.

"A girl," Aunt Faye announces.

"A precious little gift from God," Mary says.

It was about eight months ago that Kat married Seymour so either he or the Duke could be the father. But like Kat says, that doesn't matter. She's ours.

The baby keeps on crying. She's tiny. Her face is raw, her eyes squished shut, wisps of wet, pale hair plastered to her head. She's one of the ugliest things I've ever laid my eyes on—but a love swells up in my heart for this little creature, a love I've never felt before, a love so powerful it startles me.

Mary takes the baby in her arms and coos at her. This is Mary at her best, doing what she believes women were born to do, and the baby stops crying.

Aunt Faye's pressing on Kat's belly to push out the afterbirth and I'm still marveling at the baby's little peach of a head and itty-bitty fingers like an opossum's. I can't believe that one day these tiny hands will take up a pencil or a rolling pin or a steering wheel, will slap someone and stroke someone, will tremble in fear and clap with joy, and I wonder what kind of woman will have these hands, what she will do with them.

Kat sits up in bed, pale and wrung out—but she has a lopsided smile. I always thought of Kat as a soft woman but she got through this like Aunt Faye said she would.

"I haven't even thought about a name," Kat says.

"You have your baby by the grace of God," Mary says. "Perhaps out of gratitude, you should call her Grace."

"Grace. A pretty name. I like that."

"Kat, baby Grace needs a feeding." Aunt Faye's voice is knowing.

Kat unbuttons her gown and Mary passes her the baby. "Funny," Kat says.

"What's funny?" I ask.

"Married three times. Three husbands. But when I finally have a child, I'm all alone."

"You're not alone," I say.

"Not a man in sight."

"We're here," Nell says.

"You're not alone and Grace isn't going to be alone," Mary says. "I have some news. I've been waiting for the right moment and now is the time. It's been three months since I've had a visit from my unwanted guest." She kisses the top of the baby's head. "Little one, you're going to have a companion."

CHAPTER 25

THE SONG OF CRICKETS and tree frogs drifts through my bedroom window when Kat comes in. It's late and I was about to put on my nightgown, but she's dressed like she's expecting guests. "I like this little room," she says. "I remember how you said, 'Cool in the summer and freezing in the winter.'" She gives a quiet laugh.

Back when Kat was married to the Duke, she laughed all the time, but in the two weeks since the baby was born I haven't heard her laugh once. Kat's a bosomy woman, but when she tried to feed baby Grace, she had no milk. The baby started bawling and Kat panicked. "Don't worry, hon," Aunt Faye told her, "happens all the time. The milk will come in a day or two." She sent for a wet nurse, a young woman named Becca, who lives in a little house down the road and has a two-year-old son just weaning. But Kat's milk never came. In the days that followed, she watched like a hawk as Becca suckled Grace— then she stopped watching and sat out on the porch.

It was getting worrisome, Kat's frame of mind, so I'm glad to hear her laugh again. She sits down on my bed and runs a finger along the seams of the patchwork quilt. She's here for a reason.

"You must miss Seymour something awful," I say.

"Sallie, there's something you ought to know. Seymour's not dead."

I'm not sure I heard Kat right. Is she lying? Is she joking? Her face is earnest, but it also strikes me as the face of a stranger. I don't know Kat Johnson one bit. "Why in the world . . . ?"

"To make things easier. We decided to go our separate ways."

I try to look Kat in the eyes, but she's staring down at the quilt.

"Thing is," she continues, "Seymour can be with women. But he"—she searches for the right words—"he'd rather be with men."

"That can't be." That simply cannot be. Kat's mistaken. To me, to anyone in Claiborne County, that notion—of a man being with another man—is all but unthinkable, something rowdy schoolboys joke about, something preachers call an abomination, but not something that ever really takes place. In France, maybe, but not here in Claiborne County. "That can't be. Not Seymour."

"Trust me. Men like Seymour can turn out to be that way."

"But he was such a ladies' man."

"Yes, he was, wasn't he? I think my first husband knew. That's why he didn't mind Seymour keeping me company, even when he was away on business."

"I still don't believe it."

"I'm sorry. I know you always had a sweet spot for him."

"You could tell?"

"Hard to miss. Anyway, you don't have to know how I found out about Seymour, but once I got over the shock, I tried to live with it. I even thought maybe I could change him. But every time he went out, I'd get all crazy, wondering who he was with, what he might be up to. And, Sallie, I have to be with a man who wants to be with me."

"Eddie. Did Seymour ever . . . ?"

"No. Nothing like that ever happened. He thought of Eddie as a son."

"What about the baby? Seymour was going to help raise her."

"That brings me to why I'm here. Sallie, I done a lot of thinking and I've decided to leave."

That stops me cold. "You can't leave. Grace needs Becca."

"I'm not taking Grace."

"That's out of the question, Kat. What are you thinking?"

"Sallie, I've got no future here." There's a set to Kat's face. "No one in this county will ever forget what happened. I never should have married Seymour. It led to Eddie's doing what he did. People will never forgive me. If I stay here I'll spend the rest of my life shut up in this house."

"You've just got the baby blues. Aunt Faye says that happens all the time to new mamas. It'll pass." I'm trying to buck her up, but truth is she's right, the people of Caywood will never accept her. Who cares? Grace needs her.

"My mind's made up," Kat says.

"To just leave your daughter? You can't do that."

"Don't tell me what I can and cannot do." Her voice is sharp but a pleading look comes into her tired eyes. "Sallie, I'm not like you. I've always needed a man. And I've always found one. But after what's happened here, no decent man in this county will ever marry me. I'm no spring chicken, but I've still got a lot of years ahead of me and I have to move on, take what's left of the money Mattie gave me and start afresh."

"You're a mama, Kat. Your baby needs you."

"I'm not cut out to be a mama. That's what my body's telling me. Can't even make milk. If I take the baby with me, I won't be able to get a job. And a woman with another man's baby—that's a tough sell if she's looking for a husband."

"But Grace is your little girl."

"I'm doing it for her good, too. She'll be better off raised by you and Faye and Mary. If I'm not around to remind everyone, people will forget that I was Grace's mama."

"She's your daughter." This time it's my voice that's sharp. "She needs her mama."

Kat stands up. "You grew up without your mama and you turned out just fine."

That's what you think, Kat, but I didn't turn out just fine. I could tell her that. I could tell her that I have only a few sketchy memories of Mama and I've missed her something awful. So many times I watched Jane fussing over Eddie, holding his hand as they walked in the garden, tucking him into bed at night and kissing him first thing in the morning, and I wondered what it would be like to have a mama tending to me like that, letting me know that I was wanted. I pretended it didn't matter, pretended all I needed was the Duke—as long as I loved him and he loved me back, I was fine. But I will never shake the feeling that I was unwanted. Any little girl whose mama disappears will always have a hole in her heart that nothing will ever completely fill. I've never told anyone that, never seen it so clearly, and I could tell Kat now, but I know it won't work, I know that her mind is made up, that's why she was able to laugh when she first sat down and I also know that even if I could twist her arm and make her give up the idea of that new life she's dreaming about, she'd hold it against me. And against Grace.

I decide to say nothing.

But I can't. I can't say nothing—I'd never forgive myself—so I tell her, "Kat, I didn't turn out fine."

"Sallie, this is what's best for everyone," Kat says like she didn't even hear me.

"Kat, I miss my mama something awful. I miss her every single day."

"I'm leaving tonight. No need for a lot of goodbyes. In the morning, when everyone wakes up, I'll be gone."

Gone. She's already gone. I take a breath and nod.

Kat smiles at me. It's a sad smile, but a grateful one.

"Will you ever come back?" I ask. "To see Grace, let her know what her mama looks like?"

Kat shakes her head like she doesn't know.

"Where are you heading?"

She shakes her head again like it doesn't matter.

"Will you take good care of Grace?" she asks.

Is there any way I can give Grace what she is about to lose? What do I say a few years from now when a little girl with a hole in her heart asks why her mama left? Some would say we shouldn't even tell her. But I'm not going to lie. "I'll promise you one thing, Kat. Grace will never feel unwanted. I won't let her."

CHAPTER 26

GRACE JUST HAD HER bath in the kitchen sink and I'm holding the damp, squirmy little creature while Aunt Faye, a safety pin in her mouth, folds a diaper into a triangle on the long pine table. It's been two months since Kat left and it has fallen to Aunt Faye to look after the baby. She loves it. The baby and the job.

"Put her right there," she says. "Real gentle."

I carefully do as she says. Being a mama comes natural to Aunt Faye, the way she cradles the baby like she's been doing it all her life, but whenever I hold Grace my arms tighten up and that makes her squirm even more and my only thought is, don't drop this little thing, whatever you do, don't drop her.

Aunt Faye brings the corners of the diaper together at the baby's belly, smoothly pins them in place, then slips a finger inside the diaper, checking the fit. "Nice and snug," she whispers.

The baby's blue eyes are wide and curious. She's beginning to take in the world. I study her face, looking for any hints of Seymour or Kat. Or the Duke. Maybe it's too soon. She's only ten weeks old and she's still just a little monkey face. She does have Kat's yellow hair.

"I wonder where Kat is," I say. "How she's doing."

"My bet is she headed to one of the ports. Lot of those naval officers back from the war will be looking for wives." Aunt Faye gently towels the baby's wet hair. "I wish Mary would stop railing against her. You can't judge someone until you've walked in their shoes."

Mary was not just shocked, she was sickened and disgusted,

she said, that Kat had gone off and left her baby behind—"What kind of woman would do that?" she keeps asking. "Like a cowbird, leaving its eggs in other birds' nests." But she loves Grace and has talked about maybe adopting her. "A playmate," she said, "for my own baby."

Mary's starting to show and I let her know I'm happy for her. "Folks always said Belle was a good mama, a loving one," I told her, "you'll be a good and loving mama too."

"I thank you for that," Mary said. "Truly I do."

At first, I'd hoped that with one baby in the house and another on the way, Mary would have too much on her mind to keep worrying about Claiborne County's whiskey makers. I couldn't have been more wrong. "I don't want my baby born in a place where such evil exists," she says over and over again.

Mary's bound and determined to drive out the whiskey makers by the time the baby comes. She and Phillip have been holding temperance rallies, Phillip taking to the podium to rail against liquor, but Sheriff Earl is still refusing to enforce Prohibition laws, and the whiskey makers have gone about their business like before. So a couple of days ago, Mary and Phillip drove all the way to Richmond—some eighty miles east—to see the Virginia Prohibition commissioner and demand that he send in state troopers to enforce the law, arrest the whiskey makers.

"Nap time." Aunt Faye's voice interrupts my thoughts. She picks up the baby and we're in the hallway when the front door opens. It's Mary and Phillip, back from Richmond.

Mary's flush with excitement. "We've found the man for the job."

"He's smart as a fox and mean as a snake." Phillip's voice is triumphant. "We'll show that sheriff of yours how to enforce the law."

Glen Lowe doesn't look akin to either a fox or a snake. He's wearing a stiff celluloid collar, silver spectacles with lenses round as silver dollars, and has a razor-sharp part in his polished black hair. He's sitting on one of the wing chairs in the parlor, his teacup and saucer balanced in hands that look like they've never held a hammer.

His wife, Clara, a birdlike woman who's pinned up her wheat-colored hair, carefully sips her tea while Phillip describes what he calls the appalling lawlessness in Claiborne County.

The Virginia Prohibition commissioner told Mary and Phillip he had only a few agents and couldn't send one out every time he got a complaint that someone somewhere in the state was buying or selling liquor. But if Mary and Phillip hired their own investigator to collect evidence, he'd deputize the man to make arrests. The investigator he recommended was Glen Lowe.

Phillip invited Lowe to Caywood to talk about the job, and Lowe got here this afternoon. He seems to be listening carefully to Phillip, but he's keeping his thoughts to himself, nodding from time to time, asking no questions.

When Phillip is done, Lowe sets his cup in the saucer on the tea table.

"I will need complete autonomy," he says. "I don't take on a job if my hands are tied. And it could get rough."

"I was hoping it wouldn't come to that," Mary says, "hoping people would see the errors of their ways."

"It's not enough to hope," Lowe says. "This situation calls for force."

"We're not going to second-guess him, Mary," Phillip says.

"What do you mean by rough?" I ask.

Lowe looks at me, his eyes glinting and sharp behind his silver spectacles. "We'll find out."

"Mr. Lowe will need your help," Phillip tells me.

"To do what?"

I'm wondering how the heck I can wheedle my way out of this, but Lowe holds up his small soft hand and says, "I don't need the young lady's help. Just get me someone who knows the names of the unmarked streets."

CHAPTER 27

STRANGERS ARE CRAWLING ALL over the county, armed to the teeth, so I need a gun, too.

It's dark, just past nine, and the October moon is casting long, blue shadows across Caywood's empty streets. Everything is still. Houses look deserted—lights out, lamps unlit, curtains drawn—but I can feel eyes on me, feel the fear of the people peering from behind those curtained windows.

Lowe joined Chalky Hurd on his mail delivery route and Chalky was happy to point out the stores, cabins, filling stations, trading posts, cafés, and roadhouses where locals are selling whiskey. Lowe set up shop in the library at the Big House, calling it his War Room, dictating reports to Clara and plastering the wall with lists, addresses where liquor was sold, and the names of the sellers.

Even though it meant deceiving Mary, I dropped hints to a few of the whiskey makers, including Abraham. "Folks have seen that fellow riding around with Chalky and have figured that something's going on," Abraham said. "We're taking what measures we can. We'll see what comes next."

It's coming tonight. Lowe's been here two months and he's finally finished putting together that list of his. A marshal from the Prohibition Commission showed up this afternoon and deputized a couple dozen men Phillip brought in from Mercer County. A few of our own teetotaling Baptists joined up too, and that surprised me—Claiborne

County men turning on one another. Lowe made sure everyone had guns and badges, and several hours ago, he sent them out to make arrests.

Word about the strangers spread across the county like a hard wind and now most everyone's indoors, hunkered down with their families, waiting to see how rough it's going to get.

I'm also waiting. But I'm too worked up to stay indoors so I'm out walking. And if one of Lowe's thugs waves a rifle in my face, I want to wave one back.

I need a gun.

I should have brought my Remington, but it's under my bed. I turn up Main Street. The Emporium's lights are on. There's that twenty-gauge in the Duke's office. That'll do it.

The store's door is locked. I knock loud and hard and Cecil comes out from the back. His eyes are sunken and the trembling in his hands is worse.

"You all right, Cecil? You ought to be in bed."

"Not tonight." A few hours earlier, Cecil says, Lowe told Sheriff Earl that as a state marshal, he outranked all the local officials—sheriff, mayor, deputies—and was taking over law enforcement in Claiborne County. He demanded the keys to the jail and Sheriff Earl handed them over.

Cecil leans against the countertop. It helps stop his hands from trembling. "Sallie, we are under siege."

"That's why I'm here. To get the twenty-gauge."

"My dear, you're not taking a popgun out of this store."

"I've got to do something."

"Nothing anyone can do at the moment. They've got the guns and badges. They've also got the Eighteenth Amendment on their side."

"We can't do nothing. What would the Duke have done?"

"He'd have come to me, mad as a sack of cats, looking for his gun, saying we've got to do something. And I'd have told him, the smartest thing to do is wait. Doing nothing doesn't come easy. For you or the

Duke. But with men like these, you've got to wait for them to slip up. You wait long enough, they usually do."

I pace around the Emporium. I don't know if Cecil is right. It's easy to say we should wait, but what will the whiskey makers do when those deputies come for them? Surrender? Fight back? How can they not fight back? But what happens then?

Through the window, I see headlights swinging up Main Street. Cars pass the Emporium, going toward the jail on Courthouse Square.

"We can't just stand here," I say.

"We're not going to," Cecil says. "There must be witnesses to all this. But you're not bringing that shotgun."

Cars are lined up at the jail and armed deputies are standing in the street holding torches. Phillip is with them. When he sees me, he looks startled and angry, but then the deputies start pulling hand-cuffed men out of the cars.

There's our tenant Chuck Driscoll in faded overalls, red clay still on his boots, and I figure he'd been doing his late-night barn check. Next comes Hobie Shotwell in a vest and tie looking like he'd been reading the evening paper in his easy chair. Then Billy Bond. One eye is swollen shut, but with the other he gives me a look that says, so you're part of this, too—and all I can think to do is shake my head. Behind Billy comes Abraham Crockett, glaring at Phillip with a hatred he's not bothering to hide.

Cecil is right. If I had a gun, I'd be sorely tempted to use it. These men are tenants, friends, kin, I've been inside their houses, I know their wives and their young ones. And now they're being herded around like livestock at branding time.

Then Lowe drives up in his black Oldsmobile. He's wearing tall field boots, and a pair of revolvers is strapped to his thighs.

"Good work," Phillip calls to him.

"It's just the beginning." Lowe looks around and his eyes fall on me. "You don't belong here."

"Miss Kincaid and I are here to make sure everything stays proper," Cecil says, "the way the Duke would have wanted."

"We're not doing things the Duke's way," Phillip says.

"I see that," I say. Cecil puts a hand on my shoulder, gently pulling me back. "I see it got rough."

"I told you it might." Lowe's spectacles glint in the torchlight. "And it did."

CHAPTER 28

GLORIA'S ON THE PORCH of her newly painted yellow house, her lip swollen, her children huddled behind her.

"You all all right?" I call out.

"Do I look all right? Men break down my door in the middle of the night, smack me in the face, drag off my husband, and now you come asking if I'm all right?" Gloria's words are angry, but there's a crack in her voice. She's terrified. Of course she is. Everyone is. Furious and afraid. Me too.

Last night, Lowe's deputies ranged over the county, banging on doors, waving guns, flashing badges, cuffing people, shoving and punching anyone who resisted or back-talked or even questioned them.

I haven't been collecting rent today, I've been listening and holding in the fury that builds with each story I hear. People keep telling me that I've got to do something. I promise them I will. Keep promising myself, too. Now I have to figure out what that something is.

"Gloria, what can I do?"

"Get my Abraham out of jail."

"I would if I could, Gloria. You know that."

"You got to tell your sister to put a stop to all this."

"Mary barely listens to me."

"Kincaids." Gloria shakes her head. "One sister sends in men to bust up your family, the other sister comes to see how you're doing."

She gestures me up to the porch. I climb the steps and her

children pull back. They don't trust me one bit. Can't say I blame them.

The front door is splintered and hanging off its hinges. Inside, the house is quiet but the violence still hangs in the air. Chair legs broken. Cupboards open and emptied. Flour and beans and glass shards scattered across the floor. The reek of whiskey.

"They smashed up just about everything, didn't they?" I ask.

"Just about." Gloria looks at me, like she still can't decide if I'm friend or enemy. "Can I trust you?"

"Gloria, I'll be honest with you, right now, I'm having trouble telling right from wrong. But I do know that you and Abraham are good people, and if there's something I can do to help you all, tell me what it is."

She touches her swollen lip, thinking. "They didn't get everything." She points through the window to the chicken coop. Its door is open and the chickens are outside, pecking in the dirt. "Abraham took your hint. He buried a hundred quarts under the litter. More than enough for bail. But with all this carrying on, we got no buyers."

Mary is resting on pillows propped up against the Duke's big mahogany headboard. Her face is the color of tallow, her eyes are puffy, her dark hair is loose and limp around her shoulders. This pregnancy has been hard on Mary, she's had terrible cramps, can't keep food down, and what I'm about to say is not going to make her feel any better, but I have to say it.

"Mary, do you have any idea what happened last night?"

"The law is taking its course." Her voice is oddly flat.

My sister thinks of herself as a good woman, a law-abiding, churchgoing woman, and I bet that's what she's been telling herself all day, that she's on the side of right. "You said you wanted to help the people of Claiborne County. I hoped you would, believed you could. But, Mary, I just got back from the Crockett house. Those deputies gave Gloria a split lip."

"Mr. Lowe and his men are doing what they have to do," she says in that same flat voice.

"Beating a mama in front of her children? And it's not just the Crocketts. Those thugs are roughing up folks all across the county."

"I can't discuss this any further. I must have peace. I must have my rest."

"No one around here's getting any peace right now."

"Please go."

Mary closes her eyes. Can she possibly be as uncaring as she sounds? As willfully ignorant? That's what I'm about to ask her when Phillip comes into the room.

"Mary is not to be disturbed." His shirtsleeves are rolled to his elbows and he looks worn thin, but also jumpy and pumped up. He pushes me into the hallway.

"Your Mr. Lowe and his deputies had quite the night. You call yourself a man of God, but those deputies you brought in are treating human beings like animals. Worse."

"You ought not have been at the jail last night, Miss Kincaid. All of this is none of your business. Stay out of Mr. Lowe's way."

"Does Mary even know what's being done in her name?"

"Leave Mary out of it."

"Mary's already in it."

"And from now on, when this door is shut, it stays shut." He gives me a push and slams the door.

Is this Mary's revenge? Is she striking back at the people of Claiborne County for the way she and her mama were treated twenty years ago? Or does she truly believe she's saving their souls? Mary is well aware of what's going on but she doesn't care. Or else she doesn't know and doesn't want to know.

Either way, it's now clear my sister and I are on very different sides.

The bells jangle when I open the door to the Emporium. It's Saturday, usually the busiest day of the week, but the store is nearly empty.

I head back to the Duke's office to talk with Cecil about Gloria Crockett. He's not there but a special edition of the *Gazette* is lying on the desk with the front-page headline,

NEGRO WHISKEY MAKER JAILED

The article describes "prominent negro Abraham Crockett," but it doesn't name any of the other men arrested, calling them "whiskey-making accomplices," and making it sound like Abraham's the ringleader of a gang of bootleggers.

So this is how the story is going to be told. That favor-currying Morris Nelson is now writing articles he thinks Mary wants to read. Nothing in the article is out-and-out wrong, but at the same time it's one big lie. Will folk swallow it? Whenever there's trouble, too many people in these parts are quick to blame the coloreds, and the article's only going to stir those people up, make life harder for Gloria and her kids, and for Abraham if he ever gets out of jail.

The door bells jangle again and I take a look through the one-way window. It's Tom Dunbar, heading this way. What's he doing in Caywood? When Tom sees me he smiles, but it's a strained, tired smile.

"I don't know why you're here, Mr. Tom Dunbar, but I sure as heck am glad to see you," I say. "Between you and your dad, we now got us a total of two sane men in Claiborne County."

I hoped that would get a chuckle out of Tom, but he just shakes his head. "All this madness has put Dad in bed. That's why I came home."

"How bad is it?"

"He needs rest. Even so"—Tom pulls the Emporium's accounting book off the shelf—"he wanted me to bring him this."

"Is Cecil seeing visitors? I'll drive you back. Or is that not allowed, now that you're hitched?"

Tom finally gives me that slow, warm smile I treasure. "We'll make an exception."

Outside, Main Street is also deserted even though it's a perfect October morning.

"I'll crank her," Tom says and grins. "Don't worry. I'll use my left hand."

The Lizzie starts on the first crank and he climbs in beside me. I notice his wedding ring. I haven't seen him since he got hitched. "Did you bring your wife?"

"Amy couldn't come."

"How's married life?"

Tom nods. "So far, pretty good. I like having someone by my side."

Someone by my side. I never thought of marriage that way and I like the sound of it. "I'm glad for you, Tom."

Tom Dunbar is married. He and Amy invited me to the wedding—a fancy affair in Georgetown, tailcoats, gowns, an orchestra, the full works—but that was around the time Kat gave birth, so I couldn't get away. I am glad that Tom is happy—and that's the truth—but he's living way off in Georgetown with his new wife and I'm afraid that's where he'll stay. I feel like I've lost a friend and a part of me wishes I hadn't told him not to wait around.

We drive past Mattie and Sheriff Earl's house. The curtains are drawn but I know they're inside. Mattie's still keeping to herself and Sheriff Earl hasn't been seen since Lowe took over law enforcement. I know I ought to drop by for a visit but I'll get to them later. Right now, I have to see Cecil.

The Dunbar house is set close to the street and rises up tall and solid, its red bricks showing faintly through a coat of faded white paint. Cecil's in a cane-backed wheelchair by the bay window, looking fragile, almost waxen, his face bathed in the soft southern light while his wife, Louise, reads to him from the *Gazette*. The story about Abraham Crockett.

"The Duke always said nothing set him at ease like the sight of Cecil Dunbar's wise face," I say. He flutters his hand weakly. "But wise Mr. Dunbar, if you're under the weather, maybe you ought not to be sending Tom out to fetch your work."

"I should put my foot down," Louise says. She's a small, soft-spoken woman who never has to raise her voice to get your attention. She always treated me like I was her niece, equally ready to hug me when I was good and spank me when I wasn't. Right now she's not hiding her worries for her husband and her dark eyes, so much like Tom's, are tense and hooded. "Outright forbid him from lifting so much as a finger," she adds.

"Checking these figures will take a load off my mind," Cecil tells her.

"I see you're reading about Abraham," I say. "That's why I'm here."

"Known that man most of my life. He and the Duke and I used to fish together when we were boys." Cecil shakes his head slowly. "Never thought Claiborne County would come to this."

I sit next to Tom on the padded seat in the bay window. "I saw Gloria and the kids yesterday. She's got a split lip. The little ones are scared half to death. So's Gloria even if she's doing her best to hide it. Cecil, I need advice and you're pretty much the only person in the county thinking straight these days."

Louise puts a hand on his shoulder. "Cecil, I don't want—"

"We'll keep it short," he says.

I tell Cecil about Abraham's hundred quarts, how Gloria has got to sell them to raise bail for him, but with those deputies manning roadblocks everywhere all the out-of-county buyers are gone.

"Gloria's best recourse is to get that whiskey over to Billy Bond's cousin Sinclair in Webster County," Cecil says. "He's buying from people he trusts. Billy could give it the go-ahead. I heard he had no trouble making bail."

"I'm not on the best of terms with Billy Bond."

"Talk to him. Make it worth his while."

"Gloria can't get all that whiskey over to Webster County. What about the roadblocks? Besides, she doesn't have a car."

"You do."

"That's a company car. I need it for work. I'm not lending Gloria the Lizzie."

"Lending's not what I had in mind."

"What, run that liquor over there myself? That's what you're suggesting?"

"I don't make suggestions, Sallie. I give you your options, just like I did with the Duke. Then you decide."

"You are less likely to be stopped," Tom points out.

"You did tell me you didn't want to just sit there doing nothing." Cecil smiles.

"And you told me you don't make suggestions," I say, but I'm smiling back. "This sounds a lot like a suggestion."

"You have to be the one to weigh the risks."

"I could get caught."

Cecil nods. "There's that. And once you open this door you may have trouble closing it."

"That's enough, Sallie," Louise says. "My husband's worn out."

Cecil does look tired, but there's a happy light in his eyes as they meet mine, the same light I used to see after he whispered something to the Duke and the Duke nodded.

"I do make suggestions, Sallie," Tom says, "and here's one. Let me go with you."

CHAPTER 29

I KEEP TESTING THE play in the steering wheel. Billy was still nursing that black eye and got right ornery at first, but when I offered him a ten percent finder's fee, he came around. Now, Tom and I are heading west toward Webster County and Abraham's one hundred quarts in the trunk are making the Lizzie's overloaded suspension squeal and groan. She wallows through curves and pants going uphill.

"We should have gone at night," Tom says. "And taken the back roads."

Maybe he's right. I'd argued that we'd be better off in broad daylight, sticking to my normal routes until we were close to the county line, acting like ordinary folks out and about with nothing to hide, not like a couple of blockade runners sneaking over the mountains in the dark. But anyone who takes a good look at us can see that the Lizzie is carrying a load, so I keep checking people in the cars coming our way. They all seem to be eyeing us suspiciously. But then again, I'm eyeing them suspiciously. That's the way it is in Claiborne County these days. Everyone eyeing everyone else.

We pass through that stretch of road with tall pines on both sides, cinnamon-colored needles blanketing the ground, and come out of the piney woods to find a line of stopped cars and wagons. We get closer and I see that a mud-splattered hardtop is at the front of the line. A roadblock. Two men carrying rifles are standing there, one of them is Chalky Hurd. I don't know the other man, a tall fellow with his fedora pushed back off his forehead. He has one foot up on the running board of the first stopped car and is leaning down, talking to the driver.

This is quite the fix we're in. Can't wait in line and give the tall fellow the chance to look over the car. Turning around and speeding off is out of the question. Might as well shout, We're the ones you're after! And with our load of whiskey that hardtop could catch us in no time.

We stop at the back of the line, and Tom stays quiet, but I know what he's thinking. We should have gone at night.

"I'll handle this," I say.

But how? What would the Duke do, I ask myself, and out of nowhere it's like I hear his voice. "When you can't solve a problem and you can't run from it and you can't hide from it, you got to make it the other man's problem."

Make it the other man's problem. I'm not sure what I'm doing, but I honk my horn, pull right onto the shoulder, and gun the Lizzie past the stopped cars. When I reach the muddy hardtop I slam on the brakes. The weight of all those quarts makes the Lizzie lurch forward, but with all that's going on, no one seems to notice.

"Stay here," I tell Tom.

"Sallie, what are you doing?"

I shake my head. Can't talk right now. I reach under my seat for the revolver, the one the Duke kept in the library desk. I'm still not sure what I'm doing but something has grabbed ahold of me, it's making my blood race and my head light and I feel like there's a strong wind at my back pushing me to go and make this the other man's problem, so go ahead, don't think about it, just get moving. I open the car door.

"Be careful," Tom says.

I leave the engine idling, step out of the Lizzie, and make a display of sliding the revolver into my waistband.

"Afternoon, Chalky!" I shout and give a wave.

"Miss Kincaid!" He waves back.

I walk toward the two men. "You boys got these cars all backed up." My throat is tight. I hope that makes me sound agitated.

"Who the hell are you?" asks the tall man. He has sunken cheeks and teeth crowded in front.

"Sallie Kincaid," Chalky says. "Mary's sister."

"These cars got to get moving." My voice sounds better now. Steady. I look into the window of the first stopped car. It's Nate Brown, owner of the feed store in Wrightsville. He nods at me and lifts one finger off his steering wheel in greeting.

"Howdy there, Nate. I know you. You're good." I wave him through.

"You can't do that," the tall fellow cries out. "I'm running this roadblock."

"That so?" Keep going, Sallie. Don't back down an inch. "What's your name?"

"Horace Platt."

"Well, Horace Platt. You're not even from this county. You don't know no one and no one knows you. No wonder cars are all backed up."

I take the revolver from my waistband and use it to motion along the next car, then I turn to Chalky. "You know everyone, Chalky. You take over."

"The chief put me in charge," Horace Platt says.

"Mr. Lowe? I'm overruling him."

"You can't do that. You're not even deputized."

He sounds angry, but he's on the defensive. Time to push hard. "I don't need to be deputized. I'm the Duke's daughter. Now, my sister wants these roadblocks, and I'm all for that, all for enforcing the law and arresting bootleggers, but you boys got to keep the darned cars moving." I shove the gun in my waistband. "Now get back to work."

I clap Chalky on the shoulder, the way the Duke always did his men. "Keep them moving," I say again and climb into the Lizzie.

Tom is staring straight ahead. I put the Lizzie in gear and swing around the hardtop, skidding slightly in the mud, and pull past Chalky and Horace Platt, the two of them arguing.

"Sallie—" Tom begins, but then he stops.

I say nothing. My blood's still racing, I'm breathing hard and my hands are tingling, but I'm also smiling. Broadly.

I can do this.

Chapter 30

Becca, the wet nurse, is suckling Grace at the kitchen table, looking peaceful and content as she gazes down at the baby. So many women are natural mamas, but the harder I try, the more I see that I'm not one of them. I will do whatever I have to do to keep my promise to take care of Grace—I would cut off my leg and spit-roast it before I would let that child go hungry—but I simply can't seem to get the hang of this mothering business.

"If you're finished, Sallie, I'll wash that plate," Aunt Faye says.

"I'll get it," I say.

Aunt Faye takes my breakfast plate. "You sit there and enjoy your coffee."

Mary's still keeping to her bed and Phillip and Lowe are out at all hours with the deputies, so we've stopped taking our meals together. Nell leaves a pot of stew or a stack of pancakes on the stove, along with a jar of pickles and baskets of corn bread and boiled eggs, and we all eat on our own when we feel like it.

That suits me fine. It's been two days since we made the run to Webster County for Gloria and since then I've steered clear of Mary. I had to do that run—not just had to, wanted to—but at the same time I'm misleading my sister, being deceitful yet again, living under her roof while working against her. If she found out about it, she'd want Phillip to take a bullwhip to me.

I finish my coffee. Time to go to work. I asked Gloria to keep quiet about the run, but looks like word of it got out because yesterday

Dale Crawford, who lives up Scrabble Road, let me know his kids are going without shoes—and by the way, he picked up on those hints I'd dropped and he has plenty of whiskey stashed away on the off chance I know someone who's buying. I expect I'll hear more stories like that today. Cecil warned me that once I opened this door I might have trouble closing it and Tom and I could well be making another trip to Webster County. If we do, it'll be at night.

I kiss Grace and Aunt Faye and say goodbye to Becca, then push through the swinging door just as the phone in the hallway rings. Nell answers it.

"For you, Sallie," she says. "Someone from Hopewell Road."

No one on Hopewell Road has a phone. I wonder who's calling and where they're calling from. Gloria? Abraham? She posted his bail yesterday as soon as she got the money. Whoever it is, no one from Hopewell Road would call the Big House unless it was absolutely necessary.

I reach for the phone.

A flock of starlings thick as a swirling column of dark smoke flies up the road, fans out, and then comes together before perching in the grand old hackberry, chirping and flickering cheerfully as if it's an ordinary day. But there's nothing ordinary about the day and the tree no longer seems grand.

The people of Hopewell Road have gathered in the Crocketts' swept dirt yard. Tom and I make our way through the silent crowd, nodding our respects, then we climb the steps to the plain pine coffin resting on the porch, and look down at Abraham's cold face.

I didn't believe it at first. Abraham, the big man who'd always been so hearty, so opinionated, so ready with a laugh or a growl, so full of life. Abraham couldn't be dead. But there he is, and he doesn't look at peace. Why would he?

This has never happened in Claiborne County before and I believed it never would, thought that things were different here, we didn't treat coloreds that way, but I was wrong, because they came for Abraham last night and dragged him from his cabin while Gloria held the children back, then strung him up from that same hackberry where the starlings are perched.

Gloria's next to the coffin with her children and I tell her how sorry I am, but she pulls back and crosses her arms. Her face is unforgiving.

"This is on your sister," Gloria says. "On all you Kincaids."

She's including me. And why not? I didn't stand up to Mary when she brought in a man saying he was going to get rough with the people of this county. But I reckon there's going to be a lot of finger-pointing. Some people are saying this is Abraham's fault. After he got out of jail, Lowe sent Horace Platt, that deputy from the roadblock, to make sure Abraham knew he was being watched. Platt started giving Abraham a rough time. Abraham took it for a while, took those hateful, hurtful words with his head down. But as Abraham himself said, sometimes his head just wouldn't stay down. He talked back. That's when Platt slapped Abraham, right there in front of Gloria and the children. Abraham slapped back.

So people are saying Abraham was too proud for his own good. You don't stand up to men like Platt. You cower down and take it. But in Abraham's mind, you take too much of it, you stop calling yourself a man.

Gloria nods at six men, broad-shouldered neighbors and kin standing at the far end of the porch, heads bowed, hands clasped behind them. They gently slide the lid onto the coffin.

I'm searching for something to say when Tom speaks up. "Tell us what can we do," he says to Gloria.

"Lend me the train fare to Detroit."

"You can't run." I blurt out the words. "You can't let them win."

"Sallie Kincaid, they killed my man, they hung my beautiful Abraham from a tree, and you're talking about winning?" Gloria's voice is deep and cutting. "Winning is not what is on my mind. Revenge is not what is on my mind. Survival is what is on my mind. Keeping my young ones alive is on my mind. As soon as I put my man in the ground, I am taking my babies to a place where they don't kill you for being colored."

"But you've got family here. Abraham was almost like family to me."

"Almost?" Gloria lets out a bitter laugh and turns to the men standing by the coffin. "She telling me she don't know?" Then she speaks to me slowly, as if explaining something to a child who is not particularly bright. "Abraham was the Colonel's son."

I stare at Gloria, dumbfounded. She returns the stare, not backing down.

I turn to Tom.

"No one knows for sure," he says.

"Abraham knew," Gloria says. "His mama told him. Everyone on Hopewell Road knows. Not all births get written down in the family Bible."

Is it possible? Abraham's mama, Etta, was sister to Old Ida, our cook when I was a little girl. I knew Etta worked at the Big House from time to time back when the Colonel was alive. I recall the stories of Abraham and the Duke hunting and fishing together as boys. I search the faces of Gloria's children for anything that looks Kincaid, but I see nothing. Could be I'm not good at seeing things I don't want to see. At least the Duke admitted he was my daddy. How would it feel to be the son of the most powerful man in the county and to be treated as a shameful secret? Mattie's always talking about family, about sticking together, about what it means to be a Kincaid—does she know about Abraham? Does Mary?

"Gloria, let's go to Mary. Explain that your children have Kincaid blood. That you're family. She'll protect you."

"Protection from Mary Canon? You really don't understand, do you, Sallie? My children may have Kincaid blood, but they'll never be family. Mary hates you because you're a reminder that her daddy strayed. My husband and my young ones are a reminder that the Colonel strayed. From his own kind, no less. So I'm getting as far away from you all as I can. And I wouldn't be asking you for the loan if there was anyone else to ask. You know I'm good for it. I got a little put away, but I don't want to choose between getting my family up north and giving my man a proper send-off."

The six men shoulder the coffin and ease it down the steps and through the crowd, and people reach out and gently knock on it. They're taking Abraham to the colored cemetery, not the family plot where the Duke and the other Kincaids—Abraham's white kin—are laid to rest.

Gloria is on her own with five kids to raise and her life is going to be so hard, harder than anything I've ever been through. I open my wallet and give her all the money I have. "This should cover the tickets and the funeral," I say. But money is not enough. If Abraham was family then Gloria is family too, and I ought to give her something more. Something special. Something that will recognize her as family. I unfasten Mama's moonstone necklace.

"Take this." I want to tell Gloria we've got a big rosewood box full of jewels the Kincaid men gave to their women and the Colonel ought to have given Abraham's mama a necklace—and a heck of a lot more—but those are wrongs I can't right. I want to tell her that for an outsider who never felt truly welcomed into the family, this necklace has been a reminder that I'm a Kincaid too, and this is my way of welcoming her, of saying, for better or worse, we're all family, that Eddie was right, we're all connected. But that's all too much to explain right now, so when I hand it to her all I say is "It's a family heirloom. The Duke gave it to my mama."

Gloria looks at the necklace doubtfully. "A colored woman with a fancy piece of jewelry? Folks will say I stole it." She hands it back to me. "I don't need me no Kincaid family heirlooms, but I do thank you for the loan."

"It's not a loan."

"Oh yes it is."

CHAPTER 31

ON OUR WAY BACK from Hopewell Road, Billy Bond's dust-covered truck comes barreling toward us. The headlights flash and I stop. Billy pulls alongside and leans out his window.

"That lowlife your sister brought in," he says, "is telling people he's cleaning up the dirt and he ain't stopping until the dirt's all gone."

"That's what he calls killing people?" I ask.

Billy nods. "Even those that got no great love for coloreds are wondering who's next. So it's high time to take the law into our own hands. There's a meeting tonight. Shorty's Garage. Six o'clock. You all might want to be there."

The truck disappears down Plank Road trailing blue smoke. I told Gloria she couldn't let them win, but of course, that's what we've all been doing ever since the deputies arrived, letting them win. Telling ourselves there's nothing we can do, it's out of our hands, and that kind of thinking has led to Abraham's death.

"I'm going," I tell Tom.

"You can't go join some uprising against your sister."

"Tom, word about our run is getting around. We can't sit this out."

When Tom couldn't talk me out of coming, he said he was coming too, to keep me from getting into trouble. Two dozen or so men are crammed inside Shorty's Garage, leaning against walls, sitting on stacks of tires, or crouching on the oil-stained floor, most carrying rifles or shotguns. More than a few men glance our way, some surprised, some suspicious.

"What the blazes is Mary Kincaid Canon's sister doing here?" one man asks loud enough for all to hear.

Billy's in the middle of the group. He nods at me, then tells the man, "She's come at my invite."

"This ain't no place for a lady," another man says.

"If I see a lady," I say, "I'll tell her that."

That gets a few chuckles, the men relieved they don't have to act all proper for me.

Tom and I find a spot in the shadows, next to a rack of wrenches coated with dusty grease. Billy's going on about forming a local militia like the old Minutemen but the men keep shouting over him, hollering about the outrages perpetrated against their families, talking about tarring and feathering those damned deputies, firebombing their cars, and running Lowe and my sister and her husband the hell out of Claiborne County.

Then, above all the commotion and cross talk, Shorty shouts, "They're here!"

All talk stops.

Shorty heaves the sliding door upward, it rumbles loudly toward the ceiling, and in the twilight we see a car stop some forty paces away. Four men with rifles get out. There's Chalky Hurd and Horace Platt, the one who slapped Abraham Crockett and got him killed. The other two I don't know.

"Drop your guns," Platt calls out.

"That's the bastard what gave me the shiner," Billy Bond says almost under his breath, but his voice carries through the silent garage.

"You're all under arrest," Platt shouts.

"Then come arrest my ass!" Billy hollers.

Platt raises his gun and fires into the air.

"They're shooting!" Billy shouts. "Shoot back!"

He drops to one knee and raises his rifle. A loud crack. Platt spins around and topples to the ground.

Chalky gets off a shot and moves toward Platt. The men from the garage pour into the street, guns up. Chalky and the two others turn and jump into the car, the tires kick up gravel, then they're gone.

Platt is still on the ground. He isn't moving.

Shorty leans over Platt, touches his face, then calls out, "He's dead."

I told Gloria we'd get him. That was in the back of my mind when I came to this meeting. Revenge. We got it. But it's not sweet, it's not satisfying, and it leaves me with a stomach-turning sense that we have set in motion something we cannot stop, that we have opened a door we cannot close.

I hear a low groan.

Little Jimmy is doubled over on the floor, clutching his stomach.

Billy kneels down next to his brother. "He's gut-shot. We got to get him to the hospital."

CHAPTER 32

"YOU CAN'T BRING GUNS in here," Head Nurse Bertha Hynes says in a voice accustomed to giving orders. "This is a place of healing."

"Think that matters?" Billy Bond says in the voice of someone who doesn't take orders. His rifle is in one hand, his pistol in the other. "This ain't over."

We just brought Little Jimmy back to surgery and Doctor Black is operating on him while we wait in Caywood Hospital's white-tiled emergency room.

Bertha looks over the rest of us. Most still have guns in hand and she seems to decide that maybe Billy's right, maybe it ain't over, because she nods and heads into the back.

"You carrying?" Billy asks Tom.

He shakes his head. Billy holds out the pistol and Tom looks at it as if weighing something, then reaches for it.

"I know you got a gun," Billy says to me. "Best get it."

Outside, the sky is dark and a glowing halo is wrapped around the moon. The hospital is in the Heights and below me the lights of Caywood are shining. It's dinnertime. Folk are carrying dishes in from the kitchen, sitting down, saying grace, giving thanks. And we're getting ready for battle.

I grope under the car seat for my revolver and stick it in my belt. I get my Remington from the back, where it's been since Abraham was killed. Just then I see a line of cars turn onto Main Street, their head-lights sweeping the storefronts, and begin the climb up to the hospital.

That shooting at the garage, everything took place so quickly I didn't have time to think. But now I do and while I'm not what you'd call calm, I'm not frightened either, just keenly alert. I notice the oil streaks on the street reflecting the moonlight, the faint whistle of a distant train, the cold barrel of the pistol against my hip, the weight of the Remington in my hands. I take a deep breath of the bracing night air and head back to the emergency room.

"They're coming up the hill," I say.

"How many?" Billy asks.

"Ten cars."

Bertha Hynes comes back. She crosses her arms and listens as Billy fills her in. Armed men on their way here. Dozens of them. She nods and locks the doors, he cuts the lights, and we all crouch by the windows.

Tom's on one side of me, Billy and Bertha on the other. We watch from the dark room as the cars come to a stop in a row facing the hospital, their headlights glaring right at us like the eyes of wild animals. Behind those headlights I can barely make out the shapes of men climbing from the cars, spreading along the street.

After a few moments, the door handle rattles angrily.

"Open up!" It's Lowe.

"You can't come in here starting trouble," Bertha hollers through the locked door.

"Those outlaws in there shot and killed one of my deputies," Lowe shouts back. "We got arrest warrants."

"I ain't opening these doors," Bertha says. "There's sick people in here."

Lowe pounds on the door with such fury that the wall shakes. He stops and for a moment all is quiet. Then a shot. It thuds into the door's heavy oak panels and we all fall to the floor. I lie there, my cheek pressed against the cold linoleum, the beams from the headlights pouring through the window right above me, filling the room with a harsh glare.

A second shot thuds into the door. There's a pause. Then all at once the men outside open fire. The window above me explodes. Shards of glass rain down and bullets ping off the tile walls.

In the back, patients are screaming.

I shift my head to look at Billy and a shard of glass crunches loudly, sharply, beneath my cheek. I touch it. Blood.

Billy points each of his brothers to a window and they take up positions as calm and focused as if they were out deer hunting.

Billy points to my window and pushes his hand down—keep low, he's saying. I get to my knees and take a quick glance outside. Those darned headlights. They're blinding. I take aim with the Remington, pull the trigger, and a headlight blinks out. Bull's-eye.

Do it again. Aim, pull. Another headlight goes dark.

My mouth is dry and all the gunfire's making my ears ring, but I feel almost giddy, kneeling here beside men my family has been feuding with for generations, all of us firing at men my own sister brought in, men who thought they could come into our county and do whatever they wanted. Now we're shooting back at you sons of bitches, I feel like shouting, how do you like it? On my right, Billy is close enough to the window that I can see his face, and I'm guessing he feels the same way.

I look to my left for Tom. He's not there. Has he been shot? Then I see him, in a corner, crouching in the shadows, shaking his head, his eyes clinched shut, his hands over his ears. I crawl over and call his name, but he doesn't hear me. He is someplace else, and I have to bring him back, so I draw back my arm and slap his face.

Tom's head jerks to one side and he stares at me, confused.

I feel a hand on my arm.

"Leave off him." It's the deep steady voice of Bertha Hynes. "He's got that shell-shock. From the war." She touches Tom's shoulder. "You come with me, hon. I need a strong man to help move these patients of mine onto the floor. Get them out of harm's way."

Tom still looks dazed, but he halfway gets up and the two of them make a crouched run into the back. Shell-shock. That someplace else was France I'm guessing, and Tom was on the battlefield again, fighting in that war he won't talk about but can't forget.

I'm not going to think about that now, can't let it distract me, because Lowe's men have us surrounded and I keep shooting back until I run out of rifle shells, then I take out my revolver.

The rounds don't last long.

I save one. A final shot. In case they come storming through the doors.

Soon, the Bond brothers run out of ammunition. No one talks. We all listen as the firing outside slows, then stops altogether.

Now Lowe's men are out of ammunition, too. But they can resupply. And they will. Then they'll come in after us. I can get one of them if I'm lucky but that's it. I wonder if they'll let us surrender or if they'll shoot us and say we were resisting arrest.

Time passes, I don't know how much. A cold wind blows through the broken windows. I look out at the moon, now high in the sky. I'm still not afraid, just numb, wondering what happened to Tom. Then in a flash I'm certain he's been shot. I have to go find him.

I'm thinking it's most likely safe to stand now, but at that moment, Tom slips through the swinging doors. I'm so happy to see him I almost forget where we are. He sits next to me and in the moonlight I see one of his shirtsleeves has been ripped off and a bloodied bandage is tied around his upper arm.

"Is it bad?"

"Nurse Hynes says I'm lucky. Bullet missed the bone. How about you?"

"Fair to middling."

That makes Tom smile. We're whispering. Why, I don't know. Seems like we should. I ask how many people are hurt in back and Tom says he doesn't know. Then we sit in silence.

"I wish you hadn't seen me like that," Tom says.

"I wish I hadn't slapped you."

"I don't remember it."

"I didn't know what else to do." I'm quiet for a long moment, considering Tom, bandaged up and shaken, a war hero but not a fighter. There are two kinds of brave people in this world, it hits me, those who fight and those who protect the ones who can't fight. "You ever talk about it to anyone?"

"Once. To Amy." He fingers the bandage on his arm. "She told me I knew what I was signing up for."

That's a darned cold thing for a wife to say to her husband. I reckon I can come across as cold, too, but even so, I decide I don't like the woman. "None of us knows what we're signing up for."

I didn't know what I was signing up for when I came here with the Bonds. Or when I brought Aunt Faye back to the Big House or when I promised Kat I'd look after Grace. If we don't make it out of here, what will happen to them? Will Mary look after Aunt Faye and Grace? Or will she send them off to Hatfield once her own baby comes? And if Mary keeps Grace will she treat her the same as her own baby or will she treat Grace like Jane treated me? Barely tolerated, never loved, and then banished. If that happens, I've broken my promise to Kat. And to Grace.

We fall silent again, backs against the wall. More time passes, hours, I'm guessing, and I keep thinking about yesterday afternoon, when Billy Bond leaned out of his truck and told me about the meeting at Shorty's Garage and Tom warned me against going. Guess I didn't know what I was signing up for. If I could do it all over again, what would I do? I like to think I don't pick fights, but if someone comes at me, I don't back down. So if I had to do it all over again, I'm all but certain I'd do the same danged thing.

I'm thinking on that when I hear a faint rumbling. Off in the distance. Engines. I look through the shattered windows. To the east the sky is starting to fade from black to gray, the stars disappearing in the first light. Below them, a convoy of military trucks with canvas tops is coming up the hill toward us.

Tom stands next to me. "The guard."

The trucks lumber up the street, then come to a halt outside the hospital. Soldiers with bayonets fixed to their rifles scramble out and form a line. A pole-thin officer puts on his steel helmet and snaps the chinstrap.

Just then, Lowe comes around from behind a car. Lowe and the officer talk for a minute, both have their hands on their hips, then Lowe shakes his head like he's disgusted, gestures to his deputies, and they climb into their shot-up cars and drive off.

The dawn light is seeping through the broken windows and I see that the white-tiled walls are pocked with bullet holes and the floor is covered with broken glass and spent shells. Billy gets up and his brothers follow him into the back. Checking on Little Jimmy.

Nurse Hynes pushes through the swinging doors, her white uniform smeared with blood.

"How's everyone doing?" I ask.

She shakes her head. "We did everything we could for that Bond boy, but he didn't make it. Otherwise, we only got a few patients cut by falling glass. It's a miracle. Tom Dunbar, you saved some lives last night."

"Who called the guard?" Tom asks her.

"I called the governor," Bertha says. "The governor called the guard."

The doors to the back swing open and the Bond brothers come through, grim-faced, carrying a stretcher with a body covered by a white sheet. Sticking out from under it is a pair of yellow leather boots. The brothers push through the bullet-scarred doors to the street and I follow, still holding my revolver with my one last round in it.

The street is empty other than the guardsmen stationed around the hospital, their olive-green trucks, and the hundreds of spent brass shell casings that glitter in the cold morning light.

Now what?

A guard officer with a black mustache is walking briskly up the driveway. He eyes the revolver in my clenched hand, thumb on the hammer.

"Ma'am," he says. "It's time to stand down."

I look at the officer for a long moment. He wants me to stand down? To surrender? I'm still strung wire-tight. Coiled for a fight. And I still have to face Mary.

"Ma'am, did you hear what I said?" His voice is sharp now. "It's over."

He's wrong. Like Billy said, it ain't over. But I stick the revolver in my belt.

CHAPTER 33

BACK AT THE BIG House, I head straight to the bathroom to clean up. I look like I've been rode hard and put away wet. I wash off dirt, gunpowder, and the dried blood from the cut on my cheek. A bandage will only draw attention so I let it be.

In the kitchen, Aunt Faye and Nell are bathing Grace. She is so tiny, her eyes big and round and curious, her head lollying around on her fragile neck. She knows nothing of the world. I don't know how to hold her but I do hope I know how to protect her, helpless little thing.

"Thank the Lord you're alive," Aunt Faye says and hugs me with wet soapy arms.

"Where's Mary?"

"Holed up in her bedroom," Nell says.

"I have to talk to her."

"Last night I told her that you were in your room," Aunt Faye says. "Told her the same thing this morning. On your cycle and feeling poorly. Sallie, are you in trouble?"

"I don't know. But lots of people are."

"Telephone's been ringing all morning," Nell says, "people wanting to talk to Mary or Phillip, but they don't want to talk."

"I'm her sister. She'll talk to me."

I hope.

*　*　*

"How did it go?" Aunt Faye asks.

"I got nowhere." It was worse than the last time I tried to talk to Mary. Phillip wouldn't even open the door. I got hotheaded and started pounding on it, but Phillip told me to go away or Aunt Faye and I both would be leaving the Big House for good. And Mary never said a word.

"Phillip doesn't think you had anything to do with all this ruckus, does he?"

"Didn't sound like it."

"How about something to eat?" Nell asks.

"Not hungry."

I sit down at the table and run my hand across the scarred surface. The kitchen is so quiet.

Nell sets a plate of fried chicken in front of me.

"In case you change your mind," she says. "It's good cold, or I can heat it up."

I'm not hungry but that chicken does have a glistening golden brown crust and then the smoky, oily smell of meat deep-fried in hot lard reaches me. I pick up a drumstick—I'm partial to drumsticks, the way they come with a built-in handle—and take a bite. The skin is crisp with Nell's peppery buttermilk batter, and the meat inside is cold and tender. I take another bite, and then another, and when I've chewed all the meat off that bone I turn it end-on and eat the crunchy white thing at the joint. Then I pick up a thigh. The taste of the chicken, being fed, nourished, tended to, makes me feel almost like a human being again.

"Dang, this is good."

A sharp knock at the front door startles us all. I tell Nell I'll get the door. If there's trouble I want to be the one who faces it.

That guard officer is standing on the front porch, the one with the black mustache who told me to stand down. He looks startled at the sight of me, then salutes sharply and takes off his hat.

"Didn't think I'd see you here."

"I live here."

The officer raises an eyebrow. "I was told Mary Kincaid Canon lives here."

"She does. I'm her sister. Sallie Kincaid."

His eyes flick across my face, sizing me up. "Major ordered me to check in with the town's leading citizens, find out what in tarnation's been going on. Is Mrs. Canon available?"

"Mary's in bed. She's with child and not feeling well."

The officer nods. "And what about her husband, the Reverend Canon?"

In his voice I hear the hard twang of a mountain boy, but he's acting the formal military man. Hard to get a read on the fellow, but the last thing I want is him talking with Phillip about what happened last night and who was there. "The reverend also doesn't want to be disturbed."

"Then how about I talk to you? You're Mrs. Canon's sister. You must be a leading citizen."

"I don't know about 'leading,' but sure, you can talk to me. I got a lot to say."

When I dropped Tom at his house, Cecil told me although the guard secured the hospital, Lowe's men still control the rest of the town. And nothing's going to stop them from making more arrests. "I surely do appreciate you all riding in this morning like the cavalry," I say as we head into the parlor, "but you ought to be out there rounding up those killers instead of making house calls." That sounded a little hotheaded and I can't get on the wrong side of this fellow, so I add, "with all due respect."

"As I understand it, Miss Kincaid, those men were brought in by your sister and her husband, and Mr. Lowe and his wife are your guests."

"Not my guests."

"Well, that leaves me with one mighty big question, Miss Kincaid. What exactly were you doing at the hospital last night?"

I clear my throat. "I took an injured man there. Is that a crime?"

"Could be. If this here injured man happened to be a fugitive from the law." His eyes flick across my face again. Still sizing me up. "Does Mrs. Canon know you were at the hospital last night? Does Mr. Lowe?"

Before I can figure out what to say, the front door bangs open. "Clara!" It's Lowe. "Bring me a shirt and a sandwich," he shouts. "Quick. I got to head back out right away."

"No," I whisper. "They don't know."

"Can't say I'm surprised."

Lowe comes past the parlor door, peeling off his dirty white shirt.

"Lots to do," he says, his voice excited and hoarse.

He sees me and stops. He knows I was at the hospital. It's over, I'm thinking, but then he says, "We're going to get the whole damned lot of them before the day is through."

So he doesn't know. But he's hell-bent on keeping at it, cleaning up the dirt, and I've got a fierce urge to grab the fireplace poker and club that smug, crowing face of his. The officer steps forward.

"What are you doing here?" Lowe asks.

"Major instructed me to check on the Kincaid ladies."

"The women in this household are under my protection. They're all fine."

"Glad to hear that, sir. Glad to hear the ladies of this household got the protection of a man so batshit crazy the governor had to send in the militia."

Lowe is at a loss for words, and I now have another urge—this time to laugh out loud and slap the officer on the back. He turns to me and salutes. "I recommend you stay indoors, Miss Kincaid, keep safe. And if there's anything I can do for you, ask for Lieutenant Douglas Rawley."

Fifteen minutes later, I'm watching from the parlor window while Lowe climbs into his Oldsmobile, then heads down the driveway.

Something's going to happen, I can feel it in my bones, and I have to be there. I grab my coat and head out.

I figure I'll have a better chance of dodging patrols if I'm on foot so I leave the Lizzie at home and walk. The day is sunny but chilly and I turn up my coat collar. Batshit crazy. Something about that phrase puts the bounce back in my step.

I expect to see Lowe's men in town but the streets are empty, and in no time I'm at the Emporium.

"Miss Kincaid!" Mr. Lewis calls out. "Heard you were there last night," he whispers in my ear. "At the hospital."

I just squeeze his arm because a man I don't know is heading our way, wearing a plaid suit you could see in the dark.

"Miss Kincaid? Of the Kincaids who run this county?"

"No one's running this county. That's why we're in the mess we're in."

His eyes light up. "At last, someone who's willing to talk. Name's Willard Smith. *Richmond Daily Record.*" He pulls out a notepad and stubby pencil. "I can quote you, right?"

Quote me? In a newspaper? I don't care what that lieutenant said, I'm not a leading citizen, but if I'm careful with my words, maybe this is the way to let the rest of the world know that Lowe is batshit crazy. I nod.

"Name's Sallie Kincaid."

"Any relation to the late, great Duke Kincaid we've heard about all the way in Richmond?"

"I'm his daughter."

He scribbles that down. "So tell me, Sallie Kincaid, what's been going on here?"

"This used to be a peaceful place but then Mr. Glen Lowe shows up, taking the law into his hands, acting like he's the doggone czar of Claiborne County."

I get all worked up describing everything that's gone on and he nods, scribbling furiously, then glances at his wristwatch. "I have to phone in what I've got. Make the early edition."

"You can use ours." I lead him to the Duke's office. "Reverse the charges."

He puts the call through, then stops and listens for a moment. "You're kidding." He turns to me.

"My editor says the governor issued a statement. Just came over the wire. Said Glen Lowe was authorized to conduct one raid a week ago, but nothing else. No one authorized him to lay siege to a hospital full of sick people. Your czar is going to be investigated for impersonating a police officer."

Outside the jail, Lowe's armed deputies are standing guard and a few more reporters are milling around in front. Smith tells them about the governor's statement and they all start shouting for Lowe. The ruckus draws shoppers and clerks and tradesmen. Word about the governor's statement spreads, and they start hollering at the deputies—shouts of anger, demands for justice, and more than a little name-calling—all from people who just the day before were meekly taking orders from these same men. I want a better view so I climb up on the watering trough in the middle of the square.

An olive-colored guard car drives up, Lieutenant Rawley at the wheel. He parks behind a battered sedan with four men inside, their hats pulled low. I recognize the driver with the long beard. It's Billy Bond's Webster County cousin, Sinclair. Lowe knows Billy shot Horace Platt, and Billy's in hiding but I'm guessing he sent his cousin into the middle of town to find out what's going on. And maybe do something about it.

Then Phillip drives up with Clara and they make their way into the jail. A few minutes later they come back with Lowe.

"Under whose authority did you attack the hospital last night?" Willard Smith calls out.

Lowe gives him a glare that could warp wood. "I have the authority."

"Who granted it to you?" another reporter asks.

"I was called in because the law was being violated," Lowe says. "I have done nothing but enforce the law."

All that gets him is angry muttering, catcalls, and low boos.

"But there is good news," Lowe goes on quickly. "We have cleaned up Claiborne County. We are finished here. And now"—he looks around—"Mingo County, over in West Virginia, has asked me to do the same thing there."

Lowe stands up on the running board of his Oldsmobile. "Watch what we do in Mingo County!"

He drives slowly through the crowd, turns onto Short Lane, and I see Sinclair Bond ease his battered sedan into the street and follow the Oldsmobile at a careful distance.

The Bonds want revenge, pure and simple. I can understand that, understand it without saying it's right or just, but Clara's also in that Oldsmobile. I have no fondness for the woman, helping Lowe plan his campaign just like she was an accomplice, but killing her would be plain wrong.

Lieutenant Rawley's leaning against his car, lighting a cigarette.

I run over to him. "There's going to be trouble."

"How's that? Trouble just got on the road for Mingo County." He gives me a crooked grin. "You folk can go back to doing the things you do up here."

"This isn't the time to be joking. Lowe's men killed Little Jimmy Bond"—I point toward Short Lane but both the Oldsmobile and the battered sedan have driven off—"and now the Bonds are going after Lowe and his wife."

"You sure about this?" No hint of a grin now.

"I know the Bonds. I'll go with you."

"That's against regulations. And my orders are to keep an eye on this crowd, but"—he drops the cigarette and grinds it out—"we best get going."

"I'll drive. I know the roads."

"Miss Kincaid, I'm one crazy bastard for leaving my post like this, but that don't mean I'm crazy enough to let a female civilian drive a Guard vehicle. You ought not even be riding in it."

"Fine, then. Let's go."

Outside town, he opens up the throttle and we roar across the valley. Then we reach the mountains and the road gets narrow with hairpin turns and skinny shoulders.

The lieutenant knows how to handle a car, that's clear as rain-water, but these roads take some getting used to and when we reach one tricky spot where the curve tightens as you go into it, I know he's taking it too fast.

"Careful here," I say.

Too late. We skid.

He wrestles with the steering wheel, but the car veers off the road and slides onto the muddy shoulder.

The lieutenant guns the engine. The tires spin and throw mud. He works the gears and guns it again. The tires spin again. He grips the steering wheel so hard his knuckles turn white then takes a deep breath and says, "You take it."

He roots around in the scrub for a tree limb and shoves it under a tire. Don't gun it, I tell myself, and I slowly raise the throttle, feel the wheels catch, and we inch back onto the road.

The lieutenant climbs in beside me. Neither of us says a word. We've lost a good three minutes.

A couple of miles on, the road cuts into the mountainside on the left and the right drops off almost like a cliff. Fresh tire ruts run through the roadside mud and then to the very edge.

I stop and cut the engine. The air is still but from the woods below we hear a ticking and hissing. Then a faint whimper.

Chapter 34

Mournful organ music fills the Tabernacle Southern Baptist Church. Mary's front-row pew is ten feet from Lowe's open casket and I have a clear view of his face. Clara is sitting beside the casket stroking her dead husband's cheek. She lost her eyesight in the crash and is wearing a black silk blindfold. She's also showing some mettle I didn't know she had, sitting up there all by herself.

Mary's keeping to her bed to protect the baby and pleaded with me to go to Lowe's funeral "to represent the Kincaid family."

"After everything that man did, you want me to go to his funeral?"

"He did it at my bidding. And I did it for my mother. And my child." She touched her large belly. "That's what we're fighting for, isn't it? So our children don't have to suffer like you and I did."

Reporters, temperance firebrands, and the just plain curious are here, not an empty seat. Phillip preaches the eulogy, calling Lowe a heroic martyr, but I keep staring at Clara and when I turn around I see that pretty much everyone else is staring at her, too. With her upright bearing and the black silk blindfold, Clara Lowe looks tragic and mysterious, even beautiful.

As soon as Phillip finishes the sermon, a photographer stands up and points his camera at Clara. A bright flash and a loud pop. Clara flinches.

* * *

The hospital looks like I feel, banged up but carrying on. Plywood has been nailed over the shattered windows and people are going in and out of the big oak doors. Then it all comes back, and I'm there again, in the dark waiting room, the blinding headlights, muzzles flashing, the crackle of gunshots. Is this what it's like for Tom? I went through one night of hell. He had months of it.

I've been to see him once and he seemed his old self, even with his arm in a sling, but that new wife of his, Amy, came down to tend to him. She's a tall, sharp-tongued city girl and she made it clear she blames me for what happened to Tom. She may be right, but I still don't like her.

I'll go inside, thank Nurse Hynes for everything she did that night, but first I have to see Lieutenant Rawley before he leaves. I find him down the hill, helping his men load metal boxes and wooden barricades into olive-colored trucks.

"I hear you're headed home," I say.

"Governor declared that the emergency is over."

"I didn't have a chance to thank you for throwing out the rule-book for me."

"Major couldn't decide if he should give me a medal or toss me in the clink. How's Mrs. Lowe doing, anyway?"

"She's bearing up. There's more to her than I thought."

The lieutenant tightens a canvas strap and tests it. "How about we take us a little stroll?"

I glance at the lieutenant's men pretending not to listen. "No law against that."

We head along Elm Street, the lieutenant walking with his hands behind his back, me moving along at a businesslike pace, keeping my arms crossed to avoid any elbow bumping. A storekeeper is scraping frost off his windows, the blacksmith is clinking away in his shop, a farm wife is holding a shopping basket on one arm and a bundled-up baby in the other.

"Everyone's going about their business," I say. "Maybe things will get back to normal."

The lieutenant shakes his head. "Only a matter of time before the guns come out again. Pass a law like Prohibition and you're all but begging men to break it. But if the governor whistles, we'll be back." He sticks out his hand. "Goodbye, Miss Kincaid." We shake and he nods. "Firm grip—always like that in a woman." He takes a step away but then turns around, like he has one more thought. "Miss Kincaid, I'm goddamned glad we met. I'll never forget the sight of you busting out of that hospital pointing a revolver."

He shakes his head and gives a little smile. "Got to say, never come across a woman the likes of you." He pauses and then his face lights up like another thought just hit him, and he breaks into a grin. "You can whale my hide for asking this, but I like to go with my gut when it tells me something, so—you ever given any thought to marriage?"

Marriage? Is he kidding? That grin is letting me know I can act like he is kidding, but he's also half-serious. And he goes with his gut just like the Duke. But I'm not going to read too much into that. "I'm not the marrying type. But thank you kindly, Lieutenant. I'm taking that as a right nice compliment."

CHAPTER 35

A LEATHER SUITCASE SITS next to the steamer trunk Mary and Phillip brought from Mercer County. But my sister's in no condition to travel.

"Who's taking a trip?" I holler.

Phillip steps out of the library. He's wearing a black suit and his clerical collar and he's guiding Clara by the elbow. She's in her black silk dress and that black silk blindfold.

"We're going on tour," Phillip says.

"But Mary—"

"Mary and I talked. It's what she wants as well. So many people have asked me to speak. And they want to meet Clara. It's vindication. Proof that we've been right all along. We can't say no. But we'll be back."

It all started a month ago with that photograph of Clara at the funeral wearing her black blindfold. Newspapers across the whole country ran stories about Lowe's death along with that photograph and the caption "The Comely Blind Widow." Then came the letters. Most were addressed "Comely Widow Lowe, General Delivery, Caywood, Virginia." The writers—both men and women—gushed about Clara's courage, purity, devotion, and beauty. Sometimes they included money or drawings or poems or even proposals of marriage.

Meanwhile, Phillip was writing to temperance leaders and newspaper editors describing how he had done "God's work" in cleaning up Claiborne County. Then he also started getting letters asking him and Clara to appear at temperance rallies.

"What about 'in sickness and in health'?" I ask Phillip.

"Mary's not sick, she's going to have a baby. I'll be back by then."

Mary. Faithful, pious, devoted Mary. She did whatever her husband asked of her and now when she needs him most, he's taking off with the comely blind widow to bask in front of cheering crowds. What a rotten deal this marriage business is.

The muffled sound of steps comes from the landing above us. It's Mary, ghostly with her pale face and white robe. This is the first time she's left her bedroom since the night of the shoot-out. She grips the banister with both hands, making her way down the stairs, careful yet determined.

"Darling, I was just telling Sallie, it's what you want, too, this tour," Phillip says. "Isn't that so? We'll miss each other but it's a sacrifice we both must make."

Mary reaches the bottom of the stairs, breathing hard, and grabs ahold of the newel post. "I feel the baby kicking. It's a boy, I can tell." She takes one of Phillip's hands and places it on her stomach. "Here." She looks Phillip in the eyes. "Feel him."

"Goodness, he's a lively little thing." Phillip glances at his watch. "We've got a train to catch."

He wraps his arms around Mary and kisses the top of her head. "Such a fine woman. Goodbye, my lovely wife."

CHAPTER 36

MARY'S STOMACH CRAMPS ARE getting worse. Aunt Faye is worried—morning sickness shouldn't last this long—so she's called in Doctor Black. Mary's door opens and he steps out.

"How's the baby?" Aunt Faye asks.

Doctor Black shakes his head and moves down the hall. "There is no baby."

"What do you mean?" I ask.

He takes off his spectacles. "There never was a baby."

"We felt it kicking," Aunt Faye says.

"Sometimes," Doctor Black says in a quiet voice, "a woman wants to be pregnant so very much that she convinces herself she is. The body actually develops the symptoms. It's called a phantom pregnancy. But that's not what's causing Mrs. Canon's discomfort." He folds his spectacles and slips them into his pocket. "She has cancer."

"That can't be," Aunt Faye whispers.

"Of the uterus." He rubs the red marks his spectacles make on the bridge of his nose. "That's the cause of the swelling."

I stare at Doctor Black and the cold, hard truth of his words slowly sinks in. The weak light from a wall sconce casts deep shadows on his creased face. I wait for him to start talking about treatments and cures, but he's silent.

"How serious is it?" I finally ask.

"Nothing can be done, I'm afraid."

"How much time does she have?" Aunt Faye asks.

"Hard to say. A few months maybe. I'm sorry." He unhooks his stethoscope from around his neck and puts it in his bag.

"What did you tell her?" I ask.

"I leave that to the family." Doctor Black picks up the bag. "She'll be in my prayers. You all will. I can let myself out."

We listen to his slow footfalls on each of the stairs.

What's the kind thing, the right thing to tell Mary? "If I were her, I'd want to know," I say to Aunt Faye. "Knowing is always better than not knowing."

"Mary's not like you. Knowing will destroy her. Let Mary keep thinking she's got a baby on the way. Give her hope. That's what I would want. Hope."

Aunt Faye goes into Mary's room and I follow. "What did the doctor say?" Mary asks.

Aunt Faye sits on the edge of the bed and strokes Mary's hair. "He said you need rest."

"I know that," Mary says. "What else?"

She fixes her eyes on me and I have trouble holding her gaze.

"Can I get you anything?" I ask.

"My husband. I need my husband."

Phillip and Clara are scheduled to appear at the Imperial Hotel in Atlanta on Saturday, so that's where I send the telegram.

MARY SICK COME HOME NOW

Phillip's reply arrives the next day.

CANNOT CANCEL PRAYING FOR YOU WILL WRITE

I send a second telegram.

URGENT YOU RETURN NOW

Saturday comes and goes. And Sunday. Finally, on Thursday a fat envelope arrives from the Imperial Hotel. Mary sits up to read it, her eyes hopeful. I pull back the curtains and raise the window to let a little fresh air into the dark, musty room. Mary holds the letter just inches from her face, studying Phillip's elegant longhand with that nearsighted squint of hers, and I watch the hope fade from her face. Then she drops the letter on the bedspread and unfolds the packet of newspaper clippings that came with it.

I sit down next to her and pick up the letter.

Dearest Wife,

With God's help you will soon recover. I miss you terribly & promise to return to your side as soon as possible, but you & I are on the verge of realizing the dream that brought us together. The tour is going splendidly, the bookings keep rolling in, I am speaking to standing-room-only audiences, though I confess many of the good people are more interested in meeting Clara than in hearing your humble husband sermonize. She is a wonderful companion with a gentle & virtuous disposition & has been so brave & sends her warmest regards. I will write again when I have more time but for now our days & nights are committed to traveling from city to city to get our message out—& we are succeeding!

Your devoted husband,
Phillip

I fold the letter. Mary is peering at a photograph in one of the newspaper clippings, as if it holds some sort of answer, some clue that could explain the letter.

"Oh dear Lord," Mary says softly. She passes it to me.

The grainy photograph shows Phillip evangelizing in an outdoor band shell, his head tilted back, his hands raised skyward, while Clara, in her black widow's dress and black blindfold, sits next to him listening enraptured. Above the photograph, the headline reads:

TEMPERANCE FIREBRAND AND
COMELY WIDOW ROUSE CROWD

"He's not coming back," Mary says.

The wind rattles the window. What can I possibly say that might provide some sort of comfort? Mary looks lost, defeated. She was so hurt when the Duke left her mama for another woman, and now Phillip's abandoned her more or less the same way, leaving her alone, unwanted.

I can't tell Mary she's better off without that pompous windbag. But I won't lie to her anymore. It's not doing her any good. "No, I don't believe he's coming back. Not anytime soon."

She looks out the window. "He's left me here. Left me and the baby." She puts her hands on her belly, pauses a moment, then turns to me. "There is no baby, is there? That's what the doctor told you, didn't he?"

Mary is staring at me fiercely, dark circles under her bright feverish eyes, like she's finally seeing everything for what it is. I'm not lying. I nod.

"But there is something inside me, right?"

I nod again.

"And I'm not going to get better."

The room is quiet save for the steam clanking in the radiator. "No one understands that the righteous are taken away to be spared from evil," Mary says. "Isaiah. Would you shut that window? It's getting cold. And the sun's too bright."

I go to the window. The bare limbs of a giant walnut tree sway in the wind—its roots have a poison that kills most plants—and the barren ground below is littered with nothing but its rotting black nuts. I shut the window and close the curtains and when I turn around Mary is watching me closely, intently, with those feverish eyes.

"I would have made a good mother, don't you think?"

"Yes, you would have."

And it's true. Say what you will about Mary, she believes in the grace and the sanctity of motherhood, she believed she was serving God's will by bringing innocent life into a world filled with evil. I hope she believes that God, at least, is still with her.

I sit down next to Mary.

"Sallie, you're about to become a very important person in this county, the most important person." Then in a distant voice, almost like she's talking to herself, she adds, "Sallie Kincaid. Of all people. Mother used to say this family was cursed. I believed I could lift that curse but instead the curse got me." She grabs my hand and squeezes it tightly. "Promise me, Sallie, not just for my sake but for yours as well, that you will carry on the work I've begun."

How do I answer? I didn't lie about the tumor and I'm not going to lie about this. "I'll do whatever I believe is best for the people in this county."

"You can't promise?"

"I promise . . ." Mary and I are about as unalike as two sisters can be. Our stories are similar in many ways, but we told them to ourselves so differently. We tried to get along, but mostly we only pretended to. Now, at the end of our time together, as she asks me to make the same promise to her that she made to her mama, we won't even be able to pretend. "I promise I'll do what I believe is best."

Mary turns toward the dim glow of the curtained window. "Mother was right. You Powell women never could be trusted."

PART IV

CHAPTER 37

DAWN FINALLY. THE EARLY-MORNING sunlight is inching across the frost-covered grass. At first it makes the frost sparkle like diamonds but after a few beautiful moments the frost melts, the sparkling stops, and all that's left is wet, dead grass.

Mary passed last night.

Sooner than anyone expected. Just three weeks after she got Phillip's letter, but in the end Mary sounded at peace, saying her conscience was clean, God was calling her, and she was on her way to heaven to join her beloved mother.

And Phillip never did come back.

Mary wanted to be laid to rest next to her mama back in Mercer County—no service, no nothing in Claiborne County—so Aunt Faye and Nell and I washed her and slipped her arms into a simple white dress. I kept wondering how things could end so badly for someone with such good intentions. Mary was so certain she was right, but the cause she was certain would save lives destroyed them, the man who swore to be loyal abandoned her, and the pregnancy she thought would bring new life killed her. I told myself not to be that certain about anything.

It was almost midnight when the men from Singer & Sons Funeral Home took Mary's body away. I couldn't sleep. I stayed up drinking hot, bitter coffee and making a list of everything that had to be done—letters to Mary's kin, debts to be paid, debts to be collected, deals to be struck, trust to be restored. It was still dark when I was finished, but I put on a plain black dress and drove over to talk with Cecil.

I've been sitting here outside the Dunbar house for two hours, waiting to see a light switched on. Waiting to show Cecil my list.

We both know what's in the will. I stand to inherit everything. The properties and businesses. And the position. The responsibilities. But the county is in a mess and I have no idea what to do. That's wrong. I have a dozen ideas. But I don't know if any of them are any good.

A light in the parlor finally goes on. I get out of the car and cross the lawn. The grass that's still in the shade is frozen and it crunches under my feet. I ring the bell then let myself in, the way I always do.

Cecil is sitting in his cane-backed wheelchair, almost like he's waiting for me. He takes in my black dress.

"She's gone, isn't she?"

I nod.

Seeing Cecil fills me with an ache. I wrap my arms around him, to feel his warmth and strength, but I'm startled by how small and fragile his shoulders are, the shoulders of a child, not a man. As the Duke's right-hand man, Cecil was a force to be reckoned with—but only because the Duke listened to him. Ever since the Duke's death, no one's listened to him, and he's been reduced to sitting here, looking out the window, wasting away. But I will listen to him. I pull up a chair.

"My dear girl." He looks deep into me with those tired, gentle eyes. "I've known you since you were born. I've spent my entire life working for your family. And now it's all come down to you."

I'm in over my head here, but no one's going to know that. Not even Cecil. "There's so much to do, Cecil." I pull out my list. "I jotted down a few things. You'll have ideas, too. What's our first priority?"

Cecil starts coughing and keeps coughing and the plaid blanket slips off his legs. I tuck it back in place and hand him the list.

He glances at it. "Sallie, my dear, I can't help you with any of this."

"Why not?"

"I've got nothing left. I thought I was going to get better, but I can't even get out of this chair."

"You don't have to get out of the chair. We'll roll it right into the office. You don't even have to do any work. Just listen and give advice."

"Sallie, we're so sorry." It's Tom, coming into the parlor, his arm still in a sling.

"We are sorry," It's Louise, right behind Tom, carrying in the good silver tray she brings out for company. "But listening is work. My husband can't go anywhere near that office. It will start him to worrying again. And it was worry that put him in this condition in the first place."

"I will give you one piece of advice, Sallie," Cecil says. "Consider getting married. You're a very capable young woman, but this is a rough business and you ought to have a man at your side."

"That's what Mary thought she had," I say. "A man at her side."

"Mary didn't choose as wisely as you will," Cecil says. "Certain people still think it was wrong for your father to divorce Belle and marry your mother and therefore it's wrong for you to inherit what rightfully belongs to others. You know who we're talking about. I believe the Duke's will to be ironclad but you've got your work cut out for you. You'll be in a stronger position with a husband at your side. And stronger still with a son."

"Cecil, I'll think about marriage one of these days, but I need an adviser now."

"I truly wish I had the strength for it." Cecil sinks back into his wheelchair.

"There, even talking that much wore him out." Louise passes me a cup of coffee. "Take this and leave him be."

"Okay. Sorry." I take the cup then set it down. I don't need coffee. I'm jittery and my stomach's churning as it is. "Tom, the plan was always for you to get your degree and then come back to work for the Duke. But you don't need a degree. Come back now. I'll pay you whatever you'd be making if you had your degree."

"If it was up to me, Sallie, I'd do it. Today. You know that, right? But it's not up to just me anymore."

"What's not up to you?" It's Tom's wife, Amy, coming down the stairs, pulling back her long pale hair, arranging it with her long pale fingers. She sits down next to Tom, crossing her long legs. She's almost as tall as he is and I'm pretty sure that's Tom's shirt she's wearing. I've met Amy only twice, briefly. She's funny in a cutting, citified way that isn't so funny when it's you she's cutting.

"I'm making your husband here an offer," I say, "to join Kincaid Holdings."

"You mean work for moonshiners."

"We're a diversified privately held corporation. He'll be my legal adviser."

"And live in Caywood?" Amy laughs, flashing perfect white teeth. "It's not just boring, it's dangerous. My husband was almost killed in that hillbilly shoot-out of yours. I was furious with him when I heard about it. With all of you."

She looks at each of us in turn to make sure we understand that we're all included in this judgment of hers, then she puts a hand on Tom's leg. "You know, honey, I think it's time we were getting back to Georgetown. Your arm's almost healed. If I start packing now, we can catch the afternoon train."

We watch Amy take the stairs two at a time.

"That woman is not shy about letting you know her mind," Louise says.

"I'll try talking to her, Sallie," Tom says, "but she can be just as stubborn as you."

Tom follows Amy up the stairs, Cecil and Louise sit there, saying nothing. They look far, far away. Out of reach. I feel like I did when the Duke sent me to Hatfield. Completely alone. The two men I had always thought I could count on won't be there for me. I'm not afraid of hard work or having naysayers mock me or doing battle with my enemies, I'm up for all that—and yet, I know I need someone by my side, not to tell me what to do, but to give me my options, to advise me to slow down, or speed up, or keep going, or do nothing. The Duke had someone. But I'm on my own. And I don't know if I can do this on my own.

Chapter 38

A CROWD OF PEOPLE is milling around inside the Emporium. I watch them through the big plate-glass window, men and women who had once turned to the Duke for help, for advice, to be taken care of, to know that in the worst of times they were not alone.

Now they're wondering if they can turn to me, if this new head of the Kincaid clan is up to the job, this young upstart who is scarcely more than a girl, who not too long ago was a washerwoman in Hatfield.

I open the door, the bell jangles, and I move through the crowd, nodding, smiling, shaking hands, accepting hugs and condolences, but right quickly the crowd falls quiet, everyone moves back like an audience and it dawns on me that they're waiting for me to say something, something that will give them comfort, maybe, or hope.

I take a deep breath and let it out slow. "As you all know, my sister, Mary Canon, passed away last night." I stop. Where do I go from here? "Mary had a good soul." That brings a low grumble of disagreement and even a few boos. "You all hush, now. My sister did what she did because she truly believed that she was doing God's work—and that God was on her side." I stop again, knowing that whatever I say next will be finely sifted, will be repeated over dinner tonight, will make its way around the county. "Well, God works in mysterious ways, and, as someone much wiser than me once said, I'm not going to tell you that God's on my side, but I do hope to heck that I'm on God's side."

That gets a relieved chuckle.

"My good sister was determined to help the people of Claiborne County, even if it meant killing us." That gets another chuckle and I remember the Duke saying that if you could get your people to laugh at a time like this, when they're facing change and feeling scared—and they're always facing change and feeling scared—they will love you for it.

"Before you right now you all see a skinny, knock-kneed gal who not too long ago lived with her aunt up in the hollows, barely making ends meet washing the stained sheets of sick people. But as you folks know, us mountain gals can be tough. We don't need ourselves any parasols or scented hankies. We can work a plow, milk a cow, shoot a buck, and slaughter a hog as well as any man."

"Wheooo!" It's a woman giving a mountain whoop.

I take a breath. "You all also see standing before you a Kincaid, born in the Big House, who grew up at the feet of the Duke, his last living child. Folks, we got us a hard road ahead and I'm not going to stand here pretending I got all the answers, making promises that can't be kept. But I will promise you this. I am on your side. I will fight for you. You can trust me."

People start clapping and for a moment I think they're making fun of me, but then I see from their faces that it's heartfelt. We're in this together.

"I'll see every one of you," I say, "but give me a minute."

The office door clicks shut and I lean up against it, steadying myself. I wipe my sweaty, shaking hands on the black dress. The Duke's heavy wooden chair, with its barrel-shaped back and swiveling seat—the chair I spun around on when I was a kid—seems too big when I sit down. Did the Duke's hands ever shake? I doubt it.

I used to come to this office every day after school and one afternoon, I must have been about seven, I was lying curled up in the corner pretending to be asleep but listening and watching through slit eyes as the Duke talked to one person after another who was asking him for help or advice. The Duke sat back with his arms behind his head while he listened, then he'd lean forward, pointing a finger as he told them what he was going to do and what they were going to do. At the end of the day, when the Duke came over to pick me up, I reached out to him.

"I thought you were asleep, Whippersnapper." He laughed and then in his pretend-to-be-angry voice he said, "You were spying on me, you little scamp."

"How come you have to help everyone with their problems?" I asked.

"Because I'm in charge."

"Is that a hard job?"

"You better believe it." He looked me right in the eyes. "Everyone thinks they want to be in charge, to be the boss, but no one knows how tough and thankless the job really is." He shook his head. "Sure, you get to give orders, but you also have to put up with endless belly-aching, kick the shirkers in the ass, tell favor seekers no about a dozen times a day, lie when necessary—and many a time it is—and accept blame when things go wrong—and many a time they do. Even with all that, everyone wants your job, or they want to tell you how to do it, or they want to try to take advantage of you, so to be a good boss you have to be steadfast and tireless, generous and kind, a glad-hander and an organ grinder, but you also have to have a hide thick as shoe leather, you have to be calculating, devious, treacherous, cruel, a real hard-ass, and, when it's necessary, truly cold-blooded. And you trust no one. But on the off chance that you do find one man you can trust, you do whatever the hell you have to do to keep that fellow."

It all seemed very important, like the Duke was telling me something he wanted me to remember but didn't expect me to understand just yet. And so I swore to myself I'd never forget his words.

"Then why do you want to be in charge?" I asked.

He smiled again, almost to himself. "There is nothing better. Nothing."

It's early evening by the time I climb into the Lizzie for the drive home, but before starting the engine I sink back into the seat.

That was humbling.

I thought being in charge meant I was beholden to no one. What it truly means is that I am beholden to everyone. And everyone came to me with their problems, men rolling their caps in their hands, women wearing worn-out shoes resoled with tire rubber, all of them struggling to find the words to describe their plight without sounding pitiful, all of them ashamed to be asking for help from this newest head of the Kincaid family, so young, some told me, they remembered when I was born. But they all said there was no one else to turn to.

On Main Street, people are heading home from work, the lucky ones who have work, who haven't been knocked flat by the cost of living, bad weather, still taxes, armed thugs destroying their whiskey. Some begged me to buy their land so they could move to a city, get a mill job. Parents were going without so their young ones would have food and children were rolling drunks and breaking into grocery stores at night to steal tinned meat.

Hearing story after story about hungry babies is what threw me the hardest. I'd promised to look after Grace and that's all these people were trying to do, care for their children. I spent the day working out lines of credit and rolling back rent increases. I also told everyone they could go back to making whiskey, that we're back in the business of buying it. Of course folks also need money for that, for yeast and sugar, to rebuild chopped-up stills. And if we're going back to buying, we need money too.

I took Cecil's ledgers out of the safe. I'm not an accountant but I can make sense of the money coming in and the money going out, and the bottom line is that Kincaid Holdings is more or less broke. The rental houses, the warehouses, the paving company, barely break even. Leafing through the ledgers, I'm bowled over. Most of the profits come—or came—from whiskey, back before Mary banned it, whiskey that people traded at the Emporium for everything from coffee and thread to nails and boots, whiskey that we stored in the basement, marked up, and sold under the counter or carted off to cafés and roadhouses, where it was marked up even more.

I thought whiskey was just a sideline, but that long-fingered, sharp-tongued woman Tom married was right. We are moonshiners. The whole business is spelled out in Cecil's precise, vertical handwriting, including a notation for "approx. $5,000.00 loss due to Mary Kincaid Canon's destruction of liquor inventory."

The sun is setting and bats are fluttering in the twilight by the time I get to the big stone pillars at the foot of our driveway. I didn't sleep last night, I've had a long day, and I'm looking forward to Nell's pork chops and a hot bath and early bed. Then I turn up the driveway and realize my day's not over yet. Mattie and Sheriff Earl's Buick is parked by the Big House. Of course she's here.

Mattie has always seemed nothing if not strong, with her wide jaw and broad shoulders and big hands, her confident stride and her air of certainty even when she was wrong. But she's been keeping to herself since Eddie's death. The last time I saw her was when Mary called Mattie and Sheriff Earl whiskey profiteers and Mattie stormed out of the Big House. Now, as she sits on the horsehair sofa next to Sheriff Earl, Mattie's shoulders are slumped, there's a yellow tinge to her eyes and a slack sadness in her face. I'm so struck by her air of defeat that it's a moment before I notice the rosewood jewelry box on the side table, the one Mattie took home with her that day after the reading of the Duke's will.

"Our condolences for your sister," Sheriff Earl says. Mattie nods in agreement.

He said your sister, not our niece. They still haven't forgiven Mary. "She was very brave in the end," I say.

"We came to talk," Sheriff Earl says.

"About where we all stand with each other," Mattie adds.

"Sounds good."

"You're running the show now," Sheriff Earl goes on. "That's as it should be."

I look at Mattie. "Is it?"

"It's what the Duke's will stipulates." Then she adds, "Of course he never thought it would come to this."

"All right, Mattie," Sheriff Earl says. "We agreed." He turns to me. "Sallie, I want you to know that as sheriff, me and my men are behind you all the way, that is if we all—if you two—can come to see things eye to eye. There's a lot to straighten out." Earl gets to his feet. "I've said my piece, and Mattie wants to have some words with you alone, so I'll go have a smoke on the porch."

Mattie and I sit in silence until we hear the front door shut. "This"—she pats the top of the jewelry box—"belongs here."

"Why now?" I ask. "After all this time."

"It's your property. Felt wrong to keep it." Mattie shifts her big hips on the horsehair sofa. "But then there's a lot that feels wrong, to be frank about it."

She looks around the room, checking to see if any of the porcelain figurines have disappeared, if the fringed shades on the electric lamps have been dusted, if the portrait of her mother is hanging true. She can't help herself.

"I know what you're thinking," I say. "This house should be yours."

"I'm not here to say anything about that." Mattie fixes me with that fierce stare of hers. Grief and regret have aged her but she's still got fight left. "I'm not here to complain—to complain about how I was the firstborn but didn't inherit because I'm a woman and instead you've inherited it all, even though you are a woman, too—and you're not even firstborn. And you're not yet twenty years of age."

Mattie still has fight, but she's also bitter. Resentful. Who could blame her? Inheritance is the luck of the draw. "You're right, Mattie. It's not fair."

"I know it. You know it. The Lord above knows it. But fair or not, this is the way the Kincaids do things. So I brought you this." She puts her hand back on the rosewood box and drums her fingers. "A peace offering. Sheriff Earl told me that I have to accept that this is the way the chips fell. And he's right. But I'm not here because of Sheriff Earl. Or me. I'm here for my daughter."

"For Ellen?" My cousin has always been a bit of a wallflower. She was there the day I came back from Hatfield and the day we jumped off the trestle, but she's always struck me as a sweet girl overshadowed by her hard-driven mama.

Mattie runs her hands over her skirt. "You know I had an arranged marriage?"

That stuns me. I can't imagine anyone arranging anything for Mattie, but it makes sense given the Kincaid way of doing things. She's never bared herself like this to me before, so I stay quiet to let her talk.

"The Duke was looking to marry off his sister and the man he came up with was Earl Johnson. Earl's a good man, I'm not bellyaching about him, but I could have been more than a man's wife. A lot more. Now Earl's talking about marrying off Ellen. I don't want that for her. I want Ellen to be independent. Like you."

"You want your daughter to be like Annie Powell's daughter?"

"Not exactly like you," she says a little too quickly. "But independent. You could bring her into the business. Ellen's good with numbers. Maybe it will even get her interested in college."

I have to be careful, do what's smart, what's right, get people on my side and keep them there. That includes Mattie. I look at the rosewood box. I've worn Mama's necklace every day since the Duke's death, but I have no interest in what's in the box.

"Mattie, you ought to keep all the jewelry."

"Sallie, that's quite the gesture. I'm glad for it." She taps the box. "This was my mama's, after all. Every piece in it has a story, and I know them all."

"And about Ellen, I could take her on at the Emporium. She can work with Mr. Lewis, start at the bottom, learn the ropes, same as me. When I went to work for the Duke, he told me he'd treat me fair, but wouldn't treat me special. I'll do the same for Ellen."

"Good." A light comes back into Mattie's eyes. "I'm glad for that, too."

With Ellen working at the Emporium, Mattie will of course be showing up all the time, a mama checking in on her daughter, she'll say, but of course she'll start bossing everyone around. Maybe I just made a big mistake. Or maybe it's not a bad idea. I'd rather have Mattie Johnson on the inside, working with me, than on the outside, brooding about how unfair it all is and maybe even plotting against me.

Besides, it will get Mattie out of her house, help put her part in Eddie's death behind her. Maybe behind us all.

I still can't forget the look on her face, the tone in her voice that day she and Sheriff Earl dragged Eddie off. As Aunt Faye said, there's a lot of blame to go around for what happened and I reckon we were all doing what we thought we had to do. That goes for Mattie too.

"Maybe you should spend some time at the Emporium yourself. Without Cecil around, I'm going to need someone to help me keep an eye on things."

"Are you offering me a job?"

"I'll pay you what we pay Mr. Lewis. We'll see how it goes, see if we all get along."

The light in Mattie's eyes becomes a glow. I hope I haven't just opened a door I'm going to have trouble closing.

"We'll get along," she says. "Don't you worry about that. We'll get along."

CHAPTER 39

IT'S ICY OUTSIDE—THE GLASS in the front hall windows is etched with frost. I put on my wool overcoat and study myself in the mirror. I am now the head of Kincaid Holdings, my second day as the most important person in the county, to use Mary's words. But I don't look like it, not in this coat with its frayed cuffs and worn fur collar.

The Duke never wore a pair of overalls in his life. "You've got to look the part," he'd say. "Look like a dirt farmer and people will treat you like a dirt farmer." That's when it dawns on me. The Packard. It's mine. I'm going to Roanoke on business and if I take the Packard, maybe I'll look the part.

Up at the carriage house, I slide open the door and there it is, long as a locomotive and the dark hard green of a new dollar bill. Two years ago, when I first saw that Packard coming through the cold mist in Hatfield, I'd never in my life laid eyes on something so sleek, so powerful, so modern. It never occurred to me that one day that car would be mine.

Now, the shiny hood is coated with a fine layer of dust but the tires are fat and full, ready to roll. I climb in. The heavy door closes with a solid clunk. I run my hand across the soft leather seats, then grip the burled walnut steering wheel. The Packard has an electric ignition switch so I don't have to crank it like the Lizzie. I simply push a button and the engine turns over, the needles in the gauges jump to attention then bounce and quiver and I can feel the throb of those sixty horses, powerful but quiet. It also has a gas pedal instead of a throttle and when I slip it into gear and ease down on the pedal, it rolls forward so smooth I hardly feel it begin to move.

I catch a glance of myself in the rearview mirror. Then I hit the brakes. I'm the same person I saw a few minutes ago in the hall mirror—a bony-faced girl still two months shy of her twentieth birthday, wearing a worn coat and trying to put on a brave front. Driving a shiny, pricey car like this doesn't make me look the part. I haven't earned it. I have quite the pair of shoes to fill, and there's nothing to be gained by announcing to the world that I don't nearly fill them.

I ease the Packard back into the carriage house and turn off that powerful engine.

Roanoke. I'd never seen a big, fancy city and always wanted to. It's even bigger and fancier than I'd expected. Noisier too. The main avenue is broad, paved with bricks—no getting stuck in the mud here—and it's packed with honking cars and clanging trolleys. Overhead the air is crisscrossed with hundreds of wires and cables like so many thick spiderwebs and you can hear them buzzing and humming. There's a store that takes up an entire block with statues of headless women in the display windows wearing short dresses. Crowds huddle at every corner and whenever a policeman blows a whistle, they surge across the street.

It's pretty overwhelming for a gal from Claiborne County and I drive real careful, trying to take it all in. I've never in all my life had to ask directions but I can't find Davis Street so I stop to ask one of these Roanoke policemen and the car behind me honks. The policeman smiles like he thinks the way I talk is funny and the car behind me honks again. At last, I find the Davis Street garage, take a breath, and remember why I'm here.

After that talk yesterday with Mattie, I did some hard thinking. There are a lot of people like her in Claiborne County, people who once looked down on me, clucked about my mama, whispered behind my back when I returned from Hatfield, and now those folks are wondering how long my memory is when it comes to old slights.

"'Forgive and forget' is fifty percent bullshit," the Duke used to say. "Forgive, but don't ever, ever, forget."

Feels about right to me.

I'm willing to deal with those people fair and square, but right now, I need someone by my side, someone who doesn't have any angle to play or hold any old grudges, someone whose loyalty is solely to me. That means someone who doesn't have any ties to Claiborne County.

And I'm hoping that someone is right here.

I called the guard armory and was told that when Lieutenant Douglas Rawley isn't on duty, he repairs cars at the Davis Street Garage in Roanoke, and I see a pair of legs jutting out from under a car. Dirty khaki pants and battered work boots.

"Lieutenant, I'd like a few words with you."

He slides out on a board with little wheels, his black hair tousled, his forehead smeared with grease.

"I ain't in uniform, so call me Rawley, like everyone does." He tosses his wrench into a toolbox and a sly smile turns up one side of his mouth. "Talk about what, Miss Kincaid? You rethink my proposal to get hitched?"

"I'm not here to fool around. I'm here to offer you a job."

"That so? Doing what?"

"Whatever needs to be done. Drive. Collect rent. Fix cars."

"That's right kind of you, Miss Kincaid, but as you can see, I already got myself a job fixing cars." He holds out his hands and shows me the dark crescents of grease under his fingernails. "It's a dirty job, Miss Kincaid. So I don't have to haul my hide over to Caywood just to be a motorman."

Rawley opens the hood and picks up a screwdriver. "I heard about your sister—and I'm sorry for your loss—but I hear not many are, seeing as how she left you with a god-awful mess in Claiborne County." He leans under the hood and fiddles with the carburetor. "Miss Kincaid, you got your work cut out for you."

"And I'm getting started."

"Are folks going back to making whiskey?"

"It's what they've always done and everyone needs money."

"Good." Rawley slams down the hood. "Problem is—with all due respect—the way you Kincaids do business is too slow by half. You all wait for buyers to come to you. Then you sell one bottle at a time. At Claiborne County prices."

"That's the way it's always been."

"I got one word for you." He leans against the car. "Roanoke. This here town's a hub. Folk come from all over to buy whiskey here. You run your stuff into Roanoke you can sell fifty, sixty gallons in one trip. Take you a month to make that much selling retail in Claiborne County."

I shake my head. "We control Claiborne County. As long as we stay there we're safe. Once we leave, anything could happen."

"That's right, Miss Kincaid. No risk, no reward. It's like in war, you don't gain ground sitting in trenches. I was in France. Up in the air but I had a damned good view of those poor sons of bitches stuck in the trenches."

Rawley pushes the car's ignition button. He listens to the engine for a moment, then switches it off. "You don't need someone to fix cars. You need someone who can get you into Roanoke. I know this town. I've got connections here. Like I said, you got yourself a mess, Miss Kincaid, and you need someone who ain't afraid to get out of the trenches. If you're looking for someone like that, someone who can come up with a plan when the bullets are flying, then change that plan when he needs to, someone who'll be working with you—not for you—then Miss Kincaid, I'm your man."

"Cocksure as all get-out, aren't you?"

"There's worse things you can call a fellow."

The man talks big, but he thinks big, too. I like that. And running our whiskey into Roanoke sure would get Claiborne County back on its feet in a hurry. "Just so we understand each other, I'm not on the prowl for a husband."

"Ah hell, Miss Kincaid. Aim high and shoot quick, I always say."

"How soon can you start?"

CHAPTER 40

MEN'S LOW VOICES ECHO through Shorty's Garage.

Those men and I are checking over the six cars we'll use on our first blockade run. Five will be carrying eighty gallons of whiskey each, more than six hundred pounds. So we braced the suspension to support the load and unbolted the backseats to make room. The sixth car—my Lizzie—isn't carrying whiskey. She's going to be the pilot, leading the caravan, speeding ahead to check out any car in front of us and dropping back to run interference if a car comes up from behind.

Rawley organized the operation with military precision.

"You handle supply, I'll take care of demand," he said. He went into Roanoke and came back with orders from pretty much every filling station, restaurant, and speakeasy he'd visited—all at Roanoke prices.

"Thirsty folks in that city," he told me. "We can sell as much as we can carry."

Sheriff Earl put together a list of whiskey makers in Claiborne County and the both of us hit them up. I'm as short on cash as you are, I told them, and can't pay you until I sell it, but I've got buyers and if you trust me with your inventory, I'll unload it all in one day.

What happens, they all asked, if you get caught?

If I'm lucky, I'll pay a fine, I told them. If I'm not lucky, I'll go to jail. You'll lose your inventory, but that's it. We're taking all the risk here, and if we pull this off, you'll make more with us overnight than you would on your own in a month.

By sundown, we had some four hundred gallons promised to us, enough to fill the five cars.

I'm wearing a flannel shirt, khaki pants, and lace-up boots, and I squat down on my haunches to check the tires. Pressure's good. Couldn't do this in a skirt. I've taken to wearing men's clothes to work on these cars and when I do, my stride is longer and I'm not afraid to put my foot up on a fender or sit cross-legged on the floor. I listen to the fellows kidding around, the clank of tools, and I breathe in the smells of gasoline, grease, rubber, and sweat. I'm in the world of men and there's something mighty appealing about it.

I push down on the Lizzie's hood to test the suspension. It rises right back up. Good and tight. "This girl will make a right nice pilot car."

"You keep talking about driving pilot, but it's too dangerous," Rawley says. "Right, Shorty?"

"I'm staying out of this." Shorty's head twitches like it does when someone puts him on the spot. "I'm just the mechanic."

"You've got spunk, Miss Kincaid, I'll give you that," Rawley says. "But for a run like this you need both the know-how and the nerve. I'll drive pilot."

"I've got the nerve, don't you worry about that. Besides, it's going to be dark and I know the roads in these parts. And anyway, it's my call, not yours."

Around ten o'clock, Sheriff Earl pulls in, driving Kincaid Paving's big truck. Deputies George and Casey throw back the tarp and Rawley whistles at the sight of all the whiskey. The jars come in every manner of size and shape, and they don't fit neatly together in the backs of the cars, so we stuff in wadded newspapers and old burlap bags to keep them from breaking. When we finish loading, the rears of the cars are sagging from the weight and the hoods are pointed up.

"Like dogs sniffing the air," Shorty says.

Just before midnight, we roll up the garage doors as quietly as we can. I pull out first, headlights on, peering down every alley and side street for anything fishy—someone watching from a window, a stranger sitting in an idle car or lurking in a doorway—but the streets are deserted, the houses dark.

This is it. No turning back.

Outlaw. Rumrunner. Bootlegger. Blockader. I don't for one second forget that what we are doing is illegal, but legal and illegal and right and wrong don't always line up. Ask a former slave. Plenty of them still around. Sometimes the so-called law is nothing but the haves telling the have-nots to stay in their place.

Besides, I'm not taking anything that isn't mine, not forcing folk to do anything they don't want to do, just helping out the people of Claiborne County who through no fault of their own are in an awful bind. Obey the law and starve. Or break the law and eat. Not a lot to ponder there.

Outside town, I switch off my headlights. Rawley is in the car behind me and in the rearview mirror I watch him turn off his lights, then one by one the lights blink out in the cars behind him. Shorty, Casey, George, and Sheriff Earl bringing up the rear. We chose this night for the full moon, and she's doing her job—glowing cool and steady, bright enough to cast blue shadows.

If we race across the lowland and move through the mountains at a good clip, we can make it to Roanoke in about three hours.

Once we get to the valley floor, I take the Lizzie up to thirty miles an hour. The wind rushes into my open window, carrying the smell of hot engine oil, honeysuckle, and the occasional skunk. I check to see that the boys are keeping pace, hoping to avoid surprises because these overloaded cars are heavy-footed as pack mules and can't make sudden turns or stops.

We reach Finch Mountain and I slow to ease through these switchback turns. We drop down the western slope and I keep it in low, sparing the brake. We clank across an iron bridge over the James River and cross Rathole Mountain and Timber Ridge. That brings us to the low hills north of Roanoke, where we can pick up the pace again.

We haven't passed a single car.

Then, about fifteen miles north of Roanoke, just as we're coming to the town of Fincastle, I check the rearview mirror once more and see a pair of watery yellow headlights about half a mile behind us. I wait a few seconds and glance again. They're closer. Seconds later, they're closer still.

I click my lights twice, the signal for trouble, and throttle up, putting some distance between me and the rest of our convoy. I get to Fincastle's Main Street, cut down a side road, turn on my headlights, and circle around to another side road that brings me back to Main Street. I stop at the intersection. Rawley's now leading our convoy and he passes down Main Street in front of me, followed by the four other cars.

A few moments later, the car that's been on our tail comes down Main Street. I wait until it gets so close that the driver doesn't have time to think. Now. I jerk the throttle, pull out in front of him, then I'm in the glare of his headlights, two blinding white spots coming at me fast. He brakes hard, swerves to the left. His right fender clips my bumper. A grinding crunch of metal on metal. The Lizzie swings sideways, slams me against the door.

I glance behind me and see the dark shape of Sheriff Earl's car racing away. I stumble out of the Lizzie, rubbing my shoulder as the other driver throws open the door of his car. He's a tall fellow in a coat and hat and when he moves into my headlights I see a leather strap across his chest, the kind that holds a shoulder holster, and even before he pulls out his badge I know he's a federal man.

"U.S. Treasury. What the Sam Hill you doing, lady?"

"Gee whiz, mister, I'm real sorry. I've just taken up driving and I'm still trying to get the hang of it."

"At this time of night?"

"It's the best time to practice, mister. No one else around. Most times. Daddy's going to kill me when he sees the car."

The federal man looks down the road, toward Roanoke and the boys, but they've all disappeared.

"They got away, didn't they?" he asks.

"Who got away?"

The man gives me a hard stare. "I can't figure out if you're the worst lady driver I've ever seen, or the best."

"We are on the move, Miss Sallie Kincaid."

"Yes we are, Lieutenant."

Rawley and I are in the Duke's office going over the numbers. Our first run to Roanoke was three months ago, but those city folk wanted more than we had, so we made the trip again and then again and now we're hauling liquor to Roanoke once a week. Every still in the county is fired up and running through the night and new stills are popping up like mushrooms after a summer rain because people know me and my boys will take every last drop of whiskey that anyone can make. We pay a fair price for it, too. No one has to worry about selling it themselves, holding it until a buyer happens along, and we've even taken to passing out square tin cans. They don't break and they make packing a far sight easier.

Some old-timers stick to their long-held traditions of whiskey making, letting the corn ferment naturally, carefully testing the proof by checking the size of the bubbles that float to the top. That means that each batch takes a week or more, and with people in Roanoke clamoring for our whiskey, most stillers are taking shortcuts like adding yeast to speed along the fermenting or pouring a bag of sugar into spent mash. The quick stuff is sharper, short on flavor and there's nothing smooth about it—folks call it firewater, mule kick, tangle leg, ruckus juice, rise-n-shine, hooch, preacher's lye, and panther piss—but long as it has the fire our Roanoke customers don't care much about quality.

So after years of scrimping and doing without, of war and shortages, of trying to coax a living out of the hard, mean ground, the folk of Claiborne County have a little spare change in their pockets, and they don't need anyone's pity or anyone's help or anyone's handouts. Meanwhile, they've started calling me and my boys the Kincaid Rumrunners.

Rawley turns back to the first page of the ledger and traces a finger down one column showing what we're paying out for whiskey, then another showing what we're bringing back from Roanoke, and he makes an approving hum.

"The real money in whiskey comes from moving it."

He's right. I murmur in agreement, but the truth is I'm having trouble keeping my mind on numbers right now. It's the heat coming off Rawley's body. He's a few inches from my arm and if I move my elbow, it'll touch his. I can smell him, too. It's not a bad smell. Not bad at all.

I'm guessing Rawley knows I get all stirred up around him. He finds ways of letting me know he's stirred up, too. A few weeks ago, he wanted to drive over to Luray Caverns and take a gander at those rocks that look like so much dripped wax. I said no. A couple of times he's suggested going to a moving picture. I said no to that, too. He keeps finding reasons for us to be alone—mostly business reasons, of course—heading into the woods to shoot an automatic rifle on the chance we might want to pick up a few from army surplus. I keep the talk on business, but even when we're going over the books we laugh at each other's jokes just a little too hard and glance each other's way a little more than we need to. Like now.

Rawley reaches for his bottle of Coca-Cola. It's beaded with water like the glass itself is all sweaty and I watch from the corner of my eye while he wedges the bottle's neck against the edge of the desk and knocks off the cap with a practiced rap of his fist. He takes a long swig and without looking my way—we're both studying the ledger—he passes the bottle to me.

The syrup coats my tongue and the fizz tickles my nose, but all I'm thinking is how I just now put something into my mouth that only a moment ago was in Rawley's mouth. It's delicious. And disturbing. At the same time. Sort of like a long-distance kiss. But what do I know? Never been courted, never been kissed.

Rawley picks up a box of Cracker Jacks he brought with the Coca-Cola. His hands are strong but slender with slightly hairy knuckles and those dark crescents of grease under each fingernail. He slides a thumb under the lid and pops it open, then tosses a handful into his mouth. Again, without looking at me he holds out the box and I take it.

They're sticky, salty and sweet and crunchy all at once when I toss them into my mouth like Rawley did. I want to wash them down with Coca-Cola, but if I reach for the bottle, I might accidentally touch Rawley's hand. Then he passes it to me again. We keep passing the bottle and the box back and forth, talking about maybe giving bonuses to the drivers, then Rawley shakes a bright blue jack out of the box. It looks like a tiny star with knobs on the side points.

"Here." He puts the jack in my hand. "For you."

It is just a trinket, a toy, but it feels like something more, a gift, an offering, and I close my fist around it so hard it digs into my skin and then I set it on the desk because I've never been kissed and Rawley can't be the first. For all his talk of working with me not for me, I'm paying this man's wages and if I let something happen there will be nothing but trouble.

Rawley picks up the jack, spins it with a thumb and finger, and we both watch it twirl around, a blue blur, until it slows and wobbles and finally topples on its side.

Two days later, we get to Shorty's Garage just as the rising sun's turning the underbellies of gray clouds pink. Even before washing the road dirt off my face I sit on the hood next to Rawley. I can smell him again, and although he's sweaty and dusty like me, I still get stirred up. Again. But I've got to keep my mind on business.

I count the money carefully, Rawley double-checks my numbers and stacks the bills. One thousand, eight hundred and forty-five dollars. After paying off our whiskey makers, we'll net seven hundred and twenty. I set forty aside for each driver, including me and Rawley, and put the rest back in my satchel to deposit into the Kincaid Holdings account at Caywood Bank & Trust.

Rawley puts twenty dollars in his wallet then takes an envelope from his jacket pocket and slips the other twenty inside.

"Paying off your debts? Some loan shark got you in his clutches?"

He shakes his head, and a peculiar—almost shy—look comes into his face. "I send a little to my ma now and then."

Rawley's never talked about his family and I've wanted to keep my distance so I've never pried. But he's given me an opening.

"You know all about the Kincaids," I say. "Tell me about the Rawleys."

Instead of answering right away, he studies the envelope. "We lived on the West Virginia side of Bluefield," he finally says. "But Pa was the best mechanic in the whole damned town. The first man in the county to start making his own cars. Only thing is, he bet on steam."

"Steam. The engines are all the time blowing up."

"I told him gasoline was the way to go but Pa wouldn't listen. I was a kid. What did I know? Built himself a car he thought was going to put Henry Ford out of business." He shakes his head. "Damned thing exploded like a keg of dynamite. Pa lost both hands. Ma became a maid to feed us seven kids. Wore herself out working over on the Virginia side of Bluefield."

"Where the ladies with the white gloves live."

"Couldn't wait to get the hell out."

"I know how that feels."

CHAPTER 41

"HOW SHORT DO YOU want it?"

"Short. But not too short." I settle down in the chair and Aunt Faye pins a sheet around my shoulders.

"That Rawley fellow sure is a looker."

"That's not why I hired him."

I don't want to talk about Rawley. I glance around the room Jane called her boudoir. I always hated that word "*boo-dwah*"—talk about putting on airs—so I call it the dressing room. But my few dresses look forlorn hanging on the mostly empty racks and the walls are still Kat's cherry-blossom pink. "We should repaint this room one of these days."

"We should." Aunt Faye runs her fingers through my wet hair. "You interested?"

"Interested in Rawley? No."

That's a lie. I recall watching Eddie tuning his piano, the way the metal tuning fork quivered. That's how I feel around Rawley. He makes my tuning fork quiver. Aunt Faye may have a hunch about it but no one is going to know.

"You interested in anyone?" she asks.

"No."

"Maybe you ought to be." Aunt Faye picks up her shears. "You don't want to go through life alone."

"I like things the way they are."

"Sallie"—she snips at my hair—"you believe you can do everything on your own and you're gosh darned good at it, but as you get older, life gets harder—and lonelier. A woman is better off married."

That's what Mary thought. And when she needed her husband the most, he left her. That's what Kat thought too, and every time she lost a husband she was in such a hurry to get married again that she didn't take a hard look at the man she was marrying.

And that's what Mama thought.

"You never got married," I say.

"Like I told you before, I got proposals but"—Aunt Faye presses her lips together—"from the wrong men. I didn't have a lot of good choices. You, Sallie, you've got good choices."

"I've already made some choices I regret—and I mostly made them when I was answering to others. Now, I answer to no one. And I don't want anyone taking care of me. Mama had someone to take care of her, and look how that turned out."

"That was one tangled-up mess, what happened to Annie. One tangled-up mess." She cups the ends of my hair in her hands. "Is this short enough?"

"No. Shorter. What did happen exactly?"

Aunt Faye stays quiet. "We never talked about it," I say.

I was in the Big House the night Mama died, but I was three years old, scared and confused, and my recollections of it all are like a handful of broken pieces that won't fit together, that don't make a whole. I remember the sound of angry voices, Mama's and the Duke's, then there was a loud sharp crack, and next day Mama was gone. Since then, all I've known—from that creepy fairy tale Mary told me—is that the Duke killed Mama. But he didn't go to prison. No grown-ups would discuss it and I learned to stop asking.

"Never talked about it," I say again.

"It's painful," Aunt Faye whispers. "Ugly."

"Not once."

The scissors click raspy and quick near my ear and locks of hair fall to my shoulders and lap.

"You were such a little thing when it happened."

"The one time I worked up the nerve to ask the Duke about it he gave me that cold stare of his and said, 'She's gone. Doesn't do to dwell on it.'" And truth be told, a big part of me didn't want to know. I was afraid of the answer. With Mama gone, the Duke was all I had, and I wanted to believe he was perfect.

"No one was supposed to mention it. Ever. When you came to live with me in Hatfield, you never once asked about it." Aunt Faye looks at me in the mirror. "I figured it was something you wanted to forget, to put it all behind you."

"I tried, but I can't. Not anymore."

"Honey, there are some rocks you don't want to look under."

"I don't want to but I got to, Aunt Faye. I'm tired of being afraid of the answer and I'm sitting here in what used to be Mama's chair, in what used to be Mama's room, and you're carrying on about how I ought to get married, but no one will tell me what happened in my own mama's marriage. Well, now I'm asking. What did happen?"

"It's a long story."

"We got time."

Aunt Faye puts down the scissors. "There's a lot you don't know, and not just about what happened to your mama."

"Tell me."

"There was something going on. Something improper." She looks out the window and tucks a lock of gray-streaked hair behind an ear. "Between me and the Duke."

Heat rushes to my face. My daddy and my mama's sister? I don't believe her. I stare at Aunt Faye in the mirror. Someone once told me that when Aunt Faye was young, she was beautiful enough to make good men write bad checks. Now, the afternoon sunlight catches the fine lines around her eyes and mouth, etched there by years of hurt and heartbreak. She's telling the truth. "Is that why the Duke shot Mama?"

"Oh no, hon. I was before your mama." Aunt Faye turns away from the window and faces me. "People all the time talk about how Annie stole the Duke from Belle, but truth be told, she also stole him from me."

Aunt Faye pulls a comb through my wet hair and says, "You know, you're right. Shorter. That's what's in the magazines nowadays." She picks up the scissors. "And I reckon it's time you hear the whole story."

Hair falls to my lap as Aunt Faye snips away. Then she starts talking. "Belle Montgomery was a proper lady from a proper old plantation family. They had an air of respectability to them. What you call old money. But the Montgomerys put every last penny of that money into Confederate bonds—believed the war would last only a month or so—and by the time it was finally over those bonds weren't good for anything but the outhouse. The Montgomerys were flat broke. Those old Virginia families always looked down on the Kincaids, called them strivers, but when the Duke's brother, Arthur, came a-courting Belle, he was welcomed. The Colonel threw the fanciest wedding this county had ever seen. On the honeymoon, Arthur dived into a lake to fetch the little Paris hat of Belle's that the wind had blown into the water. Hit his head on a rock and died without ever coming to.

"Arthur was always the Colonel's favorite. Everyone's favorite, to tell the truth. So handsome and strong, everything came easy to him. The Duke—he was just Henry back then—was kind of scrawny and awkward as a boy—all the time shooting guns, drinking hard, always trying to prove himself to the Colonel, but the Colonel was a hard man and let your daddy know he didn't measure up.

"The Colonel was plum hollowed out by Arthur's death but he didn't want to lose his ties to the hifalutin Montgomery name, and he decided the Duke should marry Belle. The Duke, he was all of seventeen at the time, figured he could finally win his daddy's favor by taking Arthur's widow as his wife, by giving the Colonel those grandsons that he wanted. Carry on the Kincaid line."

So, as a boy, the Duke was scrawny and awkward like Eddie. That's why he was so sure Eddie could change, because he did—for his daddy. The Colonel hated the weakness in the Duke, and the Duke hated it in his own son. Because he feared it in himself.

"I always thought how different everything would have turned out if"—Aunt Faye's voice cracks a bit—"if only Arthur just let that little Paris hat float away."

I wait for her to go on.

"Well," she says, "Belle always had a lot of help at the Big House. She was four years older than the Duke, and by the time she hired me to do laundry and mending she was no fresh blossom. I had quite the figure back in those days and from the start your daddy took a fancy to me. He was a hard man to resist—you should have seen him in his prime, not scrawny anymore, a big buck—and pretty soon, we had us a little thing going on, meeting upstairs in the stone wing. The Duke, he was good to me, bighearted, gave me trinkets, sweets, and a little cash now and then. A gift, not payment, of course. A token of appreciation."

The snip of the scissors is strangely loud. So is the rustle of Aunt Faye's dress as her arms move. A gift. A token of appreciation. That's how it began. How Aunt Faye first told herself it was okay.

"Did Belle know?"

"Belle was good at looking the other way. I wasn't the first. It came with being married to the Duke." This thing between her and the Duke went on for about a year, Aunt Faye says. Meanwhile Annie was working as a maid for a family in Richmond—that's where she got all her la-di-da ideas about clothes and fabric and jewelry—but it didn't work out, so she came to Caywood, and seeing as she had a real talent with needle and thread, Belle hired her as a seamstress. "Annie had looks, there's no denying that, but she had something more. It was like electricity. She just lit up a room. All Annie had to do was flash that smile of hers and show a little leg, and men got stupid for her. The Duke was no different. And he fell hard."

Aunt Faye tugs at both sides of my hair. "It's uneven." She makes a few quick snips.

"What did you do when the Duke went after Mama?"

"What could I do? Like I said, I didn't have any good choices."

"Did it bother Mama, what had gone on between you and the Duke?"

"Of course it did. That's one reason Annie wouldn't settle for being the girl on the side. And the more she told the Duke no, the more crazed he got. He did everything short of forcing himself on her, which wasn't his way."

Instead, Aunt Faye tells me, Annie promised the Duke that if he'd divorce Belle—who hadn't been with child since Mary was born—and marry her, she'd give him the son he'd always wanted. "I warned her, 'Careful, hon, you're playing with fire.' You know what your mama told me? She said, 'I like fire.'"

Aunt Faye holds the scissors up. "Short enough?"

"No. Shorter. And in time Mama got what she wanted."

"Or so she thought." Aunt Faye's voice becomes hushed, like she's telling me something I ought not know. "The Duke had come to believe that marrying his brother's wife was unnatural. A 'violation' was the word he used. As robust as they are, the Kincaid men don't seem to father a whole lot of children, but the notion took hold in the Duke's mind that this violation was the reason why Belle hadn't borne him a son and so, using that as his cause, he demanded a divorce. Belle wouldn't give it to him. She was a God-fearing, churchgoing woman who believed in till death do you part, but Judge Barrow is a Kincaid on his mama's side, and he granted the divorce."

So, Mama didn't quite trick the Duke into getting rid of Belle, but she did make him an empty promise, one she knew she might not be able to keep. But the Duke knew that, too. He was just cooking up an excuse to do what he wanted—leave his wife for Annie. All these lies, lies that trapped everyone. For the sake of marriage. The whole thing is sickening.

"It was quite the scandal." Aunt Faye's telling becomes almost matter-of-fact, like we're going down a well-worn road, one she's traveled many times in her mind, and doesn't see how startling each turn is to me. "Divorces were pretty much unheard of those days. Tore Claiborne County right in two. Belle went back to her family in Mercer County. She took Mary—who must have been about nine—with her. There was talk by some Montgomerys of revenge, but nothing ever came of it. And nine months later to the day, you were born."

"A girl." I'm the reason that Mama and the Duke's marriage fell apart. They put all their chips on one big bet—me being a boy—and they lost.

Aunt Faye nods. "Both the Duke and your mama put the best face on it and told each other that the next one would be a son." Aunt Faye strokes my head with her free hand. "Who knows if it was because you were a girl, but Annie didn't take to being a mama. She was all the time complaining about staying at home, 'stuck in the house,' she'd say. 'I miss the gal I used to be,' she kept telling me. She wanted to carry on just like before she was married, drinking and flirting and dancing on tables."

"Carrying on is fine if you're the girl on the side," I say, "but it wasn't what the Duke wanted from his wife."

"Annie was real clever, I got to give her that, just busting with ideas and opinions, and she was all the time telling the Duke what he ought to be doing—grade the roads, build a power station, stock more up-to-date clothes at the Emporium, let her run the place."

"And the Duke hated to be told what to do."

"Something he passed on to you. Anyways, two years after you were born, Annie had that awful stillborn—that little boy—"

"No one ever told me about that." My words are almost a whisper but I'm thinking, for the love of God, the things this family keeps quiet about are the things that matter the most.

"It was hard on her. On them both. And then Annie found out she couldn't bear any more children. That was when things started going downhill. Fast. Annie turned into a real shrew, the Duke came up with reasons to get out of the house most nights, and when he came home their awful screaming fights made the windows rattle."

Aunt Faye puts the scissors in her pocket and takes the little silver brush to my hair. "How's that?" she asks.

"Good. That's enough. What finally happened?"

"It was sixteen years ago. May nineteenth. I'll never forget the date. The Duke went out after dinner and your mama started in on the peach brandy. By midnight, she'd spent the better part of four hours tippling and stewing. As soon as the Duke came through the door, Annie started saying ugly things, hurtful things, things a woman ought not ever say to her husband—about his manhood and all. The Duke had been drinking too, and he started shouting back, calling Annie nasty names, a drunk and a whore and a slut. I could hear them from the kitchen."

"I could hear them from my bedroom. I remember that."

"Those two'd had more than their share of fights before but never one this bad. Your mama busted things when she was angry—china, figurines, nice crystal—and I heard glass smashing. Then I heard the Duke yell, 'Put that down, woman. I'm warning you.' And then I heard the shot."

"I heard it too." I can't forget it, the sound of that shot, no matter how hard I try.

"I ran up the hall and just then I saw you come flying down the stairs. The Duke opened the door, he was in the library, and I saw the gun in his hand. He said, 'Take that girl back to her room.' I carried you upstairs and when I came down, the Duke was still standing in the same spot, the doorway to the library, so I couldn't see inside, and he said to me, 'Send for the sheriff.'"

"His brother-in-law."

"The Duke told Sheriff Earl that Annie had picked up the Colonel's sword and swung it at him. Sheriff and Judge Barrow decided it was a case of self-defense. No need for a trial."

"But was it really self-defense?"

"Only Annie and the Duke knew."

Aunt Faye brushes the hair clippings from my shoulders.

"Not too short?" she asks.

"No, it's what I wanted."

She pulls off the sheet. "There. You're done."

I stare at myself in the mirror. A woman I barely know is staring back. She's older. Not a child, and yet still a daughter. The Duke's.

Annie Powell's. For the first time, the broken pieces are starting to fit together. And yet, I don't know if Mama truly threatened the Duke—or if that was just an excuse he seized on to get rid of the wife he no longer wanted, just like he did with Belle. Maybe it was both.

Aunt Faye tilts her head and gives me an uncertain smile, waiting to see if I'm going to hold anything she said against her. Mama's sister. She bedded my daddy and while she didn't land him, like Mama did, she did survive him, and Mama didn't.

I'll never marry.

"It wasn't easy"—she squares her shoulders and takes a deep breath—"me telling you all that."

"Aunt Faye, I had no idea what you'd been through. It must have been hellish. And it sure wasn't easy hearing it all. But thank you. For telling me. And thank you for taking me in when Mama was gone."

Aunt Faye's smile turns grateful. I look at her, at her tired eyes and worn face. "Funny, you started out trying to talk me into marriage."

She smiles once more, but this time it's a wistful smile. "I did, didn't I?"

CHAPTER 42

THE ROAD TAKES US west, across the Webster County line and into Cedar Valley. This is one rough patch of earth. Gaunt cattle lift their heads to watch us drive by, their eyes thickly ringed with flies as they stand there in the drought-stricken July heat, flicking their tails in grazed-down fields full of granite outcroppings and spindly cedars with shredding bark. Most farmers will tell you that the only good cedar is a dead cedar, but Cedar Valley is lousy with them, cedars lining the hedgerows, cedars crowding the road, cedars sprouting up like weeds to reclaim any idle land.

Rawley lowers his window. "I said it before, Sallie, and I'm going to say it again, this is a waste of our time."

"It's worth a shot." Ever since that talk with Aunt Faye, I've thrown myself into work. That's all I want to think about. "I can talk sense to Billy. I understand him and he understands me."

Rawley pulls a cigarette from his pack. "Not just a waste of time. It's bad tactics."

"Any darn fool can start a fight. We've barely recovered from the last one."

He lights his cigarette and blows the smoke out the window. "Let your enemies know you want to parley before the shooting begins and they'll think you're scared of them."

"Once a fight gets started, it takes on a life of its own. You saw that in France. Some fool shoots some archduke no one's ever heard of and the next thing you know, the whole damned world's at war. So talking's worth a try."

I'd hoped that teaming up with the Bond brothers against Glen Lowe's thugs would put an end to the decades of bad blood between the Bonds and the Kincaids, but these mountain feuds are hard to kill—particularly if the Bonds are a party. Those boys nurse a grudge the way they work a chaw of tobacco, storing it between cheek and jaw, bringing it up every now and then to chew on it, squeezing a little more flavor out of it before packing it away again—and never, ever spitting it out.

A roadhouse brawl started it up again. What the brawl was about—cheating at cards, a woman, a bad joke—doesn't matter. What does matter is that Billy's brother Rick mixed it up with Earl's deputy George Bailey, who's like a son to Sheriff Earl and in the eyes of the Bonds that makes him a Kincaid.

That brawl was followed by a second brawl about what was left unsettled in the first brawl—only this one involved a whole passel of Bonds and Kincaid kin and friends—and soon enough, the brawling was regular, each one brought about because of the one before it. Then two days ago, George was robbed while making payments to whiskey makers out by the Webster County line. The men who took his money wore masks, but one of them had on a pair of high-topped boots made of fine yellow leather. I'd figured the Bonds would have laid Little Jimmy to rest in his boots, but they must have decided that the best way to honor his memory was to pass the boots along to one of the brothers.

I turn down a dirt lane and we go by a scruffy grove of cedars on the left, and on the right a wasteland of a hillside, a former logging site littered with dead treetops and pocked with thick tree stumps, the virgin forest clear-cut decades ago, but the rotted leaves and wood chips so thick on the ground that new growth has a hard time pushing through.

Finally, we come to a hand-lettered sign. LONG SHADE. Behind it is a good-sized cabin made from squared-off cedar logs chinked with white clay. Even with the Lizzie's engine running, I can hear the screeching and crowing of the Bond roosters, known as the meanest fighting cocks in these parts.

Long Shade is the Bond brothers' new headquarters. Billy moved their operations here, hooking up with his Webster County kin after Glen Lowe was killed and Billy figured Claiborne County was a little too hot. The timbers are hand-notched and I'm guessing the cabin's a hundred years old, built before the feud started, and I'm hoping that's a good sign, that some things around here go back even further than this confounded fight.

Two boys I don't recognize—but I know those sharp Bond cheekbones when I see them—are sitting on the porch with rifles. I wave a white kerchief out the window and holler that I'm here with a business proposal for Mr. Billy Bond. The boys pat us down, acting all respectful and gentlemanly when it comes my turn.

Inside, the light is dim, the ceiling low, and I take in the smells of woodsmoke and tobacco and unwashed bodies. My eyes adjust to the dark and I see about a dozen Bond cousins perched on stools or slouched against the wall, hats shoved back and pistols in their belts. Billy Bond's lolling in a rocking chair, a rifle in his lap and a pack of sad-eyed coonhounds drooling at his feet.

"Well, well, well, fetch me the smelling salts," Billy says. "It's the Duke's daughter, boys. A Kincaid, come all the way to Cedar Valley to pay the Bonds a visit. And it's an occasion. First time a lady's ever set foot in this clubhouse."

I glance around. This place feels like a fortress, with racks of guns and rifles, shooting ports in place of windows, and shelves stacked with canned goods and boxes of ammunition, bullet molds and a shell crimper. But the room also shows pride of place, with a couple of bearskin rugs and a twelve-point rack of antlers mounted above a stone fireplace blackened by years of soot. "Nice little setup you all have here," I allow.

"We think it's right cozy." Billy rubs the grimy creases in his neck.

Rawley moves up beside me and crosses his arms.

"You know my point man, Rawley," I say.

Billy ignores him and waves his hand at a low stool. "Have a seat."

"I believe I'll stand." There's no way I'm sitting at Billy Bond's feet. "Haven't seen you since before Glen Lowe was killed."

"Shame what happened to that fellow." Billy slides a rag along the barrel of his rifle and the blue steel glistens, sleek and shiny even in the dim light. He drapes the rag on the stool. "So what brings you here?"

I can pull this off. Billy's pigheaded but he's always had a firm grip on what's best for the Bonds. Appeal to that. "Billy, the Kincaids and the Bonds have known each other for a long time—"

"This is the same old ragged-ass speech you make every time you come a-crawling, claiming that your grandpa didn't steal those eighty-eight acres of bottomland from my grandpa."

"The Colonel didn't steal that land and you know it."

"Highway robbery it was."

"Anyway, that was some sixty years ago. We got a more immediate problem."

"You want us to forget about those eighty-eight acres? Course you do. You all stole them. But we ain't going to forget."

"Billy, the Bonds and the Kincaids joined up to take on Lowe and his thugs. We don't have to be enemies. There's enough whiskey buyers out there for all of us. We can share the roads. We can work out an arrangement. We all don't have to go to war. So if you're willing to forget a sixty-year-old land deal, we're willing to forget what happened the other day."

"What happened?" Billy looks around the room wide-eyed. "What is she talking about, boys?"

"You know damned well what happened. You talk about highway robbery. Our man was ambushed right across the county line."

"Come to think of it, I did hear about that. Got no idea who did it. And anyways, someone takes it into his head he's going to rob someone in Claiborne County, not much I can do about it." He looks around the room again. "You boys do pretty much what you want, ain't that right?" That gets a few chuckles.

"Billy, you don't want a war with the Kincaids."

A smile tickles his face. "I do believe I'm being threatened."

"No. Warned."

"Lookie here, Miss Kincaid, we don't need some young lady—and I hope you don't mind me calling you that because underneath that man's hair and those men's britches I do believe that's what you are— we don't need some young lady, especially if she's a Kincaid, coming into our headquarters giving us warnings, telling us Bonds what we want and don't want. We make up our own minds about that." He points his rifle at the door. "You know the way out, Miss Kincaid, but call again anytime. We're always happy to entertain young ladies."

Rawley's face is dark and I know what he's thinking. He's thinking we didn't just waste our time, we have been mocked and belittled. But he's holding it in.

"One more thing," Billy says. "You been doing all the talking." He points the gun at Rawley. "Why'd you bring li'l sis?"

Rawley steps toward Billy, as if he can't take it anymore, he's going to do or say something, but with all these armed Bonds around us, he can't. And everyone in the room knows it.

I grab his arm and pull him out onto the porch, doing my best to ignore the sound of the men behind us howling with laughter. We climb into the Lizzie and sit there listening to the crowing of those damned Bond roosters.

"You were right," I say. "Hit back."

Chapter 43

THE *GAZETTE'S* DELIVERY BOY drops the bundle of newspapers on the Emporium's long counter. I take a copy and there it is, on the front page, lower right-hand corner, my advertisement.

FEAR NOT

WE KINCAIDS ARE NOT LOOKING FOR TROUBLE, BUT TROUBLE HAS COME LOOKING FOR US, AND WE WILL NOT RUN FROM THIS THREAT. THE BUSINESS WITH THE BONDS WILL BE LIMITED TO THOSE WHO HAVE CHOSEN TO TAKE UP THE CAUSE. ORDINARY CITIZENS HAVE NOTHING TO FEAR. IF YOU ARE AN ORDINARY CITIZEN AND ARE HARMED OR FEEL THREATENED IN ANY WAY, YOU COME TELL IT TO SALLIE KINCAID.

I told Rawley we'd hit back, and we did. The week after my talk with Billy Bond, Sheriff Earl's spies learned that the Bonds had a shipment of liquor in a roadhouse just across the county line. We tied up the night guard, and carried off all the whiskey. It was payback for the robbery of Deputy George, but of course the Bonds felt they had to hit us for that. So they drove into Caywood and shot up a couple of patrol cars. All they did was shatter some glass and set a few radiators to leaking—but the war was on.

Some of the younger fellows on both sides are only a few years out of grammar school and they act like it's all a lark, smashing windows, slashing tires, and setting outhouses on fire.

But it isn't all a lark. People are getting hurt. Shorty's mechanic Leroy ran into Rick Bond at Pogue's Crossing, they both pulled guns, and Leroy took a bullet in the calf. It was just a flesh wound, but folks are talking about little else, so I took out my advertisement.

Mattie comes out from the back and reads the advertisement over my shoulder.

"Not the worst idea in the world," she says. "People are scared. You?"

"I'm not. Don't know why. I know I should be."

Mattie's been at the Emporium seven months now, and she can't help bossing everyone around, but the place has never looked better. "You know, Sallie," she says, "when your daddy and Arthur and I were growing up, the Colonel used to tell us the Kincaids were never happier than when we were fighting. He'd go on about how, back in Scotland, we Kincaids fought the highlanders who tried to rustle our cattle and the English who tried to take our land, then we fought the Irish when they wouldn't let us take theirs, and when we came to Virginia, we fought the Indians for the same reason, then the English again with a lot of talk about defending freedom, then the Yankees with a lot of talk about defending slavery. When we were defeated, we still declared victory—but we also swore revenge. I wish I could say we were always on the side of right, but that would be a lie. We fought people for doing to us exactly what we did to others, fought them for wanting the same rights we had. 'Fighting's in my blood, and that means it's in yours,' the Colonel used to tell us. So, Sallie, it's in your blood, too."

"I've never picked a fight in my whole life," I say, "but if someone comes at me, I won't back down."

Mattie smiles. "That's what we Kincaids are all the time telling ourselves."

A week later, I'm down in the basement when I hear hollering in the store. I run up the stairs and join the crowd at the windows. Rumors are swirling around that the Bonds have made themselves an armored vehicle and sure enough, here it comes, lumbering down Main Street. It looks like that homemade truck I saw in the Bonds' front yard—but now it has a water tank in back. Gunports were cut in the sides of the tank, and rifle barrels are jutting out.

People are terrified, running down sidewalks, ducking behind parked cars. But the Bonds don't fire a single shot. It's a show of force, pure and simple, I figure, proving that with this new tank of theirs the Bonds can go anywhere they want and we can't do a thing about it.

Unless, it hits me, we make our own tank.

The next day Rawley comes back from Roanoke driving a one-ton truck. We reinforce the suspension, weld on a water tank and steel plates, and cut us some gunports on the sides.

Our tank is the ungainliest contraption I have ever laid eyes on. With all that armor, it weighs so much that it creeps uphill, but going downhill, the brakes smoke, and it sucks gas like a thirsty elephant. Still, our tank is a source of great pride for all of Claiborne County—a sign of modern technological ingenuity.

One perfect September morning, we're rolling westward and I'm up in the hatchway scanning the road ahead when the Bonds' tank comes around a bend. I close the hatchway lid and join Sheriff Earl and Deputy George in the belly. It's black as pitch save for the long shafts of light slicing through the gunports. Sweat trickles down my back in the stifling heat and I'm alert, like that night at the hospital, not what you would call calm, but not shaking with fear either.

My Remington in hand, I peer through my port. The Bonds' tank draws up beside us and gun barrels slide out. Both sides start firing. The Bonds' bullets banging off our metal plates make a god-awful noise and the gun smoke has nowhere to go, so we can barely breathe. But our armor holds. After what's probably less than a minute but feels a lot longer, the Bonds stop firing. So do we. I watch through the port as they pull in their guns and the tank sits there for a moment then rumbles off.

In the weeks that follow, no one reports any more sightings of the

Bond tank. Our tank ends up in the lot behind Shorty's Garage. Weeds sprout around it and youngsters and grown-ups alike come from all over Claiborne County to gawk at the contraption. The young ones climb inside and shoot imaginary guns through the ports, the grown-ups finger the pocked metal plates and nod their heads as they discuss the finer points of the Battle of the Ironclads.

CHAPTER 44

THE FIRST HINT OF fall has shown up in the trees along Plank Road where men from Kincaid Paving are spreading a new layer of macadam. A steamroller behind them is flattening the gravel, and I'm perched on the Lizzie's bumper, overseeing it. Good roads. Just a few years back, ten miles was a long way to go. Farm families were stuck on their land for months at a time because of impassable roads, but now we've built decent roads up into the hollows so most days of the year folks can get out and about for work or pleasure or shopping or schooling. They're buying cars before bathtubs because, as one told me, you can't drive to town in a bathtub. And more and more, women are behind the wheel. Getting the right to vote was well and good, but it's cars and roads that have done the most to change things for women, giving them the freedom to go where they want without needing the help of a man to harness the horse to the wagon.

I reach into a bag of apples and start slicing one with my pocket-knife when a car comes along our newly macadamized road and out steps Willard Smith, that reporter from the *Richmond Daily Record*, a photographer in tow.

"They told me at the store where I could find you," he says. "Last time I was here I wrote that this county needed someone like the Duke's daughter running things. Looks like I'm quite the prognosticator."

"Cheap flattery. It always works with me." In his article about the hospital shoot-out, Smith quoted me calling Lowe "the czar of

Claiborne County," and described me as "the second daughter of the legendary Duke Kincaid, a forceful and even fiery young redhead who the simple people of Claiborne County should be turning to for some sorely needed leadership."

I didn't much care for my friends and neighbors being called simple, but I'll admit that I got a kick out of the way he described me. I point to the other bumper. "Have a seat. And an apple."

Smith smiles, shakes his head, then pushes back his derby—a gray felt number with a small, striped feather tucked into the hatband. Looks like a blue jay feather. Come to think of it, Smith's a lot like a blue jay, pushy and chattery, zipping around collecting quotes from people the way a jay collects shiny things like bottle caps.

Smith tells me that he heard about the Battle of the Ironclads. Also saw my ad in the *Gazette* letting ordinary citizens know they have nothing to fear. "What can you tell me about this gang war between the Kincaids and the Bonds?"

"Gang war? That what you call it?" I take a bite of apple. "Our so-called gang is nothing more than friends and kin who stand up for ourselves when we're attacked. We're not robbers or hoodlums, but we don't run from trouble."

"Folks are calling you the Queen of the Kincaid Rumrunners."

"I'm just a Claiborne County gal minding the family business."

"Bootlegging."

"Kincaid Holdings is a diversified corporation with a variety of operations."

"Including bootlegging."

"Don't know what you've heard, but we're just doing what we've always done in these parts."

"But it's now illegal. Says Uncle Sam."

So far, I've been pretty cagey. Just how blunt should I get? If I can make the case, this natty newspaperman could get readers all over the state to see that we're not the dangerous hill folk that city people seem to think we are, that we up here in Claiborne County are just doing what we have to do to survive.

"Your Uncle Sam, not ours." I lean in close, like I'm sharing a secret. "Uncle Sam don't hold a lot of sway around here. We pay him all these taxes and our hard-earned money goes into the pockets of politicians who dole it out to the fat cats who bribe them. Your Uncle Sam doesn't look out for us, so we take care of our own around here. I protect my people."

"Protection. Some would call that a racket."

"I keep my people safe. I take care of them."

"How so?"

Willard Smith's looking at me, eyebrows flared, stubby pencil poised, eager to scribble down my words. This reporter is not a bad fellow, but he doesn't understand that here in Claiborne County we might look like we're breaking laws, when in fact we just follow a different set of laws. I try to explain it in a way that a pencil-pushing city man can grasp and I find myself laying it on a bit thick.

"I pave the roads. I make sure widows have coal in winter. I buy shoes for barefoot children. I put a new roof on the Hatfield schoolhouse. No one else is looking after these people, so I do. You call that a racket?"

"But Prohibition—"

"Big old ugly word that means you ain't allowed to do something. A bunch of numbskulls in Richmond and Washington who think they're smarter than everyone else pro-hib-it-ing other people from doing what they got to do to keep their families from starving to death. Seems downright un-American to me."

Willard Smith asks if his photographer can take a picture of me and all the brave Kincaid boys who are working for and defending the good citizens of Claiborne County. "All those people counting on you for protection will see it," he says. "So you should be holding your guns. Maybe even standing in front of that tank of yours."

Three days after Willard Smith's visit, when I show up at the Central Café for my eggs and grits and gravy plus the latest Claiborne

County scuttlebutt, Rawley's sitting at my booth, the one nearest the door.

"Pardon me, miss," he says real loud, his eyes all sparkly and playful. "Are you the one and only Sallie Kincaid I've been reading about in this here newspaper?"

He holds up the *Richmond Daily Record* with the front-page headline:

SPECTER OF FEAR AND VIOLENCE
STALKS COUNTY AGAIN

Under the headline there's a photograph. I'm in the middle of it. Me, Sallie Kincaid, leaning against the tank next to Rawley, the Remington in my arms. I'm stiff and formal but Rawley's all smiles, looking handsome and relaxed. Around us are the boys, perched on the tank's bumpers and running boards, cradling rifles and shotguns, rakishly cocking an eye, cutting up for the camera.

Folks all over the state read the *Richmond Daily Record*. How many will see this picture? Thousands? Tens of thousands? And when they look at me, what will they see? A rough hillbilly gal? A criminal gang leader? A fighting spirit?

Josie, the waitress, brings over the coffeepot.

"I always wanted to meet someone famous." She pours my first cup. "Didn't think it would be someone I knowed my whole life."

"Josie, the only thing famous around here is your peach pie," I say. "Bring me a slice."

I start to read.

THE OLD TENSENESS AND HEAT-OF-BATTLE FEELING HAS RETURNED TO THE RUGGED TERRAIN OF REMOTE AND MOUNTAINOUS CLAIBORNE COUNTY.

WHEN MEN MEET ON THE STREET CORNERS IN THE TOWN OF CAY-WOOD, THE COUNTY SEAT, TALK IS OF THE GANG WAR. WHAT IS SALLIE KINCAID GOING TO DO? WILL THE QUEEN OF THE KINCAID RUM-

RUNNERS STAND FOR THE ATTACKS ON HER MEN? IS HER REPLY TO BE A PITCHED BATTLE WITH THE BOND CROWD, PERHAPS IN THE CAYWOOD TOWN SQUARE, OR ARE HER MEN TO MAKE REPRISALS ONLY WHEN THEY CAN FIND SINGLE BOND GANGSTERS BY THEMSELVES ON TOWN SIDE-WALKS OR COUNTRY ROADS?

The article goes on to quote the governor saying that the commonwealth will not waste more taxpayer money—"squander scarce resources" is how he puts it—by sending the guard to Claiborne County a second time.

Willard Smith describes me as a "raw-boned mountain girl with a deep up-hollow twang who eats her apple off the point of her pocketknife." And whenever he quotes me, he makes me sound like some hillbilly yokel, pronouncing "far" like "fur" and "the government" as "th' guvmunt." But he also writes that "Claiborne County could give city dwellers a lesson on women breaking new ground, for out there, it is that mountain girl who is calling the shots. She is as wily as a cougar—and as feared and respected as one, too."

I put down the paper. "I can't tell if that reporter likes me or thinks I'm a hick."

"Are you kidding," Rawley says. "That city boy couldn't get enough of you."

Queen of the Kincaid Rumrunners. That reporter fellow is having a little fun with me. But if folks want to call me a queen, even as a joke, I reckon I can live with it. Daddy loved being called the Duke, and a queen outranks a duke. What would he make of that?

I take a big bite of Josie's peach pie. It's still warm from the oven, with a flaky lard crust, and you taste the fruit before the sugar. "Josie," I call out. "Pie don't get any better than this."

"Maybe we'll start calling it the Queen Sallie Special," Josie hollers back.

* * *

Later that morning, Rawley and I are in the Duke's office when Louise Dunbar wheels Cecil through the door. He looks gray and frail in his cane-backed wheelchair. I stand up and reach out my arms in welcome. "Cecil, how you feeling?"

"Like death warmed over." His voice is faint and raspy.

"I didn't think he ought to leave the house," Louise says, "but he insisted."

Cecil holds up a copy of the *Daily Record*, his hand trembling. "What the Sam Hill's gotten into you, Sallie?" he asks. "You've gone and all but admitted to the world that we're nothing but rumrunners here. And that reporter made us out to be a bunch of rubes."

Before I say anything Rawley speaks up.

"Mr. Dunbar, no offense, sir, but that there newspaper has got power. Influence. It tells people what to think. Sallie and me, we got to be smart, we got to rope that power and ride it."

"Young man, there are things that you brag about and things that you keep to yourself," Cecil says. "The Duke understood the difference. I don't expect you to, but I thought Sallie here had better sense. The Duke would never have approved of this, Sallie, and neither do I."

I'm still of two minds about the article and I wonder if Cecil's right. Or if he's living in the past. "I'm sorry, Cecil, but when I asked you to be my adviser, you said you didn't have it in you." I hope that came out gentle.

"Sallie's turning to me for advice now," Rawley says. "And, again no disrespect, but times are changing, new opportunities coming up all the time, and in the last few months Sallie and me, we've been making a heck of a lot more money than you and the Duke ever did."

"Sallie, you're right," Cecil says. "I'm not your adviser. I regret that. And I wish Tom had taken up your offer." He points at the newspaper. "So, you think this was a good idea?"

Back when I was growing up the Duke's name made its way into pretty much every issue of the *Gazette*. When the Finch River flooded, he congratulated the "soggy but brave volunteers" who built the dike. When a teacher retired, he thanked her for "thirty years of turning rascals into scholars." When a dirt road was paved, he called it "Claiborne County's pathway to the future." I loved reading the Duke's words, not only because he was my daddy, but because like most folks I felt better knowing the Duke was on top of all things big and small in Claiborne County. And now, I figure, everyone who reads this newspaper will know that Sallie Kincaid is on top of all things big and small in Claiborne County.

"Truth is, Cecil, Rawley's right. Times are changing. This is good for Claiborne County. Good for all of us. Lets the world know how we see things. I think the Duke would have loved it. We're going to frame that article and we're going to hang it out front where everyone can read it."

Cecil sinks back into his wheelchair. "Louise, I've said my piece. Take me home."

Louise pushes the wheelchair through the door. It bumps over the threshold, making Cecil's head bob weakly, and I feel a stab in my heart. I remember all those times I watched Cecil sitting next to the Duke, whispering in his ear, sometimes telling the Duke things he didn't want to hear, protecting him from himself. That's what Cecil was trying to do for me, but I told him he was wrong and sent him packing—and I wonder if I'm making a mistake, if I've lost my bearings, if I've gone astray and just let the last sensible man in Claiborne County roll out the door.

CHAPTER 45

WENDELL COOKE, THE SENIOR senator from Virginia, is speechify-
ing on the courthouse steps about the fall in farm prices and the rise in
the cost of living, about men not long out of war hopping freights and
filling city streets to seek jobs that aren't to be found, about strikes and
communists, about how each is caused by the other and how they'll
be the ruination of us all if we don't vote for him come November—
particularly us ladies now casting our own ballots.

I'm in the small crowd below him, wondering if the senator is
going to steer clear of me on account of Willard Smith's article, but
when he wraps up his speech, he comes down the steps and holds out
his hand. "I knew the Duke and I'm glad to meet his daughter," he says
then gives me a playful wink, like he's in on the joke. "I hear you're a
coming power in these parts. Think of running for office one of these
days—just not mine."

The people around us laugh, like the idea of a woman senator
is funny, and I laugh too. At the same time thinking, sooner or later
there will be one.

I feel a tug on my sleeve and turn to see a woman wearing pearls
at her throat and ears and around her shoulders there's a fox stole with
the critter biting its own tail. She has eyes the pale blue of a winter sky,
lipstick the color of ripe cherries, and a wide smile that lets you know
she's naughty and you can be, too.

"Sallie Kincaid, I'm Georgette Rheims," she says in a throaty
voice. "I've been reading all about you. My husband's one of Wendell's

biggest supporters and I tagged along just to meet you." Then she adds in a whisper, "I want to go along on one of your blockade runs."

I laugh. She squeezes my arm with a grip stronger than you'd expect from a lady wearing a fox stole. "I'm serious."

"We don't take passengers."

"Of course you don't. Make an exception."

"It's dangerous."

"That's why I want to go."

"I don't give joyrides. I'm a businesswoman."

"If it's business, name your price. My husband goes on his safaris. I can pay for an adventure, too."

"You are serious, aren't you?"

Her naughty smile comes back. "And I always get my way."

That night Georgette Rheims is beside me in the Lizzie. We're roaring through the dark countryside, headlights off, and she keeps glancing down at my pistol on the seat, then at the cars behind us.

After Georgette made her proposal, I telephoned Rawley, who was in Bluefield visiting family, and asked what he thought of letting this rich lady ride along with us to Roanoke. He said he'd heard how some society folk think blockade running is a great lark, so why not take the lady's cash. Besides, it never hurts to have friends in high places.

We're still in the valley when I see headlights in the rearview mirror. I swing into the oncoming lane, slow to let the convoy shoot by, and then swing back so we're in front of the car with the headlights.

"Trouble?" Georgette asks.

"We'll find out."

The other car gets close then pulls into the left lane to pass us. I swerve in front of it, and the driver honks and swings into the right lane. I swerve again and he bumps us from behind.

Georgette shrieks, I wrestle with the steering wheel, then the driver bumps us again.

We come to a tight bend. I slam on the brakes. The car behind us catches our rear fender and both cars spin sideways. I screech around and back into the other car, forcing its front wheels into a ditch, then I throw the Lizzie into forward, open up the throttle, and we rocket away.

Georgette bursts into laughter. She pounds the dashboard with her fists, holding her sides and stamping her feet on the floor, the laughter coming in gales that make her gasp for air.

"I almost wet my drawers," she says when she finally catches her breath. "No one will believe this. You must come to Richmond. You'll let them all know I'm not making this up."

I check the rearview mirror. The other car's headlights are fading in the distance. I don't tell Georgette the driver is Rawley. He wanted to make sure my rich-lady passenger got the thrills she paid for.

CHAPTER 46

THE SOUND OF THE telephone ringing downstairs wakes me. Gray light is seeping through the closed curtains and I wonder who's calling at this hour. Nell's room is at the back of the kitchen, next to the laundry room, and I hear her answering the phone before I even get out of bed. There's a pause and then she shouts up the stairs, "Sallie, you best come quick!"

I'm pushing the Lizzie to its limit, downshifting into turns and roaring out of them, holding the steering wheel with a vise-like grip, leaning stiff-necked into the windshield as if that's going to get me to town faster.

The Bonds. They bombed the Emporium. I can scarcely put the words together. But I have to stay calm.

This damned feud. At first, a lot of the boys were treating it all like a game, but then, two weeks ago, things turned deadly, as I feared they would, when the body of Shorty's mechanic Leroy was found lying in a stream, a bullet hole in his forehead. Three days later, Billy Bond's cousin P.J. turned up just as dead in a Webster County cornfield. And now this. It's not a feud, it's war. Anything goes.

Fighting clean is well and good if you're in the ring, the Duke liked to say, but if you're fighting for your life you don't play by any rules, you fight dirty, you hit back where it hurts the most, you kick them when they're down, you fight using everything you've got, you fight to win.

I cover the mile to Caywood in record time. Townsfolk are gathered in the street, the deputies holding them back. They look frightened and bewildered because people in these parts don't go around planting bombs that could kill innocent bystanders. That's what happens in the big cities.

The Emporium looks war-torn, its front wall blackened with soot, windows broken, and the porch roof dangling at a pitiful angle. So the bomb missed—that could have been on purpose—and the Emporium, the beating heart of the town, hasn't been destroyed, but it's maimed and scarred and the sight of it shakes me to my bones.

Rawley and Sheriff Earl come through the gaping doorway.

"How bad is it?" I ask.

"Storefront is a complete loss and all those windows got to be replaced," Rawley says.

"But inside it's not too bad," Sheriff Earl adds. "Shelves down, inventory scattered, a lot of broken glass. Could have been much worse."

"We all know who did it and those sons of bitches are going to pay," Rawley adds, his blood clearly up.

"You need guards," Sheriff Earl says. "Around the clock. One here. One at the house."

"Maybe I should move in," Rawley says.

"Good," I say.

"People will talk," Sheriff Earl says.

"Let them."

"The Bonds have upped the stakes again," Rawley says, "so now we do, too."

Up the stakes. Like a poker game—only we're playing for our lives here. Poker's never been my game. I'm no good at bluffing and I hold on to a losing hand because I hate to fold even when I know I should. But Rawley's right. And I'm in. "How?" I ask. "The Bonds have guards all around that clubhouse of theirs."

"Sallie, I told you I could come up with a plan in the heat of battle," Rawley says. "And I got us a plan."

* * *

She's a pretty thing, yellow as a buttercup, the upper and lower wings held fast by wooden braces and crisscrossing wire struts that glint in the early light. She's known as a Jenny, Rawley told me, she's what won the war for us, and if you can fly her you can fly anything. The man tinkering with the engine is Al Cane, a daredevil pilot who fought in the skies over France alongside Rawley and now does loop de loops at county fairs and gives people rides for a dollar a pop. Al agreed to rent us the plane because he and Rawley were war buddies, but he told Rawley that if anything happened to his Jenny he'd feed us both into the propeller.

Dawn is the best time to fly, says Rawley, the air is calmest then—something to do with relative temperatures, Eddie could explain it—so just as the sun is starting to light up the sky, we climb onto the Jenny's lower wing, and I crawl into the front seat while Rawley gets into the rear. I've never seen an airplane up close. It's made of canvas and seems flimsy as all heck. The cockpit is snug—not a lot of wiggle room—and I study the dials and gauges and switches on the instrument panel. I could probably figure out what they're for, but not now. I don't need to know. I'm the bombardier.

I carefully tuck the bombs at my feet. Rawley and I made them last night, wrapping sticks of dynamite around bottles of nitroglycerin and binding them together with copper wire. At first Rawley wanted Sheriff Earl to go with him, but there was no way I was going to pass up a chance to fly in an airplane. Besides, this is my battle and I'm going to be the one who fights it.

I'm not looking to kill anyone, but I have to let the Bonds know that I can and I will if I'm pushed to it. Like I told Mattie, I've never picked a fight in my life, but if someone comes at me I won't back down. Still, the thought of what we're about to do gives me a chill, even though I'm wearing thick gloves, a leather helmet, and a lined jumpsuit Al loaned me. Hit them, Sallie, I hear the Duke say, hit them where it hurts the most, fight to win.

I pull the goggles down over my eyes, Al grabs the wooden propeller and spins it. The engine sputters and coughs. He spins it again. Sputter. Cough. On the third try it roars to life and I feel the whole plane throbbing in the soles of my feet and the seat of my pants.

The Jenny's nose swings to the left, her tail to the right, so that we're facing a wide cow pasture. The roaring gets louder, the throbbing stronger, and she pulls forward, bumping, picking up speed, faster, faster, then the bumping stops and the ground falls away beneath us. Now we're climbing into the dawn light, the engine roaring and smoking right in front of me, the wind shrieking through struts and wires, but the noise is so loud and constant that I pretty much stop hearing it and I feel almost weightless, like a bubble floating to the surface.

Rawley circles the pasture. Down below, Al is watching us. I wave wildly and he gives back a weak wave, probably wondering if he made a terrible mistake and will never see his Jenny again.

We head west and I look down at the patchwork of rolling Virginia countryside—the white farmhouses and red barns tiny as matchboxes, the rusting silos, the black Aberdeen-Angus grazing in pastures, the stubby rows of cut corn curving along the slope of the land, the dark groves of evergreens climbing up to the blue-gray mountains in the distance, the creeks coming out of those mountains, twisting through mowed hayfields like shiny silver ribbons—and the joy and awe that swell up inside me almost make me forget the misgivings I have about our plan to drop bombs on the Bond brothers.

Rawley banks north and we come to Claiborne County. I'm longing to fly over Caywood—maybe swoop down close enough to give people on the streets a wave, let them see we're not taking this lying down—but the town's off to the east, and we have business to tend to in the west.

We reach Finch River Road and follow it across the mountains into Webster County. From up here, the clear-cut forest looks jagged and raw, like an unhealed scar. Before I know it, we're over Cedar Valley and then Long Shade itself. Thin white smoke rises from the chimney of the clubhouse, a few cars are parked alongside the road, and a few more are out back near the chicken coop but there is not a soul in sight. I'll aim to drop the bomb squarely in the front yard.

I turn my head to look at Rawley and he gives me a thumbs-up. I duck into the cockpit, pull off my gloves, and hold the first bomb between my knees. I strike a match, but as soon as it stops flaring the darned wind snuffs it out. Got to be quick. I light another match and this time I get the fuse sparkling. Now I give Rawley a thumbs-up, he drops one wing, and we go into a dive. The clubhouse comes barreling up at us and before I know it, the roof is so close I can see the moss on the shingles. Then, just as Rawley pulls back on the stick, I hurl the bomb.

We're climbing now, steeply, the engine screaming, and I'm thrown against the back of my seat. I twist around and look down. But there's no loud boom, no exploding fireball. There's nothing. Our bomb was a dud.

A few men run out of the house, see us, then run back inside.

Rawley eases up on the stick and the plane levels off. I light another fuse and we dive a second time. The house comes rushing up, I wait until I'm close enough to see those mossy shingles again and I hold the bomb out. Even before it leaves my hand, I feel it coming apart. We didn't wrap the copper wire tight enough. Another dud.

Men come running out of the house again, this time with guns. Rawley throws the Jenny into another climb that makes the engine scream, then levels off. I light the third fuse and we turn in to our final dive.

We're heading right at the men in the yard. They start shooting at us. Rawley wobbles the rudder and the wing flaps to dodge the bullets and that throws me to the side so I'm off-balance when I toss the last bomb. Rawley banks sharply and I turn back to see one of the parked cars burst into flames and smoke, then roll over. No one was in that car. That's what I think. What I hope.

The men keep blasting furiously at us, but they grow smaller and smaller as we fly away.

*   *   *

The Jenny's wheels all but clip the treetops as we glide down into the cow pasture. Al Cane runs toward us waving, delighted to see his plane back safe. We touch the ground with a gentle jolt and bounce along the grass.

I raise my arms, fists clenched. We did it. We defied gravity, we defied death, and we defied the Bonds. All in one morning.

Rawley cuts the engine. Silence. I turn around to look at him. He's grinning, glowing like a jack-o'-lantern. I am too. All of a sudden, we both burst into laughter.

I climb out of the Jenny and my feet hit the solid, steady earth just as Al reaches us. He frowns and sticks his finger into a couple of bullet holes in the fuselage, but I give him an extra forty to cover the repairs. Rawley and I walk back to the Lizzie—I'm half-skipping like a schoolgirl, feeling pretty much the way I did after my first ride on the Defiance Coaster—and we're talking about the duds, about that third dive, about dropping the bomb while the Bonds were firing right at us, about how it will be a heck of a long time before those Bond brothers forget the sight of that yellow Jenny hurtling down at them.

"Who's the li'l sis now?" Rawley hollers at the sky. "Who's the li'l sis now?"

I have trouble starting the Lizzie because I'm laughing so hard, then I stop laughing and look at Rawley. He stops laughing, too, and then he leans over and kisses me. On the mouth. His mouth stays on mine, and it's all wetter than I thought it would be, wet and slippery, warm too, and I start returning his kiss with a dizzy, drunken craziness because I had no idea it would feel like this, no idea that I would want it this much. Then I pull back.

"Let's go home," I whisper.

He nods.

We don't say much on the way back. When we get to the Big

House, no one's outside. I drive past it, up to the carriage house, and slide open the heavy doors.

I take Rawley by the hand and lead him to the old tack room.

"Well, what did you think?"

"No one can know."

"Of course."

"Not a word. Or a hint. Or a look or anything."

"I promise."

"And this doesn't change anything."

"Of course not. So what did you think?"

"It was fun."

"Fun?"

"Yeah. Real fun."

"Anything else?"

"Not as . . ."

"As what?"

"Not as . . . awkward as I thought it would be."

"Nothing awkward about it."

"But what happens next could get awkward."

"We'll keep it simple. So, fun? That's all?"

"Fun. But no one can know."

CHAPTER 47

CARPENTERS ARE CLAMBERING ALONG the spindly scaffolding in front of the Emporium. Rawley and I are watching them patch her up and bring her back to life, this store that was my favorite place on earth when I was a girl. The carpenters have pulled down what remained of the porch, replaced glass, built a makeshift staircase of raw lumber, and we're back in business, customers ducking cautiously when they scurry in and out beneath the scaffolding.

"It looks naked without the porch," I say.

Rawley grins. "Some things look better naked."

"Watch yourself."

He winks at me.

Rawley has always been cocksure, but ever since that first time together he's become downright reckless. Truth be told, I have too.

After our bombing run, Rawley took to staying in the stone wing as a guard. The second night he was there, when I was getting ready for bed, I heard Aunt Faye shut her door and I couldn't let go of the thought that—if I wanted to—I could slip downstairs, cross into the stone wing, and go up to Rawley's room. And that was what I did—making sure that Rawley took precautions, like before, so I didn't have to worry about getting in a family way like all these unmarried women who end up giving away their babies. I told myself just this one more time, but of course, it happened again. Then again, and I've been sneaking over to the stone wing every night like some prowler.

During the day I do my best to act professional and Rawley tries to do the same, but sometimes he can't quite wipe that little smile from the corner of his mouth and there's a twinkle in his eye, the sense of a shared secret—and then I'll see someone else watching us and I can tell that it really isn't a secret at all, that people know something is going on, even if they don't know exactly what.

Russell Hunt, the head carpenter, jumps off the scaffolding and walks over, shoving his hammer into his belt. "Miss Kincaid, you decided how you want the storefront to look yet?"

How I want the Emporium to look. It's a bigger question than I'd have guessed. I'd thought that I would make it look the same as it used to—rebuild as it was, make folks feel that nothing has changed. But a lot has changed. And maybe when we lose something, that's our chance to replace it with something better.

"I haven't had time to think about it," I say.

"We could make it more modern," Rawley offers. "Like the stores in Roanoke. Maybe get one of those revolving doors. We can afford it."

Is that what I want? Is that what the people in Claiborne County want?

"Put your own stamp on it," Rawley continues. "It's your store now."

It's mine, but it's not. The Emporium has to be loved by the people who shop here. They have to trust the store. I want it to feel up-to-date, but not so much that they feel left behind. I bought a picture book of Roanoke and I want to take a good look at the photographs of the stores, figure whether the folks of Claiborne County would feel welcome going inside such hifalutin buildings. "I'll let you know tomorrow," I tell Russell.

Back at the Big House, I'm in the library thumbing through the book—these places are so very fancy—when I feel Rawley's hands slip around my waist. Then he puts his face in the crook of my neck and I feel his heat, the heat that makes my knees—and my common sense—get all wobbly. But not here. Not now. Nell could peek through a window. Grace could come crawling down the hall, Aunt Faye right behind her. I pull at Rawley's hands but he won't let go.

"You're going to put your stamp on something, I want to do the same," he says. "Let's get married."

My chest tightens. A marriage proposal is supposed to be romantic, supposed to make a woman feel all lovey-dovey, but Rawley's still got me in his arms and I can't breathe. I'm trapped. I push him away, hard. He lets go, but he's standing between me and the door, the same door the Duke was blocking when Mama got killed. I can't get away. I look around and see the Colonel's sword on the mantel. The sight of that sword—the sword that got Mama killed—while standing in the room where she died and listening to a man press me to marry him, it all sets off something dark inside me.

I reach for the sword—I've never touched it before, have always been leery of it—and pull it out of the scabbard. It feels good in my hand, light and balanced, like it's a part of my arm. No one's going to trap me.

"Ever see this?" I ask.

"I know what it is."

"The story is that Mama drew it on the Duke. Like this." I raise the sword and without thinking I swing it through the air above Rawley's head. He ducks and takes a step back.

"Sallie, have you lost your goddamned mind?"

"Maybe it's true." I can't help myself. I swing the sword again. "Maybe she did try to kill him. Like this." I swing the sword once more. "Maybe he deserved it."

"Give me that damned thing." Rawley holds out his hands and just like that whatever it was that had ahold of me lets go and I'm myself again and Rawley's himself again—a man who asked me to marry him, not a man out to trap me—but it all leaves me limp as a wet rag. I hand him the sword.

"Sorry. I don't know what came over me."

"Sallie, did you hear me just ask you to marry me?"

"Sure did."

"And?"

"There's so much going on right now."

"All the more reason."

"I like things the way they are."

"I don't." Rawley slides the sword into its scabbard and puts it back on the mantel. "People have figured it out, Sal. I can see it in their eyes. I'm sick of sneaking around like I'm doing something wrong. We can have us the finest wedding Claiborne County has ever seen. Or we can just run off to Roanoke."

"I have to think about it."

"What is there to think about?"

A lot. There's a lot to think about. A lot to talk about. Children. Is he one of those men who has to have a son? And what if I don't give him a son? And what if some pretty young woman comes along and promises she will? Then what? We know all about getting sweet and hot and sticky, Rawley and me, but what do we know about being husband and wife? About taking vows and keeping them?

But all I say is, "A lot."

Chapter 48

Rawley's fingernails are clean for a change. I like a man with grease under his fingernails, you know that he spends time beneath the hood of a car, but Rawley looks pretty danged good cleaned up, too. He's wearing a black bow tie and a black jacket with shiny lapels. I'm decked out too, more than I've ever been, and I tug at the silver satin gown Aunt Faye made me. The darned thing is so tight you can count my ribs.

"I look like a hood ornament in this dress."

"You look so good you ought to be illegal. I'm having trouble keeping my eyes on the road."

We're in the Packard, on our way to Georgette Rheims's New Year's Eve party and Rawley's behind the wheel. Ever since that crazy stunt with the sword, I've been trying to be a little more proper, and letting the man drive is one way of doing it.

I finger Mama's moonstone necklace, wondering what Georgette will make of Rawley. She invited me to this party saying she wants to introduce me to some eligible men, but I asked if I could bring a fellow who wants me to marry him. Funny that I'd tell Georgette something I've told no one in Caywood. I figure I can trust her opinion, seeing as how she doesn't have a horse in this race.

"Who is this fellow?" she asked. "What does he do for a living?"

"A mountain boy from Bluefield. Then a pilot in the war. Now he works for me, that is, with me."

"I see." Then she added, "Bring him. I can size up a man by the time he says hello."

We get to Richmond with its cobblestone streets and glowing cast-iron streetlamps, then we turn onto Monument Avenue, passing statues of generals who lost the war but are posed like they won it. Georgette's house is grand as a fine hotel, with a steep roof, turrets, gables, gargoyles, every window blazing with electric light. Rawley lets out that long, low whistle of his. I know how he feels. I thought Roanoke was a big, fancy city, but it doesn't have houses like this. I've heard that the snoots in Richmond don't even drink much moonshine, favoring the branded stuff smuggled in from those islands off Florida.

Inside, a line of guests snakes across the black-and-white marble hallway. Georgette is welcoming them, and beside her stands a burly man with a five o'clock shadow who looks both bored and amused. Must be her husband. Next to Georgette, a little red-eyed monkey chatters nervously and pulls at the gold chain around his neck. Behind him, a lime-green parrot sits in a gold birdcage made to look just like Georgette's house. I keep expecting the parrot to say something clever, but all it does is shriek.

When we get to the front of the line, Rawley makes a show of bending down and kissing Georgette's hand.

"What a handsome couple," she says. "Sallie, meet my husband, Gustav Rheims, the smartest lawyer in Virginia."

"Who doesn't practice law." He smiles and reaches out. He grips harder than most men do when shaking a woman's hand, but I grip back every bit as hard and he seems to like that. "Call me Gus."

"He looks for loopholes," Georgette says.

"Suckers obey the laws. Crooks break the laws. Smart people find the loopholes in the laws."

"Obey, break, get around—I don't pay much mind to that sort of fine sifting," I say. "Just do what needs to be done."

Gus tilts his head and eyes me with interest.

"Isn't she marvelous, Gus?" Georgette asks. "I told you you'd like her."

"Heard you and my gal Sallie had quite the wild ride," Rawley says to Georgette. "Quite the pants pisser."

"We did indeed."

"Heard you had a real hang-tough on your tail." Rawley can barely hide his grin.

"He was no match for Sallie."

"Ain't a lot out there who are." Rawley reaches out to shake Gus's hand.

"You must be the motorman," Gus says.

Rawley's grin disappears.

"He's my partner," I say. Looks like Georgette's husband is one of those men who just can't help themselves, got to test other men, see who's top dog.

"My apologies," Gus says, still smiling.

"Everyone sticks his foot in a pile from time to time." Rawley slaps Gus on the arm.

As we walk away, Rawley says, "Your friend's oversized penguin of a husband just insulted me."

"Don't worry. You gave as good as you got."

We go from the hall into a long room filled with gold-framed oil paintings. There's one big as a barn door of Roman soldiers carrying off plump, naked women. There are also gold eagles mounted on wall mirrors, gold cupids leaning on clocks, and gold women holding up marble tabletops, their gold breasts boldly popping out of their gold Greek gowns. Back in Claiborne County, I'm what you'd call rich. I'm not a Vanderbilt, but I do have a flush toilet, I pay the bills on time, I never go to bed hungry unless I'm too tired to eat, and when my shoes get holes in them, I buy new ones. I have a maid, for crying out loud. A Packard. That's rich. Or so I thought. Until I took a gander at all this. Maybe I should have stayed in Claiborne County and gone on thinking I was rich. But I'd never laid eyes on anyone like Georgette, and I wanted to see how she lives, wanted to know if I'd envy her life, or resent it, or simply feel out of place. And truth be told, I feel all those. All at once.

Open doors lead to a back garden where there's a heated pool house with a blue cement swimming pool, all lit up with underwater bulbs that make the water glow. On the far side, a band is playing brassy tunes and all around us, men and women are dancing, not buck stepping or flatfooting or jigging the way we do in Claiborne County, but flapping their elbows and kicking out their feet like they have ants in their pants.

Georgette comes in and introduces us to her guests, going on about our daring and decidedly illegal run through the wild mountains in the dark of night. The men are in tuxedos, the women are a blur of shimmering silks and mincy little shoes, with painted faces and pouty lips, soft voices and softer hands that they rest limply in mine. They exchange quick glances, each checking the other's reaction to me. The men chuckle and the women titter.

"Your friends are looking at me like I just fell off a turnip truck," I whisper to Georgette. She leans in close and I can smell her perfume. Not delicate like Jane's lilac, but spicy and wild, like witch alder.

"They find you fascinating," she whispers back. "You'll have them eating out of your hand in no time."

"I think I scare them."

"They scare easily. I don't. That's why we're alike. You and me. We're both fearless."

She's got it wrong. I'm not fearless. Just afraid of different things than most people.

Georgette seats me next to Gus at one of the tables flanking the swimming pool, then sits down beside Rawley. Gus introduces the weak-chinned woman across from me as Countess Something-or-other from Budapest.

"A title in search of a bank account," whispers the man on my right, a flush-faced fellow with a pouty lower lip and pudgy hands. He tells me he's Barclay Farmington of the Albemarle Farmingtons, and I figure that he's one of those eligible bachelors Georgette wants me to meet.

I start to introduce myself, but he cuts me off. "I know who you are." He points an unsteady finger at me. "The Queen of the Kincaid Rumrunners."

"Not a name I use."

He lifts a bottle of fancy scotch whiskey that he has tucked between his feet, fills his glass and drains it, and I realize that Barclay Farmington of the Albemarle Farmingtons is completely soused.

"The Kincaid Rumrunners," he says. "Quite the title for a bunch of hillbillies with shotguns."

"Careful, mister," I say. "Us hillbillies are easily provoked."

"So I hear. Feuding. Throwing bombs."

"A grown man who can't hold his drink shouldn't—"

I'm interrupted by a meaty hand on my arm.

"Ignore him," Gus says in a low voice. "The Farmington money has been in the family so long that they like to pretend they didn't swindle anyone to get it."

"Jellied salmon," a waiter announces and places a plate in front of me.

"From what I hear, Miss Kincaid," Gus says as he ties his starched white napkin around his neck, "when you're not endangering my wife's life, you're pretty good at what you do. Minding the family business, as you so discreetly put it in that interview."

"I reckon I'm doing all right. I can afford salt for the beans now— but not paintings of Roman soldiers carrying off naked ladies."

"Not yet." He takes a sip of wine. "We're a lot alike, Sallie, you and me."

"Georgette just told me she and I are alike."

Gus shakes his head. "You're not alike. I love Georgette, but she's easily bored. That's why she has her thrills. And her pets. You may drive like the devil, Sallie, but you're not a thrill seeker. I know all about your years washing laundry in that little town."

My face flushes. "How do you know that?"

"I'm a lawyer. I perform due diligence on the people my wife is interested in. Don't be coy, Miss Kincaid. I was a runner for a numbers racket when I was still in knee pants. We both grew up hungry. And when you grow up hungry, you're always hungry." He raises his wineglass. "To the hunger."

At the other side of the table, Georgette raises her glass and calls out, "To satisfying the hunger."

Then the countess starts going on about the last days of the Hapsburgs and batting her eyes at Barclay Farmington, who's talking about the money to be made in cattle futures if you have the stomach for it. Rawley is telling Georgette stories about dogfights in France. Georgette is sitting close to him, very close, resting her chin on one hand and gazing at him, then out of nowhere she drops the other hand below the table and Rawley jerks back, looking startled, and as soon as I realize what happened I want to hurl my plate of jellied salmon at Georgette. Testing him. But then Rawley lets out a laugh and he reaches under the table and Georgette jerks back. She also laughs and gives him a playful smack across the cheek. That's Rawley. Thinking under fire.

If Gus has noticed any of this, he doesn't let on. Georgette looks across the table and winks at me. The waiters start clearing the plates, Georgette stands up, beckons me with her finger, and I follow her outside.

"Did you just do what I think you did?" I ask.

"I told you I'd size him up." She laughs, deep and throaty. "And he sized me up. All in good fun." She puts her arm around my waist. "Come with me."

Georgette leads me into the mansion and up to the second floor. "Here's my necessary room." She opens the door to a bathroom the size of a parlor. The walls are tiled with mosaics of palm trees and pyramids, the vaulted blue ceiling is inlaid with gold stars, and the tub is so deep and wide you could practically swim in it. In Hatfield, Aunt Faye and I went all winter without a bath, toting water from the well into a house that was so danged cold we'd wash our hands and faces but not our hair or privates, and I'm still haunted by the feeling of growing up unclean. Rank and greasy. With a bathroom like this, I could soak and scrub for hours until I finally got clean—absolutely, completely, truly clean.

The bathroom has a second door and we go through it into

Georgette's dressing room, where she kicks off her shoes and starts unfastening the buttons of her beaded gold dress.

"Georgette, I'm glad you and Rawley hit it off," I say, "but—"

"He's handsome." She lets the dress fall to the floor. "But you can do a lot better." She pulls off her silk stockings and garter belt, slips her chemise over her head, and stands there, four paces away from me, wearing nothing but her skimpy silk drawers.

Do all rich city swells act like this? Shameless. Back in that little house in Hatfield, Aunt Faye and I worked so hard to respect each other's privacy, knocking on the privy, turning away when we changed clothes. I keep my gaze locked into Georgette's pale blue eyes but I can't help noticing small breasts and dark nipples.

"You're his meal ticket," she adds.

"Watch what you say, Georgette."

"You don't want to be someone's meal ticket, my little pigeon. You want someone who's going to be your meal ticket."

"I don't need any damned meal ticket."

"Every woman should marry up—if she can. And if she wants, she can keep a man on the side. A man like Rawley. After she comes to an arrangement."

"An arrangement? That's what you have?"

"Every marriage is an arrangement." Georgette slips her thumbs into her drawers and bends over, sliding them down until they're a white silk puddle at her feet. She steps out of them and stands there naked, like she is waiting for me to size her up. I look away, look at the rows of dresses and gowns and blouses, at the shelves of hats and gloves and shoes, but there are full-length mirrors everywhere and I see Georgette in all of them—the pale shoulders, the tiny waist and curving hips, the flaunted privates. "Any man you marry should bring you something—money, position, title. Rawley brings you nothing. I sat you next to Barclay Farmington. His family has ten thousand acres in Albemarle County."

"He's a complete jackass. And a sloppy drunk. If Barclay Farmington's what's out there, I'm marrying Rawley."

"So Barclay didn't strike your fancy. There are others. Put yourself on the market. See what you can get."

"That sounds an awful lot like whoring."

Georgette laughs her throaty laugh again. "Every woman has her price." She walks back into her bathroom. But she leaves the door open and calls out, "Your mother did."

How does Mama figure into this talk? I glance around and in one of the mirrors catch sight of myself looking like a floozy in this silver dress. "Why would you know the least thing about my mama?"

"Gus always does his due diligence." I hear the sound of tinkling. The woman is taking a pee while talking about my mama. "Anyone who asks around about Duke Kincaid and his daughter Sallie hears about your mother. Annie Kincaid had an arrangement, but she didn't stick to it. That's why things ended badly for her."

"You're saying it was her fault?"

"Your mother made a promise to the Duke and she didn't keep it. Whose fault was that?"

The toilet flushes. Georgette comes through the doorway, her privates still flaunted, but now all I see is her face—that smiling red mouth and those pale blue eyes—and I feel a powerful urge to slap that face or punch it. Mama deserves a better defense than that, but I've been caught off guard and I can't think what that defense might be, so I just stand there, staring dumbly at Georgette as she shimmies into a sleek white bathing suit that shows a lot of leg.

"It's almost midnight," she says gaily, then slips on a white silk robe and knots the sash. "Time to welcome in nineteen twenty-two."

"Why did you say all this?" I finally ask.

"I'm doing you a favor, pigeon. Most women don't learn from their mothers' mistakes. They repeat those mistakes. I want better for you."

Can she possibly mean that? I'm still at a loss for words, feeling half-witted and foolish, and I follow Georgette back to the pool house like a kicked but loyal dog. Inside, I scan the crowd for Rawley but there are so many black-haired men in black jackets that I can't spot him.

Georgette steps up on the diving board then drops the robe. Men and women cheer and clap, hoot and whistle while Georgette stands there, hands on her hips, soaking it all up. Then she sashays to the end of the diving board and stretches her arms high above her head. Gus takes out a pocket watch and, in that booming voice of his, starts counting down the seconds. Guests join in and when they reach "One" they shout, "Happy New Year!" and a butler hits a gong and Georgette bounces high off the board, spreads her arms in a perfect swan dive, and knifes into the water, her legs so straight she barely makes a splash.

Gus lumbers over to the edge of the pool and, still wearing his dinner jacket, jumps in with his legs tucked, hitting the water rump first with a splash so big and violent it startles me and for an instant I see the Duke hitting the lake—but around the pool, everyone's laughing and a couple of men peel off their jackets and dive in, then a curly-haired woman strips down to her lacy little underclothes and jumps in still wearing her tiara. After that, everyone goes wild, some ripping off their clothes as they dash to the pool, others making the leap in their tuxedos and gowns.

I'm usually game for just about anything, but not tonight, not after my talk with Georgette, and I'm standing at the edge of the pool, watching all those rich ninnies ruining their clothes frolicking in the churning water when I feel a pair of hands on my back. They shove me hard, off balance, out over the water, I'm going in, and I twist around as I fall and see the doughy, drunken, laughing face of Barclay Farmington.

I hit the surface with a smack, then I'm sinking, my nose and mouth filling with warm pool water. I try to kick and claw my way back up, but this darned satin dress, it's tight around my legs, and the fabric, it's waterlogged, heavy, it's weighing me down. Down and down, until I feel my high-heeled shoes hit something hard, the pool bottom. I try to kick the shoes off but they're buckled too tight. I wrench my arms around, got to unhook this damned dress, but I can't reach the back. My lungs are burning. I have only a few seconds left before I start taking in water. Above me, in the pool's blue glow, I can make out swirling arms and legs, drunken guests horsing around. I grab ahold of a man's leg, but he thinks I'm playing, kicks me in the face, and I lose the last of my air. I am choking. Drowning. Everything is a blur. I hear a muffled explosion, then the water is filled with tiny bubbles, a shape, someone has dived in, is swimming down toward me.

Rawley.

Chapter 49

I RECKON THERE'S NOTHING more blissful than feeling warm and snug when it's freezing cold outside. The radiator is hissing and split oak logs are blazing away in the library fireplace. Rawley will be here any minute and I sit down at the desk and look through the window for him. The sky is pale and heavy. Snow is on the way. The killing frost came early this year and the New Year brought in a brutal cold front. The creeks are edged with ice, the reeds coated with whiskery white frost, and the ponds frozen solid enough to fool you into thinking you can walk on them. It's going to get colder, or so say the old-timers who read the rings around the moon and the thickness of tree bark. But we'll make it through. The people of Claiborne County are taken care of.

Every town in the county has its own little mayor, the unelected man who solves whatever problems he can before people turn to me, and Rawley and I paid a call on those mayors to get the names of folk—the old, the infirm, the crippled veterans, and the young war widows—who will struggle to get through the winter. We put split wood in their woodsheds, canned goods in their cupboards, and wool coats on their young ones.

We could do all that because of the money we make running whiskey into Roanoke, and that's Rawley's doing. It's true I'm paying Rawley's salary, but I'm not Rawley's meal ticket, as Georgette put it. He's not some freeloader. We're partners. And that's why when he pulled me half-drowned out of Georgette's pool and wrapped his jacket around me, I whispered to him, "Get me the hell out of here and I'll marry you."

That pool. Mama's moonstone necklace is lying at the bottom of it, I'm sure of that. Rawley and I were already on the road when I reached up to touch the necklace, but it was gone. Must have come off when I was thrashing around in the water. Rawley wanted to go back and look for it but I said no. Returning to that vile place, diving into the water to search for it while Gus and Georgette and Barclay Farmington and all their guests looked on smirking and tittering about it all—that was out of the question.

Four weeks have passed since the party. Almost every day I tell myself I'll call Georgette to see if she's found the necklace but I keep putting it off. I'm not afraid of the Bonds or Glen Lowe's deputies or federal agents chasing me through the dark night, so why have I gone yellow when it comes to this rich lady?

I can't let her get the best of me. I just can't. I reach for the telephone. By the time I'm patched through my palms are sweaty.

"Sallie Kincaid!" Georgette sounds downright thrilled to hear from me.

"I called to thank you for inviting us to your marvelous party." Did that sound as phony to her as it did to me?

"You left before the real fun began."

"We had a long drive back." That's another thing I do around Georgette. Make mealymouthed excuses, duck from telling the truth. "Please thank Gus as well."

"Certainly. And your Mr. Riley. Have you made a decision?"

"Rawley. I'm marrying him." Finally, something simple and true.

"The motorman."

"Georgette, he's not—"

"Well, you do make a striking couple. You'll be noticed wherever you go. That counts for something. But don't forget, my pigeon, every marriage is an arrangement."

"So you said." I can't beat Georgette at her game. I have to stop trying and get to the point of my call. "One more thing, Georgette.

When I ended up in your pool that night, I lost my necklace. A moonstone necklace."

"After a party like that I always have a basket full of goodies people leave behind, but I don't recall any moonstone necklace. How about a splendid pair of marcasite earrings?"

"The necklace means a lot to me. The Duke gave it to—" I catch myself. I stupidly blurted that out, but I don't want to say one word about Mama. If I do, I might not be able to stop myself from telling Georgette what I really think of her, of her and her so-called arrangements and her chained monkey and her snooty friends and her naked poses and her smug advice, and that's not going to help get the necklace back.

"Then I shall look high and low for it."

"Thank you."

"And we must get together again, Sallie. Soon."

"I'd love that." One final phony lie.

I hang up, certain I'll never see Georgette again. Or Mama's necklace.

I'm still staring at the telephone when Rawley comes in toting a hefty-looking cardboard box.

"Those tile samples you ordered."

I tell him about my talk with Georgette.

"She and her overstuffed penguin of a husband can kiss my hillbilly ass. We got other things to think about. Sallie, it's time to let the good folk of Claiborne County know we're getting hitched."

"There's too much unfinished business right now."

"We'll take care of it all, me and you, as husband and wife. Let's put an announcement in the *Gazette*."

"Then you'd have to move out. It wouldn't look right, a woman living in the same house as her intended. We could just slip off to Roanoke, go to City Hall like you suggested, and come back married."

"As long as I can bring Ma."

"I'm looking forward to meeting that woman. And I'll bring Aunt Faye."

"Let's do it then."

"Soon as we get a break in the weather."

Rawley squeezes my shoulder. "I'm heading out again, to the depot. That shipment of yeast and sugar is due in."

I watch my intended close the door. That phone call with Georgette put me out of sorts and talking with Rawley about getting hitched doesn't make me feel any better. Maybe it's just cold feet. But there's something else. If I'm going to marry Rawley I'm going to have to call Tom in Georgetown, tell him about the plans. He'll think that when I told him I never wanted to get married, I meant I never wanted to marry him. That's going to hurt Tom, a man who's only ever been good to me, but there's no way around it.

I cut open the cardboard box with my pocketknife and lift out the tiles. They come in squares, rectangles, and hexagons and the colors have fancy names like cerulean blue and parrot green and blood orange.

I'm bringing the Big House into the twentieth century. There are two bathrooms, one under the stairs on the first floor and another built in a closet on the second floor. They were a source of envy when the Duke installed them—first indoor bathrooms in the county—and they're downright grand compared to our outhouse in Hatfield—where I froze my rump in the winter and fought off green flies in the summer—but they're cramped and stuffy, dark and windowless, and you still have to tote the hot water from the cookstove. So I'm turning Jane's old boudoir into a bathroom.

Looking at these tiles, however, I get to wondering if the whole idea of a newfangled bathroom is vanity, pure and simple—after all, a bathroom is a place to get in, do your business, then get out, not to loll around pampering yourself. But then I find a tile that's a simple soft white—the color of cream. Clean. Like I want to feel when I wash up after a long day.

There's a knock on the door and Aunt Faye leans into the library.

"Sal, hon, I got to talk—"

"What do you think?" I hold up the cream-colored tile.

She barely glances at it. "Real nice. But I got to talk to you. We do. Nell and me, that is."

She opens the door wider and there's Nell, standing behind her.

"Only if Nell tells me if she likes this color."

Nell has a good eye and strong opinions and I expect her to be forthright. Instead, she's staring at her feet. Something's wrong.

"I'm going to just come out and say it." Aunt Faye takes a deep breath. "Nell's in a family way."

"Oh Lord. Nell?"

She nods, still looking at the floor, her red-knuckled fingers gripping her strong arms.

Poor Nell. She's terrified. How long has she been living with this secret? "Don't worry, Nell. We'll make this right. Who's the daddy?"

Nell bites her lip. She finally looks up, but turns to Aunt Faye, not me.

"You do know who the daddy is, don't you?" It comes out sharper than I mean for it to.

"Yes, ma'am," Nell says, clearly insulted, then adds, "There was only one."

"Well, then who is it?"

Aunt Faye cuts in. "That's where it gets a little . . . sticky."

"Oh, dear," I say. "He's married."

"No, ma'am." Nell shakes her head.

"That's a relief. So, let me ask again, who is it?"

"You see," Aunt Faye begins, "back when it happened—"

"Just tell me who the daddy is."

"Rawley," Aunt Faye says in a small voice.

"Rawley?" I stand up so fast and hard that I knock over the chair. "You've been with Rawley?"

"It happened only the one time." Nell finally looks up at me. "Back in September. Miss Faye said you said you wasn't interested in him."

I see Nell's face, it's all I can see, her eyes filled with hurt and shame, and I hear her words, but mostly what I hear is the blood roaring in my head and I'm not thinking, I go wild, like a snarling, wounded animal, charging around the desk, slapping the face of this woman who betrayed me—and she just takes it, head bowed, so I slap her again, and now she's crouching down, holding up her hands to protect herself, so I smack those hands, screaming that I gave her a job, I gave her a place to live, I trusted her, and this is how she repays me.

Aunt Faye is pulling at my arm, yelling at me to stop. "For pity's sake, Sallie, have mercy on the girl. It was him that come on to her."

"And she couldn't say no?" I'm still screaming. I knock Aunt Faye's hands away. "My own kin? My own cousin?"

"Please, Sallie, get ahold of yourself." Aunt Faye's voice is firm. "It wasn't Nell's fault. And she's not your cousin. She's your sister."

Sister? Is that some sort of a joke, some sort of trick meant to spin my head around? "What did you say?"

"Nell is your half sister."

That couldn't possibly be true. Could it? I stare at Aunt Faye, trying to make sense of what she just said, then look down at Nell, cowering and trembling, her face wet with tears, her hair pulled out of the tidy little bun she always keeps it in. "Mama had a baby before me?"

"No, Sallie." Aunt Faye straightens her shoulders and holds up her chin. "I did. Nell is mine."

"But that makes her my cousin and you said—"

"Nell is also the Duke's daughter."

It's like Aunt Faye's words open a dark, gaping hole in front of me and I feel I'm about to fall into it so I grab the edge of the desk to keep from going down.

Nell is trying to stifle her sobs, pushing the loose hair off her face, wiping at her runny nose and her pink, teary eyes. I look back and forth between her and Aunt Faye, then around the room for something solid and true, something to help me right myself. The books on the shelves, all histories, no novels, the Duke had no interest in stories that weren't true. Is this story true? The Colonel's sword on the mantel. The one that Mama supposedly raised against the Duke.

Is that story true? I look at the portrait of the Duke over the mantel, like I'll find the answer there. But he just stares across the room, stares at the portrait of the Colonel, as if none of this is a concern of his, as if none of us exists. I'm all the time hearing the Duke talking in my head, clear as a bell, but now he's not saying a thing, not telling me what to think or what to do, what to make of all this, and even if he did, I very well might tell him to shut the hell up.

"I still don't understand," I say.

"Like I told you that day I cut your hair, before he met your mama, the Duke and me had a thing going on."

I nod. A year after she started working at the Big House, Aunt Faye goes on, she found out she was with child. The Duke sent her away to live with his relations in Amelia County until she had the baby. It was while she was gone that Annie started working at the Big House. After Aunt Faye had the baby—a girl, of course—she figured the child would have a better life if she was raised by the Duke's cousin Ava Porter, who'd been married for five years without conceiving. Same choice Kat made, Aunt Faye points out. The Duke promised that he'd take care of the child's expenses as long as it was all kept quiet.

So all these years, I not only had cousins living on Hopewell Road, I also had a sister a few miles away that I never knew about, a sister that the Duke, the man I adored, never mentioned. I look back at his portrait and he seems different to me now. It's like I'm seeing him at a great distance, as if I'm up in that yellow airplane, and he's way down on the ground—and he seems very small.

The year Nell turned fifteen, Aunt Faye tells me, the Duke sent for her to work as Jane's maid, but Nell didn't know the Duke was her daddy until after he died and I brought Aunt Faye back to the Big House. "When she was just a little thing, it would have hurt her to know," Aunt Faye says. "But I couldn't very well live in the same house without telling her. And Nell being a grown woman now, well, she had the right to know."

Nell is watching my face. She doesn't look like Aunt Faye, but she does have the same coloring—the dark hair and porcelain skin—

and now I see for the first time that she has that high Kincaid fore-head. Why had I never noticed before? Could I be that blind? Maybe I didn't want to see it. Back when I was little, with Mama gone, I did my darnedest to believe my daddy hung the moon and scattered the stars. That meant there were many things I didn't want to see. I've been doing pretty much the same danged thing my whole life.

"I was waiting for the right time to tell you," Aunt Faye says. "It's a lot to take in at once, so back when we had our big talk I just told you about me and the Duke."

Nell wipes at her tears and puts her hair back in that tidy little bun. I remember most of the time the Duke treated Nell like just an-other maid, ordering her around in an offhanded way, telling her to mop the mud off the porch or put another log on the fire. But every now and then I caught him watching Nell, and if he saw that I noticed, he'd quickly look away. Now I realize that he was looking at Nell the way I occasionally caught him looking at me, like I reminded him of something he'd worked hard to forget. A lapse in judgment. A mis-take. But you never know how your mistakes are going to turn out.

"How did it happen?" I ask Nell. "With Rawley."

"He noticed me. Most people don't even see me—I'm just the help—but he said I'd caught his eye the very first time he saw me. Told me his ma had been a maid, sweet-talked me, made me think he wanted to marry me."

"He proposed?"

"I thought he did. What he said was anyone who wouldn't want to marry me would be a fool. So he didn't out-and-out propose. I reckon you could say it was my fault, I reckon I heard what I wanted to hear. He was hugging and loving on me. But we were together just the one time, and after it happened I kept on waiting for him to say something or do something, but aside from giving me a wink every now and again, he acted like we never did nothing at all. I'm real sorry, Sallie. I hope you can find it in your heart to forgive me."

"He took advantage," Aunt Faye says. "Rawley's the one you ought to be thrashing."

"No," Nell says, almost sharply. "Please. I don't want to get him in trouble. I know you're the one he wants, Sallie, but I'd make him a good wife, too. I'd do anything for him."

"You know what," I say, "I believe you would."

"Tell him that, Sallie. You're good at talking to people."

Tiles.

I'm sitting here alone, staring at the stacks of shiny, brightly colored tiles. Cerulean blue and parrot green and blood orange. What the blazes was I thinking? I haul off and sweep every last one of those ridiculous tiles onto the floor. A loud clatter. Then silence.

I don't feel better. What I feel is sick, head-spinning, stomach-churning sick.

Now what?

But I know what.

I look out the window. It's started to snow. Tiny, timid snowflakes. The driveway is empty, but Rawley will be coming up it shortly, and we've got to have a talk, a serious talk that I don't want Nell or Aunt Faye to hear.

I slip on my overcoat and head for the front door thinking about what I'll say—Do I beg? Do I lecture? Do I threaten?—then it hits me I might need more than words, so I go back to the library, load two rounds into the Remington and take it to the Lizzie. I drive down to the squat stone pillars at the foot of the driveway and park, leaving the engine running, then I sit there and watch the tiny snowflakes beading on the windshield.

The Duke. I spent much of my life with that man inside my head, and for the last two years, I've been doing my best to honor his memory, trying to do what he would have done, recalling his words, hearing his voice so clear it was like he was standing right beside me. And yet, all this time I never really knew who he was. This man whose approval I so craved. He loved being loved, but he never truly loved anyone back. He took what he wanted from people, then once he got it, cast them aside.

And then there's Rawley, the man I was going to marry. He's like the Duke in ways I didn't see. Or didn't want to see. Georgette said she was trying to stop me from repeating mistakes my mama made, and much as I cannot abide the woman, that's what I was about to do, marry a man who's a lot like the man Mama married, a man who's happy living with lies, who never once breathed so much as a word about how he'd been with Nell, who was never going to tell me about it, who also takes what he wants from people then casts them aside.

I've been gnawing on these bitter truths for half an hour when Rawley's Ford comes up Crooked Run Road. It's snowing harder now and I flash my headlights. He stops. I get out and lean on the Lizzie's hood. Let him come to me. Rawley steps out of his car. He's smiling but he knows something's going on and his eyes have that alert look they get when he's sizing up a situation.

"Why the welcoming committee?" He leans over to kiss me but I pull away. "Everything okay?"

"I had a chat with Nell."

"Yeah?"

"She's in a family way."

He shakes his head and stares off into the snow. "Now why don't that come as a surprise?" Then he looks right at me. "She tell you who knocked her up?"

"She says you did."

"The hell?" Rawley lets out a short, sharp laugh. "And you're buying it?"

"Is it possible?"

Rawley starts to say something, then instead reaches inside his jacket pocket, pulls out a pack of cigarettes and taps one loose. "Come on, Sallie."

"Is it?" I ask again. "Because if she says you're the daddy and you say you're not, we're going to have to conduct us an inquiry, cross-examine both parties—"

"Sallie, this is me you're talking to. Rawley. Your man."

"—And we're going to see if Nell recalls any details about your body parts—details that most people wouldn't know."

"Come on, Sallie."

"Details that I, however, would be able to corroborate. Do you really want that?"

Rawley lights his cigarette, the tip glows orange, and he exhales slowly. "It happened just the one time," he says.

Admitting the truth only when you're forced to—that's a far cry from genuine honesty, and something inside of me shrivels up, leaving a burnt, empty feeling, but I can't think about that now, so what I say is "Why didn't you at least take precautions?"

"Heat of the moment. And it was before you became my gal, so it wasn't like I was cheating on you. Besides, could be some other man's baby."

"She said you were the only one."

"And you're saying you believe her?"

"Yes, I do believe her. So, Douglas Rawley, you are going to marry Nell Porter and give that baby a daddy."

Rawley takes another draw on his cigarette, then studies it, watching the smoke curl up into the falling snow. "Sallie, Nell's a sweet gal," he says, "and she's not too hard on the eyes. But I didn't make it through the war and move to Caywood and help Sallie Kincaid get into the blockade-running business and make us both a lot of money and convince Sallie Kincaid to marry me—I didn't do all that just to end up marrying Sallie Kincaid's maid."

"Nell's not just a maid, Rawley. She's my sister. My half sister."

Rawley's looking at me like he's not sure he heard me right. "How's that?"

"Nell is the Duke's daughter, too."

Rawley pauses for a moment, then lets out another sharp laugh. "And her ma?"

"Aunt Faye."

"Jesus H. Christ." He throws down his cigarette and steps on it. "The Duke."

"I just found out myself." I hear my voice softening. Don't go weak, Sallie.

Rawley must have heard it too, because he grins ever so slightly and cocks his head. "So, I only did to Nell what the Duke did to Nell's ma. And you and me, we can do what the Duke did. We can send Nell away. She can have the baby somewhere else. We can pay someone to raise it. Happens all the time. Look at Grace."

His words are like a kick in the gut. So this is how they do it. This is how daddies toss aside their own children like they were yesterday's newspaper. I'm almost grateful that Rawley's showing me his true colors. That makes this easier. "It's not going to happen this time." I hear the grit coming back into my voice. "Marry her, Rawley. You can keep your job. I'll give you a house. Nell won't have to work. She'll be Mrs. Douglas Rawley. You'll have a good life."

"Sallie, the Duke didn't marry Nell's ma and I'm not going to marry Nell. I've got plans. We've got plans."

The two of us stand there in the cold, staring at each other, the fine snow settling on our shoulders and hair, both of us refusing to budge, both of us stunned by the sudden loss of something that just a few hours ago had seemed so solid, so good, so true.

I'm the first to move. I reach into the car and pull out the Remington. "I'm not asking you to marry Nell." I point it at Rawley's chest. "I'm telling you to."

Rawley looks at me evenly. Unafraid. He taps out another cigarette and strikes the match with his thumbnail. He pinches out the flame.

I touch the trigger, the curved steel cold against my fingertip, and sight down the barrel at Rawley as he draws on his cigarette. I could kill him. It's just a twenty-two, but this close, aimed right at his heart, I could pull the trigger and watch Douglas Rawley die in the snow, just like the Duke watched Mama die. I could do it. I could. But I'm not going to shoot him, shoot an unarmed man, the daddy of my sister's baby, the man who pulled me out of that swimming pool. Even so, I hate him—hate this man with a passion you can feel only for someone you had loved. I don't want to kill him but I do want to hurt him, for hurting me, for hurting Nell, for hurting the child she's carrying, a child he doesn't want to ever see—for being such a good-looking, smooth-talking, double-crossing cad that he almost got away with it. So I take the Remington by the barrel and swing the butt at his head. Maybe he's faster than me—or maybe my heart's not really in it—because he catches the gun with his left hand, then draws back his right hand.

"You going to hit me?" I ask. "Is that the kind of man you are?"

He doesn't say anything, just searches my face with those dark eyes of his, but I stare back without flinching, without fear, without softness, and when he doesn't find what he's looking for he simply turns away and walks toward his Ford.

"Douglas Rawley! You get in that car and drive off and I swear you'll never set foot in Claiborne County again!"

He shakes his head without looking back. Then he does it. While I stand there, my Remington in hand, Rawley climbs into the car, races the engine, and drives away.

The red taillights disappear into the snow.

CHAPTER 50

THE TRAIN PULLS TO a stop with clank and a sigh and a puff of white steam. I see Tom Dunbar looking through one of the windows and wave at him with both hands.

The last two days have been rough. I spent a good chunk of them telling Nell she didn't need Rawley, didn't need a husband at all, she could stay on at the Big House, we'd all raise the baby together, give Grace someone to play with. But I also spent a lot of time trying to convince myself that I didn't need Rawley either. Or any man. I could do it all on my own. Manage the businesses, lead the runs to Roanoke, and keep us all safe.

I'm aching to talk to someone who will help me believe everything I've been telling myself, so when I telephoned the Dunbars last night and Louise said Tom was coming back this morning, I offered to pick him up.

"Tom Dunbar, showing up in the middle of the week. The last time you did this I was in Hatfield."

"Dad called and told me what happened," he says. "I wanted to see for myself how you're doing."

Tom. The sight of him comforts me. In his face I still see the boy I once knew, the boy who ran errands for the Duke and sometimes let me help him. He looks tired. Tired but kind. "You heard right. Rawley and I had a set-to. He's gone. But I'm fine. Where's Amy?"

"She's in Georgetown. Guests are coming for dinner tonight. She's not happy that I won't be there." Tom shakes his head and gives me that wry smile of his, but it quickly disappears. He takes me by the hand and leads me to a bench. It has warmed up since the snow, and water is dripping from the depot roof. "I'm sorry about Rawley."

"I don't need him and I don't need anyone's pity. Rawley's gone. Good riddance. I'm fine. Great. Period. End of story."

"I know you better than that, Sallie." He squeezes my hand. "Always putting on a brave front. You don't have to tell me what happened, but if you want to, here I am."

I think back on it all and the hurt I've been working so dang hard to keep down rises up into my throat. I can't get the words out. Tom sees me struggling, squeezes my hand again, and at first I falter, but then the words all come tumbling out—Nell is carrying Rawley's baby, he refused to marry Nell, wanted to send her away and pay someone else to raise the baby.

"What a heel. And poor Nell. What's she going to do?"

This is just like Tom, showing concern for Nell when so many are going to snicker or pass judgment. "I'll take care of her. The baby too. We'll all be like a family." I decide to tell him the rest, too. "Turns out we are family." I do my best to smile. "Me and Nell."

Tom nods.

"You knew?"

"Not for certain. Mother's always had her theories. Dad knew everything, but he's never said a word."

"Aunt Faye wants to keep it secret. But Nell thinks people ought to know. It's up to her. No point in trying to hide it."

"Nothing to be ashamed of."

"Nell's my sister and she's also my cousin. What would your Georgetown friends think of that?"

Tom chuckles. "They're more inbred than us hillbillies." He takes a deep breath. "You got anyone in mind to take Rawley's place? At Kincaid Holdings, I mean."

"No one."

"You offered me a job a year ago. Is that still on the table?"

"I thought Amy doesn't want to live in Caywood."

"She doesn't. I'd come without her."

"You and Amy, it's not going so well?"

"At first, everything was fine, but now . . ." He lets the words trail off. "Amy is so smart and ambitious and funny, but truth is, I can't make her happy whatever I do."

"Tom, I'm sorry. Marriage. It's nothing but trouble." I pause. Tom's being so honest with me about his marriage, but I haven't been truly honest with him about me and Rawley. And I've got to. The rumors are out there and I'd hate for him to hear it from someone else first. "There's something I haven't told you, Tom. Something I should have told you earlier, but I was waiting for the right time. I know this isn't the right time, but I have to tell you anyway. Rawley asked me to marry him—and I said yes."

Tom takes a breath and forces a smile. He's hurt and I'm the one who hurt him. Maybe I should have kept quiet, but I'm sick to death of secrets and lies. "Tom, that time a while back, when you and I talked about marriage and I said don't wait around, I wasn't ready to get hitched."

"But that changed when Rawley came along."

Tom doesn't usually talk like that. Sharp. They're the words of someone who's been wounded. "I talked myself into it, Tom. Or let myself get talked into it. Everybody is all the time telling me I have to get married. Truth is, I wasn't ready then and I'm still not. I don't know if I ever will be. And this whole business with Rawley makes me feel like I've just dodged a bullet. So, Tom, if you and Amy split up, my heart goes out to you, truly it does. But don't do it to be with me—even if we tell each other all we'd do is work together. I won't let it happen, Tom. I won't. My mama broke up a marriage, and I swore to myself that I would never do the same."

Tom nods, like he understands, like he's not going to argue or use any more sharp words. He leans back.

"It wasn't fair to put you on the spot at a time like this," he finally says, "but I had to give it a shot." He takes out his pocket watch, stares at it longer than he needs to, then gives me a smile, a real one this time, but it's also rueful.

"It's still early. I have time to say hello to Mom and Dad and catch the two-twelve to Washington. Get back for that dinner party after all. Try to make Amy happy."

PART V

CHAPTER 51

LAST NIGHT'S RAIN HAS left Caywood looking freshly washed. Tin roofs gleam in the May sunshine, the sycamores cast dappled shade on Main Street, storekeepers have propped open their doors to catch the breeze and invite the shoppers inside. I slow the Packard to dodge the puddles and finally find a parking space at the end of the block.

I drive the Packard all the time now, except for the Roanoke runs, and it feels right, seeing as how in the four months since Rawley hit the road, I've been doing everything on my own, like I told everyone I would, and holding it together—for the most part.

But everything's a trade-off. In bed at night I do miss lying next to a man, miss it something awful even though I had such a small taste of it. Sometimes I feel so alone, so damned alone. I'd rather be alone though, than bound or beholden to someone.

Besides, I do have a new man in my life. Fellow by the name of Jake. He's Nell's baby, a little charmer with Rawley's coal black eyes and olive skin. From the start he's had a powerful grip that I call the Kincaid clench. The Big House is livelier than ever—what with little Grace turning two and running around as light-footed as Seymour, so maybe he is her daddy after all. Nell and Jake have moved into the stone wing, and she keeps saying what with a baby, a mama, and a sister all under the same roof, she's never been happier.

We're a family. There are two kinds of family, those you're born into and those you put together from pieces that don't go anywhere else, and this is one of those families. Five of us now. Like mismatched buttons that still keep your shirt closed. I've thrown myself into fixing up the house, buying modern kitchen appliances. Our new electrical washing machine dances around the floor like a lunatic but gets the stains out. We also have a new bathroom, with nickel fixtures, cream-colored tiles, and steaming hot water piped up from a fancy new electric water heater in the basement.

Nell wanted to go on cleaning house, earning her and Jake's keep, but I told her she had her hands full with the baby so I hired Becca, Kat's old wet nurse, to cook and clean. Her husband, Virgil, makes repairs and takes care of the garden. I told them to call me Sallie, but they said they could never do that. They call me ma'am and Virgil takes off his cap when he sees me, the both of them generally acting the way people acted around the Duke. They're not the only ones, and I'm not sure I like it. Then again, I'm not sure I don't.

I'm busy as the Duke ever was—planning runs, leading them, collecting rent, checking in with every town's little mayor, going over the police blotter with Sheriff Earl and the Emporium's books with Mattie, all the while worrying about the Bonds. When I get home Grace is usually in bed and Aunt Faye warms my dinner and from time to time after a rough day I catch myself snapping at her. I apologize—she laughs it off—and then I tell myself I can't be taking my moods out on others, because this is what I always said I wanted, to work, not to be idle and pampered like Georgette, not to feel stuck at home like Mama, but to work. I try to be good to people, to be fair, but I know that at times I can sound hard.

I walk past the Emporium's sparkling new plate-glass windows. Inside, I see Mattie giving Ellen and Mr. Lewis the day's orders. She rules the clerks with an iron hand—that Kincaid clench—but the shelves are full and the floor well-scrubbed. She keeps talking about raising prices—the same way she hiked rents two years ago—and I tell her we'll do that only when our costs go up.

I'll stop by the Emporium later. First, breakfast and the latest Claiborne County scuttlebutt. At the Central Café, Josie pours my coffee and slides the *Richmond Daily Record* across the table.

"That story's just like one of them dime novels." She points to a headline.

LAWYER KILLS WIFE IN JEALOUS RAGE

I spread out the paper and read.

POWERFUL RICHMOND ATTORNEY GUSTAV RHEIMS YESTERDAY SHOT AND KILLED HIS WIFE, THE SOCIALLY PROMINENT HOSTESS GEORGETTE RHEIMS, THEN TURNED HIMSELF IN TO THE POLICE, AUTHORITIES SAY.

I stare at the words. Something inside me becomes unglued. I left the New Year's Eve party disgusted by Georgette—and I never did hear back about Mama's necklace—but there was something about that woman that drew me to her. She had figured out how to get what she wanted. She'd made her arrangement. Georgette said things went wrong for my mama because she hadn't kept to the arrangement in her marriage. Now she's been killed by her husband just like Mama. What happened to Georgette's arrangement?

Each morning, my table at the café is piled with newspapers and I read every word I can find about the case. The details are hideous, but riveting. The reporters are treating the story like it really is a dime-store novel, calling Gus the "loophole-loving liquor lawyer" and Georgette the "luscious and lusty gold digger." Turns out Gus and Georgette were bribing Senator Cooke for permits to sell "medicinal liquor"—one of those loopholes that made Gus rich. But Georgette learned that a federal agent was onto them. So she turned on Gus to save her own hide, helping the agent collect evidence against him, then they started having an affair. But Gus's government spies told him about it. He found her swimming in that pool he'd built for her and that's where he shot her.

Those reporters dug into Georgette's past and learned that her daddy was a rich textile-mill owner who went bankrupt and that her mama killed herself by swallowing a bottle of poison. Georgette was ten when it happened—older than me when my mama was killed, old enough to understand and to remember.

Could be I was too hard on Georgette. I'd figured that she'd had an easy life, but maybe that was another thing I didn't want to see, that hiding behind the rich, spoiled woman was a hurt, angry little girl with a hole in her heart. We both lost our mamas when we were girls, but she never once mentioned it. She knew everything about me, but I didn't know the first thing about her. Never had the chance to ask. What would she have told me if I had?

Two weeks after Georgette was shot, Josie hands me that day's *Daily Record*. "This story gets crazier and crazier," she says, tapping the headline:

LIQUOR LAWYER'S DEFENSE: TEMPORARY INSANITY

Gus found another one of his loopholes.

"What kind of woman would betray her husband like that?" Josie asks.

"A woman who thinks marriage is an arrangement."

"I sure can understand why that husband of hers did what he did," Josie says.

I stir my coffee. Can Gus get away with murder? If the jurors think like Josie, he sure will.

"That woman," Josie goes on, "she asked for it. In my opinion."

I take a sip of coffee. I remember Georgette saying she always got what she asked for, but I keep that to myself.

"What do you think?" Josie asks. "You think she got what she deserved?"

"Some people will make that case, but no, I don't." I leave it at that and Josie moves on to the next booth.

She got what she deserved.

That's what some people said when Mama was killed. It is what you tell yourself sometimes, a way to make sense of things, a way to make you feel safer, that people who get hurt bring it on themselves. But it's such a lie. Lots of folks don't deserve what they get. Eddie, for one. Abraham Crockett. And lots of folks don't get what they deserve.

Will Gus?

CHAPTER 52

I'M SQUEEZED INTO A bench in the last row of the courtroom, but I can still see Gus's back, his bulky shoulders straining in his tight black jacket as he hunches over his legal briefs.

It's the final day of the trial. I kept telling myself I wouldn't come, that I'd passed through Georgette and Gus's world and once was enough, but ever since the trial began I've been fighting a powerful hankering to come to this courthouse.

Then yesterday I couldn't stand it any longer, had to be here when the verdict was read out. I reckon it's because ever since that talk with Aunt Faye about Mama I've wondered what would happen in a court of law to a man who killed his wife and claimed it was her fault, that she'd driven him to it, that she got what she deserved.

I am about to find out.

Temperatures are near a hundred today so even with the courtroom windows open, everyone inside—reporters, curiosity seekers, some faces from the New Year's party—is shiny with sweat, men wiping their foreheads with handkerchiefs, women fanning themselves with pretty silk fans or hats or anything at hand. The twelve men on the jury file into the room and the spectators lean forward, eager and excited. The prosecutor starts his closing argument, recounting the facts in a gray, dry manner, droning on about law and order, about crime and punishment, about how one man cannot be judge, jury, and executioner. Gus provides the only theater, shaking his bald head in disgust every time the prosecutor makes a point. "Gentlemen of the jury," the prosecutor says in closing, "Georgette Rheims may not have been a saint, but that does not justify her own husband killing her in cold blood."

The prosecutor sits down. Gus, who's defending himself, walks slowly to the jury. He starts off talking a little about the legal definition of temporary insanity—but he talks a heck of a lot more about marital vows, about loyalty and love, about honoring and obeying, about the agony and despair, the pain and humiliation that can drive a sane man mad, completely mad, when a woman breaks those vows, betrays that man, utterly destroying his manhood. "I stand before you a broken man," Gus says. "But if you feel I have not suffered enough, by all means, punish me more, send me to my death."

After deliberating for twenty-four minutes, the jury files back into the courtroom. The foreman passes a piece of paper to the judge, who declares, "Not guilty on the grounds of temporary insanity."

People in the crowd leap to their feet. Men cheer and clap, laugh and hoot and light cigars. Some women look grim and one is crying, but others are cheering right along with the men. I'm disgusted but not shocked. I had a feeling it would turn out like this, the husband acquitted because the wife got what she deserved, and that's what would have happened if the Duke had been tried for killing Mama. Her name would have been dragged through the mud and he'd have ended up shaking hands with the jurors, just like Gus is doing now.

I push through the crowd up to the rail. Gus sees me and comes over.

"I had a hunch you might show up," he says.

"Why?"

"Just a hunch. Why are you here?"

"To see if you'd find the loophole. You did."

"The loophole just let the jurors do what they wanted to do. My job was to make them want to do it."

"Georgette said you were the smartest lawyer in Virginia."

"Congratulate me." He holds out that thick hand of his.

I shake my head. "For killing your wife and getting away with it?"

"You're blunt, Sallie. One of the reasons I liked you from the beginning. I'm blunt, too." He pauses and I see a hint of a smile. "Do you know why Georgette looked you up in the first place?"

"Might be she wanted another exotic pet." I wait a bit for a reply but Gus just looks at me, still with that hint of a smile. "She said it was on account of how we were alike. She said we were both fearless. But we also both lost our mamas when we were girls. Could be that had something to do with it."

"Georgette told you what happened to her mother?"

"No. I read about it in the newspapers, how her mama killed herself because her daddy went bankrupt."

"The newspapers got that wrong. It was the other way around. The mother killed herself first. His life fell apart afterward."

"Why'd she do it, then?"

"Georgette's father was having an affair. With their maid." He pauses again with that same darned hint of a smile. "And can you guess who the maid was?"

How the heck would I know? That's what I'm about to ask, but I stop short before the words get out because all of a sudden I remember what Aunt Faye told me, that Mama had been a maid in Richmond when she first left home. But it hadn't worked out.

I feel the blood leaving my face.

"Do you think," Gus asks, "that my wife showed up in your godforsaken little town in Claiborne County because she was curious about some two-bit blockade runner? Georgette wanted to get to know the daughter of the woman who destroyed her family."

I stare at Gus, still at a loss for words. I can't move.

"By the way," Gus goes on, "Georgette found that necklace of your mother's but she wanted to keep it. Seeing as how Duke Kincaid never did any time for killing his wife, I've been carrying it around as a good-luck charm." He reaches into his pocket and then holds out his hand. There, in a little tangle in his upturned palm, are the pale moonstones and their silver chain. "It worked," he says, "so here, you can have it back."

Chapter 53

I HAVE TO GET away. Away from this loud, hot, stinking courtroom, filled with jeers and cheers and cruel laughter, with the smell of sweaty bodies and cigar smoke. I snatch the necklace from Gus without looking at his smirking face. Mama's necklace, my one link to her, had been a talisman that made me feel protected and hopeful, but after what Georgette and Gus did with it, Mama's necklace seems dark and ugly, something with a power that is almost evil. It feels scorching hot in my hand, like it could burn, and I shove it in my pocket and force my way through the crowd.

I stumble out onto the street. I need air, fresh air, but the stink of the courtroom, Gus's sour breath, has seeped into my hair and my clothes, into the pores of my skin. The Packard is parked in the punishing sun and inside it feels like an oven. I slide down the window but before I've gone a block, the stench of death floods the car. A slaughterhouse? A dead horse rotting in the street? Death, it seems, is everywhere. Death and pain and deceit and filth.

It comes from folk placing themselves above the law. And what about me? "I just do what needs to be done," I told Gus. That's what he and the Duke both told themselves before killing their wives. God help me. I'm not that different from them.

Clean. I have to get clean. It's all I can think about on the drive home. I want a bath, I need a bath, a bath so hot and scalding it will leave my skin red and raw and clean.

By the time I get back to the Big House, the sun is down and a few lightning bugs flicker in the tall grass. Inside, everyone's asleep. I go to my new bathroom and turn on the electric sconces that fill the room with a soft light and make the nickel fixtures glow. I twist the faucets and clean, hot water gushes forth. The water's so hot I wince, but I force myself to settle in, I can take this, I need it. I wash my hair and use the boar-bristle brush to scrub my skin and my armpits and the soles of my feet—my entire stinking, shameful body—with lye soap.

I climb into bed. Sleep comes in no time, but it's a fitful sleep. I dream of water that burns and fire that cleans, of smoke and flames, of Mama and Georgette. And Eddie and Abraham and Mary. I toss and kick, trying to wake up, but the smoke grows heavier. Then I sit up coughing.

I'm awake. I can still smell smoke. Real smoke.

It's black as pitch. I stumble out of bed and turn on the light. Smoke is seeping beneath the door. I throw it open and hit the hall light. More smoke, dark and thick, drifting up the staircase and hanging in the hall. I get down on my knees, pull my nightgown up over my nose and crawl to Aunt Faye's room. I shake her and shout but she only mumbles and shifts around, so I slap her face and shout again and now her eyes open and she starts coughing. "Fire!" I shout. "We have to get out!"

Now Grace.

She's in the alcove next to Aunt Faye's room, curled up under the sheets. I shake her. Nothing. I shake her again. Still nothing. Please, God. I scoop her up—her arms limp and legs dangling—and run in a crouch to the stairs. Smoke is now pouring up the stairway. The hall light goes out. All is black. I take a deep breath and climb down into the dark, holding Grace's weightless little body in one arm, my hand cupping her head—don't drop her, don't drop her—my other hand on the rail, feeling my way step by step.

I reach the landing, then the first-floor hallway. The air is thick with smoke. So much smoke. Baby Jake and Nell. They're in the stone wing. I've got to get them. But limp little Grace is still in my arms, and I have to get her out first.

I put my hand over my mouth. Try not to breathe. The hallway floorboards are hot beneath my bare feet. I reach the front door, open it and a big gust of air sweeps in, feeding the fire behind me with a roar.

Outside, there's air. Clear, cool air. I take deep gulps. I shake Grace. Nothing. I shake her again. The hospital. I have to get her to the hospital. But that would mean leaving baby Jake and Nell. I can't do that. Please, Grace, breathe. Do it for Jake. I don't know if I'm doing this right, but I read about it once and I put my mouth on hers and blow air into it. Once, twice. Then she coughs, makes a gurgling noise, and lets out a wail. Thank you, Grace. Thank you, God. Thank you.

I carry her into the middle of the yard and try to lay her on the ground, but she is crying and gripping me with both arms. I hear shouts in the distance. "Come get this little girl!" I yell, then tell Grace, "You'll be safe here, people are on the way and I have to go back for baby Jake and Nell, they're both still inside." I pry her hands off me, and run back into the house.

I start to cross through the parlor to the stone wing, but bright, hot flames are climbing up the curtains, eating the wallpaper, and the fierce heat stops me. Try to push through it. Can't. Try again. Cannot do it. Can't get to the stone wing. Not from here. Have to go out and around to the back of the house. And where's Aunt Faye?

I stumble onto the porch and down the front stairs, my throat raw from the smoke. I'm coughing so hard I fall to my knees. People are gathered in the yard, eight, maybe ten, their faces golden in the fire's glow, and Becca is holding Grace while the others are shouting and pointing. I look back at the house, at the stone wing, and there, at a second-story window—it's Aunt Faye. Nell is next to her, clutching baby Jake to her chest.

Flames are curling out of the first-floor windows, spraying orange sparks into the dark sky. Without thinking, I get up and run toward the stone wing's little front door, but I hit the heat again—a wall, solid and punishing—and I can't get any closer.

"Jump, Nell!" I shout. She can't hear me. The roar of the fire is too loud. She seems frozen.

"Throw me the baby!" I shout.

She stands up there, staring, paralyzed by her two choices, both unthinkable—to leap from the second-story window with her little baby in her arms and risk crushing him, or to toss him out the window and trust that I'll catch him. She can't. Can't do it. Nell can't do anything that might hurt her baby.

Then Aunt Faye looks straight at me and all of a sudden she yanks baby Jake out of Nell's arms, leans across the windowsill, and with more strength than I thought she had in her, she heaves him in my direction.

Baby Jake falls toward me, naked except his diaper, his arms and legs splayed out, small and completely helpless, tumbling down to whatever awaits him, coming at me slowly, like he's underwater, and I think to myself, please, God, I know I've done a lot that's wrong, but please, God, have mercy, please let me do this one good thing, please help me catch this baby.

And then with a solid, heavy thump, baby Jake lands in my arms, almost knocking me to my knees, and I clasp him to my chest, thinking, thank you, God, Thank you. Thank you for helping me finally do something right, maybe the one important thing I've ever done.

I'm holding the baby and watching while Aunt Faye helps Nell clamber to the sill—two black silhouettes in front of the yellow-orange flames boiling behind them—but Nell stops, frozen again, gripping the sides of the window. "Jump!" People are screaming. "Jump!" But she can't, and again it is Aunt Faye who moves, wrenching Nell's arms loose and shoving her hard.

Nell tumbles awkwardly out the window and lands with a thud on her side. Men from the crowd rush forward and try to help Nell to her feet, but she sags in their arms.

I am still standing there clutching baby Jake, frozen myself now, my eyes on Aunt Faye as she pauses, waiting for the men to carry Nell clear so she can jump. She puts one foot up on the windowsill, but just then, the fire behind her explodes with a loud crack and she falls backward.

No!

God is sparing Jake but taking Aunt Faye.

But then she's there again, Aunt Faye, in the window, only her nightgown has caught fire, and she pulls herself onto the windowsill and jumps, arms outstretched, flames rising from her sleeves like a pair of burning wings.

Chapter 54

SOME SAY THAT WHAT doesn't kill you makes you stronger, but that isn't always so. Many a time, what doesn't kill you leaves you broken and crippled, unable to fight the next fight, or sometimes it leaves a wound in your heart so deep and ugly that it never truly heals, leaves you bitter and angry, unable to forgive the world for its cruelty.

Aunt Faye is lying in the hospital bed, her arms and shoulders slathered with thick white paste. Nurse Hynes keeps giving her sips of laudanum for the pain. Doctor Black was just here. He believes Aunt Faye will recover, but she will have scars—deep, ugly scars. Aunt Faye was always so proud of her beauty, even as it was fading, and now she's scarred. To my mind, scars are a small price to pay for coming out alive, for saving her daughter and her grandson. I hope Aunt Faye will see it that way too.

Jake and Nell are fast sleep in the chair next to Aunt Faye, Jake in Nell's arms. Grace is also asleep, curled up at the foot of Aunt Faye's bed, none of them bothered by the morning sunlight streaming in.

I look out at the street where Glen Lowe's deputies were lined up behind their cars that night shooting at us. That night. It feels like a lifetime ago and it also feels like yesterday, me and Billy Bond hunkered down side by side, returning fire back in that brief stretch before we started trying to kill each other. The Bonds. Did they set the fire? Did they do this to Aunt Faye?

Or did I? Was it my fancy new water heater, the one I bought to make the Big House feel grand and up-to-date?

"Where are they? Which room?" Mattie's voice echoes down the hallway, interrupting my thoughts. The house she loved, the house she grew up in, the house she thought rightfully belonged to her, has burned down on my watch. I go to the door, bracing myself for her fury, and when she sees me she raises her arms. I flinch and clench my fists, fixing to be hit and hit back, but instead Mattie wraps her arms around me.

I'm taken aback—I can't remember the last time Mattie even so much as touched me.

"I'm sorry, Mattie," I say. "So very sorry about the Big House."

"I am, too. But it's gone. Crying won't bring it back. Getting angry won't bring it back. It was just a house, I keep telling myself, and the things in it were just things. Maybe in time I'll come to believe it." Mattie looks over my shoulder at Aunt Faye. "How is she?"

"Doctor Black says she'll make it."

"The little ones?"

"They're okay. We're all okay."

"That's what matters. That you all are alive. The Kincaids have picked up and moved on from worse than this. That's what we're going to do now. Pick up and move on. I'll throw a potluck dinner tonight. Bring everyone together." Mattie's trying here, trying her best to rally us, but then she stops. "I can't help it, Sallie, I am angry. Angry as hell. If lightning struck the house, I'd accept it as fate, as God's will. But this wasn't God. It was arson."

"It could have been my new electric water heater. A short."

"It was the Bonds. I know it. Know it in my bones."

The Bonds. They're never going to go away. I've tried everything—met every move, countered every threat—and it just keeps getting worse. How do I kill this beast? I look into Mattie's eyes, those hazel Kincaid eyes that used to seem so hard and cold to me, the eyes of a foe, but ever since I put her in charge of the Emporium, she's come around, she's changed. But maybe it's not Mattie who's changed, maybe it's me, I've changed toward her, brought out a different side of her. There's got to be a way to do something like that with the Bonds.

"Mattie, can you look after Grace? I have some business to tend to."

CHAPTER 55

DARK THUNDERHEADS ARE ROLLING in from the west, so low they feel like a ceiling. Good. We could use the rain. With this dry spell, ponds have turned to mud holes and the Lizzie's tires are kicking up clouds of dust. And a rain will put out what's left of the fire.

I'm still wearing the nightclothes I had on when the fire started and by the time I get to the Bond house, I'm a dusty, soot-stained mess. One of the Bond women tells me I can find the brothers up at their timber stand, cutting wood, all I have to do is follow the sound of the saw. I can hear it a mile away, and when I get to the clearing, the brothers have jacked up an old car, taken a wheel off, and replaced it with a circular saw they're using to rip logs.

The noise is hellacious and when Billy cuts the engine, stopping the saw, the silence is almost as loud. He picks up a shotgun leaning against the truck.

"Unarmed," I call as I step out of the car, "and alone. I came to talk."

I hold out my hands to show I'm hiding nothing. They're not shaking because I'm feeling no fear. And I know I look a fright, but I'm also feeling no shame. I'm here to put an end to this.

"Morning, Miss Kincaid." Billy takes in my sooty nightclothes. "Heard you all had a fire. Shame about that."

"Could have been a lot worse."

"Heard it was bad wiring from some fancy new water heater you put in."

"Might have been the wiring. Might have been someone tampered with the wiring to set a fire."

"You saying it was us?"

"I'm saying no such a thing. Don't know. Don't want to know. Didn't come here to find out if you did it—because if you did, Billy, I would have to kill you. Kill you all. But there's been enough killing, enough score settling. I got young ones to raise and you Bonds do too. So I came here to make peace."

"Peace? That so? How you planning to do that?"

"Sell you back that bottomland. Those eighty-eight acres."

"That you all Kincaids stole from us."

"You say we stole. We say you sold. So to make matters right, I'm prepared to sell those eighty-eight acres back to you. Same price as what we paid for them."

"Two dollars an acre?"

"That's right."

"You're fixing to sell us that fine bottomland for two dollars an acre?"

"If it puts an end to this fighting."

Billy slowly lowers his gun, then raises it again. "What about all the money you Kincaids made off the land since you stole it? You planning to give us any of that?"

"Knock it off, Billy. I'm letting you do the stealing this time, and you know it."

He spits tobacco juice into the dirt. "Me and my brothers, we'll have to think on it."

"You all do that."

I climb into the Lizzie as big fat raindrops start to fall, drumming on the hood, making dark spots on the ground. I look back at Billy and he gives the tiniest nod. It's the mountain way of parting on good terms. Unless I imagined it.

Chapter 56

Late that afternoon, Grace and I are staring at the charred, soggy remains of the Big House. All that's left standing are four brick chimneys, some blackened timbers, bent water pipes, and the walls of the old stone wing. The smell of smoke hangs heavy in the air, woodsmoke but also the sharper smells of burned rubber and paint and linoleum.

That storm was one of those short drenchers, the skies opening up and pouring down more than an inch in less than an hour. All that water sure did put out the fire.

Sheriff Earl and a couple of deputies are down in the basement, kicking through the smoldering ashes. He figures it started in the basement near the new water heater, but can't say what caused it. And like I told Billy, I don't want to know. Either I caused it, or I just made a gift of a deal with those who did.

Wind carried sparks up to the carriage house and it caught fire too. Inside the blackened timbers is what's left of the long, green Packard, its tires melted like wax, the paint blistered and peeling, but its lines still elegant and grand.

"All gone," Grace says.

"All gone," I agree.

What do I do now? How do I go on? I don't have the answer. And I'm not going to get it from the Duke. I haven't heard his voice in my head since that day Aunt Faye told me he was Nell's daddy.

Sheriff Earl and the deputies have been holding up odds and ends that for some reason survived the fire. A shoe. A few of the piano's ivory keys. Nell's cast-iron frying pan. Just then, Sheriff Earl gives a shout. He pulls the Colonel's sword out of the soggy ashes and passes it to me. The ornate handle is still warm to the touch. I slide it out of the scorched scabbard.

"It'll clean up just fine," he says.

I run my finger along the delicate carving at the hilt. The sword the Colonel carried in the war, the sword the Duke said Mama raised against him, the sword I swung at Rawley. Not a lot of reason to get teary-eyed over this particular relic. "No. It's part of the past. Best left there."

I toss the sword back into the charred pit. It lands with a muffled clunk and ashes swirl up. Good riddance. As long as I'm saying goodbye to the past, I reach into my pocket for Mama's moonstone necklace. I've had no desire to put it on since Gus gave it back to me—hard to believe that was only yesterday. I start to throw it into the ashes after the sword, but right before it leaves my hand I hear a voice in my head.

"You hold on to that," the voice says.

It's not the Duke's voice. It's a woman's voice.

"You hold on to that."

The voice is both strange and familiar. Then it comes to me. It's Mama's voice. I'm certain. Mama. My memories of her are so few, so faint, pushed into the dark corners of my mind by all those people pretending for most of my life that she never existed, letting me know one way or another that I must forget her, forget everything about her. But now, staring at the necklace, I have a sudden memory of her so clear and bright it feels like she's right here.

I'm sitting on Mama's lap looking up at her and she's wearing this very necklace, the moonstones glowing pink and blue against her pale throat. I'd heard her and the Duke fighting, loud and angry and cruel, and I'd run into their room. The Duke stormed out and Mama picked me up and held me close.

"My Sallie, my daughter, my precious girl," she said, "if something happens to me and one of these days I'm not here for you, people will say things about me. Unkind things. But you should know that I made the choices I made for you, Sallie. I wasn't going to let you be cast aside like Faye's baby girl. No one was going to pretend that you never happened, that you were a mistake. You weren't a son, but you are everything you ought to be. You are wanted. You are loved. You got that, Sallie?"

"Yes, Mama."

"Good. Now you hold on to that. You hear me, my brave, clever, strong Sallie. You hold on to that."

The wind from the west picks up, sweeping smoke away and bringing in clean, fresh air. Up above the smoldering ruins, the half-moon is hanging in the blue sky, faint and white but bright enough to be seen in the late afternoon.

I'm not sure if I'm remembering what happened or just finally understanding it, but all these years, I've been hearing stories about Mama as told by others, and now, I finally understand the story as Mama would have told it.

She didn't destroy Georgette's family. Georgette's daddy did that, lusting after his pretty maidservant, a young woman all on her own.

When the same thing happened a few years later, Mama was not going to let another man take advantage of her. She held out. But she didn't destroy Belle's marriage, either. The Duke should get the blame for that.

And then, when the Duke turned on her, when she could see it was only a matter of time before he got rid of her too, she fought back, not just because she was headstrong and willful. She saw what had happened to Belle and Mary, sent away, as if they'd never existed. She fought back for me.

I squeeze Grace's hand.

Hold on to that.

Can I trust that voice? Can I trust a sudden, out-of-the-blue memory of something that happened so many years ago? And why should I believe those words? I surely don't feel brave, clever, or strong, don't feel like I'm everything I ought to be. Could be I'm imagining the whole thing. People are all the time hearing voices that aren't there, tricking themselves, making up reasons for why things happen when there is no reason, pretending there's hope when there is no hope.

I'm startled by a hand on my shoulder. It's Tom. I was so deep in my thoughts that I didn't hear his car drive up.

He hugs me then steps back and studies me in that careful way of his. "How are you holding up?"

"I'm trying, Tom. I'm working on it."

Tom kneels down in front of Grace. "How about you? Are you okay?"

Grace nods.

"My little gal's tough," I say.

"She takes after her Aunt Sallie." Tom stands back up.

"How are you holding up, Tom? How are you and Amy?"

"It's over. I moved back into the boardinghouse a couple of days ago."

"You as much as told me it was coming—but I am sorry. And that's the truth."

"We're both better off."

"Still, you put so much hope, so much belief into something and then it just disappears."

Tom nods and looks at the smoldering ruins. "There was a lot of history in that house—both good and bad. You had time to think about where you go from here?"

"No. I can't." My voice starts to falter but I keep talking. "It's an unholy mess, Tom. I don't know what to do. I don't trust myself. I don't have the answers. I'm lost."

"You'll find the path, Sallie. And you'll rebuild. You've got a family that needs a home."

"I don't think I have it in me."

"Sallie, you got more fight in you than anyone I know."

Do I tell Tom about Mama's voice? If anyone would understand, he would. "Tom, if I told you I just heard my mama talking to me, would you think I'm crazy?"

Tom gives me that slow smile of his. "Sallie, if you just heard your mama talking, I think you'd be crazy not to listen."

I show Tom the necklace. "I was looking at this, it was Mama's, and I was fixing to throw it into the ashes, but I heard her voice saying, 'You hold on to that.'"

"Sounds like good advice to me." Tom takes the necklace. "Here, let me help you put it on."

I turn around. Tom's hands feel warm and gentle on the back of my neck. Tom telling me to trust the voice, to trust myself. I want to hold on to that. Hold on to him.

"When are you going back?" I ask.

"I'm staying for this dinner Mattie's throwing tonight. It'll be good to see everyone. Then I'll catch the morning train to Georgetown."

"Stay. I need you."

"You mean you need a lawyer?"

"Could be I need a lawyer. Could be I need a husband. Could be that's what I need. Tom Dunbar, marry me."

Tom grins and strokes my cheek. "Sallie, you're not yourself. You're not thinking straight. Once you're back on your feet, you'll feel different. Then we can talk about it." He pulls out his pocket watch. "We all should be getting ready for this dinner." Then he looks at me with a face as kind and wise as Cecil's. "Sallie Kincaid, I will always love you, but I don't know if you'll ever come around to the idea of being someone's wife."

Tom kisses my forehead, his hand lingers on my cheek for a moment, then he turns to leave. I have a powerful hankering to grab him around the waist, outright refuse to let him go, but he's right, this is not the time to be talking marriage, and after last night I'm not thinking straight, so instead I watch Tom walk slow and easy back to his car. He's also right about rebuilding. I have a family to look after. Aunt Faye, Nell, Jake, Grace. And Jake and Grace are the ones carrying the family into the future, Kincaids without the Kincaid name—and to hell with all that nonsense about who's a real Kincaid and who's not, about sons who rule and daughters who serve, about who's an outsider and who belongs, who's legitimate and who's born out of wedlock, who lives in the Big House and who lives in a Sears house and who lives on Hopewell Road.

I run my fingers through Grace's hair, fine and honey-colored like Kat's. "We best get back to Aunt Mattie's and change."

"Is that where we live now?"

"Just for a little while. I'm going to build us a new house. Different. One that suits us better."

"Good."

Tom starts his car, then waves to us.

"I've known that man my whole life," I tell Grace while we wave back. "When I was your age, I used to ride around on his shoulders. And then, when I got older, he was the fellow who taught me how to drive a car."

"He's a better driver than you?"

"Oh no, I'm much—" I stop, watching Tom cross the bridge over Crooked Run. "We're different. He's more careful. I'm faster."

"Then who's better?"

"Let's just say I always get there first."

I take Grace by the hand and we walk away from the smoking ruins. "And one of these days, as soon as your legs get long enough to reach the pedals, I'm going to teach you how to drive."

I'll teach Jake, too. If he's like his daddy, he'll be a demon behind the wheel. But maybe Grace will be the one who loves cars and Jake will want nothing to do with them, like Eddie. That will be fine by me.

Eddie. Sweet Eddie. Out there somewhere, traveling at the speed of light. Godspeed. Eddie, you were so smart. So much smarter than me. But the words of that poem you left behind, they were wrong. You don't always kill the things you love. You do everything you can to hold on to them. And sometimes—when you're standing in the right place and your heart's willing and a little baby comes hurling down at you from out of the sky—sometimes you even save the things you love.

ACKNOWLEDGMENTS

THIS BOOK OWES ITS life to the sharp penciling and heavy lifting of Nan Graham, a brilliant editor, candid critic, and dear friend. She read more drafts of the manuscript than I want to admit but never lost faith. I'm also deeply grateful to Margaret Riley King, a fierce and loving advocate and agent. Many thanks to Brian Belfiglio, Susan M. S. Brown, Sophie Cudd, Tracy Fisher, Sabrina Pyun, and Sylvie Robineau.

I often turned to my brother, Brian, for his wisdom, insight, and humor. And I will always be beholden to my husband, John Taylor, who took every step of this journey with me—sometimes ahead, sometimes behind, usually beside—but always there.

Some characters and scenes in this story were inspired by actual people and events. A woman named Willie Carter Sharpe was known as the "Queen of the Roanoke Rumrunners." She was said to be the best driver, man or woman, in Franklin County, Virginia, racing down mountain roads with an open throttle and piloting liquor caravans that carried a total of some 200,000 gallons of moonshine. Much of what is known about Sharpe came out during the Great Moonshine Conspiracy Trial of 1935. I read court transcripts and newspaper accounts of that trial, and a particularly enlightening book about it is *Spirits of Just Men: Mountaineers, Liquor Bosses, and Lawmen in the Moonshine Capital of the World* by Charles D. Thompson Jr.

Feuds and battles between rival bootleggers were common, and one of the most violent took place in Williamson County, Illinois.

Scenes such as the shoot-out at the hospital, the tank battle, and the airplane bombing of the club house were culled from newspaper reports about similar incidents there, as well as *Bloody Williamson: A Chapter in American Lawlessness* by Paul M. Angle; *A Knight of Another Sort: Prohibition Days and Charlie Birger* by Gary DeNeal; and *Brothers Notorious: The Sheltons, Southern Illinois' Legendary Gangsters* by Taylor Pensoneau.

Gustav and Georgette Rheims bare some resemblance to the Ohio lawyer George Remus and his wife, Imogene, whose story is told in a number of books, including *King of the Bootleggers* by William A. Cook. The Reverend Phillip Canon has parallels to Virginia minister James Cannon, the subject of *Prohibition and Politics: The Life of Bishop James Cannon, Jr.* by Robert A. Hohner. And, because the Tudor dynasty provided the earliest inspiration for this story, I'm grateful for the exhaustive research and thoughtful writings of so many historians, especially Alison Weir, Chris Skidmore, and Peter Ackroyd.

The peculiar alliance of religion, nativism, racism, and progressivism that led to Prohibition is well-documented. The books I found the most useful include *Last Call: The Rise and Fall of Prohibition* by Daniel Okrent; *Prohibition: Thirteen Years That Changed America* by Edward Behr; *Bootleggers and the Beer Barons of the Prohibition Era* by J. Anne Funderburg; *Moonshine: A Cultural History of America's Infamous Liquor* by Jaime Joyce; and *Mountain Spirits: A Chronicle of Corn Whiskey from King James' Ulster Plantation to America's Appalachians and the Moonshine Life* by Joseph Earl Dabney.

I relied on hundreds of other books and articles from and about the period. Among those I'm most indebted to are the writings, both fiction and nonfiction, of Virginia author Lee Smith; *Savage Peace: Hope and Fear in America, 1919* by Ann Hagedorn; *Only Yesterday: An Informal History of the 1920s* by Frederick Lewis Allen; *Three Generations, No Imbeciles: Eugenics, the Supreme Court, and Buck v. Bell* by Paul A. Lombardo; *The Story of American Roads* by Virginia

Hart; *Treasury of Early American Automobiles, 1877–1925* by Floyd Clymer; *Tales from the Deadball Era: Ty Cobb, Home Run Baker, Shoeless Joe Jackson and the Wildest Times in Baseball History* by Mark S. Halfon. And without *Green's Dictionary of Slang* (online), the characters would have cussed curse words that weren't yet around.

ABOUT THE AUTHOR

JEANNETTE WALLS WAS BORN in Phoenix, Arizona, grew up in the Southwest and West Virginia, and worked as a journalist in New York City. Her memoir, *The Glass Castle,* was a *New York Times* bestseller for more than eight years and has been translated into thirty-five languages. She is also the author of the bestselling novels *Half Broke Horses* and *The Silver Star*. Walls lives in rural Virginia with her husband, the writer John Taylor.